Child of Fire

The moon hung low on the horizon, and a wolf howled in the darkness. Marda shivered and groped in the folds of her cloak for her flint and steel. It needn't be a big fire. It only had to burn long enough to say some words. She struck flint against steel and watched the sparks fly. Were her hands too shaky to aim aright? No, a curl of smoke showed that a spark had fallen true, and quickly the fire blazed orange.

"By Enath." The words caught in her throat.

There was no time for fear. Go through with it. She took a deep breath and quickly said, "By Enath, I summon you. By Elun, I summon you. By Anchytel, I summon you."

The world did not change. The fire burned. The niche remained empty.

Then a voice behind her said, "By Enath, Elun, Anchytel, we have come. Who are you and for what do you summon us?"

Marda scrambled to her feet and faced the shadowy mass of horsemen. Instinct screamed at her to run, but she held her ground. Surely she would have heard earthly horsemen and these men were mounted on horses that shone with the moon's pale light. She raised her chin and said, "My name is Marda Trefsdottir and I will that you put my son safe in my arms again."

Other Avon Eos Titles in
THE WILD HUNT *Series by*
Jocelin Foxe

THE WILD HUNT: VENGEANCE MOON

JOCELIN FOXE

THE WILD HUNT
CHILD OF FIRE

AVON • EOS

This is a work of fiction. Names, characters, places, and incidents either are the product of the author's imagination or are used fictitiously. Any resemblance to actual events, locales, organizations, or persons, living or dead, is entirely coincidental and beyond the intent of either the author or the publisher.

AVON BOOKS, INC.
1350 Avenue of the Americas
New York, New York 10019

Copyright © 1999 by Linda Reames Fox and Joyce Cottrell
Cover art by J. K. Potter
Published by arrangement with the authors
Library of Congress Catalog Card Number: 99-94997
ISBN: 0-380-79912-X
www.avonbooks.com/eos

First Avon Eos Printing: December 1999

AVON EOS TRADEMARK REG. U.S. PAT. OFF. AND IN OTHER COUNTRIES, MARCA REGISTRADA, HECHO EN U.S.A.

Printed in the U.S.A.

WCD 10 9 8 7 6 5 4 3 2 1

To Daniel Boyd Fox,
for his (almost) unending patience

Character List

THE HUNTSMEN

Walter—a knight, leader of the Wild Hunt, cursed 247 years after the fall of Reasalyn.

Hamon—once ruler of the Principality of Saroth, cursed in 268.

Eleylin ("Ellis")—last heir of the Rensel Empire, a sailor from Onsalm who prefers to live in the present, cursed in 302.

Thomas—lawyer and politician, former member of the Council of Amaroc, cursed in 315.

Michel—merchant's son from Iskandroc who preferred selling cities to selling mercery, cursed in 349.

Payne—a courtier from Yesacroth, descended from Amloth, and cursed in 439.

Reynard—a street entertainer and thief from Rayln, cursed in 511.

Ulick—a warrior of the eastern Sueve, cursed in 596.

Justin—an apothecary and alchemist of Manreth, cursed in 650.

Bertz—a farmer and headman of his nonate of the monotheistic Stros, cursed in 880.

Garrett—a member of the gentry of the Tributary Lordships, cursed in 908.

THE TARSEANS

Marda Trefsdottir—the summoner, a woman acquainted with loss.

Robin—her son, who is lost.

Sella—a neighbor, who is searching.

Poul—Sella's brother.

THE SUEVE

Dayan—called "Fire-born," who is rankled by a loss.

Ketai—the current Khan, beset by family problems.

Ridai—Ketai's brother, a frustrated man of honor.

Aslut—a shaman, who seeks gain from a foreign prophecy.

THE BARAJIANS AND THEIR SUBJECTS

Kaiyun Chrysogon—a princess who possesses one thing of value.

Tita Maimai—the Kaiyun's chief waiting woman.

Lord Wiraz—an envoy to the Khan, a snob.

Lord Dovir—Wiraz's shadow.

Ofarim—the governor of Lakandar, a man of great ambition.

Ferahim—commander of Silasar Fortress, another man of ambition.

Valaker Amval—an old soldier with a thankless job.

Zakar—a reader of entrails with important friends.

Banturim—a slave dealer with a government contract.

Medrim and Fidrach—Banturim's agents.

Ivreim—a reluctant member of the governor's guard.

Tiramet—an Eskedi soothsayer, a woman holding a tiger by the tail.

Reshalon—an Eskedi merchant who pays his debts.

Naroc—Reshalon's friend who speaks Tarsean.

Alsen and Dirac—Naroc's nephews.

Olm—the head of a charitable brotherhood.

THE DEAD, REVERED AND OTHERWISE

Peter—Marda's husband and Peter's father.

Tekar Khan—late leader of the Mahar.

Tulat—servant of a young prince.

Ortas—the lawgiver of the western Sueve.

Amloth—Ortas's grandson, the first leader of the Wild Hunt.

The Deities

THE HIGH GODS OF THE RENSEL

Enath—Goddess of Fire. The patroness of warriors, artisans, and all those who use the fire of the mind. Symbolized by the half-moon.

Elun—Goddess of Water. The patroness of women, children, and those deserving pity. Symbolized by the full moon.

Anchytel—Goddess of Earth. The patroness of those who delve for the fruits of the earth and of deeds done in darkness. Symbolized by the new moon.

OTHERS

Theyyad Haldan (Tiat Altan in Eastern Sueve dialect)—the Sky and War God of the Sueve.

Lugan Mahar Khan—Great Father of the Mahar.

Bakshamai—The Barajian Goddess of the Moon and Lady of Mercy.

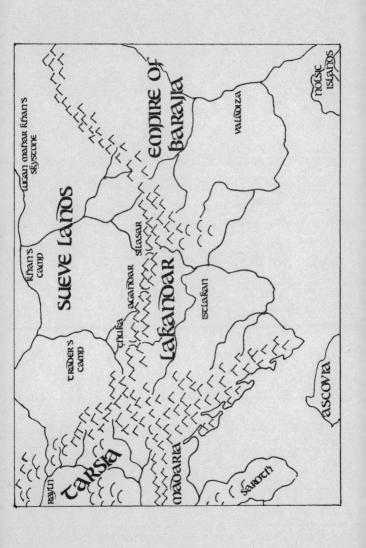

full measure. Stretch on the steppe. She would not
weak for the five lands they would be a con-
hundred. Or such a thing, he would begin with
buy. Would have it be confident.

Prologue

If the Magnary river had not cut its bed through
the rampart of mountains that separated the five
lands of the Rensel from the steppe beyond,
Ortas would not have been able to lead the western Sueve to the borders of the Rensel Empire
and his son Tarses would not have been that
Empire's destroyer. There would have been no
Wild Hunt, for Ortas's grandson Amloth was the
first man cursed to be the Rensel Goddesses'
tool and do each summoner's bidding or burn if
he failed.

If the kingdom Tarses founded had not had its
base in Sueve custom some thousand years earlier Richenza Indes would not have had the ancient status that allowed her to defy the Royal
Family of Tarsia and by summoning the Wild
Hunt set their destruction in motion. Certainly
she would not have been able to set the Huntsman she freed from the Goddesses' curse on the
throne.

But, as in every other time the balance was
disturbed between the steppe and the five lands,
a weakness on one side or the other of that mountain gap pulled trouble to the weaker side. If Tarsia were weak then there were those among the
eastern Sueve, the Sueve who had stayed true to

1

their ancient customs on the steppe, who would find in that weakness the opportunity they sought for greed and for ambition. At such a time, the weak might well be thankful there was a Wild Hunt to be summoned.

Full Moon

The woman pulled the coarse folds of her home-spun cloak around her and huddled in the meager protection provided by the few remaining stones of the ruined villa.

This has to work, she thought. If the Wild Hunt could put a king on the throne and start her troubles, they could mend them as well. If there was a Wild Hunt and not just wild rumors. Where could she turn if there was not?

She'd soon find out. The light had nearly faded from the sky and the forest below was black, alive with the first sounds of nocturnal animals. The moon hung low on the horizon. Must she wait till it was high? The stories she had heard of the Hunt didn't say.

A wolf howled in the darkness. She shivered and groped in the folds of her cloak for her flint and steel. She crawled across the cold fragments of tessellated pavement to the niche in the south-ern wall. Peter had told her that the niche had been a shrine for the household goddess back in Rensel times. How long ago that day had been when he had shown her this secret place, his eyrie, and they had lounged on the sun-warmed pavement and like soaring hawks watched the villagers scuttling like field mice distant and far below.

Her eyes filled with tears and she wiped her sleeve across her face. Tears were no help. She pulled her pouch from her belt and dumped the leaves and twigs it contained in front of the niche. It needn't be a big fire. It only had to burn long enough for her to say some words. She sat back on her heels and spread the cloak to shield her kindling from the night wind. She struck flint against steel and watched the sparks fly. Were her hands too shaky to aim aright? No, a curl of smoke showed that a spark had fallen true and quickly the fire blazed orange.

"By Enath." The words caught in her throat.

This was no time for fear. Go through with it.

She took a deep breath and said quickly, "By Enath, I summon you. By Elun, I summon you. By Anchytel, I summon you."

The world did not change. The fire burned. The niche remained empty.

Then a voice behind her said, "By Enath, Elun, Anchytel, we have come. Who are you and for what do you summon us?"

She scrambled to her feet and faced the shadowy mass of horsemen. Instinct screamed at her to run, but she held her ground. Surely she would have heard earthly horsemen and these men were mounted on horses that shone with the moon's pale light. She raised her chin and said, "My name is Marda Trefsdottir and I will that you put my son safe in my arms again."

The middle-aged brown-haired lead rider asked in the same voice she had heard before, "And why is your son not safe and with you?"

"He was carried off by the Sueve five days ago when they burned my village."

A horse shifted abruptly, its saddle-fittings jingling. Marda looked toward the noise and locked eyes with the horse's rider. He was black-haired, stocky, with an arrogant, high-cheekboned face—a Sueve. She stepped back, tensed to run.

The leader said quickly, "Ulick is one of the Hunt. He is as bound by your command as any of us. You need not fear him."

But she did. She started to shake.

The leader leaned down to her. "Is there shelter near?"

"No."

He reached down and swung her up to sit before him. "Then show us the way to your village."

The road that had served the decrepit Rensel villa where they had been summoned was gone a thousand years and more and the hillside the woman had climbed was too steep for the horses.

Not, Ulick thought, that there was any danger to the horses or the riders—only to the woman named Marda who rode with Walter. She must be kept alive till the next full moon so that her son could be returned to her. Her words made that imperative; the others had told him often enough of the fate that would befall them if they did not heed the letter of her command.

A lost child? A fine reason to put men's souls in jeopardy. He counted off the Huntsmen he had seen in the moonlight—Walter, Hamon, Ellis, Thomas, Michel, Payne, Reynard, Justin, Bertz, Garrett, and himself.

Two less than last time. It was true, then—Alesander and Brian had been held, had escaped the curse.

The freed men were fortunate. If the men still cursed failed, eight of them would burn, body and soul, and Justin would lead the Wild Hunt. Aye, and fail again they would, if that happened—Justin had too much love for his wineskin and too much hate for himself to be trusted. Not that it would matter to Ulick, for he had been cursed before Justin—he would burn. Only the three newest Huntsmen would survive.

A child taken by Sueve. That meant they were near home—he didn't recognize the area, they were still in the forested hills that formed the boundary between Sueve grazing lands and the Kingdom of Tarsia. But the steppe lay beyond and free riding. He could find his way easily enough.

Would Walter have the wit to give him more than the usual menial tasks? Walter was wise in many things but Ulick had seen him misjudge his men from habit a time or two. And that could be fatal.

As if in answer to his thoughts he felt a nudge in his

mind; Walter wanted him to come forward, out of his place in the line of Huntsmen. Ulick guided his horse past the men who had been cursed before him. But he didn't go too near; he stayed a little back and remained silent, hoping Marda hadn't noticed his advance.

"What happened when your son was captured?" Walter asked, "How long ago?"

"Five days ago. I was in the meadow looking for a strayed lamb when I saw the smoke from the village. I ran to the river and saw people running away. I hid among the reeds. I thought Robin would be safe—that Sella would have gotten him away with her children." Marda's voice caught in her throat. "But the Sueve rode along the far bank and I could see Robin slung over one of the horses. I couldn't do anything."

Better for her she hadn't tried.

"You're sure it was your son you saw?"

"His hair—so red—I couldn't mistake it."

That would explain why the child had been taken. Red hair made for a fierce warrior; they wouldn't harm him. Didn't she understand that?

"Do you know their tribe?"

"They were Sueve."

That, apparently, was all she knew. Further questioning elicited no more. She'd seen nothing that could identify them.

"Has there been trouble over grazing?" Walter asked.

They might be able to identify a tribe who felt their territory had been violated.

"No. We farm where we have always farmed."

Why attack dirt-turners if their land was no use for herding?

"Where is the child's father?"

"Dead, they tell me."

"How?"

Had the woman lost man as well as son to Sueve? She asked no blood-price for that.

"Four years ago. In the duke's war against the king." Her voice was angry. Why? Men went to war. Sometimes they didn't return.

"Which king did your duke fight?"

"The new one. The one you made." No need to strain to hear her anger now.

"The one we made?" Walter paused, "King Alesander?"

"Yes."

Ulick heard a sharp intake of breath from at least one of his companions.

"How long has he been king?"

Alesander should have taken the throne soon after their last summoning. How long had the Wild Hunt slumbered this time? Not as long as the three centuries between the previous summonings, certainly.

"A year before Peter left. Five years maybe."

Not so very long. He looked to his right: where rains had collapsed the hillside, he could see rolling farmland beyond. Beyond that would be the plain.

Suddenly he wanted to cut free of the others, to see if the centuries he had been told were long sped had truly passed. The time reckonings of the other Huntsmen made little sense. Were his sons and their sons and their sons' sons long ago dust and memories? Nothing left but cairns too long forgotten to be honored?

He had buried the other questions, the other mysteries that would never have answers. He'd learned to leave them long ago, except when, like Justin, he succumbed to drink.

Walter still questioned the woman and Ulick forced himself to listen.

"Did you go to the authorities for help?"

Marda snorted. "Yes, and got no good of it. The governor doesn't want trouble stirred up with the Sueve."

"How did you know to summon us?"

"The men who returned after the duke's defeat told us stories. They said you killed the old king and made the new."

Ulick could guess the cause of Walter's silence. He did not like the Hunt to be conspicuous and too many people who had seen Sir Walter Martling then could now guess he was Walter of Jacin. Far as they were from the Tarsean capital where that moon had been spent he might still be recognized.

Walter rarely ran out of questions, but that last answer seemed to have left him with little taste for more. The Hunt rode in silence, picking its way down toward the fields.

2

First Day

Ulick smelled the village before he saw it. He'd learned to bear with the smells of the Westerners, even the stench of their cities. But this, the smell of fire, smoke, and death, he had known and hated long before his cursing. It hovered over the fields as the Huntsmen rode toward the eloquent silhouettes of ruined buildings stark in the red light of the rising sun.

All that remained of ten houses and their outbuildings were the charred timbers of their frames and the stone chimneys of two of the larger dwellings. A raven rose cawing from a fence post as the Hunt and the woman who had summoned them halted on the common that had been the village center.

A man's body sprawled next to the ruin of a cottage; the arrow that had killed him protruded from his back. No one had returned to bury their dead.

"We'll have to search. The Sueve might have left something behind," Walter said.

Ulick didn't think there was anything to find; the raiders hadn't lingered—just come, snatched what they thought valuable, and burned. Fletching changed from man to man, not tribe to tribe.

Walter helped the woman dismount.

8

"Which way were the Sueve riding when they left?"

Marda pointed roughly northeast.

Ulick could see mountains to the northwest and southeast. This was where they parted for the Great River, the land too hilly and forested to interest his people. The river would be north of them, and northeast—where Marda said the raiders had gone—would be the open lands of the Sueve.

"How far to Rayln?" Walter asked Marda.

"Two days' walk."

Less than a day's ride. This village should have been safe except in time of war.

"Show me where you saw them go," Walter said. Marda squared her shoulders and led him beyond the houses.

As soon as they were out of sight Reynard changed his clothes and took the reins of Walter's horse and his own. The woman might wonder about their changed appearance, but she would not witness it.

Ulick did not leave his horse's appearance to Reynard's choosing. So near home he did not want to ride a horse that, however magical, looked like the animals of the Westerners. He'd put up with riding the tall, ungainly beasts for too long. He wanted one of his people's steeds, small and swift and hardy—a black mount like the one who had led his people out of the underworld. He would need the guidance it promised.

The creature appeared in his mind vividly, as if it had been a part of his years-long dreaming, and he saw his mount change shape to match his vision.

Satisfied, he reached up to braid his hair. The Rensel Goddesses' predilection for the long hair of their empire was no embarrassment to him—the Sueve wore long hair as well—but the other Huntsmen's eagerness to be shorn made him smile despite the grim surroundings. Ellis beat Bertz to be first. This summoning to a land beyond Tarsia meant that for once Ellis would not have to pretend to be a Selinian mercenary. He could appear as he pleased. The other Huntsmen seemed just as pleased not to be playing parts and had altered their clothes to their pleasure.

Garrett looked from Huntsman to Huntsman, toting them

up on his fingers, then pointed a single thumb in the direction Walter had gone.

"Eleven," he said. "We were thirteen last time. Alesander and Brian must be free!"

"The woman said as much," Payne pointed out. " 'The King you made.' Alesander and Brian have succeeded—or rather their women have—where so many others have failed."

"That means—" Garrett began, but Hamon waved him to silence.

"It means what we all know it means. Walter said to search for anything these damned barbarians left behind." Barbarians. Ulick knew the word and didn't like it, but he pretended he hadn't heard and walked the boundaries of the village to see what he could find. This task would mean long riding and fighting at the end of it. How many of his less "barbaric" companions were up to it?

Hamon, Ellis, and Payne had been nobles among their own peoples and bred to fight. All had ridden long with the Hunt, long enough to learn discretion and obedience. Long enough to swallow their pride and do what was needed.

Bertz and Garrett were more recently cursed. He had only two summonings to judge them by. He had worked with Garrett during the last summoning in Tarsit and found him to be a competent fighter but young for his age and indiscreet, a type not unknown among the household men of a Khan before battle hardened them. Bertz he knew little of save what Garrett had told him, and Garrett hated the Stros. That hatred was based on warfare between their peoples, though Ulick could see as little difference between one Lordship and another as these Westerners could see between Sueve and Sueve. Both men were from the north, from the area called the Lordships on the fringe of the Tarsean Kingdom. Garrett had been a lord's household man; as far as Ulick had heard, Bertz had been a farmer, and at best a village headman.

The other four Huntsmen were townsmen and more likely to be liabilities than not. Thomas had been an official, a lawspeaker; he at least had discretion and the habit of authority. Justin was a learned man—when he was sober. Reynard was from Rayln, the great northern trading city, not far from this village. He might know enough of the Sueve to be an asset if he kept his fingers in his own pouch—he'd been trained as a thief but was a quick learner. Ulick decided to take the boy aside and impress upon him how disastrous a theft or any transgression of the proprieties could be in their dealings with the Sueve.

He doubted that any warning would have an effect on Michel. Too bad they couldn't leave him behind. A moon acting as Michel's body servant in Yesacroth had taught him that Michel was soft, self-indulgent, and casually cruel, so spoiled by an indulgent father that his undoubted intelligence was almost more a liability than an asset.

Even now, while the others worked, Michel sat on the grass by the roadside, his clothes unchanged from the finery of Tarsit, and complained. "I don't see what good it does to search. There's nothing to find."

"Then shut up," Ellis said as he and Garrett pushed a downed section of fence upright, revealing a man's body. Garrett gagged and backed away retching. Ellis frowned. "We'll have to bury him. When the woman gets back we'll ask if there's a burying ground." Ellis leaned over and jerked the arrow from the man's chest. "Anything you recognize?" he challenged Ulick.

Ulick wiped the arrow on the grass before he examined it. Death was ugly, no matter how it came. He had had time for a cursory glance at the fletching when Walter returned with the woman. Walter had served a khan of the Western Sueve before they had absorbed Rensel ways. He should understand their eastern kinsmen. His age—he was past forty—and habit of authority would earn respect among the Sueve that his discretion should keep him from forfeiting.

The woman Marda was hard to judge. It had taken courage and determination to appeal to the authorities and then to the Hunt to regain her son. But her bristling distaste for him made Ulick wonder if she could hide her feelings. She would be a liability if she could not. Her looks shouldn't cause trouble. She was past youth, about thirty, he judged. Her hair was brown, though it showed red glints where the sun struck it. She was tall, her grey eyes were level with his, and the long hand that clutched her cloak around her was hardened with work. Men wouldn't fight over this woman, though the Westerners would not think her plain. She looked strong, but she'd need to be if she didn't want to hinder them.

"How well do you know the area?" Walter asked Ulick.

"We camped within a few days' ride the last years before I was cursed."

"Can you identify the tribe that raided this village?"

Ulick shrugged. "After so long? I don't know. The range of a number of tribes shifted in my time, but rain had been sparse to the east. We moved for the herds."

"Which way do we go? Follow the river?"

"And end up in the soft ground—the marsh? No. Most likely east and south. If we can't find their track we will have to ask if any of the camps or solitary herdsmen have seen their passing. A large war band will be noticeable."

Walter nodded and turned to Marda, "Did they take captives besides your son, any livestock?"

"There were other children—some from other villages—and many sheep."

"Would that slow them down?" he asked Ulick.

"The sheep perhaps. They would take the children because they are small and not as troublesome as adults. And," he looked directly at the hostile figure next to Walter, "because they can be trained to be warriors or sold."

Marda stiffened and Walter put a hand on her shoulder. "I think you should help the others. You know what doesn't belong here."

The woman strode off without looking back. Walter frowned after her. "I'm trying to convince her you aren't the enemy."

"I know—to her we're all the same."

Walter nodded slowly. "It doesn't make the task any simpler."

"Find a child—what could be more simple? No one has to die this time." Last summons their task had been to destroy the royal house of Tarsia. It had been underhanded and bloody.

"One child somewhere on the steppes. It's like finding a field mouse among the wheat."

The Huntsmen worked silently, some searching and some setting up camp. The arrows they brought told Ulick nothing, except that they were made in the same way they had always been made. He was surprised that so small a thing could comfort him.

The sun had climbed halfway to the zenith when they heard a rumbling sound and voices. Marda turned tensed to run. She had no reason. The rumbling was a cart, and besides, the Sueve who had done this had no reason to return.

She must have recognized the cart as soon as it came into sight. "Sella!" she called to the fair-haired woman who rode beside a tall man who looked to be her kin.

Walter caught her before she ran to them, "These are folk from the village?"

"Yes, Sella is. Poul is her brother. She must have gone to Ilton to stay with his family."

Sella scrambled down from the cart. "Have you seen Anya?"

Marda shook her head.

The woman's voice was clogged with tears. "We've been to the other villages where folk took shelter, but no one remembers seeing her! She's too little to hide on her own." Her gaze focused on Marda. "Where is Robin?"

"The Sueve took him. I saw."

"Did they have Anya?"

"I only saw they had Robin."

Sella looked at the men who had stopped to listen. "Who are these people?"

"I couldn't get anyone to help me rescue Robin, so I . . ."

Walter stepped forward. "She went to Rayln and we came to help her."

Marda glanced at Walter; she seemed to understand.

"They took other children, ones Anya knows," she said. Ulick nodded; she'd promised nothing, but Sella looked less frantic. Well spoken. "Maybe we can salvage some of her things, let's look."

Ulick joined Hamon in setting up camp. The strangers would speak more freely without his presence. "Someone will have to find food," Hamon was saying when one of the women screamed.

Ulick ran to where Walter and Marda held Sella back. This had been the largest house in the village and the stone chimney that rose like a tower amid its timbers testified to its builder's pride. "Keep her back," Bertz ordered from where he stood among the rubble. "She should not see. The child climbed into the oven to hide and suffocated when the house burned. Let us do what is necessary."

Poul handed Ellis his cloak for a shroud and Ellis joined Bertz at the chimney. Poul tried to pull Sella away but the mother wailed louder.

"There's nothing you can do," Walter said. "Let them work."

Sella shook with great wracking sobs. Her eye lit on Ulick. She pulled free of her comforters and ran at him. "This is your fault. Your kind did this!"

He spread his hands. "Not my tribe. We don't destroy for no reason."

She opened her mouth to scream at him again as Walter and Poul caught her.

More to put his thoughts into words than to calm a woman who was beyond reasoning, Ulick continued, "This is senseless. If sheep and slaves were what they were after, there was no need to burn. This was no encroachment on grazing. This land has long been under plow. Why destroy so much for so little gain?"

Walter left the woman to her brother's care. "Is that what you see here? Wanton burning? What Sueve would do this?"

"Tribeless men seeking plunder, but this goes beyond what was necessary. They had to know these people couldn't pursue them."

"And no sign of their camp?"

"None. They came, took what they wanted, killed those who tried to stop them, and burned the rest. I doubt they even knew the child was there."

"Then this task is harder than I thought."

"Perhaps not. Such a band would attack Sueve, too. Word would spread of attacks as wild as this. I think we need only ask to follow their trail."

Marda's eyes were wide with fear.

"Robin—would they hurt Robin?"

Ulick shook his head emphatically. "No, he is valuable, or they wouldn't have burdened themselves with him. Either they wanted him to sell or they wanted him for a future warrior. They will keep him well in either case."

She pressed her lips together and nodded.

Bertz helped the couple dig a grave in the burial ground. There were other graves to dig as well. More people than the child had died, but the small grave seemed to take the Stros the longest and had the most care lavished on it.

Ulick wondered if Bertz, too, had left children behind when he was cursed. Ulick took care not to recall the faces of his sons and daughters. They made him remember too much, mourn too often. He wanted to find a cache of liquor and join Justin in downing it.

For Sella and Poul, the Hunt had to pretend to be like other men, so they ate what food could be scavenged from the village stores and some pretended to ready themselves for sleep when the sun set. As the others sat in desultory conversation, trying not to disturb the mourning couple, Walter sat next to Ulick at the fire. "I think my first move should be to go to Rayln and talk to someone on the governor's staff. If these Sueve have raided more than these few villages, they should have some idea of who they are."

Ulick agreed and Walter summoned the other Huntsmen. Ulick was again startled by the uncanny mental call coming from this ordinary looking man. Obscene somehow that here, on the very edge of the steppe, the realm of the Sovereign Winds of Heaven, the power of three Rensel goddesses should flow so strong.

When the others had joined them Walter said, "Garrett and Reynard, you will go with me to Rayln to gather information and buy supplies and horses for the journey. Supplies will be tight in the neighboring villages. We'll leave when the strangers," he nodded at Sella and Poul, "are safely asleep.

"The rest of you will widen the search. Thomas, take Payne and Justin and follow the trail from here. Ulick and Bertz, take Marda and escort these people back to Ilton and question any other survivors. Then go to—what was the other village they mentioned, Besinton?—and see what you can discover there. Eleylin, Hamon, and Michel, you ride to the first village the raiders hit and see if you can find out anything. I'll call you together when I return from Rayln."

Reynard shifted from foot to foot, then spoke up. "Sir, there is an old trader's rendezvous on the edge of the steppe, a hill you can see in all directions. We could meet there."

"As good a place as any," Walter agreed, "and a step further on our journey." He rose and walked toward the tethered horses, talking to Reynard.

Ulick watched the others disperse in the moonlight and wondered if there were other things as stable in the changing world as a trader's rendezvous dictated by the very form of the land. What changes would he find in his homeland?

3

Second Day

Walter paused in the castle gateway. So far Rayln had been a fool's errand. He had cooled his heels half the morning waiting for one official after another to make time for him and not one of them had given him more than a word or two before referring him to yet another unavailable subordinate. He hoped Reynard and Garrett had had better luck and stopped himself from summoning them. No, they had their own tasks. Better just go to the alehouse and wait.

The alehouse fronted the main square of Rayln just outside the castle and should be patronized by the garrison. He should be able to learn something as well as quench his thirst.

He took his ale from a barmaid and joined a group of soldiers at a long table by the fire, but their talk was of the Lordships and the northern frontier, rather than the Sueve or what went on in the capital. Odd, how much he wanted to know what had happened in Tarsit. Usually there was a generation at least between one summoning and another. Lately there had been centuries. But even long ago, early in the Hunt, when there had been intervals as short as this five years, he had not been so consumed with curiosity. Why? Because Alesander and Brian had escaped? He still could not grasp the enormity of that fact. To escape, to have a way out . . . how did one deserve that? Why did one deserve that?

The table had emptied while he was lost in thought and Walter started to get up to go in search of new gossips when a grey-clad man sat down opposite him. Walter recognized him from his abortive attempt to speak to the governor earlier. This was a clerk from the governor's office.

The man sipped his ale, eyeing Walter over the rim of his flagon.

Walter considered him. This clerk ought to know the needed information. What was the best approach?

He needn't have worried. The clerk set down his flagon. "You'll never get straight answers at the castle. They're afraid of their own shadows."

"Oh?"

"Afraid they'll be held responsible if anything goes wrong. There's been too many changes in Rayln since the rebellion and everyone covers his ass."

"That's a universal failing."

"Isn't it? Just more prevalent here."

"I've just come from serving in a dinky garrison in the backwoods of Irkeldra, where nothing happens so nothing can go wrong." That ought to explain his accent and his ignorance. "Is it really that bad here?"

"Worse. Last thing the governor wants is word spreading that he has trouble with the Sueve or anyone else, for that matter. This king doesn't tolerate idiots like the last did. The officers suspect everyone of being a spy."

"But all I want is information on the Sueve and their raids."

"They want to know why and for whom."

"I was hired by a peasant woman named Marda Trefsdottir to rescue her son."

"She didn't mention having money to hire anyone when she accosted the governor."

"Would it have made a difference if she had?"

The clerk retreated into his ale.

Walter continued, "Look, I don't know where she got the money but I'm from the south. I need to know what is happening among the Sueve. Can you tell me anything?"

"Not a lot. Just about the time Robert Feracher, the grand duke of Brenzin, rebelled the former khan of the Mahar Sueve fell ill, and the various contenders for the khanate were set on proving their mettle by raiding. Since everything was in an uproar here—Feracher, may he burn in the nethermost pits, had stripped the garrisons of his strongholds and pulled the able-bodied men from his lands when he marched on the capital—Tarsia made a fertile hunting ground. There were Sueve raids, Stros raids, the Lordships refused their tribute. It was chaos."

"So, the Sueve raids have been going on for three or four years?"

"No, once Feracher was defeated and the king moved north and pacified the country, we were able to restore order. Besides after the new khan was elected there was no point to the raids. Only outlaws and tribeless men have anything to gain."

"But they still raid the frontier?"

"These are the first we've heard of in nearly a year. From what the woman said and other reports, a band of twenty or so unidentified Sueve raided three villages in the Tarrozian district and disappeared into the steppe. Not enough to risk relations with the khan."

Was that a warning? And was this loquacious and informative little man acting on his own or as an unofficial envoy from the governor?

"Is my search for the woman's son considered a risk to Tarsean-Sueve relations?"

The man shrugged grey-clad shoulders. "Depends on what you do. Just don't expect official help."

"I see." Walter sipped his ale. He wanted information on Tarsit, on Alesander and Brian, on Richenza, and even on Tredgett. Could he get this man to provide it? Probably not about Brian. He asked "You didn't like Feracher?"

The man smiled wryly. "Loathed him even before he rebelled, and I freely admit it. He always wanted something and acted like it was his right to take what he wanted when he wanted it. When the new king was elected, I was afraid he was going to cave in to Feracher completely; he made one concession after another to buy his cooperation. But Feracher eventually asked for too much, and with Arin defeated, the king could say no. Feracher couldn't stand to be gainsaid and rebelled. I never was so glad to see a head on a castle gate as I was to see his. Not that there aren't those who still feel otherwise. That's why the king restored Feracher's brother to some of the family lands."

That answered some of his questions, but not the important ones. How had Alesander become king? What about Richenza? Was she his queen, or had she been one of the concessions Feracher, her betrothed, had demanded? What question could the man he was supposed to be ask which would elicit an answer?

"His brother, not his son?"

The clerk raised an eyebrow. "Thought that was notorious. Never married. Found out his betrothed was the king's whore practically on his wedding day."

"That was when he rebelled?"

"No, being Feracher, he repudiated her and asked for her lands as a sop to his honor."

"And the king agreed?"

"Had to, I guess, with the Arinese army besieging Iskandroc."

Walter wanted to ask, "Did the king marry her himself?" but that would be too well known. Finally he asked "So, why did Feracher rebel?"

"The king refused to let him dictate who would be of his Council."

They sipped their ale in silence. Walter had more questions now than when he started. But, he reminded himself, they had no relevance to the task at hand. He looked up to see Reynard in the doorway and warned him off. If this clerk was a government spy, then the less he knew, the better. He rose. "Thank you for the information."

The clerk nodded shortly.

Walter left the alehouse and gestured for Reynard to follow him. When they were out of the public square he asked, "Horses and supplies bought?"

"Yes, Garrett is waiting on the outskirts of town."

"Good. Any information on the Sueve?"

"Very little. Garrett talked to a trader just returned from the steppe."

"He can tell me what he learned on the ride."

*   *   *

Bertz reined in at the crest of the hill waiting for Marda and Ulick to come up with him. The village below, Besinton, Marda had named it, showed signs of Sueve attack, but they were minor compared to the devastation in Marda's village. One cottage had had its shingle roof half-burned, some haystacks were charred heaps, some fences were knocked down. This larger village must have been able to fight the Sueve off. Had the villagers noticed anything that would identify which Sueve had attacked them? He turned to Marda. "You say the miller's daughter here was one of the captives?"

"Yes, I recognized her hair, the palest blond, almost no yellow in it, like silver gilt."

"Would they have taken her from the mill there?" Bertz gestured toward the substantial mill by the stream.

"Possibly, but she was a gadabout. She could have been anywhere."

Anywhere there were men, the woman Sella had intimated yesterday. No loss to lose her kind to the Sueve. But the boy, Marda's son, and the dead girl—they shouldn't have suffered. The boy at least could still be saved. One child saved.

He eyed Ulick on his small dark mount. "Do you think these people will talk in front of a Sueve?"

Ulick cut in before Marda could answer. "Do you think either of you could identify a tribe from their descriptions?"

Bertz shrugged. "The sooner we identify the captors, the sooner we can save the boy. And I don't need to remind you, do I, the task is safely over and we don't burn. Follow or not, as you think best." He gestured Marda to precede him to the village.

They aroused no little curiosity and anger with their Sueve companion, but by the time Marda had convinced the villagers that Ulick was a tame Sueve, Bertz had concluded that the man's presence had actually loosened their tongues more easily. Whether those tongues wagged to any purpose was another question. Apparently here too a Sueve was a Sueve. If the Stros had been so undiscerning of their enemies in his time, they would have perished. But Tarseans were soft, always had been.

A garishly clad woman handed Ulick some token on a string or thong. Ulick frowned over it, then tucked it in his caftan.

The crowd was thinning. Marda was leaning down, talking quietly to a respectably veiled brown-clad woman and a few children stood at a distance, gawking at Ulick. There was nothing more to learn here.

"We should go," he told Marda.

She nodded and bade the woman farewell.

Once they had left the village behind, he asked Ulick what the woman had given him.

"That's for Walter to know, not you," Ulick answered then softened at the look on Marda's face. "I can't be sure until I examine it more closely. Let's make for the camp."

4

Third Day

It was a good place for a rendezvous, Thomas thought. This must be the last hill till the rising moon. No wonder traders traditionally chose it for their last stop before venturing out into that featureless plain of waving grass that undulated before him.

"Any sign of Walter or Ulick's parties?" Ellis had joined his vigil on the hill.

"To tell the truth I wasn't looking for them. I was contemplating that endless sea of grass. Intellectually, I know that travel is stimulating, but this is a journey I'd rather not take."

"Give me the real sea any day."

"Ulick wouldn't agree with you."

"No, he certainly wouldn't." Ellis laughed. "Do you think this is some cosmic revenge and our hindsides will pay for Ulick's belly?"

"I'm trying not to think about that. A moon on the plain with Michel and Justin should count as two moons of punishment."

"Three. By the way, who do you want to cook? Justin or Hamon?"

"Truthfully? Neither, but Justin was setting up to cook."

"And Hamon relieved him of the job when we rode in. Do you want to do anything about it?"

23

"Not really. Since neither of the competent cooks has rejoined us, I don't think it's worth the effort."

The wind shimmered through the long grass. Thomas pulled his robe closer. "It's a very foreign country we're going to. I wish we had more warriors."

"We could use Alesander."

"Yes." Thomas stopped, at a loss for words.

Ellis didn't add anything either, but stood gazing northwest toward the mountains far in the distance.

Apparently the realization that freedom from the curse was possible was as personal a thing as what happened between summonings. He hadn't heard but one Huntsman speak of it and he had been quickly silenced as though his words were ill-luck.

"Dinner's ready." Justin had climbed the hill to join them. He looked at the plain to the east and shuddered. "I'd rather burn than go there."

Ellis clapped him on the shoulder. "Those are the alternatives in a nutshell, but I'm told they brew a drink from mare's milk that makes it all go away."

Justin snorted and led the way down the hill to where Payne, Hamon, and Michel sat about the campfire.

Ulick, Marda, and Bertz rode in before Michel and Payne had finished quarreling over who got the drumsticks of the chicken Justin had roasted. As contribution to the scanty feast, Bertz and Marda unloaded bread, and to Bertz's disgust, a skin of drink that proved to be mead.

Thomas chewed the coarse peasant bread slowly, considering that this was as civilized a meal as he was likely to eat for this moon's circuit. Didn't the Sueve drink blood from their horses? The sheer thought made the scrawny hen taste like capon.

The mead was being passed around and Hamon and Payne were amusing themselves by improvising verses to a southern drinking song when Walter, Reynard, and Garrett rode in leading a string of pack horses. The singing stopped and Marda, who had retreated from the campfire, returned.

Garrett and Reynard dismounted quickly, but Walter sat for a moment, surveying them like a stern schoolmaster.

Thomas rose. "Any news of the Sueve?"

Walter grimaced and dismounted. Reynard took the horses and disappeared into the darkness.

"Have you eaten?" Justin asked, and when Walter shook his head, produced the portions he had hidden from Michel.

Walter ate his and said nothing till Reynard returned. When they were all assembled, he said, "I want to know what you found first. Eleylin. You followed the Sueve trail back to the first village they raided. What did you find?"

"More arrows similar to the ones we already saw." Ellis nodded to Hamon, who pulled three arrows from inside his saddle-roll and handed them to Ulick.

Ulick moved closer to the fire to examine them.

"Anything identifiable?" Walter asked.

After a moment Ulick shook his head. "No, nothing specific to any tribe."

"Thomas, did your party discover anything by following the trail of the Sueve and the stolen sheep?"

Thomas nodded to Payne, who answered, "They followed the river after they passed Marda, then swung up into the hills. They made camp about two miles from here, but I didn't see anything that made it remarkable. Perhaps Ulick could see something I didn't. Then they moved southeast into the plain."

"Ulick, we should examine that camp come daylight." Walter said. "What did your party find in Besinton?"

Thomas thought that Ulick hesitated before he answered. "More people who can't tell one Sueve from another. Vague descriptions that could fit any tribe on the steppe."

"Just as I feared," said Walter. "From what Garrett and I learned in Rayln, the official line is that there is peace on the steppe enforced by the new khan of the Mahar. Any previous raiding is explained as the result of the illness of the earlier khan, and any current raiding is to be ignored in the name of fostering diplomatic relations. Though from what Garrett learned from a recently returned trader, raiding even among the Sueve tribes themselves has been minimal since a new khan was elected. Ulick, I never heard of the Mahar. Do you know them?"

"They were a clan of the Trevardin in my time. One of the three tribes of the eastern grazing lands."

"Explain. The western Sueve after they conquered Tarsia

were semi-settled by my time. They had 'hin,' which, I was told, meant encampments but actually were set territories. Do the eastern Sueve have such territories?"

Ulick answered, " 'Hin' must be the same word as our 'yin,' which means an encampment of more than a few days' time. The clans have grazing ranges, not fixed boundaries, like farmers."

"So they shift around like Ortas, first leading the Sueve into Rokhelsan?"

"In time of drought, we shift with the grass."

"What tribes are we likely to encounter?"

Ulick shrugged "It's been a score or more generations since I rode the steppe, but in my time. . . ."

Thomas watched Walter as he listened to Ulick's description of the political situation on the steppe. He seemed alert, more alive than he had been for several summonings. But then the task Marda had set them was straightforward and morally unobjectionable. Rescue a child. It might call for fighting, but it didn't call for murder or murky intrigues. He personally might find this task too full of physical exertion and too lacking in mental stimulation, but it was just what Walter needed. A moon to let his conscience heal after the questionable bloodletting in Tarsit.

Thomas wondered if Walter had inquired about Alesander as well as the task at hand. He'd have to wait for Walter to bring it up. If Walter was letting the past be past for once, Thomas didn't want to open wounds by mentioning the bloody business.

Hamon rose from squatting next to him, and Thomas looked around to realize that only he remained with Ulick and Walter. Reynard and Payne were gone, probably with the horses. Justin and Michel were finishing the mead, while Hamon sat down to join Garrett and Ellis's conversation. Bertz was standing alone, looking up at the moon as it began its descent to the west. The woman was asleep by the fire, wrapped up in her cloak with another grey one over her. Grey? And Bertz wore only a tunic. Unlike him to share, but she was a woman of his class, even if she were not Stros.

Walter had noticed it too. His gaze was intent and he

was frowning slightly, as if distracted by a thought he didn't want to follow.

Ulick paused.

"Was there something else at Besinton?" Walter asked.

"Yes, but I'm not sure what it means, and it would upset the woman." Ulick reached into his caftan and pulled out a small pouch on a thong. He fingered it slowly. "It's a shaman's amulet."

"Does it point to a tribe?"

"No, not really."

"But then?"

"It's an amulet to bind wolf-winds to the owner's will. A thing of evil."

Walter said nothing but pushed himself to his feet. He looked down at Ulick sitting cross-legged by the fire. "I wish the daylight were here so we could search their camp."

5

Fourth Day

Ulick surveyed the deserted campsite silently. It was Sueve—they had burned dung, even though firewood was easy to obtain. In this wooded country, caravans rarely resorted to the fuel that so offended their nostrils. The men who had taken Marda's son seemed to be as careless here as they had been at the village. They must know that their looting had made them enemies, but they had made no attempt to conceal their camp— the fire had been in plain sight, and scattered about were the leavings of their meals and dis- carded items taken in their raids. They had even left a sheep carcass to rot in the grass.

They were not well led. Ulick was even more sure now that these were tribeless men. The am- ulet now in his caftan might be the reason at least one was an outcast.

That was bad. If they were part of a tribe, their khan could be appealed to, or the boy simply bought back. These men would have no tribe to return to, no set territory to range, and if they lingered anywhere too long, they risked being challenged by the tribe that claimed the grazing.

He looked for some clue, any clue to whether they would return to the grasslands or stay to raid another village. He didn't want to tell Walter the trail was cold.

On the edge of the encampment stood a cairn of stones—not a mourning cairn, though; it was too large. The stones were loosely piled, covering something. What? These men had left their refuse lie. He pushed away a few of the round stones—so many must have taken most of a day to gather—and saw what he'd expected.

"I need help," he said, without looking up. Garrett and Bertz joined him and in moments they had uncovered a body, a Sueve body, dead only a few days. It had been covered by stones to keep the wild beasts from it. Fear of being haunted by the dead man had made his comrades perform that small service.

The man was loosely wrapped in a few garments; when Ulick pushed them aside Bertz drew back, his jaw suddenly clenched.

The Stros pointed to the three deep, festered wounds in the dead man's belly. "Manure fork," he said, his voice taut before he walked away quickly.

The wound wouldn't have killed at once, which explained why the raiders had tarried. It also explained why they had left so hurriedly—they wouldn't want to linger in a place which might harbor a ghost.

The dead man's clothes caught Ulick's attention. He rubbed the cloth in his fingers, and then rolled the body on its side to pull the caftan away. As he did the corpse's arm and back were exposed.

Ulick's grunt of surprise drew Walter.

"Have you found something?"

He nodded, but didn't answer as he bent to confirm his suspicions.

"Mahar," he said at last. "Unless things have changed very much."

"How do you know?"

"Look at his back and arm."

Walter surveyed the body, then knelt to look at the indigo blue designs on the skin.

"What are they?"

"Pigment driven into the skin with needles. Only the tribes that camp between the Tangar Mountains and the south bank of the river you call the Magnary practice this. I saw no sign of it among the few Sueve mercenaries I met in Tarsit last time."

"I see."

"Then there are these." He gestured at the clothes.

"What about them?" Walter asked.

"Silk."

Michel, who had wandered up from doing nothing to watch the others work, took exception. "That's not silk, silk is smooth and . . ."

Ulick smiled. "Silk sold to rich western merchants is smooth and shiny. Silk sold cheaply to the eastern Sueve is this stuff. I'm told the thread is the waste from the thread spun for the fine silk. Anyway, look at the shirt—that's finer."

"Why would a Sueve wear silk to raid a village?" Walter asked.

"Because it's light and comfortable and provides some protection from arrows."

Walter raised an eyebrow.

"Silk's strong. Bits of it aren't driven into a wound. And I'm told a skilled healer can unwind the cloth in such a way that the arrow follows its original path when it is removed, and doesn't make a great hole. But it's too costly for the western tribes. In my time only a few great khans could afford it and then only as tribute or booty. But the Mahar often got silk as gifts from the Barajians. Most of the khan's guard would wear it, which leads us to this man."

He prodded the body with his foot. "I don't think he was part of the any khan's household recently, but I think he was at one time. The shirt and the markings would only be found on someone who belonged to a powerful clan."

"You said the raid looked like the work of tribeless men, so you think they no longer belong to the Mahar?"

"Yes. You said that there was a new great khan. It sometimes happens than some clans or individuals quarrel with a new leader and leave."

"What do you suggest?"

"Continue to follow them," Ulick said, and Walter nodded resignedly. As they mounted to ride back to their encampment Ulick passed Michel, who was staring at the carefully restored grave.

"Needles. Into the skin with needles." He looked as if he wanted to be ill.

Dayan Fire-born, son of Tekar Khan, turned the Barajian sword so that he could see the mysterious patterns that lived in the metal. Never in all his sixteen years as the son of a great khan had he seen a weapon quite like this. The Barajian caravan they had encountered was too well defended to raid—even the hottest of his followers had admitted that—but for once Dayan had something the Barajians would trade for.

"You have the sword from your father," said Aslut the shaman.

"Yes, but it is not so fine as this." He swung the new weapon to test its balance.

Aslut took the blade and pointed it first to the sky then to the ground.

"A blade is the source of a warrior's strength." He handed it back to the youth. "Take this, if you will, but do not discard the other. It will take much blood to give this weapon a spirit as strong."

"Jidai says we could trade some of the captives for it, but that we would do better to trade for salt and tea."

"Jidai has the soul of one of these traders in worthless things. Your spirit says you should have this sword."

Dayan frowned at the weapon. "I wish Tulat were here. He would know which we should get." He missed Tulat, who had been a great warrior long ago, and deserved a better death than four lingering nights from a wound inflicted by a peasant.

"Tulat was no more than your servant. He could tell you nothing you do not know already, if you look into yourself."

Aslut had said that, or words like that, many times, but did he understand how *hard* it was to look into himself for the value of a sword?

"We will sell the white-haired girl. All she does is cry." He didn't look at the shaman, afraid he would divine what it was that Dayan had not quite been able to do with her.

"Women are always weeping."

"My mother didn't—doesn't."

"Your father's spirit tells me that you must purify yourself from the taint of her blood."

Dayan nodded. She was Barajian, and Barajians were a
strange people.

"This woman weeps too much."

"A warrior's pleasure is the pain of his enemies."

"Being sold to Barajians should be pain enough."

"As you choose. She is of no matter."

A rider approached the camp. Dayan recognized him as
a Tarsean who lived on the fringes of the plain with a Sueve
wife in something that was neither a true yin nor a Tarsean
farm. In exchange for being left in peace, he had given
good information on which Tarsean villages were weak
enough to raid.

He hailed Dayan and Aslut as he rode into camp, ignoring the idle stares of the Barajians sitting around their
campfire.

"You have news," Aslut said when he had dismounted.

Dayan tried not to stare—he always found the man's
reddish brown hair and pale eyes disconcerting. Was everything blue through eyes like his?

"It took me long enough to find you. I thought you were
going back north."

"Your news?"

"My sister's married to a clerk in Rayln. He told her a
funny story. A woman accosted the governor in the street
a week or so ago about her son who had been taken in a
Sueve raid."

Dayan clenched his fist on the hilt of the new sword.

"And?" Aslut prompted.

"The governor brushed her off. But a few days later a
man who said he was working for her turned up asking
questions. I think he plans to follow you."

"What could one man do?"

"He may have companions. Besides," the Tarsean
paused, "there was something strange about the whole
thing."

"What?"

"This woman couldn't have had any money, or much of

anything, after you finished with her village. How was she paying him? Mercenaries take money."

"You think someone else is paying him?"

"There are people who would benefit if the current governor looked as if he couldn't keep the borders safe. One of them might pay this mercenary to find out who was raiding."

Aslut nodded slowly and Dayan frowned. It was too soon to attract the attention of the Tarseans. Ketei wouldn't dare touch him for now, and by the time he did, Dayan would be strong enough to defeat him. But the Tarseans were different. Aslut had assured him that they wouldn't bother about the small villages, but there was no blood tie to guarantee it.

"If I were you," the Tarsean said, "I'd stay away from the villages."

"You are not me," Aslut said. "Did the woman or her hireling describe the boy?"

"My brother-in-law didn't say."

Dayan looked at the little group of captives they had taken. Five were boys.

Aslut dismissed the Tarsean, who sauntered over to gape at the Barajians' wares, and stood watching the horizon, which was just beginning to darken. When Dayan turned and started to go to Jidai to tell him what he wanted to trade for the sword, Aslut put a hand out to stop him. Dayan waited obediently until the shaman spoke. "I have dreamed."

Dreams, the shaman had told him, were not like spirit journeys. A spirit talked plainly if you spoke his language and knew the prayers to say and the offerings to make. Dreams told truth, too, but were harder to read.

"What did you dream, Aslut?"

"Three nights ago. I marked it because I saw the moon a night past full when I woke so I knew it spoke of something that had already happened." He paused as if trying to sharpen the memory: "I dreamt of wolves—wolves beneath a full moon, hunting. Led by a lean black wolf with grey eyes."

"What does it mean?"

"I searched for the answer in my belly, but I thought it

was good. Perhaps that one of the hunting gods had taken up your cause."

"Now you don't think so?"

"No. The black wolf—he must have been the man we have heard of."

"But why a wolf? Why a full moon?"

"I will find an answer soon."

"I should get rid of the boys, shouldn't I?"

"No, that would not be wise. You must have warriors taught to serve you from before they were men."

"Some of them."

"As you will."

"Jidai thinks the fire haired one would be a good warrior. He has quick wits—we have to watch him all the time."

"Too quick, perhaps. But you must choose as your spirit tells you."

"I'll talk to Jidai—"

"Wait." Aslut turned his full attention back to this world. "Tell Jidai to do something more useful than inspect the salt for dirt."

"What?"

"The Tarsean. He'd sell information about us as easily as he sells information about them. Tell Jidai to make sure he doesn't get home."

"But I promised him I wouldn't harm him if he gave us good information! I would be breaking my word."

"You swore an oath to your father to fulfill your destiny. Which of your oaths is more important? To the one who gave you your life, or to this *obtil*?" He used the most pejorative term for one who wasn't Sueve. "If the khan of Rayln sends armies to stop you now, he will find you weak. You will fail your father."

Dayan hesitated and Aslut stepped away from him. "You must do as your spirit dictates," the shaman said. "I am only your servant."

"I—I'll tell Jidai."

"As you will."

6

Fifth Day

Marda had never ridden for so long. It was just past midday, and she felt as if every bone had been jarred out of place. It was increasingly hard to keep silent and hope that they would rest—or did she want to stop? Every painful jounce brought them nearer Robin. How far had they traveled? How could you tell when one mile was like another—all grass and sky, with no sign of life except the occasional hare startled by their passing?

Were they truly following the right trail? These men—the Wild Hunt—seemed so certain, but how could anyone be sure? So many of them seemed to be great lords of some sort or another. What would they know of trailing Sueve?

The Sueve they called Ulick seemed to be the one they consulted most; but whatever Sir Walter said, she wasn't sure he wouldn't lead them astray or into a trap.

Marda wanted Peter again: not to tell her what to do, but to tell her what she'd done was right. But then she'd never stopped wanting Peter; sometimes she was just able to put the longing aside. She could have married again, but none of the men who'd made their tentative advances had measured up to Peter, or her memory of him.

After four years she wasn't sure what was truth and what was not.

The riders slowed to a halt. Ulick had risen in his saddle and was scanning the horizon. She saw what had caught his attention—even she could smell the smoke, and yes, there was a grey wisp to their north.

Walter rode up to the Sueve. "What is it? The raiders' camp, do you think?"

"Could be. Or a solitary encampment. I don't see any reason the raiders would make camp this early. But then, I've not understood anything these men have done since we started."

"It won't take long to check—we can leave someone here to mark where we stopped. If it's just a herder's camp we can pick up where we left off."

Ulick nodded. Walter turned to consider the men who rode behind them.

Michel immediately put himself forward. "I'll stay! I couldn't ride another foot."

Walter nodded and turned to Marda. "You should rest too."

Her body wanted desperately to agree, but the plump blond Michel made her uneasy. He talked too freely of his skill with women. Without Sir Walter near she wasn't sure how he'd act.

"No, if they have Robin I'll know him."

"It won't be safe if this is a war band."

It took all her courage and anger to shake her head. "No, I will go with you."

He frowned, but instead of forbidding her, Walter turned to Ulick and Payne. "Ride ahead and scout the camp. We'll rest here until you return."

They came back quickly.

"Only a herder's encampment," Ulick reported. "They might know about the men we're after. I think there's been trouble of some kind—the herds are close in and the men are on guard."

"Better find out."

The Sueve camp was smaller than her village—a single family, she heard Ulick tell Walter, who would only rejoin the rest of their tribe a few times a year to trade, except in time of war.

The tent looked like a dirty white mushroom on the green grass, though as they drew closer she could see that it was decorated with strange curling designs in dark reds and browns around its sloped top and the bands that girdled its middle. The smoke curl had come through a hole in the roof. Four mounted men and a boy not much older than Robin waited warily just outside the boundaries of the encampment as the party rode up.

Ulick spoke to the men in Suevarna. A greeting? She wasn't sure. The conversation went on. Whatever Ulick was saying didn't seem to reassure the Sueve.

Finally the oldest man nodded. He called out over his shoulder and the square white entrance to the tent was pulled aside and several women and children emerged. The men dismounted and Ulick, with a nod behind him to do likewise, followed suit.

"They don't like it that I'm working for an outsider woman," Ulick said to Walter, "but they have had trouble with a group I think is the one we're looking for. We've been invited into their tent, where I hope we'll learn more."

"How should I act?" Marda said. "I've never . . ."

"Just stay silent," he said. "I'd prefer they forgot about you. Take food when it's offered. And as for the rest of you—" his look encompassed the Huntsmen, "Less than three drinks of the koumiss would be considered insulting when the skin is passed." He looked back to Marda. "Remember what we learn could help us find your son."

The tent was dark and noisome, but bright with unexpected color. Fiery red and bright pink cloth covered the furnishings and hung to hide the latticework that made up the frame of the tent. She knew some of it was trade cloth from Rayln, but other stuff was woven or embroidered with exotic designs and must have come from far to the east.

The oldest man sat on a chest opposite the door and the other men sat on his right. The women bustled around, serving food. The children stayed outside, but occasional giggles and high-pitched voices gave notice that they were daring each other to spy on their strange guests.

Marda and the Hunt had been seated slightly to the left

of the entrance. It seemed to be a customary seating plan, since Ulick appeared to know exactly where to go.

The conversation between Ulick and the older man resumed and Marda's frustration grew; she could interpret neither gestures nor expressions. She was not, it seemed, alone in her dilemma. Behind her she could hear two Huntsmen whispering.

She glanced briefly over her shoulder—the youngest huntsman, the one called Reynard, was speaking to the tall one, Garrett.

"Ulick's just explaining which tribe he's supposed to be from and who his father and his cousins and all are. I hope he keeps it straight."

She hadn't expected Reynard, who she'd been told had been raised in Rayln, to understand the Sueve language, but she was grateful for the translation.

The talk went on to matters of no import, and she grew impatient, especially when the wineskin began to make the rounds. She took one drink because she'd been told to, but the strong stuff that smelled and tasted like sour milk nearly choked her—she noticed several of the Huntsmen felt the same. She only pretended to drink the next two times and after that she was able to politely decline.

An eternity seemed to pass before Ulick broached the subject of the raiders. He described what he had found at their camp.

"The old Sueve says that these sound like the men who attacked this camp a few weeks ago," Reynard said. "They ran when these people fought back."

Marda saw Ulick snort and ask something else.

Reynard translated the reply: "Seems they've been raiding since cold moon—last autumn, I guess. There's talk of hunting them down, but no one wants to take the responsibility."

Ulick frowned and started to reach into the front of his caftan, then seemed to stop himself.

"Why?"

Even Marda understood that word.

"First, he says, because the new Great Khan of the Mahar, while he claims no responsibility for the party, refuses help in stopping them. Gossip in the winter camp was that the leader is one of his kinsmen." The old one paused. "And second, because of their shaman."

"A spirit-caller?" Reynard seemed puzzled as he translated Ulick's phrase.

"Yes. There was thunder in the sky for three nights after we drove them off, and a wolf wind. It frightened the sheep, so we lost ewes in the lambing. Also, my son Eber was injured in the raid, and has not fully healed." One of the men at his right nodded and Marda saw he held his left arm stiffly at his side. "If it wasn't that my wife knew how to draw out the evil I think he would have died."

Marda clenched her fists. These were the people who had Robin?

"Ulick is asking what kind of magic he works," Reynard whispered to Garrett. "They say he has a man-skin drum."

In spite of herself Marda let out a cry; as soon as it left her lips she felt a hand press on her shoulder and she turned to look into Bertz's face. He shook his head warningly, and she bit her lip to keep from speaking, but she continued to shiver.

Ulick spared her a swift glance, then turned back to the Sueve leader. This time he reached into his caftan and drew out the pouch he had been given in Besinton.

One of the older women knelt to take it—her nose wrinkled as she looked inside. She spoke to Ulick, expounding over the contents, Marda thought, but Reynard no longer translated.

All she could think of was Robin being killed by this Sueve shaman. When the others rose, Bertz had to take her arm to help her to her feet.

Outside the tent the coolness of the spring breeze revived her a little, but she was silent as Bertz helped her mount. Ulick paused to speak to the oldest Sueve, and while Marda waited, the woman who had examined the pouch came to Marda and said something.

Ulick looked over his shoulder and translated, "She wants to know how old your son is."

"Eight, almost nine years old."

Ulick replied to the woman, who glanced briefly at the children chasing each other in the grass. She took something from around her neck, another pouch, and held it up to Marda.

"She says to take it; when you find your son, it might help if the shaman has bewitched him."

It was only a small felt purse on a leather cord that smelt of herbs and had something hard inside.

"Tell her, 'Thank you,' " she told Ulick. She clutched the little gift as they rode away.

Marda kept her counsel until they set up camp in the twilight. Then, with the food on the fire and the horses settled for the night, she turned to Ulick, who was seated with Walter.

"Why didn't you tell me about the pouch? You knew something was wrong!"

Ulick sighed as if he had been expecting this and wasn't pleased about it.

"I wasn't sure it meant anything. The man who lost it could have carried it for years. These are tribeless men, and they will flaunt that sometimes by wearing magic that is anathema to their tribe."

"But you knew that Robin could be harmed by this shaman."

Reluctantly Ulick nodded. "But I've told you they aren't likely to hurt him. He's valuable to them, or they wouldn't have taken him."

"And if the shaman needs another man-skin drum?"

"I don't think your son would be of use to him. The higher the blood of the one whose skin is used—whose spirit is trapped in the drum—the more powerful it is. The son of no one at all, your son, would have little power. Almost any Sueve would be a better choice."

"He didn't use the man he left at the camp."

"He had no time. But I still don't think your son is in danger."

Walter rose and put his hands on Marda's shoulders as she tried to marshal words to voice her fear and frustration.

"Marda, we are tracking your son as quickly as we can. Try to believe what Ulick says. He is here to help you, too."

"So you say," she answered, and walked away. Ulick,

she noticed, went the opposite direction and stood at the edge of the firelight, staring off at the horizon. She didn't sleep much better than the men she had summoned that night, and she saw his figure black against the sky until nearly morning.

7

Sixth Day

The sun was halfway to zenith and the almost quarter moon was sinking in the western sky when the Hunt came upon what by now even Thomas recognized as an abandoned camp. Trampled grass, dung, a fire ring with ashes— this was like the other camps they had stopped at, only larger. Ulick swung off his horse eagerly and Bertz and Garrett soon joined him. The three quartered the ground like hunting dogs, while the others watched them or scanned the horizon.

Ulick grunted and stooped to pick up something.

Walter dismounted. "What is it?"

Ulick rubbed whatever it was with his sleeve, then held it out. "A coin, I think."

Walter took it and gestured to Thomas to join them. "I don't recognize the type. It isn't Sueve?"

"No Khan ever minted coins," Ulick said. "And most coin from trade ends up as trinkets for the women."

"Thomas?"

Thomas took the coin and let the sunlight play across it. "Gold. Surprising someone would leave without it. Does it look like they decamped in a hurry?"

"No," said Ulick. "I think some sizable party

42

was already here when the raiders arrived. There is another fire ring over there. They didn't burn dung. There is a cross trail north-south where the trail we follow has been heading east-northeast. I think . . ."

"I found this." Garrett joined them.

"A Barajian wineskin," said Ulick, "I remember those horn spouts."

"And I think the coin is from the Nolsic islands off the Barajian coast," said Thomas. "Can we assume a Barajian trade caravan?"

"Probably," said Ulick.

"Were they here at the same time as the raiders or before or after?" Walter asked.

"The same time, I think," said Ulick.

"Garrett?"

"I agree."

"Bertz?"

Bertz rose from squatting near the fire ring. "The tracks mingle rather than cross. I think they were here at the same time."

"What do Barajians trade with the Sueve for?" Walter turned to Ulick.

"Horses, hides, fur, and amber from the forests to the north," Ulick answered, "and slaves."

"Damn!" Walter turned and walked away.

Thomas followed.

Walter stopped when he was well away from the cluster of people and horses and stared at the mountains that made a purple rampart on the southern horizon. "Barajia." He paused. "That's assuming that they traded the boy. But they might not do that, since Ulick says they keep young male captives for warriors. Maybe they just sold the women." He shook his head. "No, I'll have to split the Hunt. Are you familiar with Barajia?"

"I dealt with their envoys when I was a member of the ruling council of Amaroc. That's about it. I've heard they've since conquered Lakandar. The expansion probably hasn't made them any easier to deal with. They were a byword for arrogance even then." Thomas studied the jagged mountains on the horizon. "I think we're due north of

Lakandar and Barajia is southeast of us, if I remember my geography."

"Both parties will need fighters." Walter turned to look at the Huntsmen, who had all dismounted. "I'll need Ulick with me. How big a party would suffice for Barajia?"

"Not many. We'd be dealing with individuals, not hordes." Thomas stopped. Somehow both he and Walter had fallen into the assumption that he would lead the party into Barajia. He looked at Walter, who was frowning over the problem of assigning his men and realized that he didn't want to go. Barajia might offer the chance of fine food and intellectual stimulation, but he would worry about the rest of the Hunt.

"Actually," he said, "we'll be dealing, in all likelihood, with traders, not diplomats, and I don't have much experience at that. You should send Hamon."

Walter hunched his shoulders in distaste.

"Hamon speaks Barajian." Thomas marshaled his arguments. "He has acted the merchant before and there is, or was, a sizable population of Eskedi merchants in Lakandar. The Eskedi are the same people as the Sartherians, even if the Sartherians don't acknowledge it. I think Hamon could blend in more plausibly and ask questions without drawing the wrong attention that an errant bureaucrat from Madaria would. They might think that I was a spy."

"You're right, as usual. What would I do without you?" Walter summoned Hamon, who sat on the ground by the fire ring talking to Payne and Michel. Hamon rose as if every muscle protested and walked toward them stiffly.

"*Ylos ton paros emias,*" he said in Sartherian, looking beyond them to the far mountains.

"What?" Walter asked sharply, annoyed by the unknown language.

"The rim of the civilized world," Hamon translated. "I never expected to see it from this side. The talk is that our quarry has crossed paths with Barajian traders. Are you sending some of us to Barajia?"

"Yes, although Thomas says we are actually north of Lakandar."

"*Maia ton misitia bi meditia,*" Hamon quoted, and translated immediately, "Land of turquoise and perfume." He added, "Corruption and intrigue, too, but the poets never mention those things."

"You should fit right in," Walter interjected, goaded by the repeated Sartherian.

Hamon smiled. "So, you're sending me. Who else?"

"No more than three."

"Reynard first.

"Why not Michel?" Thomas asked. "He was trained as a merchant and speaks Barajian."

"Reynard can juggle, which draws an appreciative crowd to question, and his skills as a thief are likely to come in handy. He's also young enough to deal well with the boy if we find him." Hamon pivoted to face Walter. "Besides, I don't want to listen to Michel's bellyaching or worry about what sink of depravity he's mired himself in. That's one of the 'privileges of leadership' I don't have to shoulder."

"Very well, you can take Reynard, but he doesn't speak Barajian," Walter said.

"The less the others talk, the less they can say amiss. I'd like Payne, too. He fights well and he can pass for Arinese. And an Arinese is much more likely to be in Lakandar than a Northerner."

"Agreed."

"Justin."

"No. We might need his medical skills here."

"So might we."

"There should be plenty of doctors and healers in Barajia if you need help. You can have either Garrett or Bertz as a second fighter."

Hamon frowned. "Not much choice there. Two yokels who only speak Tarsean but can fight and track. Shall we flip a coin? No, I take that back. I'll take Bertz. He's the better cook."

"So be it," Walter agreed. "I suspect that the boy is with the raiders, but I can't take the chance that he's not."

"And we get to make a useless holiday excursion into Barajia."

Walter started to rejoin the group by the horses.

"Two things," Hamon stopped him. "One, if you're

wrong, how do we identify the boy without his mother being there?"

"I'll have her describe him to you," Walter dismissed the question.

"Two, how do we summon you if we find him? She said 'safe in my arms.' Just finding the boy doesn't satisfy the terms of the summoning. You can summon us over any obstacle or distance, but how do we summon you?"

"I'll sense if you're successful."

"Wonderful." Hamon glanced aside at Thomas as if asking him to acknowledge the absurdity.

"And you know very well that I can sense where any of the men are and find him." Walter ignored his sarcasm.

"It's the boy you need to find," Hamon continued. "What if we find him and lose him again, or he's somewhere we can't stay with him? I realize you don't like to share your powers, especially with me, but we need some way of marking the boy so you can find him no matter what happens to us."

Walter turned to Thomas. "Do you still have the coin?"

Thomas handed it to him.

Walter drew his dagger and held its point against the coin, which melted away from it as Thomas watched startled. Walter was usually so shy of displaying his powers. He must be impatient to have Hamon and his goading presence gone, to be so blatant, or was he doing this to make clear to Hamon who was leader and who follower?

"That should do." Walter let the sun glint off the now pierced coin. "An ornament that should go unremarked in Barajia and I will sense where it is."

He tossed the coin to Hamon, who caught it as if it were ordinary and dropped it into his purse.

"Do you have other objections to voice before we rejoin the others?"

"Before I and my matched set of redheads hit the trail? No."

"Then we'll ask Marda to describe her son minutely to your group and you can go."

8

Seventh Day

The balmy weather that had eased the Hunt's search changed in the night. Icy winds drove out of the west, hurling stinging rain that drove at their backs and down their necks. No shelter was in sight—even when they stopped to eat at midday the cold slashed at them.

Marda ate the cold food without tasting it. She watched Sir Walter confer with Ulick; the men's demeanor spoke of trouble. Their sudden silence when she joined them confirmed her suspicions.

"What's wrong?" she asked.

"Ulick thinks we have lost the trail."

The Sueve frowned. "We crossed another track and I'm not sure we followed the right one."

"What will we do?"

"Keep following this one until we find out one way or the other."

"Besides," Walter said, "I'm not sure that confronting the raiders directly is a good idea when we don't know their strength. We've too few fighters now that the others are bound for Lakandar."

"So?" Ulick asked.

"I think we should see the Mahar great khan."

"Why?" Marda demanded.

"We need to know if the raiding party was sent

by him or is under his protection—the other Sueve intimated he might not want them touched. In that case we
must act discreetly. On the other hand, he might consider
them a problem he hasn't decided how to handle."

She gave up trying to argue; they were too convinced
that Robin was safe with the savages who had kidnaped
him. All she could do was stand back and listen as they
tried to decide where to search for this great khan.

All they could be sure of was that his encampment was
somewhere east of them, which didn't change their direction significantly. It just meant that they would look for
small outlying camps like the one they had visited, instead
of avoiding them.

So they rode, scanning the horizon for signs of life until
a solitary girl on foot showed them the way.

She wasn't quite in her teens, herding a ewe with twin
lambs. Her black eyes were round with surprise at the appearance of a party of strange men, but she didn't seem
frightened. Was that because her camp had not been bothered by the raiders yet?

Ulick questioned the child briefly and reported that her
camp was nearby to the north. They sped on their way until
the girl was out of sight. Then Ulick pulled up.

"We need to tell a different story this time," he said.
"This late in the day we may have to stay the night."

"Oh, can't we just politely decline?" Michel protested.
"The smell . . ."

"No, in this weather that would raise questions which,
even if not asked now, could cause problems later. More
news gets from camp to camp than you might imagine."

"Then what should we tell them?" Walter asked. "You
said the other Sueve didn't like the idea of your working
for an outsider woman."

"I think I know what to say." He glanced briefly at
Marda. "I'll tell them she's my wife."

"What!" Marda nearly choked.

"They'll know that it's not unusual for an Ortasjian to
take outlander wives. If I tell them Robin is my adopted
son, they'll understand why I'd travel so far to find him."

Justin pulled himself upright with an effort. "What about
the rest of us? Your brothers, maybe?"

"No. I'll tell them you were fellow soldiers when I hired out to fight for the Tarsean duke. Since you don't have loyalties among the tribes, I brought you to help me."

"Plausible," Walter said after a moment's thought. "It seems a reasonable explanation."

"No, it doesn't!" Marda said. "How can they believe you when I don't understand a word they're saying? If I'm married to you I'd have learned *something*."

"You're very stupid," Ulick said, then apparently thought better of it as she glowered at him. "We've been living on your farm. No need for you to know anything. Later I'll try to teach you a few common words."

"What else do I have to do?"

"Stay quiet." He frowned. "And we'll have to share a bedroll when we're staying in an encampment."

For a moment all Marda could do was open and shut her mouth like a fish. Michel grinned and she didn't know whether she wanted to hit him or Ulick more.

Before she could make up her mind, all the Huntsmen except Sir Walter and Ulick looked to their leader, then ambled their steeds out of earshot.

"Is this necessary?" Sir Walter asked.

"Yes," Ulick answered. "It would raise too many questions otherwise." He sighed. "And if it looked like my wife refused to sleep with me, it would lower me in their eyes. It's going to be difficult enough to explain why I brought her along."

"Do you understand, Marda?" Sir Walter asked.

"Yes, but—"

"We're not dealing with tribes that follow Ortas' laws," Ulick said. "It's going to be hard to convince them to help us."

"I don't trust him." There. She'd said it.

"Marda—" Sir Walter began, but Ulick interrupted him.

"This is not my idea of how to spend a pleasant night, either," he said sharply. "I'm no more fond of the idea than you."

That surprised her. The Sueve had never before dared speak plainly to her anymore than she had dared speak of him to Sir Walter.

"It's the surest way to convince them to give us information about your son," Walter added.

She looked from one man to another, trying to think of another argument or alternative. Nothing occurred to her.

"All right," she finally conceded, "But if you dare—"

"He won't," Sir Walter assured her, "You have my promise."

"Easy for you to promise," she answered. "If it's necessary, we'll try it this time."

Their approach must have been heard—people gathered in the center of the triangle made by three squat tents. But no mounted men on horseback waited ready to drive them off. The Hunt was less a threat than a curiosity.

Still, they weren't immediately invited into the tent, as they had been by the smaller family. They waited in the wind and the sharp spatter of cold raindrops as Ulick made his explanations to the men.

The oldest man was tall for a Sueve, she thought. Taller than Ulick and the other Sueve, anyway. His dusky pink caftan was of the same slubby silk that the dead Sueve's had been. In fact, the whole camp had a far more prosperous air than the small one they'd stopped at days ago. The people seemed better fed and their clothes were dyed and embroidered in bright colors.

She knew when Ulick explained about his foreign wife—the Sueve men turned to inspect her. After that she could find no shape to the talk.

Then abruptly the oldest Sueve, the chief of the encampment, Marda was sure, half-turned and called out to someone in the tent. A woman emerged. Her glossy black hair was piled high on her head and held in place with small sticks of carved bone.

The chief spoke briefly with her and Marda saw her look over the company appraisingly—counting the numbers, Marda understood, and probably cursing her husband for his inconvenient hospitality. Peter had done the same often enough to her.

They were served mutton, boiled in the great pot. Bowls were dipped into the steaming liquid as each took his portion. It was not much different from a meal at home, except that the mare's milk wine was as revolting as it had been before.

During the meal there was more incomprehensible talk, but it seemed to flow naturally, as if Ulick conversed rather than questioned. She regretted that Reynard had gone with the other party. She wasn't sure if another Huntsmen spoke the Sueve tongue, and they remained silent.

Sir Walter was frowning—did he understand what was being said, or was he as frustrated as she? No, he was watching Justin, who had held onto the wineskin. The city man started a little and glowered at his leader. Then the wineskin was hurriedly passed to the next man, Michel, who barely pretended to drink from it.

She'd thought for some time that Sir Walter had a way of speaking to his men that she couldn't hear, and this was more proof. There were other things she wondered about these men as well. Did they ever sleep? She'd never seen them do so. They were always awake when she fell asleep and awake when she woke.

That disturbed her more than sharing a bedroll with Ulick. It was one thing if they both merely slept—but to lie the night with a man who had nothing better to do while you slept than to think what thoughts, make what plans? Or to—

She shoved the thought away. Time to worry about that when or if it happened.

Marda could hear the rain and wind outside. But inside it was warm and the flickering firelight lit the faces around her and made even the ones she knew strange and enigmatic. The talk, unintelligible as it was, took on a familiar rhythm. Were they telling stories? The chief Sueve was speaking now with sweeping gestures, as her grandfather had when he told tales.

As the talk continued, her surroundings faded, became more distant. Images danced in the fire and she imagined that they were part of the tale the Sueve was telling. She had almost grasped their meaning when she jerked awake.

Ulick noticed, and laughed shortly as he spoke to the other Sueve. There was a stir among the company and everyone began to rise.

She tried to look unconcerned as she and Ulick laid out

their blankets to make a mutual bed near the entrance to the tent. If her hands shook, she decided, the Sueve could attribute it to tiredness. She couldn't quite bring herself to meet Ulick's eyes.

But when they were done he glanced briefly toward the entrance to the tent and left, joined a moment later by Sir Walter. Relieved, Marda nestled into the blankets and surrendered to the sleep that had almost claimed her earlier.

She awoke later to the sound of deep rolling thunder. At first she forgot where she was, and the feel of a warm body against her back meant only that Robin was there. Then memory surged in on her peace.

She was stark awake, and afraid to move. Somewhere beyond the dimming coals of the fire, a child woke and whimpered its fear of the storm. Marda had curled herself too tightly into a protective ball and her muscles hurt. She relaxed. Ulick faced away from her, toward the tent entrance. Was he watching for someone or something?

Wet wool smelled like wet wool, she realized, even mixed with the smell of bodies and the smoke of many dung fires. The sound of the rain on the felt was strangely muffled, making it hard for her to judge how bad the storm really was.

A crash of thunder frightened the child and it screamed. A woman's voice, half-soothing, half-annoyed tried unsuccessfully to quiet the little one. Another voice, a man's, whispered hurried words to someone unseen. The child continued to cry, answering between sobs.

She had to roll over and half sat up to do so. Ulick instantly rolled toward her and put a warning hand on her shoulder.

"What—?" she started to ask, but he hushed her.

Then, as she lay back, he answered.

"The child is afraid of the wind," he said. "They've had other bad storms like this—wolf winds."

"Sent by the shaman?"

"Perhaps." He listened, but the child had finally been soothed. "But not this one, I think. It's already letting up. A storm sent for evil would last all the night and longer." He settled on his back. "Go to sleep. We've a good day's riding before we reach the great khan's camp."

She crooked her arm under her head and closed her eyes. The rain had settled to a soothing, monotonous patter and the thunder grew fainter and more distant. She slept.

9

Eighth Day—Last Quarter

The yin of the great khan of the Mahar was a short ride from where the Great river was fed by one of its tributaries. The smoke from its many tents was visible for a distance, which reassured Ulick that the Mahar were not at war.

A small rise gave him a good view of the encampment. The tents were clustered in small groups by tribe and clan around the white tent that would be the great khan's.

The scene was peaceful—many sheep and goats grazed on the new grass, and beyond them, horses were herded. The very familiarity ought to have been comforting, but . . .

The other Huntsmen and Marda stirred restlessly behind him. Walter was watching him. "Is something wrong?"

Ulick scrutinized the camp. "It's too big."

"It *is* a great khan's camp."

"It's as big as a winter camp, but the snows have melted. No one should be here but the great khan, his kin, and his household. There are far more than that."

"I don't understand."

"Tribes camp together in winter, but by this time most should be where there is grazing for their herds." He shook his head over the picture.

54

"The only thing I can think of that would keep the tribe together so late into the spring is war, but this isn't a war camp. They burn fires freely; they camp with water on two sides, so that they could not flee. And I can see young men tending the herds."

"None of the small camps spoke of war," Walter conceded.

"And they've just elected a new khan, so it's not that."

"Is it dangerous to approach?" Michel was close behind Walter.

"I don't think so, but be cautious." Ulick looked at the encampment. "Perhaps it's only a wedding."

The camp was open, but a guest did not have the privileges of a tribesman—Ulick led the Hunt to the eastern entrance. All the tents faced that direction, away from the wind, and everyone could see and know they were on honorable business. Two tents flanked the well-beaten path into the camp; standing between them were armed men.

There were guards—wary, but not hostile. They summed up the seven men before them, but made no move.

"What is your business?" one of them asked.

Ulick did not dismount. Behind him, Walter and Garret moved back and out, to give themselves a better view, and to shield Marda.

"I have business with Ketai Khan," Ulick said.

A man emerged from one of the two flanking tents.

"Who is it who has such urgent business?" he asked. He was a broad man, almost square, but what must once have been a strong, hard-muscled body was going to fat. He limped heavily and a puckered white scar ran from the corner of his eye to his chin. It gave him an expression of sardonic humor that fit ill with his ponderous bearing and hard eyes.

"Ulick Assaga Nu." Ulick of the Black Horse. That should keep them guessing.

"Ortasjian?" Of Ortas' People.

"Yes." The man waited expectantly to hear more—tribe and clan—but Ulick did not tell him.

"You've come far." Ulick nodded, and when it was obvious that no more information was forthcoming, the man continued. "And your business with Ketai Khan?"

"Is with the great khan."

The man pursed his scarred lips for a second, then replied, "I have some authority to speak for Ketai Khan. I may be able to help."

"I am looking for my son," Ulick said.

"What makes you think he is here?" The man looked genuinely puzzled. "We haven't taken any captives since the new khan was chosen."

"One of the men who took him wore Mahar clan markings on his back."

"What markings?"

"A stag and a hawk with great claws."

One of the guards said a word—a name, perhaps—that Ulick didn't catch. The speaker scowled at them and they shut up.

"This should not be discussed here." He gestured to the entrance to the tent from which he had come.

"I will deal only with the khan," Ulick said.

"The khan is busy with some Barajian yellow robes." His wry smile seemed genuine as he shared the mild insult. "He'll not be free under this sun. Tell me and I can put your story to him in the morning."

"Not until I know you can aid me."

"I am Ridai. Ketai Khan is my brother, as was the old khan, Tekar. I am commander of the dayguard."

Not so trusted a position as the commander of the nightguard, but Ketai Khan would need a warrior who could still fight for that most important post, and this man would not be such—not with a lame leg. He was trusted, however—no doubt of that.

"It's a long story, and my wife will have to tell part of it—I was elsewhere when my son was stolen."

Ridai's gaze turned to the rest of Ulick's companions, but his expression did not change.

"Come, then, there's food and koumiss and shelter for guests."

The people of the Mahar camp did not look frightened or worried by the strange band of travelers who rode into their camp. A few children ran to hide behind their parents, who only laughed and pointed. But Ulick saw something else—no tent they passed lacked a token to ward off evil:

animal masks, hoops and staves hung with feathers, shards
of mirror—bought dearly from the Barajians, even though
it was worthless trash to them—and blue objects of every
shape and description.

It was not unusual to see such tokens—someone had
hung one on Ulick's own tent after he had been cursed,
before he had been taken by the Goddesses. Little good it
had done, too. But every tent in a great khan's encampment? These people must have something to fear—wolf
winds, perhaps?

The tent they were brought to was little better than a
herdsman's, but near the khan's tent and those of his household. That could mean one of two things: that they were
honored guests, or that they were being put in the most
secure part of the camp so they could be watched or de-
tained.

The fire in its center had burned down to a few coals,
but Ulick could see that the fuel had been wood—wood
which must have been imported from either the west or the
east. An expensive luxury. He sniffed—it was no common
firewood; it had a strong sweet smell—aromatic wood.

Ridai noticed his wrinkled nose. "We had some of the
Barajian yellow robes here. I'll have their stink cleaned
out."

Michel started to say something—he undoubtedly liked
the cloying scent—but Walter must have stopped him. The
exclamation drew Ridai's attention to the other Huntsmen;
Ulick could almost read the question in his eyes.

"These are my sword brothers," he said. "We owe each
other many lives." It was truth, in a twisted sort of way.

He wasn't sure that Ridai was satisfied, but he asked no
more questions with his eyes or his mouth.

Food was brought, and koumiss, and they settled about
the rekindled fire as Ulick began to tell the story—or as
much of it as Ridai should know. He called on Marda for
details from time to time, translating, though he suspected
that Ridai understood some of the Tarsean.

"Describe again the dead man you found," Ridai said,
when they had finished. He looked grave as Ulick repeated
the description of the marks on the body.

"A bad way to die," Ridai commented, as he stared out

the door of the tent. He shook his head and returned to the
men about him. "I must tell this to the khan."

"Do you know who these men are?"

Ridai scowled. "Perhaps. I cannot say more until I con-
sult with the Khan."

"You mean until the Khan tells you what more you can
say!" Ulick stood up. "If you know who these so-brave
warriors are who steal women and children, tell me."

Ridai waved a placating hand and Ulick sat, but remained stiff and angry. "If they are who I believe them to
be, this touches the khan and his kin. I cannot tell you more
until the khan gives me leave."

"And if he doesn't?"

"More is at stake than one child."

Walter leaned past Ulick. "Tell your khan that if it is his
kin we seek, then there are many in the west who believe
the warriors of his tent are cowards. These men ran when
faced with opposition, and killed children and women. Nor
is it only among the outlanders that his blood will be
thought ill of. We stopped at more than one camp that had
been attacked. And we're told they send wolf winds, as
well. Does the khan countenance this?"

Ridai looked as if he wanted to challenge Walter for his
presumption. Instead, he struck both his fists on his thighs,
once, furiously.

"I cannot say more until I speak to Ketai Khan." Ulick
stood, and Ridai with him. He put out a restraining hand
as Ulick started toward the door to the tent. "I can promise
you one thing." Ulick waited. "You will not find the boy
without his help." When that did not placate Ulick, he continued. "Wait a little. If it is as you say, the khan may
choose to help."

"One night," Ulick answered, and Ridai nodded.

"This tent is as yours," he said, and left them.

"Well?" Walter said, when they were certain they were
alone.

"Do you think there's any chance the khan will help us
against his own kin?"

Michel scowled across the fire at him. "Is that what he
said? That we're chasing some of the khan's family? Won-

derful. I say we should get out of here now." Michel was already rising to grab his saddle pack.

"Not yet," Walter said, and Michel reluctantly sat back down.

"Ulick, what do you think?"

"I can't be sure until I know more. If the khan is protecting his kinsmen then we may be in danger. On the other hand, he might find us a convenient way out of a difficult problem."

"And that is?" Thomas asked.

"From what we have heard, the old khan's illness and death caused a great deal of disruption—there must not have been an obvious candidate to succeed him. All the men older than fifteen who were within four generations of kinship to a former khan were eligible. The rivalries can be bitter, and sometimes men leave the tribe when they are defeated.

"If that is what happened, then the khan is caught in the middle. On the one hand, he cannot let his honor be compromised by the actions of his kin. On the other, he cannot be responsible for harming men of the khan's blood."

"Where does that leave us?"

"We are nothing to do with him. If we should 'accidentally' pick up some information that would lead us to these outlaw kinsmen of his, why, that would be the will of Heaven and not his responsibility."

"Do you think he knows where they can be found?" Walter asked.

"Perhaps. But if he chooses to help, he might be able to tell us something useful." He paused for a moment. "One more thing may work for us."

"Yes?"

He described the amulets he had noticed were so plentiful, and pointed to something hanging unobtrusively near their door—a chip of blue stone with a hole drilled through it, strung on a leather thong. "These people are afraid of something. Something that only holy spirits can ward off, or Blue Heaven itself. I think that's why the camp is still together."

"These 'wolf winds'?"

"Yes. The khan may want to send us to find his kinsmen

because he doesn't know how strong their shaman really is. And we're expendable."

"Shit," Michel said.

The north wind cut through the pass above them and swirled the fallen snow in eddies through the deserted courtyard of the caravansary. Bertz buttoned the top button on his hooded cloak so the wind wouldn't pull his hair free from his hood and turned his back to the wind. Hamon should be finished with the border guards soon. Reynard and Payne had watered and fed the horses and rejoined him.

"Any trouble?" Payne asked.

"No sign of it," Bertz answered. "But Hamon didn't talk as though it should take this long."

"Maybe he's pumping the guards for information on the caravan." Reynard squatted in the lee of the central well.

"Let's hope so," Payne said. "This place gives me the willies. Too many blank windows and closed doors. There should be more people."

"Would you be outside in the wind if you didn't have to be?" Bertz asked.

"No. But I can feel their eyes."

"So let's give them something to see." Reynard sat on the well's rim and took three silver coins from his purse. He tossed one into the air so it spun and flashed in the pale sunlight, then added a second and a third to form a ring of moving sparkles.

Bertz glanced at the doors and windows that faced the courtyard. They were the only travelers there. Hamon had ascertained that before going to the guardhouse. But the buildings didn't feel empty. Were there other residents, the staff of the caravansary or the guards' families? Apparently some residents could be lured with legerdemain, for one of the formerly closed doors was open a crack.

Payne nodded to Reynard, who shifted his position to give the unknown watcher a better view. Soon two small heads, one above the other, were peering around the door.

Reynard added two copper coins to the circle he was juggling and grinned at the children. The smaller child toddled into the courtyard, his eyes as round as the flashing coins. The elder yelped and hurried after him. He, or she—

the children were so bundled up against the cold that it was impossible to tell—grabbed the toddler and kept him from coming closer, but was wonderstruck enough that he didn't retreat to the safety of the doorway.

Bertz's daughter, Minka, had shown the same round-eyed wonder and lack of fear when she had watched him at the forge, and he had let her stay, although it wasn't a woman's place to watch a man's mystery, because she was as enrapt by the process of forming things as he was.

The wind made his eyes water, and he turned away. These were alien children, Bertz reminded himself. They were nothing to him.

The door to the guardhouse opened and Hamon strode out. Reynard caught his coins and flipped the coppers to the children who caught them and scurried inside.

"Any news of the caravan or Robin?" Payne asked, as Reynard left to fetch the horses.

"The caravan is two days ahead of us, which means it has probably already reached Istlakan, its destination." Hamon glanced around the courtyard. "The guards seem to have believed my story about being separated from the main caravan, but I'll be happier when we're away from here."

"So will I," Payne said, "and not just because it will be warmer once we're out of the mountains. The very wind here wants to pick my mind."

"Was Robin with the caravan?" Bertz repeated Payne's question.

Hamon glanced at him sharply. "There wasn't an opportunity to ask. The guards were edgy and suspicious enough without asking about things the person I'm pretending to be wouldn't be interested in. Something's got them worried."

"Raiders?" Payne asked.

"Maybe." Hamon was distracted by Reynard's arrival with the horses. Before he could mount, Payne cleared his throat loudly. Hamon turned.

One of the guards walked briskly across the courtyard toward them. He started to say something and stopped abruptly staring from Reynard to Payne.

Hamon said something to him in Barajian, and the guard

frowned, replied shortly, pivoted, and hurried back to the guardhouse.

"What was that about?" Payne asked.

"I don't know," Hamon swung up into the saddle, "but I'm not staying to find out. Let's get out of here."

"Gladly." Payne led the way through the gate onto the mountain road beyond.

Ninth Day

The palace tent of the Khan of the Mahar appeared less a dwelling than a portable audience chamber, though Thomas had no doubt that it served both functions. And just like every other audience chamber Thomas had ever been in, petitioners were forced to wait in it much too long. At least he could entertain himself by watching those whose business was deemed more important than the Hunt's.

Most of the people admitted to the Khan's presence ahead of Walter, Thomas and Ulick seemed to be Barajians, whom the Sueve called "yellow robes." Ulick had explained the reference last night. The color was Barajian imperial livery, and the officials wearing it were considered cowards by the Sueve. The joke was in how the robes were supposed to have become yellow.

He wondered what the Barajians' business was. Their spokesman was tall and supercilious, sporting robes of an obnoxiously bright yellow boasting a prominently displayed badge of rank—Thomas tried to recall which rank the green enamel duck represented. Watching the Khan and the Barajian, he decided he had rarely seen a better example of two men so obviously contemptuous of each other attempting polite negotiation.

"Any sign they'll be finished soon?" Walter whispered.
Ulick shook his head.

"I wish we could hear." Thomas discreetly shifted his
weight off the buttock that was numb.

"Probably arranging a hunt with the emperor," Ulick
said. "The Barajians seem to feel it fosters goodwill, and it
gives the emperor a chance to gauge the Mahar's mood and
strength."

"Like a Tarsean king descending on some hapless duke
and eating him out of house and home for weeks at a time?"
Thomas asked.

"Very much."

Now and then Thomas caught a word or phrase of the
conversation, but his Barajian was rusty and without a context the scraps he caught were meaningless.

At length the Barajians departed, sweeping past the party
of Huntsmen without even a glance. The khan conferred
among his own people, showing no sign of summoning
them, however.

Strange, that the preparations for a hunt should be so
complex.

Another group entered the tent. Women, this time, with
an escort of Sueve and Barajian guards. The party had a
hurried air as if on an urgent mission, but they waited for
permission to approach the khan.

The women weren't Sueve—their robes were the full
stiff garments of Barajia—but they didn't appear to be
slaves or prisoners.

The woman at the center of the group, obviously the
focus of the escort, crossed her hands impatiently in front
of her. Thomas caught a glimpse of the angle of her jaw,
and the way her earring danced against her cheek, and his
mind flooded with bittersweet memory.

Mencia.

But then the woman turned to survey the Huntsmen
seated near the door. She wasn't Mencia, of course, but she
was beautiful by any standard. She had the oval face of a
Barajian goddess, with large black eyes under thin curving
brows. Her black hair was elaborately arranged in braids
and loops, studded with golden ornaments. Her glance
paused on the Huntsmen—Tarseans and Madarians could

not be common visitors to the Mahar camp—but she was clearly distracted.

She was only left to wait briefly before the khan beckoned her forward.

"Who is she?" Thomas asked.

Ulick shrugged. "His wife?"

Thomas couldn't imagine this woman married to a barbarian khan, but while her attitude was respectful it was not servile. She spoke quickly, anxiously, with worried gestures. He caught a few tantalizing phrases—she wanted something delayed. The emperor's hunt? Thomas couldn't tell. Whatever it was, the khan appeared regretful but adamant.

She argued, her consternation increasing, but she kept her composure.

Old memories intruded on his study of her, overlaid them, like reflections in a pond. *Mencia.* Mencia, trying to convince her husband that he shouldn't do something he was set on doing.

Mencia.

He'd thought he'd locked that particular set of memories away very securely.

Walter nudged him. "You're staring. It might be taken the wrong way."

Walter was right. Thomas turned as if to speak to Ulick, but he watched the dais from the corner of his eye.

She must have won some concession from Ketei Khan; she looked less worried as her party departed.

She gave the Huntsmen another puzzled glance as she hurried out.

"Nothing," Walter said. "Not a single hint that the khan might help us." They had waited most of the day. It was dark by the time they had returned to the tent where Marda and the others waited, and they had had to postpone any discussion during the meal they'd shared with Ridai's men. It was late now, the camp was quiet.

"He didn't tell us to leave," Ulick said. He had a point, but Walter still scowled.

"You said we'd leave if you didn't get any cooperation," Marda said. "I don't want to stay here."

"As I explained yesterday, it is a very delicate matter." Ulick was being determinedly patient. "And he at least agreed to see if he could learn anything about the party that raided Marda's village."

"He was lying," Walter assured him. "He knows who's responsible."

"I see." Ulick looked thoughtful. "I still think there's a chance he might help us."

"What will we do if he won't?" Marda asked.

Walter crouched near where she sat by the fire. "They're bound to do more raiding. We'd have to keep watch on the outlying encampments and follow them when they hit."

"How—" Marda began, but Michel, who had been sitting on the other side of the hearth, put down the wineskin and headed for the entrance to the tent.

"Where are you going?" Walter asked.

"Out. Even you have to take a piss sometimes."

"Be careful."

"What trouble could I get into here?" Michel disappeared into the darkness. They were better off without him for a while. His only contribution had been a stream of complaints.

"How can you keep watch on all those little camps?" Marda continued. "They're so spread out."

"We can separate—and meet at nightfall each day." Walter looked at Ulick. "Most of them will stay in one location for a few days or weeks, won't they?"

"Yes, but you're going to have to think of some plausible excuse for your spying. Someone's bound to notice. Tarseans aren't exactly common this far east."

Ulick was right.

"I still," Ulick continued, "think the khan will help eventually."

"We can't wait forever."

"Two more days? Ridai seems to favor us—that should help."

"Two days. No more."

Perhaps Hamon had had more luck. Walter fervently hoped so.

Tenth Day

The crisis had begun, as they so often did, in the middle of the night. The Hunt had quieted, and Thomas was lying on his back in his bedroll, staring at the sky through the tent's smokehole and wondering about the woman who had petitioned the khan, when curt voices and angry footsteps outside portended the arrival of a dozen armed Sueve. They had taken Walter and Ulick and left the rest of the Hunt under heavy guard.

Shortly after dawn the remaining Huntsmen had been escorted into the great palace tent, leaving Marda behind as a hostage for their good behavior.

In the hours since, Thomas had grown tired of sitting and listening silently to conversations he couldn't understand.

Michel appeared to be the problem. He stood surrounded by guards on the far side of the khan's great palace tent, wearing a restraint resembling an unsupported pillory round his neck and hands.

Seated before the khan was a party of Barajians, one of whom had opened his embroidered silken robes to show a deep, fresh cut across his forearm—the sort of wound incurred when defending oneself from a knife-wielding opponent.

67

Walter and Ulick and the rest of the Hunt were seated opposite the Barajians before the great khan. At least they did not appear to be prisoners and the khan was listening to Ulick when he spoke. But . . .

"What did the brat *do*?" Garrett whispered. Like Michel and Thomas, Garrett had no Suevarna at all. Ellis and Justin could both at least order an ale in the western dialect. If the Sueve had had ale, anyway.

"I think they're saying he tried to assassinate the khan's wife," Justin said.

"Widow," Ellis corrected.

"That's stupid. The khan's sitting there. How could she be his widow?" Garrett asked, annoyed.

Ellis shushed him, and leaned forward to listen. "She's the old khan's widow."

"Why should the Barajians be concerned with a Sueve woman?" Thomas asked, and both Ellis and Justin shook their heads.

"They'll probably try to kill us all anyway," Garrett muttered, resting his hand where his knife had been before the Sueve guards had removed it.

"No," Ellis said, "Ulick seems to have talked his way out of that. Now he's trying to argue the khan out of throwing us out of camp—except for Michel—they want to keep *him*."

And that would mean they'd spend the next nineteen days riding around this endless sea of weeds trying to find one small boy, with no clue as to where his captors might be.

Of course Hamon might find the boy; at least he was unlikely to run into problems like this one. Walter should have insisted he take Michel with him. Even if Michel spent the entire trip in drunken roistering, he was less dangerous that way than bored.

Ellis let out an exasperated sigh. "The khan is saying we must leave at once and be out of sight by sundown."

Garrett cursed.

Thomas moved from his place near the back of the clump of Huntsmen and, as unobtrusively as he could, crouched next to Ulick.

"What is the evidence?" he asked.

He'd startled the Sueve and it took him a moment to answer. "They found him in the dowager's tent with his knife drawn."

"What does Michel say?"

"He hasn't been allowed to speak. He doesn't speak Sue-varna and the Barajians won't trust any of us to interpret for him."

"He speaks Barajian."

"Badly."

"Ask if there is anyone else who speaks Tarsean in the camp."

The request sparked more debate. The Barajians were especially vocal; they didn't seem to like the idea. But Thomas noticed that the more the Barajians argued, the more the khan scowled. He had been right yesterday, the khan didn't like the Barajians. At length the Sueve leader consulted with one of his men who hurried away.

Thomas studied the khan while they waited. Ketai's age was hard to judge—he could have been thirty or fifty. He was stocky like most of the Sueve, though somewhat taller. His yellow-brown eyes were shrewd, and he spoke little. He was not stupid, or easily misled.

A little murmur of voices heralded the arrival of a familiar procession. The woman he had seen yesterday, the one who so reminded him of Mencia, took her place next to the khan on the dais.

As if they had choreographed it, the Barajians reared up on their knees and then fell forward onto their hands and touched their foreheads to the ground.

An important female Barajian, then.

Ulick turned to him. "From the earlier talk, I think that's the old khan's widow."

"A Barajian wife—a very noble Barajian wife?"

"Sometimes, when it serves the Emperor of Barajia's purposes, he gives a great khan one of his sisters or daughters."

The dowager's gaze passed over her own countrymen and the Sueve to the Hunt. She surveyed them for a moment, then said, "My Tarsean may be very poor. I have learned it from slaves."

Her accent was heavy, but more than understandable.

Was it wise to trust the intended victim of a crime as an interpreter? Normally he would have asked Ulick to protest, but who else would the khan trust, since he wouldn't trust any of the Hunt?

Thomas studied her for a moment. He could object, but Walter would know if she lied whatever tongue she spoke, and besides, this might placate the Barajians.

"Your Highness speaks the tongue well," Thomas said, guessing at her title. She inclined her head in gracious acknowledgment.

"And you are?"

"Enandor Thomas Chadener," he said, using the title he had held on the Grand Council of Amaroc. No one should recognize it, but it might give him an edge in this status-conscious company, and no one was likely to know how long it had been since anyone had held that office. "I am a lawspeaker." He deliberately used the rough translation of the term lawyer rather than the word itself, hoping she would understand the nuance and use it.

The khan seemed amenable to the change in spokesmen.

"First, Your Highness, could you tell us what you saw occur in your tent last night?" Thomas asked.

"Almost nothing. I was awakened by screaming and sounds of a struggle. When a lantern was lit, I saw that man"—she gestured to Michel—"being held by the guards who sleep in the outer chamber of my tent. I was told he had a knife."

"But you did not see one?"

"No."

Not much help. But at least Thomas didn't think the incident had been disturbing enough to turn her mind against Michel and color her words. She gave two translations—one in Sueve, the other in Barajian. He could follow enough of the Barajian to know it was a fair paraphrase of what had been said.

"Are the guards who captured my companion here?" The dowager beckoned two men from the group which had come with her.

Through the dowager he asked the men what had transpired.

"They say that all they know is that they heard someone

running through the camp, and then suddenly this western outlander was in my tent waving a knife."

"They said they heard him running?"

"Yes."

What had Michel been up to? Time to find out.

"Please ask the khan if we may listen to my companion's story."

The guards dragged him, wooden yoke and all, and dropped him before the khan's dais. He knelt as much because his legs wouldn't hold him, Thomas thought, as because it was wise. His face was pinched with fear and peevishness.

"What were you doing in Her Highness's tent last night?" This venue wouldn't allow for much subtlety of question and answer, so he might as well come right out with it.

"I was being chased. I didn't know whose tent it was."

"Who was chasing you?"

"Some Barajians."

"Why were they chasing you?"

"How should I know? I couldn't sleep, so I walked around, then someone came out of a tent and attacked me. I defended myself and ran and then more people came after me."

"Why were you attacked?"

"I don't know. I was minding my own business. Maybe he was with someone else's wife."

The silence from the Barajian contingent grew ominous as the dowager translated.

Thomas asked Michel a few more questions, trying to ascertain the route he had taken in case any Sueve could corroborate his testimony, but Michel had no idea what direction he had been going or where he had been until he had ducked into the dowager's tent.

"May I ask your countryman a few questions?" He thought she smiled faintly at his request, but she turned to the injured man. They argued.

"Lord Wiraz agrees," The dowager finally informed him.

"Why did you attack my companion?" he asked.

"I did not attack him! I was leaving my tent to relieve myself and I saw him sneaking with his knife already drawn, on his way to Kaiyun Chrysogon's tent."

Kaiyun was "princess," he knew that. And Chrysogon? It sounded much like the word for "golden." *How wonderfully appropriate.*

When Michel heard the translation, he let out a howl of indignation. "That's a lie! He wasn't in his own tent! I saw him before that!"

The Barajian was addressing the khan and the kaiyun now.

"He wishes his turn at questioning the prisoner."

That was the khan's decision, not Thomas's, so there was nothing to do but stand aside and see what transpired.

The Barajian method of cross examination seemed to consist of standing over the prisoner and shouting accusations. The princess's soft-voiced translations of the Barajian official's words made an almost amusing counterpoint.

That technique might work in a Barajian court with the full authority of the emperor behind it, but it merely served to provoke Michel.

"Why would I want to assassinate your kaiyun?" He shouted back, finally. "I don't even know who she is!"

The translation—given, Thomas thought, with a certain amount of enjoyment—seemed to take the Barajian aback. He stopped his questioning abruptly and returned to his place.

Thomas addressed the khan. "I believe I see what has transpired. My companion, sleepless, was wandering through your yin and ran into this gentleman," he gestured to the injured Barajian, "who, thinking he was an assassin, attacked him. My countryman acted to defend himself and ran. Lost in your encampment, he hoped to save himself by hiding in one of the tents, and by great misfortune chose Kaiyun Chrysogon's. An assassin would hardly run noisily to his victim's tent. This is all a misunderstanding."

He listened intently to the Barajian translation and noted that the princess inserted into the narrative a few adjectives stressing the youth of Michel and the great size of the camp.

The Barajian's comment was brief and sardonic.

"A likely story."

The khan stood up. The kaiyun, the Barajians, and everyone else rose with him. He spoke briefly to the woman, who translated, "The great khan says he will consider the best course of action."

Now why, he wondered, as he and the rest of the Huntsmen not accused of any crime were escorted back to their tent, would a Barajian princess know Tarsean? And why hadn't she just sent the slave from whom she had learned the language to do the job?

"Who was lying?" he asked Walter, as soon as they were in the tent.

"The Barajian lied about everything. Michel was mostly truthful, except that he knew why he was attacked."

"Could it have been over a woman?"

Walter shrugged. Marda demanded to know what had happened, so they busied themselves explaining the situation to her.

"Now that we know 'yes,' 'no,' 'please,' and 'thank you' in Barajian, what other useful phrases can you teach us?" Payne asked Hamon, as the four Huntsmen sat around the campfire sharing the meat pastry and the fruit that Hamon had bought earlier in the day at a market on the outskirts of Istlakan near which they were camped.

"More wine?" Reynard licked his fingers. "That's a useful phrase, since we're going to the taverns for news."

"Useful only in moderation." Hamon shifted to lounge against his bedroll. "Wine is *carso* and a cup is *dan*. The plural is *danta*, so a cup of wine is *dan se carso*, two cups *bar danta se carso*. Three is *val*, four *deren*."

"And after a few you could just hold up your fingers." Payne raised his hand with three fingers and thumb extended.

Hamon laughed.

"It's not that funny."

"It could be. You'll get a fight, not a drink, if you make that gesture in Barajia. Keep your thumb in."

"You mean it's like . . ." Reynard made a gesture Bertz had seen made in arguments in Tarsit.

"No, it's more like—" Hamon put his thumb through his clenched fingers. Payne gave a low whistle and Reynard's mouth formed an O. The three Huntsmen looked at each other and laughed.

Bertz rose, unnoticed in their merriment.

"So don't use that gesture unless you want a fight. Now, if I send you to the tapster, what do you ask for?" Hamon asked Reynard

"*Val*, no, *deren danta se carso*?"

"*Val* was correct." Bertz said. "I'm not going with you." Hamon looked up at him measuringly.

"What good would I be?"

After a moment Hamon said,"Do as you please, just don't get into trouble."

Trouble? I'm not the one going drinking, Bertz thought, but he said nothing and busied himself with the horses.

Reynard teased a few more Barajian phrases out of Hamon and soon the three were gone laughing together into the red light of sunset.

Bertz drew water from the well and spilled it into the trough. The horses pricked their ears and the dun, his horse, ambled over and drank. *They're as rested as if we had not ridden them for days and the last three nights*, Bertz thought, and the horse looked up as if it had read the thought. Hamon's horse shook its black mane and whickered across the stony pasture as though it laughed at him.

Demons, not horses. He had to get away.

Bertz fled down the dusty lane to the road. Hamon and the others were not in sight and Bertz shrugged. He really did not want to go into the city whose walls loomed on their ridge two miles away. The road was little wider than the lane he had left and full of choking dust from the traffic of farmers returning home from the city markets.

The road they had traveled from the frontier had been paved and had had inns and what Hamon had told them were official posting stations at fixed intervals along its length, but Hamon had avoided the highway once they were in sight of Istlakan. He had hired the use of this out of the way pasture and gone alone to the market to buy their dinner. Bertz did not question his caution. Beautiful things were treacherous and Istlakan had been beautiful at first sight that morning, its golden walls glowing above green fields netted with silver water channels. Up close the walls were tan stone and the roads dry with dust. And the barley stood high in the fields when at home it would scarce be time for sowing.

God, how he wished he were home.

A harsh shout in incomprehensible words jerked him back to the present and he jumped aside to let a string of donkeys, their straw panniers bouncing with emptiness, pass. He started after them in the lavender twilight.

Why am I here? He turned off the road to walk along the raised bank of a canal that reflected the red sunset like molten metal. *Why did God let me be taken by demons?* He had been doing God's bidding when the Stros had raided the unbeliever's villages. He had been following the Brotherhood's orders when he led the attack. Why, then, had the woman's curse been able to touch him? Ever since he had smelt the smoke of the Tarsean village the doubts had haunted him. The sight of children's bodies seared in his memory. Was he cursed for that? They were unbelievers. So the Brotherhood had said.

They had rejected God.

He had argued. "Reason with them, show them the truth," he had said.

They had their chance; they rejected it, he had been answered.

Not the children, he had thought, but he had obeyed and children had died. Slight bodies twisted, trampled in the mud amid the embers of their villages. The woman with the blood on her face had cursed him in the names of her Goddesses—demons—and his heart had gone cold. But he had trusted God.

Why did God abandon me? Bertz rubbed his belly remembering the wound he had suffered in Tarsit. *Are the Goddesses more powerful?*

The sun had fallen and the canal waters beside him were leaden in the failing light.

Or had his pity for the unbelievers displeased God? Had he been abandoned to their demons to learn the error of his thought? Or perhaps to learn their weaknesses, their secrets? Perhaps he could earn God's forgiveness and no longer be alone among the aliens and their strange ways.

A dark shape loomed before him, black against a sky that showed the first glitter of the stronger stars. It looked like a gate with an arch over it, but when Bertz came closer he could see that the arch was a bridge that carried a road across the canal and the gate—did it hold back the water? The embankment prevented his knowing, so he climbed up to the road and scrambled down the far side. He was examining the heavy timbers that formed bridge and lock in the poor light of fading twilight when the clamor of many horses' hooves on the paved road made him look up.

The horses slowed, and he could hear men's shouts and their laughter as their horses' hooves thudded on the timbers above him. They couldn't have seen him, so why had they slowed? The thuds were random, as though they were milling about, and their shouts were words now, incomprehensible except for one: "Eskedi." Wasn't that what Hamon was pretending to be, an Eskedi merchant?

The timbers creaked above him, and the men laughed. Then someone screamed shrilly. A woman's scream. The men laughed louder. Clothes fell over the parapet to drift into the canal below as though a basket had been emptied. The woman pled with them, her tone unmistakable. Bertz edged out of the shadows under the bridge to look upward. A basket appeared on the parapet and more clothes spilled. The woman screamed again. Not only clothes had been dumped this time, a cloth wrapped bundle fell faster than the rest and splashed into the water. A baby's indignant wail mingled with the men's laughter and the jingle of horse mountings as they continued their interrupted journey.

Bertz dove into the canal and swam to where the baby floated. Its wrappings would too soon pull it down. He grabbed the bundle and held it to his chest as he searched the canal banks for a landing place. The baby's outraged wail reassured him that it had come to little harm so far. He heard a call from the far bank and swam carefully to where the woman had scrambled down from the bridge. She knelt on the embankment and he handed the baby up to her outstretched, indecently bare arms. She clutched it to her, murmuring, and he swam to gather some of the still floating clothes.

After a moment she called something and gestured to the embankment beside her. He tossed the clothes up, but she shook her head, long earrings jangling, and said something else he couldn't understand. Finally she laid the baby down and knelt to hold out her hand. He took it and she pulled him up beside her.

"*Amedu*," she said.

That was "thank you" in Barajian. What was "You're welcome"? "*Katzu*." He finally remembered the word Hamon had taught them.

She rose and led him to the road. He grabbed the wet clothes he had salvaged and followed her. More clothes were strewn about the bridge, as well as three empty baskets. She said something that sounded like a curse and one-handedly started cramming the dry clothes into the largest basket.

Bertz righted one of the smaller baskets and dropped the wet clothes he carried into it, then busied himself in gathering the rest. When he looked up, finished, she had filled the largest basket and nestled the baby on top of the clothes. She slipped her arms through its handles to carry it on her back. She reached for the remaining baskets.

"I'll carry them." Bertz said. She understood his gesture, if not his words, and waited while he put the basket half-filled with wet clothes into the other empty one, then she led the way up the road away from the city.

This wider, paved road had buildings dotted at intervals along it. Bertz looked at the woman in the light of the torch at a door as they passed. She had dark eyes and black curly hair that escaped the shawl she had covered herself with. Her slight build and swarthy skin reminded him of Hamon. If she were Eskedi, then Hamon should pass for one.

Torches bobbed in the road ahead. The woman beside him tensed.

Someone in the other party shouted and the torches came faster. Bertz started to set down the baskets to free his knife hand, but the woman cried out and ran forward. She was met by a young man who dropped his torch to run to her. He hugged her, then took the baby from its nook in the basket on her back and cradled it as she talked and gestured. Soon they were surrounded by a score of jabbering, gesticulating men.

Bertz set the baskets on the ground. He was no longer

needed. He walked back to the canal. The walls of Istlakan rose before him, illuminated by the torches spotted along their battlements. He was almost at the bridge again when he heard hooves rapidly coming up behind him. He ran to the bridge and slid down the embankment, fearing that these were the riders who had harassed the woman earlier. But it was only a single rider galloping toward the city, wearing the same uniform as the guards at the border station in the mountains. Bertz frowned. Could he be a messenger? Hamon had said their horses' special abilities had given them more than a day's time before even the fastest post could arrive if the border guards were suspicious enough to inform the Governor about them. This messenger was not half a day behind.

Bertz shrugged. It was unlikely that the messenger carried news of them. The wind was cold on his damp hair and clothes, and now that there was no one to witness it, he reluctantly gathered his thoughts to change his clothes to dry ones. Then he retraced his previous journey along embankment, back road, and lane to return to the pasture where the horses waited.

The other three Huntsmen were already there, although he had not expected them until midnight. They had rebuilt the fire and Payne and Reynard sat near it with a wineskin and dice between them. Hamon lay wrapped in his blankets on the ground on the edge of the firelight.

"Where have you been?" Payne asked.

"Gone swimming?" Reynard chimed in.

Bertz grunted. "Did you find out anything about the merchants who might have bought Robin?"

Payne and Reynard looked at each other then glanced at Hamon who sat up.

"Well, did you?"

"No," Hamon said.

"It was odd." Reynard tossed the dice in his hand. "You'd think we carried a plague. They either wouldn't serve us, as though we were invisible, or they'd seat us apart from the other patrons, who ignored us."

"They watched us when we weren't watching them," Payne corrected.

"So we learned nothing." Hamon pulled his blankets back around him and lay down.

Payne and Reynard went back to the wineskin. Bertz unrolled his bedroll in the dark beyond Hamon. He stretched out watching the stars wheel in the black sky above them, the only familiar thing in this alien land. He could not sleep, of course, but the weariness of days in the saddle pinned him to the ground with iron force.

Reynard and Payne had long before banked the fire and unrolled their bedrolls, and the crescent moon was rising over Istlakan when Hamon rolled over to face him.

Bertz turned his head. "Is there another word that sounds like Eskedi?"

"No, why?"

Bertz told him of the horsemen and the woman and then about the messenger.

Hamon lay still beside him. Finally he said, "I wondered. I wondered if they were staring at them." He jerked his head toward Payne and Reynard. "Or staring at me."

"A goat!" Garrett said. "A dead goat?"

Thomas leaned back and watched Ulick—he was learning to judge the man enough to understand when he was exasperated. A few hours after the hearing before the khan, Ulick and Thomas and Walter had been summoned back to the palace tent to hear the khan's decision.

"Yes," Ulick said. "Since Ketai Khan is unable to ascertain who is lying, he has decided that we and the Barajians are to compete in a 'tuan barkha,' which translates loosely as 'goat grabbing.' The winner's story will be accepted as the true one."

"Some of the men in the border lordships compete to see how many sheep they can steal from the Tarseans," Garrett said, "but not dead ones."

"The point is to get a goat carcass free of the other riders."

"Riders?" Justin, who had been sprawled against his bedroll, apparently uninterested in the conversation until now, sat up.

"Yes."

"Can't I get out of it?" Justin was easily the poorest horseman among the Huntsmen.

Thomas answered, "The khan insisted that we all must participate, except Michel. We asked for a trade—Michel to ride and you to be hostage—but he wouldn't agree."

"Michel would be much more use than I."

"As it turns out, they agreed that Marda and another hostage could be traded for Michel—but you weren't considered of sufficient status to guarantee that we wouldn't decamp with Michel."

"So who doesn't have to do this?"

There was a moment of silence, and Walter finally answered, "Thomas."

Justin scowled, "Damn you! You've gotten out of the dirty work again."

"You just have to stay out of the way. None of us expects more than that," Walter told him.

"Explain how this works again," Justin begged.

Ulick explained, "A goat carcass is dropped in the center of the riders. Any rider who gets free with the goat has scored. Normally each man who scores wins a prize from the khan and the status it gains him, but we're to compete for tokens from the khan. If we have more tokens than the Barajians at sunset tomorrow, we will be considered the victors."

"But what are the rules?"

Ulick shrugged. "No weapons, and try not to kill anyone—clear off if someone falls off his horse."

Justin shook his head in bewilderment, and Ellis took pity. "Wasn't it common in Manreth for apprentices to play football on holidays?"

Justin grimaced in distaste, "I avoided it, but if you mean a drunken pack of men running wild through the streets in ostensible competition for a ball, yes."

"Think of that—with horses."

"I see." Justin didn't look happy.

Garrett said, "Doesn't sound much different from some of the games we played at home, though it usually wasn't a goat we were grabbing. How many men on a side?"

"If the khan were throwing a real tuan barkha, there

might be fifty or sixty or more riders. We will each have ten."

"Who are the other four on our side?"

"Ridai volunteered," Walter said. "He couldn't convince the khan to decide in our favor, but Ridai has offered himself and three others for the tuan."

"That should help," Garrett said.

"I hope so. We're against Barajian cavalrymen, but we'll have six men with experience playing this game."

"Six men? I count five," Thomas said.

"The duke I served may have used a bastardized Rensel title, but at heart he was a Sueve khan. We played tuan barkha, or something much like it, to amuse him on great occasions. The only difference I see is that we had a marked circle, which was the only place it was legal to drop the carcass."

"How civilized," Justin said.

"Our horses should give us an edge." Garrett frowned. "How long does this last?"

"From high noon to sundown. Roughly six hours—normally a tuan is days long, but the Barajians want this settled quickly."

"Why are there all these damned Barajians here, anyway?" Ellis asked. "Why would the khan put up with so many in his camp? From what I've seen, he doesn't like them."

"I asked Ridai," Ulick answered. "Apparently they are here to escort the Kaiyun back to the capital of Barajia."

"She's the emperor's sister," Thomas added. "Michel chose the worst possible tent to duck into."

"Have we discovered more about what happened?" Ellis asked.

"They still won't let anyone talk to Michel, and I don't dare try for fear the khan might change his mind," Thomas replied.

Marda, who had sat alone, silent and despairing most of the day, finally spoke up. "If you win, will they tell us where Robin is?"

They were all silent for a moment, then Ulick answered her, "Perhaps. If we are good enough, just perhaps."

12

Eleventh Day

"Shouldn't we go with you?" Reynard asked. "My juggling always draws a crowd."

"You heard what Bertz said last night." Hamon stuffed his purse into the folds of the sash that held his jacket closed. "I don't think I want to draw a crowd."

"Take me," Payne suggested. "I understand the market lingo even if I don't speak it fluently, and you could use another man in a fight. That's what you're afraid of, isn't it?"

"If something happened to both of us, who would translate for them?" Hamon nodded at Reynard and Bertz, who were still seated finishing the coarse bread and dates they had all breakfasted on.

Payne was obviously groping for another argument, so Hamon explained. "The incident Bertz described suggests the Eskedi are not popular with at least part of the population. I hope that that prejudice doesn't extend to Sartherians."

"Hence the get-up?" Reynard interjected.

"Hence the get-up." Hamon adjusted his calf-length full robe so that it hid his dagger. "I should be back by midday; if I'm not . . ."

"We'll send your horse after you," Reynard suggested.

Hamon frowned and Reynard sobered. "That would draw the wrong attention. Don't do anything unless I don't return by nightfall. Understand?"

Reynard nodded.

Hamon took Bertz's route of the night before and soon stood beside the main road into the city. There were enough lodging places outside the walls on this road that no one would think it odd that a well-dressed stranger would enter Istlakan on foot through these gates. He mingled with the passing traffic of horsemen and pedestrians, pack animals, and litter-bearers who crowded the road.

The guards at the gate were shouting and pushing at a string of pack mules one of whose panniers had slipped to dump its load of melons in the gateway. They barely acknowledged his passage through the tunnel-like entrance under the thick city wall.

The morning sun cast sharp shadows that made the angular mud-brick and stone building seem like a child's piled toy blocks. The main road cut cleanly between the gate and the palace centered on the riverbank on the east side of the city, but on its flanks, all was congested confusion. Near the wall, where the buildings were mostly single-storied, an occasional moplike crown of palm fronds or silver-green spray of olive branches revealed a garden behind the featureless walls that faced the maze of irregular lanes. Beyond, in the city center, the buildings rose four to six stories in piles dissected by shadowed passages that opened off the main road and quickly lost themselves in the clutter of stalls and awnings which crowded all the space near the main road.

Unexpectedly the road widened into a square and the stalls reduced themselves into a kind of order. Under the eyes of guards in city uniform buyers and sellers noisily carried on their business. Hamon bought a handful of apricots and settled beside the booth to study the layout of the market.

The central area with its bustling crowds had food stalls. The south side seemed to be country people selling eggs, more produce, baskets, and straw-stuffed mattresses. The north and west sides had cheap metalwork and textiles interrupted by wide wooden gates that opened onto crowded closes. The best wares would be stored and sold in those protected shops. As he wiped the juice from the last apricot from his chin, a slight, dark man in a sleeveless robe emerged from a small door cut into one of the wooden gates to a still closed passage, looked around warily, then hurried across the square carrying a small casket and disappeared into another door in a closed gate.

"Eskedi dog!" one of the guards spat after him.

Time to establish that I'm from Saroth. Hamon asked the fruit vendor where to find an honest moneychanger and followed her directions up one of the crowded closes. In the dark shop he changed his Sartherian coins, along with a few from Arin and Avrian he had added for verisimilitude, into Barajian viels and rymoks and inquired in hesitant Barajian about the location of the slave market.

The moneychanger looked up from the scale he was weighing the coins on. "Domestic or exotic?"

"Exotic. I haven't come this distance for a weaving maid."

"Then you should try the Court of Leopards behind the main slave mart."

Hamon dropped the coins the moneychanger handed him into his purse and went back out into the dazzling sun of the marketplace. He followed the man's directions up the main road toward the palace, down an intersecting road to another smaller square near the river and its dockside noise, then down a twisting close to a courtyard with a fountain whose black cat-headed spouts had apparently given it its name. The houses which bordered it all had great open double doors, but few displayed their wares in the street.

He crossed to one that did and looked over the sad display of three children from Tatomy who looked as though they would rather cry or sleep than play the drum and tambourines they held.

"Don't see what you want?" The sharp-faced man who sat in the shade beyond them roused himself to make his spiel. "Plenty more inside. Slave for every task and taste. Best selection in Istlakan."

Hamon cut him short. "These seem a trifle shopworn. I'm looking for something fresh."

The man whistled and three attendants rushed out to escort him inside. Soon Hamon was examining a parade of slaves from all the trading routes Barajia knew, but none of them was a red-haired boy from Tarsia.

It was much the same at all the other shops along the square. Only the quality of the goods differed and the sophistication with which they were presented. Finally, in one of the more elegant shops, seated in an alcove off the main reception room, Hamon sipped chilled fruit juice and frowned at the sweaty, scantily silk-clad, overly made-up Avrinese boy who simpered at him.

"I'm looking for something fresh and exotic. These catamites are four to a fita in Saroth. Don't you have anything northern? Sueve or Tarsean? Unspoiled?"

"Not trained. I can't show the untrained stock without Master Banturim's approval."

"So fetch him."

"He's not here."

"And you'd waste the chance for a sale?"

The young man seated beside him on the flowered carpet hesitated arranging his robe across his knees. He clapped his hands and told the attendant. "Send number sixty-three."

The water splashed from a spigot on the tiled wall into a fluted basin, and a pigeon perched cooing on the rim of the open roof of the main room where the slaves had been displayed. Soon the attendant returned with an older woman and a shawl-wrapped girl. The woman unwrapped the shawl as though displaying a treasure, but the girl had learned no showmanship and stood passively. Her red eyes and nose suggested that she had been bawling. She wasn't bad looking. She had silver-gilt hair and a high-breasted, long-legged body, but she stood stiff as a broom. The woman prodded her with the short stick that swung from her wrist, and the girl arched her back so that her breasts showed more prominently. Not satisfied, the woman slapped her on the rump.

"All right, already," the girl muttered in Tarsean, as she shifted to let her tunic fall open to display one leg from ankle to hip.

Hadn't there been talk of a girl with gilt hair taken by the Sueve raiders? Hamon didn't want to buy this sullen girl. She'd be a nuisance. But how else could he ask about Robin?

"Fresh indeed," Hamon said, "but it isn't a girl I require. Now if . . ."

Before he could finish, an older man entered and rushed across the tiled floor, berating his embarrassed host. "Only Master Banturim decides who sees the special merchandise."

His host retreated rapidly and the woman grabbed the girl by the arm and hurried her away.

"Then when can I see Master Banturim?"

"Tomorrow. Come back tomorrow." The man escorted him out and stood, arms folded, in the doorway.

Hamon stood in the hot sunlight of the Court of Leopards. The sun was past its zenith. He shrugged. The other huntsmen were waiting. He might as well buy them food and return to the camp. And see what Master Banturim showed him tomorrow.

The exchange of Marda and Thomas for Michel was silently formal. The flat stretch of ground just beyond the camp where the tuan barkha was to be played had had a small dais erected for the khan and several other spectators, including the kaiyun and the wounded Barajian.

In his yoke Michel looked more sullen than scared. When the Sueve guarding him unfastened it, he set about rubbing his arms and shoulders as he went to join the other huntsmen. Thomas noticed that he tried to say something, but was hushed by Walter.

The Sueve guard held the yoke and looked from Thomas to the khan, but the kaiyun said something in a low voice. The khan shrugged and waved the yoke away. Relieved, Thomas allowed himself to be escorted to a place beside and slightly behind the fascinating lady who had just rescued him from an uncomfortable afternoon's confinement. He was also in easy earshot of the Barajians, who chattered away oblivious to the fact that Thomas understood almost every word they spoke.

He settled back to spend the afternoon, enjoying, if not the tuan barkha, then the company he kept.

*   *   *

Walter scowled at Michel as he joined the other Huntsmen and the Sueve who were to help them.

"Walter, I . . ." he began.

"Never mind. I don't know why, but you've put us to a great deal of trouble and you're about to put us to more."

"But—"

"Listen." He explained what they were about to do, cutting off Michel's increasingly frantic attempts to speak. "Do you understand?"

"Yes." Michel was sullen now. "We get hold of a dead goat and try to get clear of other riders. Disgusting."

"Maybe. But, Michel," Ellis said, "Do you know what happens if we lose?"

"What?"

"You get handed back to the Sueve and we leave."

Michel turned white.

They mounted and rode to the tuan field.

Walter surveyed the competition. The cavalrymen were none of them very young, but all of them were large and looked as if they had much experience on horseback. Not men to back down easily—this had to be a less dangerous pastime than war.

One of the Khan's men was holding something that had once been a goat—the head and the hooves had been cut off and the legs neatly split to give a better grip. That was what he remembered from his younger days. Gods, even if he hadn't been cursed, it would have been nearly ten years since he had joined in the sport. He hoped he remembered enough.

He glanced at Ulick next to Ridai at the front of the riders nearest the goat. A shout went up as the khan's representative dropped the carcass and the frantic press of horses began.

He lost track of the goat almost at once as the riders surged forward to form a tight circle around the carcass. Ridai's men were experienced and eager for the sport—they had hands on the carcass almost at once, but the cavalrymen were close behind.

Upper body strength was important in this, as important as control of your mount, and a foolhardy disregard for your own safety. None of these men lacked those qualities.

But Walter saw a difference from the tuan he was used to—even in the duke of Hersin's time the game had been played for individual glory. This game was not. The Hunt had a stake in playing as a team—the cavalrymen, it was apparent, did as well. They were obviously trying to block Ulick. Walter smiled grimly and commanded his mount into the press.

Thomas's immediate impression of the spectacle was chaos—a whirlpool-like frothing of bodies and horses with neither rhyme nor reason. The Barajian's supercilious discussion behind him was distracting because it was much more understandable.

"Beasts. A sport for beasts," said the one in the sky-blue brocade robe.

"What did you expect?" his companion, Lord Wiraz, still nursing his injured arm, replied. They were keeping their voices low—the khan must speak a little of their tongue. "Only uncivilized drinkers of blood would have a sport such as this."

The formation of horses changed and almost miraculously one was free of the rest, its rider bent nearly flat over his saddle, the carcass, grasped by one ridiculously thin leg, swinging at his side. Another rider closed on his flank, trying to snatch the goat from him. The lead rider feinted a swerve toward his pursuer, who veered and was left behind.

The victor, Thomas realized, was Walter, who circled the main body of riders triumphantly and dropped the battered carcass in front of the dais. The leader of the Hunt looked uncharacteristically pleased with himself as he held out his hand for the horn token the khan dropped in it. He wasn't even winded.

Behind Thomas, the Barajians stirred angrily.

"Did you tell the fools what would happen if they lost?" Lord Wiraz asked.

"I told them that one would be chosen by lot and beheaded as soon as we reached Istlakan if they were not victorious."

So that was the stake the cavalrymen had in this. Their lives. Too bad they didn't realize that they were competing against men whose stake was their souls.

The kaiyun had heard the conversation, too, and she cast a appraising glance at her countrymen, who did not seem to notice.

As he turned back to watch the vortex of riders reform as the carcass was dropped, the kaiyun's glance intercepted his.

"Your companion seems to have surprised Lord Wiraz," she said.

"He has often been underestimated."

"Only by the unobservant. He has the eyes of a sage."

"Your Highness is most certainly not to be counted among the unobservant."

A minor camaraderie established, they watched the incomprehensible competition proceed. At length another rider broke free—a Barajian cavalryman. And not long after that a second Barajian received a token.

Thomas had half forgotten Marda, but she showed signs of distress at this development. He turned swiftly to reassure her that the sun was still high and the battle barely begun.

The kaiyun noticed too.

"Is she so fond of the little golden-haired one?" the kaiyun asked dubiously.

"No. She has more at stake than even your men, Your Highness," Thomas said. "We had hoped the great khan could aid us in finding the men who took her son in a raid a few weeks ago—aid which will certainly not be forthcoming if we lose today."

"Her son." The kaiyun lifted her chin, the little spark of amusement in her eyes abruptly gone. "Why do you think the khan can help you find him?"

"Ulick says the men who raided her village were Mahar."

"Tell me—" She looked toward the khan, who was utterly engrossed in the spectacle before him. "No. This is not the time."

To Thomas's disappointment, she fell into an abstracted silence.

Walter had lost track of time, all he could count now were the khan's victory tokens—five to a side. Ulick had become skillful at avoiding the cavalrymen set to impede him, and

Ridai's men had done more than their share.

There had been a brief pause to replace the carcass. The last score had been disputed, but in the end, Garrett had been given his token when the khan had decreed that he held enough to count. Even Ketai Khan had been amused at the young Huntsman's gleeful shout of victory.

Now they were again whirling in a tight circle, each man kneeing his horse forward to get near the goat: only Justin hung back on the outskirts, as he had been told.

Ulick swept forward, wresting the carcass from a cavalryman, and Ellis and Garrett swung out to let him get free. He spurred his mount forward, but another Barajian gave a vicious kick to his own mount and headed at Ulick with the obvious intent of forcing him back into the press where the Barajians would have a chance at the prize.

But the man misjudged his own speed and the two horses collided, bowling Ulick's horse over on top of him. The carcass hurled through the air to land next to Justin. The alchemist stared at it for a second, glanced up, and saw that all attention was on the injured riders.

Leaning down awkwardly, he grabbed a leg, and, as he was spotted by three Barajian cavalrymen, took control of his uncanny mount and rode headlong away from his pursuers. They hadn't the ghost of a chance of catching him, though, and looking as amazed as everyone else Justin rode to the khan to get his token.

Turning back, Walter saw Ulick limping to his horse.

"Can you still ride?"

Ulick grimaced. "For now. I may not be able to score, but I can cover the others."

"Don't incapacitate yourself. I need you for more than this." Ulick nodded grimly and they joined the rest of the riders.

Thomas saw that the sun was low, just touching the horizon. Ulick had said they would declare the victor when half its face was hidden. He had lost track of the score, but he thought the Hunt had an edge. Their mounts were not spent as the Barajian's were. Walter had had Ulick stipulate that a change of horses was not allowed. The Barajians could not know what a sacrifice they had made.

But Ulick was visibly in pain and hanging back, cutting in only when one of his companions needed help.

"Your men ride well," the kaiyun said, speaking for the first time since Thomas had explained their quest to her.

"Desperate men do," he said.

"Desperate to save someone else's child?"

"He is Ulick's son, too."

"Ulick is the Ortasjian?"

"Yes."

"Why do you help him?"

"He has helped us."

"You are a long way from your homes."

"So is the boy we seek." On impulse he added, "The child is only eight."

Her beautiful hands had been still all day and he had wondered that anyone could stay so quiet, but now he noticed that she rubbed them together, the fingertips of one hand circling the back of the other, then changing. Something had touched her.

"I will see if the khan will help you even if you lose. I have a little influence with him."

"We would be grateful. You have already gone to a great deal of trouble for us."

She smiled again. "That was more for my benefit than yours. Otherwise I would never have known exactly what happened. Everything would have been kept from me for my own good."

Thomas shook his head, "I've never understood why anyone would prefer ignorance."

"Nor I—" She broke off. "Look."

A new rider held the goat—Thomas recognized Michel's stocky form. He wasn't quite free; a Barajian sprawled across his own mount to grab the carcass. Michel threw himself forward and sideways, pulling the goat away, and his horse kicked with both its hind legs. Barajian horse and rider fell back as Michel rode triumphantly clear of all opposition.

"I think," the Kaiyun said, "that gives you the victory."

The sun was a scarlet half-circle on the horizon. The khan rose as Michel approached, holding the carcass at arm's length. He hadn't had a chance to change from the

Tarsean clothing he had been wearing when captured. The silks were tattered, and Michel's face was filthy, but he looked maliciously triumphant as he took his token.

The khan spoke.

"He's asking for each team to show its tokens," the kai-yun translated.

The Barajians' tokens clicked onto the carpeted platform—twelve. Then the Huntsmen's, one by one. Twelve—then Justin surrendered his small, valueless prize—thirteen for Walter's party.

Marda was sobbing softly next to him—why, when they had won?—and the kaiyun turned toward her.

"Hush," she said gently, "you will surely find *your* son."

As he moved forward to congratulate Walter, he wondered why she had spoken it just that way.

The attendant entered and turned the hourglass for the second time since Master Banturim had been escorted to the anteroom outside the governor's audience chamber. The official seated on the bench beside him gave an exasperated sigh before settling his shoulders back against the wall.

Banturim was equally exasperated but not surprised at the delay. The sounds of men marching and countermarching in the large courtyard behind the governor's quarters undoubtedly meant that the governor was reviewing his precious guard. Only when he stopped playing soldier would he attend to business. Six officials of rank fidgeted on benches or paced the anteroom. They had been here when he came. He'd be lucky to be home by supper.

The noise from the courtyard crescendoed to a ruffle of drums, then mutated to an occasional voice, and the officials on the opposite bench hopefully put their papers in order. But when the attendant returned, he waved Master Banturim into the audience chamber. Gratified and alarmed, he wondered what the governor wanted so urgently.

The governor stood on the dais while a servant unfastened his gilded breastplate. He unbuckled his plumed helmet and dropped it into his chair of state. "Well, where are they?"

"Where are who, Your Excellency?"

"Don't play coy with me. I'll pay your price. The other

Children of Fire. A messenger from the Thuka borderpost brought word of a straggler from the caravan who had two redheads with him. You aren't trying to hold out on me to sell to another buyer, are you?" The governor frowned, his heavy white brows lowering over his beaked nose. Banturim had always thought the effect was marred by the governor's weak chin, which not even his beard and flowing mustache could conceal.

Why hadn't Medrim told him there were more slaves coming? Banturim bowed to give himself time to think. "Your Excellency," he said finally. "You must remember that the message came by official post. The horses—the messenger, perhaps—were changed so that you would learn the news sooner. My poor agents do not have those resources. They are still on the road, and then, of course, the slaves must be rested and cleaned up before I present them to you. Be patient."

The governor seemed mollified, so Banturim ventured a request. "Could I speak to the messenger? I would like to know of my merchandise's condition at Thuka."

The governor assented, and soon Banturim was escorted to a room in the barracks. "You are the messenger from Thuka who came in last night?" The lanky man who had been pointed out to him looked up from a dice game.

"Made the whole ride myself," he boasted. The other men at the table looked suitably impressed.

"Wonderful stamina. You deserve a reward for your diligence." Banturim dropped a viel into the man's hand. "Could we speak apart?"

The messenger followed him into the courtyard.

"Did you see the travelers at Thuka?"

"Yeah."

"Describe them."

"Is this a test?"

"One that has a prize." Banturim flashed a gold coin.

"There was an Eskedi man who came in and talked to the officers and a guard who stayed with the two redheaded slaves in the courtyard."

"Describe the redheads."

"I only saw them from the window. One was a grown

man and the other was a youth who juggled in the court-yard."

Banturim flipped him the coin. An Eskedi with two red-headed slaves—that didn't sound like Medrim's doing. Was someone trying to cut into his business with the governor?

He hurried home. "Medrim!" he shouted as soon as he entered his courtyard. Everyone from the doorkeeper to the cleaning maid shaking a carpet in a window turned to gape. Medrim came running from the back of the house, robe flapping, brushing crumbs from his jacket. Fidrach poked his head out of the showroom.

"Yes, Master." Medrim bowed hurriedly.

"Are there more slaves coming from Suevia?"

"No, just the ones that came with the caravan."

"You didn't contract with an Eskedi to acquire more?"

"An Eskedi?" Medrim sounded scandalized. "Of course not."

"Did any of the other merchants in the caravan?"

"Not that I know of."

"Find out."

"Master Banturim?" Fidrach bounced up from his third bow. "There was a man here in your absence. He claimed to be a Sartherian but he looked Eskedi."

"Did he have slaves to sell?"

"No, he was buying. He wanted something fresh."

Medrim cut in. "This idiot showed him the untrained Tarsean girl."

"He asked about boys." Fidrach recaptured the conversation.

"Was he particular? Did he ask about redheads? Children of Fire?"

"He didn't have time. Medrim, here," Fidrach relished the chance to score against the superior agent, "chased him away before I could learn more."

Banturim swore fluently.

"I told him to come back tomorrow," Medrim ventured.

"You'd better hope he comes, or I'll sell you for a mill slave. Meanwhile, investigate the other dealers. Two red-headed male slaves were brought past the guard post at

Thuka. I don't want anyone stealing my business with the governor, so find out who has them."

Medrim bowed himself through the courtyard and out the gate.

The Tarseans had a legend of a ghost who sat at his own funeral feast. Ulick couldn't remember which blood-feud among the Royal Families of that kingdom had induced the dead king to intrude upon the occasion, but he knew how the ghost must have felt. It wasn't that no one welcomed him to the victor's celebration the khan had decreed, but too many other images came between him and the others around him. He stayed silent, apart in his thoughts, if not his body.

Perhaps it was because the scene was familiar and yet not. If he closed his eyes Ulick could hear his father's voice going on about the tuan just as the khan did, and the women serving could have been his wives or his sisters. But if he opened his eyes, he was surrounded by the Hunt and half the plain and many centuries away from that scene.

He took another drink of the koumiss. The pain was the problem. He had gone the afternoon riding after his fall, but now, without the excitement of the tuan to make him forget his hurts, he was beginning to notice it more. Particularly his knee, which had doubled under him when his horse had fallen. The drink helped, but to drink enough to kill the pain would lead to other problems.

He had been here long enough, he judged. He could leave politely. His companions seemed to be behaving, and Walter would ensure they did nothing wrong.

Ulick rose unsteadily, and the khan caught his eye.

"Ulick Assaga Nu." He had almost forgotten the by-name he had given Ridai. "Are you leaving us so early?"

He inclined his head courteously. "It has been a long time since I rode in a tuan, and I fear I am not as young as I was then, O Khan."

"Which of us is?" There was no answer for that, so Ulick waited. "Go then, if you will. But I remember you came here in search of something. Come to me tomorrow and I will see if I can aid you."

"Most certainly, Great Khan."

Standing in the night air outside the palace tent, he was briefly disoriented by the same strange overlapping of past and present. Home and yet not home. He found his way through the camp as if it had been his own. But the tent was not his—it was dark and dirty felt, without the clan markings his had boasted.

He pulled aside the felt door—his tent had had a wooden one—and saw Marda sitting alone huddled before the half-dead fire. Marda was certainly not his wife—even in the dim light he couldn't have fooled himself about that. The present, and the pain, came back in a rush.

Her face was blank as he entered, but she looked beyond him, hoping for the others to follow. When no one did, she looked hurriedly back into the fire. She was still afraid of him, but he was too bone-weary and sore to care.

Marda had spread out the blankets to make their bed as she had every night. Always before he had been careful not to join her until she was asleep, but now he went to the pallet wanting only what rest the three Tarsean Goddesses would allow him.

He dropped to his knees and realized at once that he had made a mistake; the pain redoubled.

He must have cried out; he heard Marda's voice as from a distance.

"Are you going to be sick?"

"No." He tried to rise but couldn't manage it and rolled onto his good leg, holding the bad one.

"Your leg." She paused. "Your horse fell on you." She knelt beside him. "Let me see."

"Leave it!"

She snorted. "Men. Always thinking they don't need help. Roll over." She was not a weak woman; she half-helped, half-forced him onto his back. With his knee slightly flexed, it hurt less. She touched it with firm, gentle hands.

"I can feel that your knee is swollen and hot even through your trousers." She rose. "Cool water will help." He heard splashing and the sound of water running back into a bucket as if she had wrung something out. He saw that she had soaked her veil as she came back to him.

"It'll work better against your skin. Can you undress?"

"Leave it," he said again.

"No. It'll only hurt worse in the morning." She was right and he cursed fate softly as he sat up. He had no trouble taking the boot off his good leg, but to bend his leg enough to reach the other was exquisite pain. Marda, with a sigh fully as exasperated as his own, took the task from him. He managed his felt stockings and his trousers.

She was right about the cloth; the coolness eased the pain as she wrapped the wet linen around his knee.

"See?" she said, as he lay back and relaxed. She returned to her place beside the fire, and they were silent for a long time. But he could not sleep, and he suspected she would not as long as they were alone.

"Why did you think I was going to be sick?" he asked.

"Peter always was when he drank."

"Peter was your husband?"

He thought her voice caught as she answered, "Yes." Another silence. "What were they talking of when you left?"

"About the tuan today, and tuans yesterday, and how they were better or worse than this one. And tales of what had happened at all these tuans and the lives of the men who rode in them."

"I see."

"But as I left, the khan said that I should speak with him tomorrow about the reason we have come to his camp."

She turned from the fire, her face animated. "Do you think he'll help us?"

"If he truly knows anything."

"What will we do if he doesn't?"

"Look elsewhere." He put his arm across his eyes. "We've promised we will find your son."

"It's easy for you to say! Robin is nothing to you!" She was angry again. When she wasn't frightened, she was angry. "I can't not know what's become of him. He is my son! You don't understand."

It was his turn to be angry. He pushed himself up on one elbow.

"Do I not? I had sons. Three of them, and lost far worse than yours, for they are lost in time and I will never know what became of them."

She didn't understand, he could see it in her furrowed brow.

"Did you think we were born to this?" he continued. "I was war-leader for my clan. I had a wife, two concubines, and five children when I was cursed. Walter had a son and his duke had the child killed. Bertz and Justin had children, too. We have all lost them forever."

"Why? How?"

"You must know Walter's story. It was known everywhere in Tarsia."

She nodded hesitantly. "But what about you? Why are you with them?"

He sank back; this was easier to remember than the other.

"For three summers the rains were sparse. Our herds were lean. Better grazing lay west, near the border. Your people, your dirt turners, didn't welcome us; they had put the grazing land we needed to feed the herds under the plow." Marda's face was grim, she wouldn't like what he said. "We fought to take the land back—it was that or starve. I led the raids. What happened at your village happened at many others. The last was the worst—they fought almost to the last man and woman—their duke gave them no help. One woman lived though. She cursed us. I led; it fell on me. Twenty-one nights passed, but my heart was a stone in my chest. When the full moon rose that last night I was taken by the Three Tarsean Goddesses, and until now, I've ridden among strange people in strange lands and I've liked it as little as you."

That last wasn't really true, he realized as he spoke, for he had learned and seen things he had never dreamt of. He understood more of men's minds than he had before and he had become eager to see what he would learn next.

Marda's grey eyes were leveled on his, as if trying to decide whether she believed him. He lay back and stared at the sky opening in the roof and saw the stars of heaven above him.

"So you see," he finished, "I will find you your son, or I will burn with the rest if we fail."

"I—" she began, but there was a murmur of familiar voices—the rest of the Hunt was returning at last.

Walter came in and looked from the woman by the fireside to Ulick with his bandaged knee. There was a question in his eyes.

"He didn't want me to tend to his knee," she said. "He's been grousing ever since." He shot her a grateful look; Walter didn't like his Huntsmen telling too much to anyone, even the one who had summoned them. She was wise enough to understand.

"Justin, see what you can do," Walter said. But the alchemist was drunk, and Ulick pushed him away before he could make the pain worse.

"Leave it," he said, "The woman's done her worst. We'll see if I can walk in the morning."

13

Twelfth Day

Walter had had to drink more than was his wont at the khan's celebration; there had been no way to avoid it. Drink was dangerous, it led his mind like a staggering sot along avenues both unanticipated and perilous.

Michel was chief in them. Walter still had not had the chance to find out what had really happened the night Michel had been found in the kaiyun's tent. Something stupid and self-serving, no doubt.

Why had the Hunt been saddled with the useless young wastrel? Surely the Ladies had some way to filter out the worthless or the unworthy who were cursed. He had no doubt that Michel deserved to be cursed—betraying Iskandroc to the enemy was perfidious enough. But if evil were the main criterion, then he should have a Hunt of only villains, and that wasn't the case. Many were simply men who had done what had seemed necessary at the time, but they had been unfortunate enough to be cursed for it.

Impossible to fathom the purposes of one deity, let alone three.

He rolled over. He wanted to get up and pace, but he'd wake Marda, and besides, with so many stretched out in such a small space, there was no room.

Eleven Huntsmen this time. Not thirteen.

He didn't know how one rated cursing, still less how one rated freedom.

Brian—Brian probably shouldn't have been cursed to begin with. Had he been allowed freedom as a sort of reparation for the wrong done him by his mother? That didn't seem likely—but none of the others had been cursed for something they so clearly had not been responsible for as the Prince—probably King now—of Canjitrin.

Alesander was another question altogether. He had not been cursed by mistake, had always admitted to killing his brother in cold blood, his reasons notwithstanding. So why allow him to be freed?

Was it only because they had by chance caught the eye of the right woman—one who could hold them at the full moon?

Had the priestess who had tried to hold Hamon been the wrong woman? No, she had chosen the wrong man.

And it hadn't been a woman who had freed Lorcan, if the stories Walter had been told by the Huntsmen cursed before him were true. He pushed the thought from his mind, he had no way of gauging what had happened all those centuries ago; he hadn't been there.

Freedom couldn't be random; there had to be some reason one deserved it. Some critical something that made it possible for a woman to pull a man from the Goddesses' grasp.

Alesander had been with them for five summonses, Brian for one. It wasn't experience, then. Or not obviously so.

Had Brian and Alesander—and Amloth and Lorcan—somehow had some virtue that others didn't?

If so, who among his men possessed this elusive quality?

Easy to pick out the ones who most certainly didn't. Not Michel. Nor Hamon. Reynard? He was still a thief at heart. Bertz—did he have to believe in the Goddesses to be forgiven by them?

Payne, Ulick, Justin, Garrett—hard to say. They kept their thoughts to themselves.

That left Eleylin and Thomas. Eleylin was angry about

his cursing, still. But so had Alesander been. Did he deserve to be among their number any more than Brian had been? He'd executed his mother, hoping the act would save his young brother. Perhaps the Goddesses held him in hope of renewing the royal line of Reasalyn and he could be freed only when the time was right.

Thomas. He tried to imagine a Hunt without Thomas advising him or distracting him when his thoughts were black. All he could remember of the time before Thomas had joined them was harsh bickering between Hamon, Eleylin, and himself.

But Thomas would top his list of men to be free—whatever pain that caused him. Thomas did not deserve the endless summonings and journeyings and machinations that this existence entailed. It was past time he was allowed to find a place where he could be happy among his books and his legal precedents.

Was there a way to anticipate the Goddesses? Could he find a woman for Thomas?

Walter smiled at the notion of himself as matchmaker and rolled onto his back. Probably not this time. Not among the Sueve. It would be dawn soon, and he needed to plan their approach to the khan.

Morning dawned in the Hunt's tent with attendant hangovers. Walter allowed Michel a little time to savor his before confronting him about his transgressions. The young Huntsman was sprawled on his belly on his bedroll, doubtless wishing he could pass out. Walter prodded him with his boot. Michel lifted his head and stared at him with bloodshot eyes, then dropped his head into his arms.

Garrett nudged him from the other side. Michel groaned and didn't move. "Somebody, get a bucket of cold water!"

Eleylin grabbed one and sloshed the water around in it noisily. Michel pushed himself up and grabbed the sides of his head in pain at the sudden movement.

"Get up!" Eleylin said. "Maybe you can find a tree to run your head into and knock yourself out!"

Walter scowled down at Michel. "Explain."

"They want to kill her!" Michel pointed at Marda.

"Who wants to kill Marda?"

"The Barajians. I guess the khan is paying them."

"The khan is paying the Barajians to kill Marda. Why?"

"How should I know? I only know what they said."

"Give me the whole story from beginning to end."

"I was bored, so I wandered around camp for a while. Just as I was going to come back I saw a Barajian sneaking out of one of the tents. He was so obviously trying to avoid being seen, I thought he might be up to something.

"He went into another tent full of Barajians—I could smell the expensive wood they were burning to mask the nasty smell of the tent. I listened, but I couldn't hear much, and what little I could hear didn't make sense. Anyway, about the time I decided to leave, I heard one of them say very clearly, 'The woman must be killed.'

"Turns out the reason I could hear him so clearly is that he was on his way out. He almost ran into me. He tried to grab me and I knifed him. He and some others chased me through camp. I thought I'd duck into a tent and explain that I was lost and they'd just bring me back here. But I ducked into the kaiyun's tent, and you know the rest."

" 'The woman must be killed'? Those were the exact words?" Walter asked, and Michel nodded. "I'm told he Barajians find your grasp of their tongue a poor one."

"I understand it better than I speak it."

"Have you ever actually heard a Barajian speak Barajian?"

"Yes! My tutor was an imperial official of the second rank. Besides, if I heard them wrong, why did they chase me when they discovered me listening?"

"He has a point," Thomas said.

Walter frowned down at Michel. "We have no way of knowing which woman they were speaking of, even if you heard correctly."

Michel rubbed his eyes. "I hadn't thought of that."

"Of course. Clean yourself up. You're filthy." Michel glowered as Walter turned to Ulick. "Your leg?"

Ulick rose gingerly, and flexed his knee a couple of times.

"Better."

"Will you be able to ride?"

"Probably. Just don't ask me to run any foot races."

"Get ready. The two of us have an audience with the khan this morning. The rest of you, stay out of trouble. With luck we should have this over soon."

The successful tuan had put Ketei Khan in an expansive mood. Given his way, Walter and Ulick would have been as drunk as Michel had been last night, before the khan finally came to the point.

Once the subject of the raiders was broached, the khan's manner became more grave.

"This was not an easy decision for me, Ulick Assaga Nu." He was silent for a time. "Tekar Khan, who died last year, had but one son of his wife. Just before the boy's birth, a shaman of the Intaki came to the Tekar's yin speaking of a prophecy of a Child of Fire. He said that the khan's son would be that Child."

Not that again, Walter thought. *Where did a Sueve shaman hear an Eskedi prophecy?*

"The khan," Ketai continued, "had not had much hope for this child. His wife had borne three other children, two of them boys, none of whom had survived to take their first steps. But the shaman's words put heart into my brother. The shaman spoke of portents, and there was a flaming star in the sky.

"Since the khan's wife had almost died with the previous child, Tekar knew this would be the last by her, and the last son is the fire-son, the hearth son. The boy was named Dayan, but was called the "Fire-born" from the time he emerged from the womb. He was a healthy babe, and Tekar credited Aslut the shaman with his son's strength." Ketai Khan sighed. "So Dayan was raised with the shaman whispering in his ear about his glorious future. His mother's women were no help; they believed, if not the shaman, that the greatness of Barajian Emperors was in his blood. By the time he could speak he was stuffed full of his own importance."

"But he was not elected khan," Ulick said.

"When Tekar died, Dayan was just sixteen. Barely old enough to be considered. He has no sense; he presumes that his destiny will carry him through and gives no heed to the damage to his followers. He had some support, but not nearly enough. The night I was proclaimed great khan, Dayan, Aslut, and a handful of followers left the camp."

"Would the boy listen to no one?" Ulick asked.

"When he was young, his mother, then Tekar, and sometimes Tulat." Ketai took a long draught of the koumiss. "Tulat was given to Dayan when he was born. He was the only man who dared argue with Aslut over what he taught the boy. It was Tulat's body you found. I had hoped that Tulat might still have enough influence to teach Dayan responsibility. Now . . . it was a bad death."

"A very bad death," said Ulick. Both spoke of more than a festering belly wound.

"So now, I have no choice. Dayan must be stopped. But . . ." Ketai drank again. He was cradling the wineskin as if it were a comfort, Walter thought. "There are many Mahar who still believe that in time Dayan will fulfill a great destiny. That his birth was a gift from Great Heaven itself. Then there are his mother's kin to consider."

"If we stop Dayan, the blame will not fall on you," Walter said.

"That thought was in my head," the khan said to Walter. "And you will find what you seek as well."

If Robin isn't in Barajia.

"And you can tell us where he is?"

"I think so." Ketai beckoned Ridai, who had sat silently throughout the conversation. "Ridai knows the place. I have kept track of Dayan's journeyings, and they return often to the area where Lugan Mahar Khan's sky stone is. Aslut says that the Great Father's spirit speaks clearest to him there. They will likely camp there. If not now, then soon."

"And Ridai can tell us where it is?"

"I can show you," Ridai said. The khan looked to his brother. "Ketai knows I've counseled him often to take action against the boy before he starts a war. I've men already picked to come with us."

That would ensure enough warriors, but would slow the Hunt. Walter weighed the choices, then asked, "How far?"

"A day's hard ride." The Sueve would ride hard; the moon wasn't half over yet. And it would be best not to offend the khan even now.

"We can't take my wife," Ulick said. Walter hadn't

thought about Marda. It wouldn't be safe to take her with them.

"Leave her with Tekar's widow. She'll be well treated."

And make a good hostage so we'll have to do what he wants. No matter. They had no choice but to find Dayan Fire-born.

"In the morning then," Ulick said.

"You should have taught me Barajian instead of fencing," Reynard complained, as he and Hamon stood in the street leading to the Court of Leopards.

"Who would have guessed you'd need to know it? The Hunt's never had to venture outside the Five Lands before. Besides, I thought you wanted to learn a gentleman's accomplishments."

"I do, but," Reynard glanced around at the towering houses with their carved doors and intricate grillwork, "this is a rich city. When I get out of the Hunt, I might find a wealthy patron for my music here."

Hamon laughed. "Always thinking ahead. You would do better in any of the Five Lands or even in Ascovia. The people of Lakandar have always thought music work fit only for slaves, and the Barajians are little better. Keep your mind on the task at hand. You know what you're supposed to do?"

"Case the joint?"

"Yes. And see if you can talk to the Tarsean girl. I'll whistle if I need you to show the slave dealer what I'm looking for."

"Am I supposed to be jealous that you're abandoning me for a younger boy?"

"Cheeky! You have a filthy mind."

Reynard grinned. "I thought Bertz was going to throw up when it dawned on him what a boy-slave was probably going to be used for."

"Bertz has led a sheltered life. I could wish you had as well."

"Boring. You can't grow up ignorant in a thieves' quarter."

"Just watch which talents you put to use today."

"Of course."

"Then let's see if Banturim has Robin."

Reynard dropped back to a proper respectful pace behind Hamon as they entered the Court of Leopards.

Hamon was greeted at the door of the slave dealer's establishment by two men who outdid each other in obsequiously bowing him inside the house, across the inner courtyard, and into the large room beyond. One provided refreshments, while the other emerged back into the courtyard and ran upstairs. He soon returned with an older man who must be his master.

Reynard, left behind in the courtyard, leaned against the far wall and considered. The houses that faced the Court of Leopards had no space between them and no windows on the ground floor. The upper story windows were small and grated. No easy entrance on three sides, then. A gatekeeper sat in a small room by the entrance. The other rooms at the front and along this side seemed to be for storage. The opposite side had a loggia on the first and second floors. Hamon had been escorted into a room beyond the ground floor loggia, and the slave dealer fetched from rooms off the upper loggia. The doors on the upper floor were draped with brightly patterned hangings. Probably the dealer's private quarters, Reynard decided, too luxurious for slaves.

No one had reentered the courtyard. If they were exhibiting any merchandise for Hamon they were bringing it in from within the building.

The stairway to the loggia filled most of the remaining wall of the courtyard, leaving space for a narrow arched passageway near the corner. Reynard walked over and peered down its shadowed length. Sunlight gilded a blank wall at the far end. A courtyard wall or a back entrance? The gatekeeper was watching the passersby outside in the Court of Leopards and there had been no sign of anyone, slave or not, at any of the doors or windows. Reynard hesitated. *I might not hear Hamon if he whistles. But I can act stupid if I'm caught. Slaves are supposed to be stupid.*

The sunlit wall formed the side of a one story block which continued around two sides of a larger courtyard. Judging from the black, open doorways it seemed to be divided into a number of small rooms. Two men in short

tunics leaned in a doorway deep in conversation and a clot
of women hung out clothes to dry. Beyond them a woman
sat by another doorway cutting up vegetables and dropping
them into a pot beside her. None of them looked Tarsean
or even Sueve. Certainly none of them was an eight-year-
old boy with red hair or even a girl with silver-gilt hair.
No exit was visible but the passage he stood in. You
wouldn't want extra exits if your merchandise could flee,
Reynard decided.

He watched for some time but no one else entered the
courtyard. *Maybe if I put on a show I could draw an audience.* Reynard sorted four silver coins from his purse.
*One thing about Barajian viels—they're big enough to
catch the light.*

A shout from the other end of the passageway stopped
him. The man who had fetched the slave dealer shouted
again and sprinted toward him. Reynard stuffed the coins
in his sash. The man grabbed him and pulled him back to
the entrance court where Hamon stood with the two other
men.

"Idiot! I told you to wait here."

"Sorry," Reynard managed to say, before Hamon slapped
him. Shocked, Reynard rubbed his stinging cheek. Hamon
had turned back to the slave dealer and his men. His tone
suggested that business was nearly concluded and Reynard
was not surprised when Hamon pushed him out the door
into the Court of Leopards a few minutes later.

"Keep walking," Hamon whispered, as Reynard tried to
stop and ask questions in the Court. "They're watching."

They reached the main market square before Hamon
slowed and let Reynard come abreast of him.

"Any news of Robin?" Reynard asked.

"They sold a boy of his description to another customer
two days ago."

"Did they say who?"

"No, but when I promised Banturim a great enough price
he offered to negotiate with the new owner. He said he'd
have word tomorrow." Hamon stopped at a fruit stall and
dickered with the woman who tended it. "I'm sorry I hit
you." He tossed Reynard an orange. "But it had to look
good."

"I'll get revenge." Reynard picked up two more oranges and juggled them as Hamon pulled his purse out to pay for them. "When you least expect it."

Hamon wasn't watching him. "Let's get back to the others."

Reynard wondered why they were suddenly in a hurry, but he asked no questions as Hamon handed him his purchases and led the way out the main city gate. Hamon grabbed his arm when he started to turn aside along the embankment. "Stay on the road. We're being followed."

They didn't stop until they reached a cluster of buildings a few miles down the road. Hamon steered them into a tavern and dropped into a seat by the door.

"Remember how to order drinks?"

Reynard grinned.

"Then get to it. We'll have to wait him out."

The setting sun dyed Aslut's white deerskin tunic the color of blood. This was the garment he wore only when he was spirit journeying to question the Sky Ones.

"What did he say? What does Lugan Mahar Khan say to me this time?" Dayan finally asked. The shaman had been silent for too long.

Dayan had seen Aslut so grave only once, the night he had told Dayan that he had not been elected Great Khan.

"Nothing. I sought him in his white palace tent and he would not speak. I entreated him with all the prayers I know. I threatened with all the threats I know. I offered gifts. I bargained, but he spoke not a word."

"What does it mean?"

"That you have displeased him."

"If he won't tell me what I've done wrong, how can I fix it?"

"I know what keeps him from speaking."

"Tell me, so I can appease him!" Dayan didn't like the way Aslut scanned the horizon, not meeting Dayan's eyes.

"Do you remember I dreamt of wolves?"

"Yes."

"I dreamt of them again last night."

"You thought they were the men the Tarsean traitor spoke of."

"They are those men. I saw them and yet . . ." Aslut frowned. "I could see through them. They were transparent, as if they were half of this world and half not. They are no mere Tarsean mercenaries, I know. They are something other."

"How can they stop Lugan Mahar Khan from speaking to me?"

"He will not speak because he believes you don't have the courage to face these half men."

"Show them to me! I will destroy them."

For the first time Aslut met Dayan's gaze.

"You will have your wish, Fire-born. I learned one thing on my journey: your uncle has sent them after you."

"I shall meet them."

"Yes." Aslut's gaze returned to the horizon. "I fear you will."

The sky was black and the torches at Banturim's door paved the courtyard with stark patterns of orange light and black shadow when Medrim returned. Banturim, who had been pacing the upper loggia since supper, rushed down the stairs.

"What took you so long? Where did they go?"

Medrim plopped on the lowest step, as though his knees had given way. Banturim frowned at his bedraggled appearance and clapped his hands. When a slave came running, he ordered food and water for his agent.

Medrim smiled wanly, started to talk, and broke into a fit of coughing. Banturim fidgeted until the water arrived.

"Well, where did they go? What did they do?"

Medrim drank, then answered. "From here they hurried to the main market, where the man bought food."

"Did they speak to anyone?"

"Just the food vendor. She's a regular, she has a stall there every market day."

"Then?"

"I thought for a moment they were going to linger to set up a pitch. The slave started to juggle, but before anyone much noticed his master hustled him away."

"Where?"

"Out of the city by the Alifar gate. They walked about

three-four miles, then stopped at a tavern off the main road."

"In Beliki?"

"On the outskirts."

"What did they do there?"

"The man sent the slave for drinks. I found a place under a stair where I could see them through the tavern door."

"And?"

"They sat and drank."

"That's all?"

"They were drawing something on the table between them."

"Did they speak to anyone?"

"The slave went back to the tapster a few times."

"Where did they go when they left?"

"I didn't see."

Banturim swore.

"I just looked away for a minute," Medrim hastened to explain. "I was under this wooden outside stair. People kept going up and down from the rooms above. I think it was a laundry. I tried to ignore them, to be inconspicuous, but there had been this bunch of Eskedi children giggling from the window. Then a woman yelled and they stopped and disappeared. I thought they had gone away, but the next thing I knew someone dumped a cauldron of wash water on me. The cauldron almost hit me as it fell. I looked up. There were three boys on the landing, pointing and laughing. A woman came out scolding and grabbed two of them and hauled them inside.

"I looked back at the tavern, and the man and the slave had disappeared. I was furious. Naturally, when the third Eskedi scamp passed me to retrieve the cauldron, I hit him. I shook him so hard his teeth chattered. Then I dropped him and went across to the tavern. I questioned the tapster, but she insisted she hadn't seen where the man and slave had gone."

"Did you believe her?"

"She played stupid, acted as if there were nothing odd about an Eskedi with a red-haired slave. After a while I gave up."

"It was dark when this occurred?"

"About dusk."

"Then what took you so long?"

"When I came out of the tavern I found six or seven Eskedi men waiting. One asked why I hit his son. I explained, but that didn't appease him. He shoved me and then they were all screaming and shoving me. I looked around for help, but everyone in the area was Eskedi. I retreated; three or four of them followed me even after I was on the main road. They caught up to me on the bridge and crowded me into the canal."

"Could you identify them?"

Medrim shook his head. "It was dark by then. The mob outside the tavern, maybe, but I couldn't be sure which three followed me." He hugged his crumpled robe around him. "I pulled myself out of the canal. The gate watch wouldn't let me into the city at first, I looked too disreputable, but they finally gave in when I mentioned your connection to the governor." He sneezed.

Banturim took pity and dismissed him. Medrim picked up the tray of food and disappeared into his room behind the ground floor showroom.

Banturim frowned after him. The Eskedi and his slave who juggled—the juggling proved they were the ones from Thuka—had gone to ground in a village with a sizable Eskedi population. Furthermore, his man had been distracted by an Eskedi ruse. Were the other two, the guard and the red-haired man, also in Beliki? He didn't have the resources to find out. Banturim sighed. He'd have to tell the governor.

Thomas hadn't realized how tired he was of the dark tent with its one eye open to the sky until he knew this would be the last night he would spend in it. No wonder the Sueve worshiped the sky—outside it covered them like a bowl, with horizon on all sides, and in their homes it peered down at them through the smokehole. He watched the smoke rise up through that aperture and waited for Walter to return. Ulick had stopped in briefly to tell the Hunt that they would head out to find the raiders the next day, but he had had no time to give them any details.

Strangely enough it was Justin who provided the solution to the boredom that was making the rest of the Hunt restless and bickering. Apparently the long period of unaccustomed sobriety—last night's debauch notwithstanding—had made the apothecary remember something of his old scholarship. Just now he was regaling the Hunt with the details of a book he had once read entitled *Travels in Suevia.* His black sense of humor had found the book's inaccuracies particularly engaging.

"The author described an unlikely ceremony involving a sheep skull and hide set up on a pole. It seems . . ."

The tent flap was pushed aside and Walter and Ulick entered. The leader of the Hunt raised one eyebrow at the joviality, and Justin explained.

"It's usually a horse's skull," Ulick said. "And it's rarely performed, except in times of flood." Was he joking? Thomas couldn't tell; Ulick merely looked inscrutable. Tarsean ways had had an odd effect on the Sueve.

"What happened? Where are we going tomorrow, and who are we going after?" Thomas asked, handing Walter a bowl.

"The khan has asked us to do his dirty work for him," Walter said. "To put a stop to his errant nephew's raiding. He leads the party we're looking for." He explained the rest between bites of the boiled mutton he dipped from the pot on the fire. "You're frowning," he said to Thomas. "What is it?"

"If Dayan is the son of the old khan and his wife, you realize who that makes him?"

"Who?"

"The son of the kaiyun—the woman who translated for us yesterday. That makes him the nephew of the emperor of Barajia. The *semi-divine* emperor of Barajia. Are we supposed to kill him?"

Walter put the bowl down.

"It isn't likely there would be time to get word to the emperor before the end of the moon anyway, and it only concerns us if they don't have Robin."

"I don't suppose an unidentified group of Tarseans killing his nephew will cause much of a rift between Tarsia and Barajia. As I recall, the Barajians pretty much view non-Barajians in the same light Tarseans view Sueve. But still . . ."

Walter was nodding. "It would be wise not to kill the boy if we can avoid it. We can drop the hot coal back in the khan's lap and head south or west, depending on whether Robin is with Dayan Fire-born or not."

"Is it more likely he's with this party, or in Barajia?" Marda asked. She been silent all day, even venturing an occasional smile at one of Justin's tall tales. Thomas didn't know what had worked the change in her, but he was grateful that her mood had lifted even a little. Walter could concentrate better without her constant harping.

"We don't know enough to make even an educated guess," Walter told her. "But with Hamon's party searching Lakandar for Robin and ours on the trail of the men who raided your village he will be found."

"Am I to go with you?"

"No. Ulick has arranged with the khan for you to stay in the kaiyun's tent." She started to say something, Thomas could see fear in her eyes. "We have an important job for you there, though, now that I think on it." Marda didn't look happy, but she let him continue. "You've just heard us say that the leader of the men we're going after is the kaiyun's son. If Robin is not with these men and we must go to Barajia, we need to know if she will try to cause us trouble because we harmed her son."

She won't do that, Thomas wanted to say. But he had no evidence to back his conviction, so he stayed quiet. Besides, Walter's plan would provide Marda with something to do besides fret.

"But I don't speak Sueve or Barajian," Marda protested.

"The kaiyun speaks Tarsean."

"She won't talk to me."

"Perhaps. Perhaps not. You may learn more than you think just watching. If she sends a messenger south while we're gone, for instance. Any small thing might help." Marda nodded uncertainly. "Good. I know you'll do your best."

He turned back to the rest of the Hunt.

"The khan is sending Ridai and ten of his men with us to help. I couldn't refuse—Ridai knows the way and we need warriors. We'll have to rest our horses as if they needed it."

"I had three offers for mine last night," Garrett said. "They already suspect they're something out of the ordinary."

Walter frowned, "Then we must be especially careful. Marda has made it plain that in Tarsia, at least, the Hunt's existence is believed. We don't want to start more rumors."

Why not? Thomas wondered. *All we'd be is one more Sueve legend.* But he didn't ask. Walter had made it too plain over the years that this was his policy and it was not to be argued with. All Thomas could hope was that Walter would act as necessary when discretion was not the better part of wisdom.

The brocade curtain fell across the doorway as Banturim left the governor's chamber. Governor Ofarim drummed his fingers on the arm of his chair. "It is undoubtedly an Eskedi plot."

"As I have warned you from the beginning, Excellency," said his companion, a thin man in dark Barajian court robes who warmed his hands at the brazier. "She is using this fable to entice and discredit you."

"No, no, Zakar, you do not know the Eskedi as I do. This proves the prophecy is true. The Eskedi also seek the Child of Fire. She spoke the truth."

"I do not trust her."

"Do not fear that because I listen to her I am distracted from our larger design. The true Child will make the other task easier."

"There is no time."

"Confess it, you are jealous."

"I am zealous for the cause which must come to fruition soon. But the emperor must not get wind of it before we strike. Your search for the Child of Fire sends whispers of ambition that could reach the emperor's ear."

The governor cupped his chin in his hand. "Two more Children of Fire. I must have them."

"This Eskedi wants the boy you already have, not the slaves he owns. Has she identified the boy as the Child?"

"Tiramet says he is too young to be certain, but it is possible."

"Perhaps she cannot tell."

The governor silenced him with a wave. "You yourself have prophesied, read omens, that tie in with the old prophecies she tells. But he must be older, in his teens or early twenties when the prophecy will be fulfilled. That is the age of the redheads this Eskedi owns. He must sell them to me."

"Unlikely, in view of what happened today, and he has the older slave hidden."

"I know, I know. We must entice them out of hiding and seize them all. And do it on such grounds that even the most squeamish cannot protest. You must devise a plot." The governor rose. "Arrange it with Banturim. He said the man was to return to his shop tomorrow."

"But Excellency, about the other . . ."

"The other goes apace. Do not worry."

Zakar bowed him from the room, his expression sour, as though he swallowed indigestible words.

14

Thirteenth Day

The Hunt were making their final preparations to depart. All through the night Marda had been aware of their low voices discussing the battle to come. She'd never felt fully a part of their plans and plots, but today she had no place in them at all. They were going to abandon her in this alien camp to a tent full of strange women.

This was necessary to find Robin. She'd only be in their way if she went with them. She recited the reasons she'd been given, but found them cold comfort. Sir Walter had tried to convince her that she'd be useful spying in the women's quarters, but that was busywork meant to ease her mind. Sometimes she thought the Hunt's leader thought her a simpleton.

So all she could do was wait—she'd always hated waiting. Peter had told her to wait, too, when the Duke's men had come to lead him and the other men from the village. What good had waiting done, then?

The horses were brought; they would leave soon. She stood in the doorway watching, wondering if there was something she could say or do, when a small group of people came around one of the tents beyond theirs—a woman in Barajian robes accompanied by two Barajian guards—come, it was clear, to fetch Marda. The woman was thin, her skin stretched tight over fine bones. Her black eyes appraised Marda as if she were a cow for sale in the market.

To shield herself from that critical gaze, Marda clasped the neck of her kirtle and felt there the thong of the small amulet the Sueve woman had given her. The Barajian woman beckoned, but Marda dove in among the Huntsmen instead. She found Ulick securing his saddle pack.

"Wait!" she said and he turned to her, his yellow-grey eyes puzzled. She pulled the amulet from around her neck.

"The woman gave this to me for Robin. I don't know what it's for, but use it if it will help," she said. Ulick took the small sack and tucked it in his caftan just as he carried the other.

As Marda turned to go with the Barajians, Ulick called back to her, "Remember what I told you after the tuan." She nodded as the Huntsmen mounted their horses, and lifted one hand in farewell as they turned to ride off.

The morning sun had scarcely dispersed the shadows in Banturim's courtyard when Hamon arrived to be welcomed with even more eagerness than on his previous visits. Within minutes he had been escorted inside, Master Banturim fetched, and refreshments brought. Banturim seemed nervous as he hurried through the polite preliminaries.

"You spoke to the boy's new owner?" Hamon asked.

"Alas, he refuses to sell." Banturim made an elaborate gesture of regret.

"Even at the price I am willing to offer?"

"Even at that price."

Hamon started to rise. "Then we have no further business."

"There is another way." Banturim fluttered a gesture to stop him.

"Yes?" Hamon sank back to the carpeted floor and let the pause in the conversation lengthen.

"If you truly want this boy, there is another way."

"Which is?"

"I could tell you who his owner is, point out his house."

"So I could negotiate myself?"

"You would have no more success than I."

"Are you suggesting that I steal the boy?"

Banturim did his best to look bland.

"I would have to want this boy a great deal," Hamon sipped the strong coffee they had been served, "and I am not sure that I do."

"But he exactly fits your needs. You wanted a boy of eightsome years. Red-haired. From the north. Unspoiled. This boy was young, strong, healthy, brought on the latest caravan. His hair was like the rising sun."

"So you say, but I have not seen him."

Banturim fidgeted with his sash.

Hamon let the silence lengthen, then said, "There was a Tarsean girl who was shown me the first day I called. Did she come on the same caravan?"

"Yes."

"Then let me speak to her."

"You would take the word of a female slave?"

"If I'm to indulge in slave-stealing I want corroboration that the merchandise is worth the risk."

"Oh, very well." Banturim rose and disappeared into the doorway from which the slaves had been brought on Hamon's previous visit.

This was suspicious: a merchant initiating a theft from a local customer, especially a theft by a foreigner who was unlikely to be a repeat customer. Hamon set his cup down on the brass tray that held the refreshments. It was even more suspicious that Banturim had asked no price for his information.

Banturim returned with the girl and the trainer who had been with her on his previous visit. The girl had learned a little in the interim; she no longer had to be prodded to stand provocatively, but she didn't seem any happier. Her eyes were red.

Hamon rose. "Master Banturim tells me you come from the north, that you arrived in a caravan from Suevia with a boy with red hair. Describe him to me," he commanded in Tarsean. Hamon judged from his expression that Banturim did not understand what was said but the enigmatic trainer probably did. He would have to be careful what he asked.

The girl looked confused. "What about him?"

"His age? His looks?"

"Eight or nine. He has grey eyes, red hair. About this tall." She held up her hand.

"His character?"

She was dumbstruck at the question.

"Come, come, are you stupid? You were with him for days."

That prodded her to speak. "I've known him for years and he's an ill-mannered brat."

The trainer raised her stick, but Hamon stopped her with a wave. "Sounds like a relative. Your brother, perhaps?"

The girl sputtered a quick denial, then went on. "He's from the next village, the widow Marda's son, spoiled rotten."

Exactly the confirmation he needed, but her words were likely to earn her a beating. Hamon felt a fleeting moment of pity. "The boy sounds both spirited and intelligent," he said to Banturim in Barajian. Then he turned back to the girl. "The boy's hair is red, not brown?" That question should allay suspicion that he sought a particular boy.

"Red as a thieving fox," she answered.

Hamon switched to Barajian. "It seems the boy is just what I sought. A pity you sold him."

Banturim dismissed the girl and trainer. "A pity indeed."

"But you will help me obtain him?"

"I will show you the house of his master. It would ruin my reputation to do more."

"And if I negotiate with him, will you expect a percentage?"

Banturim overrode the question. "No—I told you, he will not negotiate. If you want this boy you must take him. My agent will show you the house, discover the safest hour, but that is all the help I can give. You must use your own men for the rest."

"And your agent?"

"He will meet you in the main slave market after dusk."

"We will need to be inconspicuous, fit in with our surroundings. In which quarter is this house?"

"In the Madresh quarter by the river, near the Palace."

Hamon bowed. "Then I will meet your agent . . ."

"Fidrach," Banturim supplied.

". . . at dusk in the slave market."

Banturim quickly bowed him out into the Court of Leopards.

Kaiyun Chrysogon regarded her tent somberly. She had never expected to dread leaving it. Certainly the Sueve considered it a fine dwelling—it was pristine white, showing that her husband had had the status and wealth to change its covering whenever the smoke from the fires darkened it. Only the brightly painted wooden door, a luxury in this treeless expanse of grass, gave it any color. She had instantly hated the tent when she was first brought to it, but then, she'd hated almost everything about the Sueve.

Hate had faded to dislike, and eventually to something warmer than indifference, and cooler than affection. Her husband's first illness had stripped away her complacency, reminding her that there could be an end to this life. To her own surprise, the idea of going back to Barajia frightened her almost as much as leaving it had.

Now she had more than an illogical fear to make her want to linger—she could not abandon her son.

Ketai had finally sent men to deal with Dayan. The day after tomorrow or the day after that she would know whether her heart was to die, her soul to wither with nothing left to love.

She smiled at her own hyperbole—too much poetry.

The unexpected noise inside the tent did not lend itself to introspection. She was at a loss to understand the cause of the uproar, until she heard an unfamiliar female voice protesting in Tarsean.

The Ortasjian's Tarsean wife—what could be the problem? The noise came from behind one of the curtains Tita Maimai had had hung across the tent to provide a modicum of privacy for the women who had followed an emperor's daughter into exile.

She waved away the men of her escort who had sprung between her and the imagined threat. "This is only women's quarreling. Wait outside."

Beyond the curtain one of her maids was sprawled on the floor, and a disheveled angry woman stood, fists clenched, confronting the kaiyun's senior maid, the formidable Tita Maimai. The tall gaunt Barajian woman was scolding the Tarsean and pointing to a tub of steaming water. A bath.

The Tarsean whirled to face the kaiyun. The stranger was dirty; she clearly needed the bath. More was wrong than the threat of hot water, though. She was frightened, true—who wouldn't be, when faced with Maimai and a tub of what looked to be scalding water?—but there was desperation beneath the surface fear.

The kaiyun remembered her conversation with the man who had called himself Enandor Thomas—this woman's son's fate hung in the balance this day, too.

"Maimai, couldn't you have waited until I returned? She doesn't understand."

"She's in no fit state to be presented to you! Just look at her."

"You'd look like that, too, if you'd ridden across country for days."

Maimai sniffed; she considered that unlikely. The Tarsean woman looked more terrified with every word.

"Maimai wants to know why you refuse to be bathed," the kaiyun said to her.

"That's not what she said!" The woman was no fool; just frightened, angry, and humiliated.

"It is, shall we say, the gist of her words."

"She didn't ask me, did she?"

"Apparently not." She turned back to Maimai. "You really should have waited for me. You've made everything worse. The khan requested we treat her as a guest, and you have treated her like a slave. She is not stupid, either—I'd be careful what you say. She understands more than you think."

"As you wish, Kaiyun. Will she let herself be bathed or will we have to put up with her smell until her man fetches her?"

The kaiyun smiled at the Tarsean woman. "Maimai offers as much apology as her pride allows her." The woman relaxed, allowed herself a brief smile as she if shared the small joke.

"The men who sent you here could not be bothered to tell us your name. What is it?"

"Marda."

A name with an edge. It suited her.

"Marda, you've traveled so far, wouldn't you feel better for a bath?"

Marda gave the tub a sidelong glance, then pushed a stray lock of dirty hair out of her face and nodded.

"But not with her—Maimai—watching."

Maimai bristled at the discourteous omission of her proper title.

"If you would keep her happy, address her as 'Tita Maimai.' She's very particular about titles, I'm afraid."

"Without Tita Maimai, then." Even with the title Marda's words sounded faintly impolite.

"As you wish." The kaiyun turned to Maimai. "She says she would rather you didn't stay. Let the others do the work. I need to speak to you."

They left Marda to the cautious ministrations of three of the lesser maids. The sounds from behind the curtain were subdued. The matter seemed settled.

"What did Ketai want?" Maimai asked. She could never bring herself to call the new khan by his title. To her, Tekar had been the khan, Ketai only his youngest brother, chief of the kaiyun's bodyguard for the years of her marriage.

"He has sent the Tarseans to 'deal with' Dayan."

Maimai's thin face grew tauter. "They are worse barbarians than the Sueve! Who knows what they will do to him?"

"We don't know enough to judge. But they have reason to be angry. He's been doing something among the Tarseans—he has at least taken captives. The Tarsean woman's son among them. That's why they've come, to find her child."

"How did you learn this?"

"A little from the khan. More from the Tarsean man who stood hostage at the tuan."

"What shall we do?"

"What *can* we do? Wait."

"We could send to His Resplendent Majesty; your brother would surely help."

"He doesn't need this vexation, even if there were time to send to the capital for his aid."

Maimai had never been prone to shows of affection—scolding was her way of showing love. Even for her that was too inappropriate now, she was clearly at a loss for what to do. Put her mind to something simple.

"We should keep busy. Whatever happens, we will be departing in a matter of days. I suppose it is time we thought about packing."

"It isn't as if we haven't moved all this every time the winds changed for the past twenty years."

"Yes, but we won't need to take everything, and then there are farewell gifts to consider."

Maimai scurried off to the chest where she kept her careful housewifely inventory of all Kaiyun Chrysogon's possessions. *Things.* Chrysogon looked about her at the golden hangings that so bravely tried to disguise a Sueve tent as a Barajian palace, at the cunningly wrought folding chairs and benches made by the emperor's artisans, given to her on birthdays and to celebrate the births of her children, the ones who had not lived and the one who did.

They had comforted her for so long, tokens that proved that she was not forgotten, that far away in the palace where she had been born someone remembered her and acknowledged her sacrifice for the sake of her father and brother. Now she wanted to burn them, every splinter, every stitch. Make a great sacrifice to the Sueve and Barajian gods—even the Tarsean ones—to plead for Dayan's life.

She'd been too carefully schooled to allow herself that release. No, she must not show outward sign of her feelings. She had shown as much as she could when Tekar Khan had died. A few careful tears, genuine but insufficient. Insufficient for a man who had been kinder than the haughty young bride she had been had deserved.

Maimai was waving lists under her nose, making suggestions Chrysogon could only pretend to listen to. The present was a shadow thing, overwhelmed by the unappreciated past and the ominous future.

What was happening to Dayan?

Maimai's discourse was interrupted; one of the maids

emerged from behind the curtain. The Tarsean woman was presentable.

Chrysogon rose, brushing aside Maimai's accounts, not heeding the woman's annoyed exclamation. There was only one person in this camp who could truly understand what it was to be anxiously awaiting word of a missing son.

Marda sat swathed in a drying cloth, allowing one of the women to braid her hair. Cleaner and calmer the Tarsean woman was not such a comic figure. She had a sturdy dignity, tinged with sadness and a too familiar apprehension.

Maimai picked over Marda's travel stained garments that lay in a pathetic heap near the tub. "She can't wear those again." She was right.

"Do you have other clothes back at the tent?" Chrysogon asked Marda.

"No. Those were all I had after—" She pursed her lips. *After what?* "I don't have any others."

"Maimai, find something. The maids will have new clothes when we arrive in Barajia. Look in their chests."

Now that their victim appeared docile, Maimai and the maids amused themselves with dressing her. The Tarsean woman remained patient, until a jacket of a particularly garish shade of pink was brought out. Even if the color had not been objectionable, it would have gone ill with the subdued red in Marda's hair. She pushed it away and it was obvious that she was tired of the game. She looked well enough in the blue jacket and skirt of deep rose.

"That's enough, Maimai. What she's wearing will do," Chrysogon said. "Bring tea and leave us."

She patted a bench near her. "Come speak with me. I get little chance to practice my Tarsean now."

Marda sat carefully as if afraid she'd break something. "Where did you learn to speak it?"

"I had a Tarsean slave and it kept my mind occupied. I can acquire books from time to time." Those would be packed to take back to the capital—they had been companions as comforting as any she had had over the last twenty years.

"What happened to the slave?"

"She died."

"Oh."

The slave hadn't been much like Marda; she'd been thinner and blonder and more defeated. A fever that should not have done more than incapacitate her for a day or two had killed her. "Your husband is a Sueve? Do you live with his people?"

"N—no." Marda seemed slightly confused by the question. Why? "We live—lived in my village." She took a deep breath and continued as if reciting. "Ulick came back with the men who fought for the duke three years ago after my first husband—my son's father—died."

"Did you want to marry him?"

For a moment she saw blank incomprehension in the Tarsean woman's face. If she was lying, and Chrysogon strongly suspected she was, this was not part of the prepared story.

Marda shrugged finally. "There was Robin to worry about."

"Robin is your son? The one you search for?" Marda nodded. "Your husband cares about him that much?"

"Why else would he look so far?" Shrewd to answer a question with a question.

"Why else indeed?" But whatever the truth was about the man Marda called her husband, she was genuinely frightened for her son. "Tell me about your son."

Marda stared at her work-hardened hands. Whatever her life was in Tarsia, it hadn't been easy. "He's like his father, but more so. He likes to do things just to see what will happen—he's always in trouble." Dayan had never been in trouble, even when what he did was wrong. Never until now. Marda was shivering; the questions about her son must have hit too close to home. "I just want Robin back, even if there's nothing left to take him home to."

"What happened?" Best to hear the worst now, she might never know otherwise.

"Sueve came—they burnt everything. Killed people, and took some of the children. I saw Robin with them."

Chrysogon clenched her hands tightly. "Did they deliberately burn?"

Killing, burning. He'd been raised to war, but Chrysogon had hoped that Dayan had understood that it wasn't something to do needlessly.

"Ulick says so. He says it made no sense."

Around the emotions the kaiyun's mind caught the contradiction.

"He wasn't there when it happened then?"

"N—no." She'd been caught beyond her planned story again. "He was gone; when he came back and found Robin stolen he asked some of his friends from when he was a mercenary to help."

Some of his friends. It was time to move the conversation away from the painful subject of Marda's son. Chrysogon considered. *Some of his friends from when he was a mercenary.* She decided that it was permissible to indulge a little curiosity.

"They must be good friends. Tell me about them. One is called Walter and another," she furrowed her brow in false forgetfulness, "Thomas?"

"I don't know them very well. I'd never seen them before two weeks ago. They're all soldiers, I suppose."

"This Thomas appears to have more learning than the others."

"He was a clerk once, maybe."

"More than that, I think." *Enandor.* Marda obviously didn't want to talk about the other men any more than she did about her alleged husband. "Would no one else help you?"

Marda snorted. "I got no help from the governor." Her contempt was genuine. She met Chrysogon's eyes and frowned a little, then she settled her hands in her lap and said, "Unless there have been more raids since our village. Then they might decide to take action."

She's trying to mislead me. What does she think I can do now? The effort was becoming too difficult; any more and she'd become annoyed with the woman's simple deceptions.

She changed the subject, trying to find something which didn't touch on the painful past or the uncertain future. But no matter what was said, Chrysogon knew that events, unknown and beyond their control, were at the forefront of both women's thoughts.

Lady of Mercy, bring both our sons to us safely.

*   *   *

"I thought you said dusk?" Payne complained to Hamon, as they leaned against one of the walls that formed the boundary of the square that housed the slave market.

"Banturim said after dusk, though I assumed not this much after." The sky was dark and glittered with stars and the square was so nearly deserted that Hamon decided that two small parties were no less conspicuous than one larger one. He gestured for Reynard and Bertz to join them.

"No luck?" Bertz asked.

Hamon shook his head.

"I hate this city," Reynard declared, as he dropped to a crouch beside Hamon. "It's like a box within a box with no outlet. It makes no more sense than the maze in a rich man's garden."

"The Madresh quarter isn't this closed in," Hamon replied. "I scouted it this afternoon. Though it does contain some rich men's gardens," he grinned down at Reynard, "I doubt they go in for topiary. No, from what I gathered, the residents are court officials and members of the old nobility of Lakandar. If we're lucky, the house where the boy is held will be near the river. We'll grab the boy, steal a boat, cross the river, and call the horses to us. Then we'll ride north to join Walter. We won't have to go back through the city."

"It's a trap," Payne muttered.

"More likely a setup for blackmail, but we—here he comes."

The huntsmen turned to watch as Master Banturim's agent entered the marketplace. His robe collar was turned up, his headdress pulled low over his eyes like a conspirator in a bad comedy. He stopped and peered from group to group that dotted the market.

Hamon whistled. The man jumped, then scurried to join them.

"Fidrach?"

The agent nodded.

"You're late."

"I had to wait till the hour was ripe, till we could be sure of the boy's whereabouts. Now we must hurry." He started across the square then up the street that led to the Palace and beyond it to the Madresh quarter. Hamon and the other Huntsmen followed.

Fidrach didn't stop until he huddled into the shadows of the garden wall of a great mansion near the river. "This is the house. The boy serves his master till the master retires, then the boy returns to his quarters, walking across the garden here."

"Unguarded?" Hamon asked.

"To the best of our knowledge. Where would he run?"

Hamon translated for the others.

Fidrach looked from face to face. "Where are the rest of your men?" He sounded shocked.

"Not your business. How do we know that the boy is not already in his quarters?"

"You see the light high on the second floor? That is the master's chamber. He has not yet retired."

"The quarters are where?"

"In the south corner. A low building."

Hamon translated for the others. "Check it out." Payne boosted Reynard to the top of the wall.

"I can see the low building and make out a path between it and the main building," Reynard reported. "The garden is empty now."

"Good," Hamon said, as Bertz boosted Payne up to join Reynard. He turned to find that Fidrach was hurrying away. "Wait."

Fidrach barely paused to whisper shrilly, "I've told you all that my master promised." Then he disappeared around the corner of an adjacent house.

Bertz was waiting to help him over the wall. Hamon gestured him away. "Keep watch," he ordered Payne. "Reynard, scout the garden. Bertz and I are going to check out a route to the river. Whistle if the light goes out."

No whistle sounded as they followed the wall to a street beyond, then separated to search for a way to the river. Just beyond the wall of another garden a lane cut down to the water's edge. Hamon called softly for Bertz to follow him. The lane was steep and narrow, a black canyon between two houses' outer walls, but it ended in a landing on the river, and twenty feet away was the water gate of an aristocratic house with a pier and several boats bobbing in the river with no apparent guard.

"Not bad," Hamon said. "With the current we should land on open ground on the other bank. Let's get back to the others."

Reynard reported no change when they returned. Hamon described the route to the river then let himself be hoisted atop the wall. Reynard dropped back into the garden as Payne and Hamon hauled Bertz to the top. Soon they were all inside.

"Bertz, stay here near the wall. Reynard, position yourself where you can see the exits from the house to warn us if anyone but the boy comes. Payne and I will grab him when he passes the arbor. There's cover there to hide. Then run for the wall and the river."

"The light just went out," Reynard whispered.

"Go."

Reynard crept nearer the house while Payne flattened himself against the dark side of the arbor and Hamon crouched behind a carved bench. Soon a door opened at the back of the house and a man with a torch stepped outside, accompanied by a child. The man put the torch in a bracket next to the doorway, gave the child a shove toward the path, and went back into the house slamming the door behind him.

The child stood looking at the door, then turned toward the path. The torchlight glinted on red hair under his cap and gold trim on a scanty tunic. The child's head drooped and his shoulders hunched as he scuffed his way down the gravel path.

"Now!" Hamon whispered as the child came abreast the bench. He rose and grabbed the child's arm. Before he could put a hand over his mouth, the child screamed as shrilly as a calf gone to slaughter. Armed men spilled out of the surrounding buildings like scum from an overheated stew pot. Hamon grabbed the child and realized the extent of the trap when the child's wig fell off.

"Run!" Harmon yelled, but it was too late. Two men were behind him before he could drop the child and draw his dagger. He sidestepped a third man and tripped him into the others' way. Payne had pushed the arbor over on his attackers, but six others surrounded him before he could flee. The sound of another mêlée near the house meant that Reynard had also been found.

Hamon jumped on the bench and kicked at an attacker, but there were too many men, too many torches. An attacker swung a spear that caught him in the back of the knees and knocked him off the bench to sprawl on the hard stone path. Before he could rise, someone's foot was in his back and his hands were pulled behind him and tied. Haman lay prone, the gravel cutting his cheek, a man's foot still on his back, unable to see anything but the shadows cast by the torches on the bench beside his head, while the cacophony faded to a silence broken only by hard breathing and the child's sobs.

Footsteps crunched on the gravel path, paused, then came toward him. His captor removed his foot from Hamon's back, grabbed him by the hair, and pulled him to his knees.

A man in dark brown Barajian court robes stood over him. "Slave-stealer," he said, and slapped Hamon hard enough that his teeth cut his cheek. Hamon awkwardly wiped the welling blood on his shoulder.

"I thank the Gods you warned me, Zakar." A man in the flowing robes of Lakandar came up behind the Barajian. "Who knows what they would have stolen next?"

"Who knows indeed?" the man called Zakar murmured. The torchlight picked out the gold embroidery on the collar and front of his brocade robe and turned the grey at his temples to silver horns. "But we have stopped them." He gestured, and the guardsmen hauled Hamon ungently to his feet.

Beyond the Barajian and his companion who was fondling the crying child, Hamon could see Payne, and, when the guards shifted, Reynard surrounded by a knot of spearmen.

"Handsome slaves, Eskedi. They will serve others now. Take him away."

Two guards grabbed Hamon's arms and hustled him through a dark arch and into the street beyond. As he stumbled over the dark pavement, Hamon realized someone was missing. *Where was Bertz?*

15

Fourteenth Day

The child's scream pulled Bertz from his post by the wall, but the rush of armed men with torches from the house and outbuildings stopped him. Payne had been right; it was a trap. He ducked behind a flowering plum. The cloying sweetness of its blossoms contrasted strangely with the scene beyond; Hamon was down, Payne and Reynard surrounded by armed men. Nothing he could do would help. Climbing the wall to escape would attract attention. The best he could do was watch and wait.

The men and torches converged in the center of the garden. There, Hamon was jerked to his feet to confront a robed man to whom the others deferred. Then Hamon was dragged away. Bertz wanted to follow and discover where they were taking him, but saw no way. His best hope was to stay hidden and escape when everyone left. Perhaps he could follow Reynard and Payne and their captors, maybe help them escape.

The robed man still stood in the circle of torch-light, talking to the effetely dressed man who had accompanied him from the house. He beckoned to one of the waiting guardsmen, who listened then went into the house. A few minutes later he returned, dragging a gesturing man.

Banturim's agent, he knows there were four of us. Bertz knew that he had to escape even before the robed man ordered the guardsmen to search. The wall was too smooth to climb, and no trees stood near enough to help him swing over to the top, but a bench stood next to the low building in the corner. From its roof he could go over the wall. Bertz ran, taking advantage of what shadows the garden provided as the torches advanced. He was only halfway to the building when someone shouted. He could hear running feet on the gravel. He reached the bench, jumped up, and started to pull himself to the roof when someone grabbed his leg. He kicked, and his assailant lost his hold.

Bertz swung himself to the tiled roof. A spearman jumped to the bench and thrust upward. The spear went over Bertz's shoulder and grazed his forehead. Blood poured down into his eye. Ignoring it, he scrambled across the tiles. He could hear men on the roof behind him. He jumped the three foot gap between building and wall, couldn't keep his balance, and fell into the street below.

He lay dazed on the pavement for a moment till an ill-thrown spear clattered on the cobbles close to his head. He pushed himself to his feet, left shoulder throbbing where he had landed on it, and ran toward the river.

Blood soaked the padded hood of his cloak, and he discarded it at the mouth of the lane he and Hamon had found earlier. The bleeding had slowed. The padding had probably deflected most of the blow, but he was still woozy from the fall and the loss of blood. He staggered down the lane and dropped into the water.

The coldness revived him, and he swam awkwardly to the pier twenty feet away. He was about to pull himself up and untie a boat when torchlight shone on the walls of the lane. He ducked under the pier and clung in the shadow of its supports as a group of guardsmen stood at the bottom of the lane. They searched the river's edge and looked for boats already on the river. Seeing none, they fell into animated discussion. One of them waved the cloak Bertz had discarded.

The cold water made even his good hand numb, and the swift current pulled him. He could not be dragged into the light. Bertz anchored himself by wedging his bad hand into an underwater crevice between the posts that supported the pier.

After further noisy discussion, all but two of the guardsmen left. The two made a further half-hearted search, poking their torch into promising shadows. Then one started up the lane and called back to his lingering companion.

Bertz loosened his grip. A suitable boat, oars propped across the bench, bobbed only feet away. If the men would just leave, he could steal it. The sound of a creaking gate, then the tromp of feet on the pier above, cut short the thought. Men milled about, one of the boats was pulled closer, and it sounded as though someone was being questioned. Torchlight glittered on the water. Someone thudded to his knees on the pier above. Bertz carefully and quickly submerged. He held himself as far under as the posts would allow and forced his eyes open to watch the dull circles of the torchlight.

Finally they receded. His lungs aching, Bertz let himself surface. He tried to breathe quietly, though his breath sounded as loud as a bellows and his heart like a hammer at the forge. Footsteps still reverberated on the pier but dwindled after a time as men left. The two guardsmen still stood in the lane. Another pier farther down river was searched, torches bobbing.

The cold was making him drowsy. He wedged his hands into the crack between the posts. Two men paced up and down the wooden planks above monotonously.

Water slapped Bertz in the face. He choked and coughed before he could stop himself. No one moved on the pier above and no one stood at the foot of the lane. He must have passed out. He freed his numb hands with difficulty and half-swam, half-floated to the still bobbing boat. He painfully pulled himself into it. His hands were too stiff to untie the mooring line, so he hacked at it with his dagger until it parted and the boat floated free. He forced himself to row, to maneuver until he was far enough away from the bank that the current could not sweep the boat into any of the jutting piers. His shoulder ached, his left arm was stiff and painful to move. He let the current take him.

The city drifted past on his left, blacker than the night sky. The crescent moon, thinner bladed than a scythe, hung just above the horizon. *What was Hamon's plan?* He tried groggily to recall. *Land on the other bank, call the horses.* He was too tired, too cold. The wind cut through his wet clothes. He could change them, he finally remembered. *Evil magic.* He did nothing.

The city was almost past when he roused himself. The pasture where they camped—that would be some safety. The path lay along the canal just beyond the city wall.

His left arm was useless. He half-steered, half-rowed with his right. He got the boat into the canal mouth with difficulty, the current bouncing it against the embankment. The lock loomed ahead. He couldn't get by it. He'd have to land.

The boat jounced against the embankment, knocking an oar into the water. He tried to stand. The embankment was high. He'd needed the woman's help before. The boat rocked dizzyingly and he fell. Pain assaulted him like a wall of flame as his shoulder hit the oarlock. He lay still then roused himself. *Robin has to be saved.*

He pulled himself to the bench, then stood. The boat rocked. It lay against the grassy embankment. He got his right arm over the top of the bank. The boat slewed out from under him. He clung to the bank one-handed and tried to get a foothold. There was none. He tried to raise his other arm. Pain burst through him. He gasped. *Help.* But there was no help.

He clung waiting for the pain to recede, then tried again. He pulled himself up a few inches and found a foothold, then another before his foot slipped. He slid back. *Rest. Try again.* He must have fainted, he told himself, for he did not hear his horse approach. It was just there, reins dangling, and the sky beyond it purple with morning.

He couldn't let go of the bank. He tried to reach the reins with his left hand. The effort made him sweat. He could not reach them. The horse lowered his head farther. Bertz tried again. Impossible.

The horse seemed as frustrated as he was. It threw back its head and neighed wildly. The morning seemed even more still in the silence that followed, and then footsteps thudded along the embankment. He could hear a woman's voice, then a man's. He was hauled from the canal and dropped on his back on top of the embankment. Black pain closed in. When his vision cleared a man stood over him, arms akimbo. The woman dropped to her knees beside him. Her black hair escaped her shawl. Does she ever keep it neat, Bertz thought groggily, recognizing her.

She must have recognized him as well—she was talking quickly as she examined his head wound. The man's expression softened.

Incomprehensible conversation buzzed over him as he stared at the lightening sky. The man left and returned minutes later. He held out his hand. Bertz struggled to sit, then let the man help him to his feet. He staggered, and the woman braced him. The man brought Bertz's horse. The three of them together got him astride it. Bertz fought to retain his balance as they led the horse to the road.

Once there the man helped the woman with some familiar baskets and paused to watch as she started toward the city. Then he shrugged, muttered something, and took the reins to lead the horse in the opposite direction.

Bertz couldn't have said how far they traveled. He fought to remain conscious against every jounce of their progress, but finally they were at a door and hands reached up for him. He surrendered to the darkness.

The westerly wind had changed at sunset the day before, from a damp breeze laden with the scent of earth and greenery to an ice cold gale, dry and howling like a pack of wolves.

"Wolf winds," Ridai had confirmed. "Aslut has sent them often since he and Dayan left." He made a gesture with his hand as if to ward something off. "They will get worse."

This morning his prediction proved to be accurate. Clouds had roiled onto the horizon, no less ominous because they weren't laden with rain and didn't voice their threat with brave displays of thunder and lightning. Instead, a sickly grey-green, they swelled and rolled.

The Hunt and the Sueve had camped a few hours ride from the mourning cairn of Lugan Mahar Khan. The Sueve looked hollow-eyed and stony-faced, as if hiding their fear. Walter refrained from telling Ridai that he would not think ill of any man who left. They would not thank him for his consideration. Still, it was a measure of Walter's unease that he would consider it at all.

His fears were confirmed when the wind slammed them in the face with shards of ice that stung like countless flying needles as the men mounted toward their destination.

They covered their faces with scarves or the folds of their cloaks and kept their heads down. The Hunt's horses were oblivious, but the Sueve's, even as hardy as they were, fought being taken into the shrieking wind and the ice.

At first Ridai tried to lead them north, out of the direct path of the wind, but it shifted direction with them, always in their faces, making it clear that it was a force sent to stop them, as if Walter had not guessed that already.

After they had nearly made a circle around the shrine, Walter drew up beside Ridai.

"We're not going to outride this—the only way to the shaman is straight in."

They agreed, though no one liked the idea.

And as they changed direction for the last time, the wind changed again as well.

This shift was not entirely tangible. The clouds blackened to blot out the light and leave the world around them nearly dark as night. But something else was in the wind besides the stinging ice. Walter no longer heard wolves— he heard women's voices, children's.

No, not plural. The same voices, again and again. Walter tried not to recognize them. How could a Sueve shaman command *those* spirits—Cassimara's, Cynric's? They must have been reborn to new lives long ago.

One of Ridai's men lost his nerve and turned and rode away in a silence more ominous than any scream of fear. The others murmured the Sueve word for "ghost" and two more soon followed the first. The Sueve did not like ghosts.

Neither did Walter.

When half Ridai's party had fled, Walter called a halt. The party drew into a circle. He inspected his Huntsmen— how were they handling the harrowing experience? Eleylin, Thomas, Garrett, and even Michel were grim faced, eyes dark, as if they too had heard the cries of voices they wanted to forget or never to know. He studied Justin most closely; if each heard ghosts from his past, Justin's would be a hundred times worse than the others', or at least, would seem so to him. But the apothecary was in a better state than he had expected. He was drawn and pale from the cold wind and bleeding from many small cuts—apparently unwilling or too uncaring to cover his face—but he seemed to have mastery over himself.

"I think we should split up," Walter said. "This wind can't come from everywhere."

Ridai scowled. "I wouldn't wager on that."

"Perhaps it will break the shaman's concentration and lessen the force for each." He debated silently for a moment, then continued, "Besides, I have reason to think it is us the shaman fears."

Ridai agreed so readily Water suspected the man was relieved. The groups made hasty battle plans with little hope they could be carried out, for they depended on the wind and the darkness being lifted.

Ridai's men rode off, the wind shrieking louder, as if to challenge them. The Hunt prepared to take their course, but Justin pushed ahead of the others and stopped him.

"Walter, I know what this is."

"Wolf winds. We've been hearing about them for weeks now."

"I know, but the book I read—*Travels in Suevia*—it mentioned 'winds with voices.' They're sent by wizards."

"Shamans—like the one we're after."

"Yes, but it said more, too." Walter waited impatiently. "It said the eastern Sueve had charms that protected them from these winds."

"What?" He didn't hold much hope. Ulick was shaking his head as if he didn't believe Justin, either.

"Herb bags, with sweet grass, hairs from the mane of a yellow horse, and stones from a gravestone."

Ulick spoke up. "Sweet grass is used for magic, yellow horses are always potent, and the stones are from a *mourning cairn*, not a gravestone."

"The writer called things wrong. I don't think he spoke much Suevarna."

"Where would we come by these things, now?" Walter asked. "I wish you'd remembered this earlier."

Ulick reached into his caftan and pulled out two small

bags hung on thongs. Walter recognized the first—it was the one Ulick had been given at the raided village—but not the other.

Ulick sniffed both, discarding the one Walter recognized—throwing it away as if it were filled with offal. The other he held up.

"Sweet grass, yellow mane and tail hairs, and a stone," he said. "Other things I don't recognize. But the woman who gave it to Marda said it might help against the shaman. She meant it for a protection charm, but I think it's more than that." He tossed it to Walter. "You take it. I think you're right—the shaman fears you."

Walter caught the light leather pouch, so small he couldn't have gotten two fingers inside it.

"But what do I do with it?" Ulick shook his head. "Justin?"

"The book said to wear it!"

Not particularly convinced, Walter put the bag around his neck. The wind howled as it had before—but the voices were gone.

"Well?" Justin asked.

"Can you still hear the voices?"

Justin showed the first sign of emotion since he'd first spoken. "Gods, yes," he replied through clenched teeth.

"I can't." Walter listened. The voices had stopped, but he could hear something else—something less macabre. It took him a moment to recognize that it wasn't his own heart beating. "I hear a drum."

"Aslut has a man-skin drum," Ulick said. "Follow it."

They rode hard now, toward the sound. The darkness still swirled around them, but Walter was no longer tormented by the ice shards, and the far more painful sound of too familiar voices. The drum kept up its steady beat, a beacon of sound in the chaos around them.

Reynard paced the room yet again. "I hate closed places."

"Sit down. Eat your stew," Payne advised him. "I've been in worse jails."

Reynard sat on the cot opposite him. "I could top you in a worse-jail contest."

"I've no doubt of that." Payne handed him the bowl. "Food's not bad, considering."

Reynard sampled it. "You're right. I wonder why. It didn't look like Hamon would fare so well."

"No." Payne frowned at the thought. "But they think we're slaves, and slaves aren't responsible for their actions; their masters are. So we're property."

"Held in escrow," Reynard relished the fancy word, "till Hamon's case comes to trial?".

"No, I suspect we're someone else's property now."

Reynard finished the stew. "Boost me up."

"Not again."

"Can't see through the keyhole and there's nothing to see but feet through the crack under the door. So if we want to find out anything . . ."

Payne groaned, but went to the wall that held the only window, a small slit near the ceiling covered by an iron grate. Soon Reynard stood on his shoulders, peering out. "See anything?"

"Same as before. A big sunlit courtyard with a lot of doors off a loggia. Every so often I see a man in uniform."

"Could be a barracks."

"Something official," Reynard agreed. "Funny thing is . . ." He paused.

"Yes?" Payne sounded impatient.

"Whenever I see anyone with his helmet off, he's got red hair."

"You're joking." Payne swung Reynard to the floor.

"Nope. Sorry." They stared at each other, then Reynard said, "The Sueve think redheads make good warriors. Do the Barajians think so, too?"

"We're in Lakandar, not Barajia proper, and I've never heard that either people shared that superstition."

"Superstitions get around."

Payne shook his head as if to clear it. "Damnedest recruiting policy I ever heard of."

Reynard grinned. "I can see you in one of those pretty uniforms, but why would they want an eight-year-old boy?"

Payne dropped to his cot. "They're in no hurry to tell us."

*   *   *

Garrett yelled a battle cry as they charged the Sueve position. It sounded real. Walter hoped this looked like a credible attack as he veered right and Garrett veered left at the far edge of arrow range. His men split behind him. Pitifully few men, and fewer still with any cavalry experience. He hoped they looked more formidable than they were in the armor Ketai had loaned them, hoped that they would provide the distraction that he needed while he rode to destroy the shaman.

An arrow thunked into the ground near his horse's hooves and he signaled to Eleylin to circle back in front of the line of archers. He rode alone to the sky-stone where the shaman chanted. If the shaman fell, Dayan's men might panic and flee. That was their only chance of victory.

He could hear the shaman's voice chanting in time with the drum. The shaman sat on the very top of the sky-stone, the tallest cairn Walter had ever seen, higher even than Garrett's head. Walter rode behind the loose pile of stones, knowing the Sueve archers would not risk hitting Aslut. His head was level with the drum. Walter drew his sword and struck not at the man, but at the drum he beat.

The drum was not just man-skin; its base was two skulls without lower jaws, joined at the crowns. His sword struck the drum in the middle and it flew up and away from Aslut, who screamed as if the blade had struck his own flesh and dove after it.

Walter flung himself off his horse and tackled Aslut. The two men rolled down the hill in an avalanche of loose stones and tiny pieces of cloth, bright glass, and countless unidentifiable objects deemed worthy to leave at the Mahar Great Father's Shrine. The shaman ended up on the bottom and Walter threw his full weight on him to keep him from reaching the drum only inches away. Then, startling even the Huntsman, Walter's horse kicked the obscene instrument, shattering it. Aslut's body thrashed and Walter pushed his face hard into the dirt and stones to keep him still. The horse battered the drum until nothing was left but shards, indistinguishable from the pebbles and dirt they lay in.

Walter rose cautiously. The shaman pushed himself up on one elbow, blood running from one corner of his mouth.

The two men stared at each other, then Aslut spoke with great effort, "If you'd been live men I could have killed you; if you'd been dead men, I could have bound you. But you are neither." He swallowed. "But I'll tell you this, not-man—this task will cost you something you do not value enough." He coughed, and his eyes grew wide as he looked behind Walter. He threw up his hand. "No!" he cried, "Not now!"

Walter whirled—there was nothing behind him when he looked back, the shaman's eyes were unseeing; fixed on nothing. He was dead.

A mounted Sueve came around the cairn. Walter clenched his hand round the hilt of his sword. But it was Ridai who looked at the corpse and laughed.

"You got him. I knew when the sky cleared." Walter looked up. The sky was lightening, and the air was still. When had that happened?

As if he were playing another sort of tuan, Ridai bent down from his saddle and grabbed one of the shaman's arms.

"When Dayan's men see that Aslut's dead, they'll know his gods have deserted him—and them." Walter nodded. "You were right; as soon as we left you, the wolf winds stopped tormenting us."

The battle was nearly over; with the aid of Ridai's men—most of the deserters had rejoined them once away from the ghost voices—the Hunt was making short work of the few opponents who had not fled.

He checked his men—Justin was standing next to his horse pulling an arrow from its saddle. Thomas was with Ridai's men herding prisoners. Where had he found the spear?

Garrett, Michel, and Eleylin were fighting the remnant of Dayan's men who had not yet fled or surrendered. Ulick was the only man not in sight.

Ridai shouted as they approached Dayan's men. He dropped the body face up.

"Here's your shaman," he yelled. "Who wants to join him?"

To give them credit, only a few of Dayan's remaining men cut and ran. Ridai signaled his men not to follow.

Walter saw bodies on the ground. Was Ulick among them—too hurt to fight? Then he saw the Sueve Huntsmen fighting a single opponent he had cut off from the others, a tall youth with a gilt decorated helmet—Dayan Fire-born. Walter sped to help.

Ulick was a good swordsman, but the boy was desperate. Dayan might not win, but he could force Ulick to kill him. The boy's death was not in their best interests.

"Your shaman is dead," Walter said, as he drew near.

Dayan scowled at him. "That is as Heaven wills," He fought on.

"Heaven willed you to kill women and children? To fight unarmed dirt-turners?" Ulick said. "What honor is there in that?"

"I did as Heaven decreed."

"Heaven or a dead man?" Walter said. They forced him back foot by foot, toward the sky-stone. "I broke his drum, but I didn't kill him." That startled Dayan. "His gods killed him. He looked in the sky and begged to be spared."

"No!"

"The only thing Heaven willed was his death," Ulick said.

"I cannot be defeated! I am the Fire-born."

"Perhaps," Walter countered. Dayan had his back to the sky-stone now. "Or perhaps the shaman lied to you."

"Did Heaven itself lie with the flaming star at my birth?" Dayan's voice was defiant but he wasn't fighting and he didn't seem to notice that neither Walter nor Ulick was either.

"No, but perhaps Aslut didn't read your true destiny," Ulick declared. Dayan had divided his attention between the two speakers. He didn't seem to know which to confront.

"Would your father have wanted you to weaken the tribe by taking warriors from it? To stir up trouble with the Tarseans? To bring disgrace to your own people?" Walter pressed him.

"I—"

"You have disgraced your father, destiny or no. All these deaths are on your head," Ulick pressed him in turn.

"No, no, I haven't! I was born be the great khan! I'll—"

He had focused on Ulick. Walter grabbed the boy's sword arm and Ulick took his sword. Dayan grabbed at Ulick, and Walter knocked him to the ground. Something round and metal that hung on a cord round Dayan's neck escaped the collar of his caftan; he clutched it as if it were some protection.

Ulick struck his hand away. "More of the shaman's magic?" He asked, as he dragged it over the boy's head.

"No! It's a gift from my father! Give it back!"

"An unworthy son doesn't deserve such a gift." Ulick thrust it into his caftan. "Stand up, and tell your men to drop their weapons unless their deaths are necessary to your greatness."

To Walter's surprise, Dayan did as he was told. Dayan's remaining men surrendered without a murmur—even now he had their loyalty, it seemed. It spoke well for him that some still obeyed him even with their shaman dead, and the knowledge that the great khan would probably execute them.

Later, after Dayan and his men were secured, they saw to the bodies of the slain—three men of Ridai's, six of Dayan's and the shaman. Ridai refused to bury Aslut.

"Leave it," he said. "If we burn him, his ashes will mingle with the wind and he'll ride with the other ghosts. If we bury him like a man, someone will have a place to make offerings. Let the animals have him."

It seemed a fitting fate, and they rode away from Lugan Mahar Khan's sky-stone—as carefully restored as they could manage, and with Dayan's men's weapons left as further offering—leaving the shaman to stare endlessly at the Heaven that had forsaken him.

Robin was not in the Sueve raiders' camp. Three other Tarsean boys, none of them red-haired, were still with them. Walter questioned Dayan and his followers.

They seemed surprised at his interest—all but Dayan— but yes, they had taken such a boy and had sold him to a Barajian caravan. Dayan sulked and would not say why; Walter didn't try to pressure him for more, which surprised Thomas. Instead, he walked off and bleakly surveyed the southeastern horizon.

"We foresaw this might be the case," Thomas said. "We've at least made sure at this end of the search. We know he's in Lakandar somewhere."

"Probably."

"Now we go after him. We've more than half the moon left. Everything is going smoothly."

Walter wheeled to face him. "No. No, it's not."

"Why?"

"Pain—since last night. I thought it was another torment from the wolf winds, but they've stopped and I know it's Hamon and Bertz. Something is wrong, very wrong—they're injured, or worse."

"Then we need to find them at once."

"We've too many entanglements here. I want to make sure these boys get back. They're victims as much as Marda's son or the child back at the village."

"Then we'll hurry. We should be back at the khan's camp tomorrow, and if we move quickly, we can be in Istlakan a few days after that."

Walter sighed and wearily rubbed his face. "I can't help wondering what's happened to Hamon—the pain keeps worsening."

"Nothing he can't handle, I'm sure," Thomas commented, and changed the subject to the Tarsean boys.

16

Fifteenth Day—New Moon

Bertz tentatively moved his left arm. The pain was still there, but it was no longer nauseating, and he thought that he could move it more freely. At least this time he didn't faint, as he had when the old woman had examined him the day before.

It must be morning again. He could hear people moving in the room above after long silence. Little light reached this underground storeroom through the grates that let in air, even at midday. He had learned that yesterday when he had been hurried down into it, just before the room above had echoed with shouts and marching feet and the crashes of things overturned roughly. It must have been a search, but Bertz wasn't sure. None of his rescuers spoke any language that he knew. He suspected that they were trying to find a common language: twice people had come not to tend to his injuries or bring him food or bedding, but merely to talk at him, then shake their heads and walk away.

Bertz rose and walked to the grate. He couldn't stay here. Somehow he had to save Robin. He suspected that he was endangering the people who sheltered him. He must leave as soon as his injuries permitted, but how could he free the boy when he knew nothing of the customs or the language? He could return to the house where they had been ambushed and try to get to the boy. No, he needed to find Hamon. Walter had given Hamon a token—Hamon had shown them a gold coin on a cord that was to mark the boy—so that Walter could bring Marda to her son. Walter would follow the token. He must get the token to the boy, but how?

The trap door opened and two middle-aged men scrambled down the ladder. One Bertz had seen before. He had been one of those who spoke at him the previous day. The other was of the same build and coloring and dressed similarly in a sleeveless robe and long undercoat fastened with a sash, but older, with grey curly hair rather than black streaked with silver.

The grey-haired man greeted Bertz in Tarsean. Bertz drew a relieved breath and answered him. The other man had listened intently; now he gestured for all to sit and spoke rapidly.

"My friend, Reshalon," the translator nodded at the other man, "wishes to thank you for saving his grandson from drowning."

"Anyone would have done as much."

"Not everyone," came the answer through the translator. "He wants to know who you are and how he can help you."

Bertz gave his name as he considered how much to tell. He needed help. He decided to keep back only the Hunt's summoning. He told them about the quest to save Robin, following the caravan, the slave dealer, and the ambush.

Reshalon shook his head over the story and fired back more questions. When they had been answered, he said, "You are in more trouble than you know. The governor himself must be involved. Troops searched this house yesterday."

"So I thought," Bertz answered. "I must leave so I no longer endanger you."

"Where would you go?"

"I don't know. I need to talk with Hamon."

The men seemed surprised at the name. "This is the leader you spoke of?"

"Yes, he was arrested, taken I don't know where."

The two men conferred. "Perhaps he was taken to the

palace, but if he was caught stealing slaves it is possible he was taken to the city prison. We will inquire."

"My other friends, would they have been taken there as well?"

The men looked at him. "Your countrymen—do they look like you? Do they have red hair?"

"Yes. Robin does as well."

"Then they are undoubtedly at the palace."

"How can you be so sure?"

"The governor seeks the Child of Fire. Your friends would be taken to him. The boy as well."

"The Child of Fire?"

"The deliverer who, it is prophesied, will restore us to our homeland. Tiramet"—Reshalon's tone made the name sound like a curse—"has betrayed all our hopes to the foreigners."

"I still don't understand. What has that to do with us?"

"The Child of Fire will have red hair. The governor is taking all males with red hair into his service so that he will control the Child of Fire for his own purposes. He takes our sons from us and raises them to be his tools. You would not be safe in the city."

Bertz remembered Hamon saying that he wondered if they stared at Payne and Reynard, not him. "I cannot abandon them. I must save the boy."

Reshalon looked stern as the words were translated. "I owe you much. If you are bound to it, then I will help you as I can. I still have contacts in the city. I will see what I can learn of your friends."

As they came in sight of the yin of the great khan late that afternoon, Ulick was suddenly reluctant to enter. It meant too many unwelcome facts: that he would have to ride to Lakandar to be among outlanders, that he would once again be relegated to a minor role in Walter's plans, and worst, that someone would have to tell Marda that they hadn't found Robin.

Word spread quickly through the camp of their return. They went directly to the great palace tent of Ketai Khan, and they had barely greeted him and presented their prisoners when a group of women entered.

At first Ulick didn't recognize Marda among them. She was dressed in strange clothes and her hair was braided into a bun. She stayed among the kaiyun's women, as if to hide herself, but her gaze searched the prisoners and the huddle of Tarsean boys.

At length her eyes met Ulick's, and since Walter was occupied in describing the shaman's death to the Khan, Ulick crossed to her side.

"They sold him to the Barajians," Ulick told her. She bit her lip. "We've already sent Hamon to follow the caravan. He'll have a lead on the boy by now." No need to tell her what Walter had sensed.

"I know. I was praying that—" She took a steadying breath and looked at the captured raiders. "Which one is the kaiyun's son?"

"The tall one."

"What will they do to him?"

"I don't know. Execute him, I imagine. He has brought disgrace on tribe and clan and the khan."

She stared at Dayan, who stood with his head up, stubborn defiance in his whole bearing.

"It will break the kaiyun, if they do."

"If it weren't for him, your son would be home safe." *And I wouldn't be here either. Is that good or ill?*

"I know. I know. But she's as frightened for him as I am for Robin. She doesn't speak, but shows it in a hundred ways." She shook her head. "When will we leave?"

"Another day, at least." She looked worried again, and he changed the subject. "Did they treat you well?"

"Mostly." Marda scowled. "They gave me a bath! There's one servant I wish I could speak Barajian to, to have a few words with."

Ulick smiled. She was changed. A good change, too. As if something that had nearly broken in her was beginning to mend. Broken, he wondered, when her village was raided, or when her husband died?

Whatever it is, hold tight to it, Marda Trefsdottir. You've a long journey yet.

Payne sat on the edge of the cot and stared at the line of light under the door. He tried to prepare himself for what might come and tried not to worry about Reynard.

Dawn had barely cast pink light into the room the first time the guards had come for Reynard. He had been returned several hours later and had had the chance to signal to Payne that he had stuck to the story they had agreed on, before Payne in turn had been hauled away to be questioned.

Payne had been taken to a series of small rooms and asked repetitious questions through an interpreter by men in successively fancier uniforms. To each he had told the story he and Reynard had concocted. He and Reynard had been bought in Rayln as debt-slaves and brought south through the Sueve lands for what purpose they did not know. They had simply been obeying their new master's orders when they were captured. They didn't know the language and were ignorant of local geography and thus had no useful information about what they had done or where they had stayed since their arrival in Istlakan. The questioners had finally given up and returned him to the cell where Reynard waited. He and Reynard had compared impressions over the evening bowl of stew and had been confident that they had been believed until the guards had returned.

It had been hours since they had taken Reynard again. Payne ran his fingers through his hair and tried not to imagine what could be happening. If slaves could be tortured for testimony, the authorities would surely have started it much earlier in the questioning. That thought was logical but not convincing. *What is happening to Reynard?*

The door to the room outside the cell creaked open and soon keys jangled in the lock. The door swung back and one of the guards gestured for him to follow. They took him through a maze of hallways, up a flight of stairs, past highly embossed bronze doors, across a large richly decorated room to a spiral stair cleverly hidden behind a wooden panel in an alcove. Half the guards stopped there, the other half prodded him up. At the top, two men stood guard at a pair of double doors. One knocked, and the doors were opened. Payne's guard pushed him inside, said a few words, and exited.

Payne looked around. This didn't look like a torture chamber. The room was nearly circular, with a domed ceiling that dripped filigreed buttresses as elaborate and delicate as icicles. The floor was inlaid marble that formed a pattern of stars within stars. A silver-haired man lounged on the carpeted silk-draped platform on the opposite side of the room. He beckoned Payne forward and said something to the room's other occupant—the Barajian who had supervised the ambush two nights before. From their tone he was asking questions, and the Barajian was increasingly impatient about answering. After a particularly sharp answer, the silver-haired man turned and said a single word.

A shawl-swathed figure stepped from one of the latticed and silk-draped doors in the outer wall and silently crossed the room to bow deeply to the man on the platform.

What was an Eskedi woman doing here? Hamon had said that the government was prejudiced against them.

The woman turned to him. Payne examined her as she examined him. She was of medium height and slightly built, even the layers of drapery could not disguise that. The fine gray wool of the outer shawl covered another of thin black silk over her eyes, but from what he could see of her lower face, Payne guessed that she was young, no more than in her twenties. He had seen this style of dress depicted in Saroth many summonings and centuries ago, and it had been old-fashioned even then. Apparently the Eskedi of Barajia clung to the ways of their ancient homeland. Or did this woman have reasons of her own to dress this way? He didn't recall any other woman he had seen in Istlakan who dressed with this archaic panoply. He had seen a woman or two with a draped shawl rather than the more usual stiff coat and veil of Lakandar, but not one had worn the full elaboration of Eskedi dress, as this one did. But from her shawl-draped head to the silver-embroidered shoe peeping from under her full closely pleated skirt, her clothes were sober colored, not the golds, rich reds, and blues he remembered from Saroth.

She walked around him slowly. The Barajian said something brusquely, impatiently, and was echoed by the man on the platform. The woman produced a pendant from within her draperies, a pale opal the size of a hen's egg that swung free within an oval gold frame fringed with pearls.

She *was* young, Payne thought, looking at the hand that
held the jewel. She studied the jewel and the old man
leaned forward eagerly. Her hand trembled slightly, betrayed by the swing of the jewel. The man whispered a
question. She answered quietly, her eyes on the Barajian
not the questioner, and the pendant quickly disappeared into
her draperies. The Barajian said something sharply, walked
to the door, and summoned the quards who had brought
Payne. After a short conversation, the guards escorted
Payne back along the route they had previously followed
to his cell. Reynard was not there.

Tiramet retired to the doorway to the wall walk that led to
her own tower apartments but no further, and watched the
stars sparkle in the moonless sky.

What was this stranger? Her jewel had blazed red in his
presence, much as it had glowed green for the youth earlier
this evening. Had she betrayed her surprise? Had Zakar
noticed?

If he had, he was not telling the governor. Their conversation was the usual exchange between Zakar's contemptuous skepticism and the governor's credulous hope.
Zakar could be biding his time. For all his obsequious
words, his prophecies, his omens of the governor's greatness, she guessed that Zakar served only himself.

She must know more of this man who made her jewel
red. Could he truly be the Child of Fire? What had she set
in motion if he was? The questions whirled in her mind,
making her feel more powerless than ever.

Zakar left. She crossed the room and knelt before the
governor.

"Excellency, I beg indulgence."

He waved for her to go on.

"I wish to question this man that we examined tonight."

"Why? You said that he is not the Child. He is old
enough that you would know, unlike the youths and boys.
Or so you have said."

"True. But he is also old enough that his former master
may have told him why he sought the boy from the caravan
so especially."

"He has been questioned about that."

"By men in uniform. Perhaps a woman can learn more. I speak Tarsean."

The governor thought it over. "Oh, very well—I will tell Captain Imrehim that you are to question him at your pleasure."

"A thousand thanks, Your Excellency." She rose, bowed again, and left the chamber.

17

Sixteenth Day

Kaiyun Chrysogon dressed carefully, arranging each fold in her golden *saltar* with exquisite care. Her maids helped as best they could, but when they thought she couldn't hear, they sobbed as if Dayan were already dead—except for Tita Maimai, who merely scolded more earnestly.

Chrysogon had been allowed to see Dayan last night. He had been sullen and uncommunicative. To her, at least, he had not defended his actions with recitations about his destiny, but he had not backed down either. Ketai Khan might not want to have his nephew killed, but Dayan's lack of remorse, his refusal even to admit a mistake, gave the khan little choice.

Her son had one slender chance, and Chrysogon must take it despite the cost to her pride.

She did not speak, but turned to the entrance to her tent beckoning to her women and her guard. She would have dispensed with the women, but each had solemnly petitioned to accompany her when she went to hear the khan decree her son's fate. She could not refuse any of them. She hoped the presence of so many of her people would make her actions that much more poignant.

The journey to the great palace tent had never

seemed so long. To make her degradation more complete, Wiraz and Dovir would witness it. Why had Ketai found their presence necessary? They had barely acknowledged the existence of her son.

Dayan stood before the khan. She recognized that stance—she had known it since he was two and had first begun to realize that he could be defiant and be heeded.

The khan had just finished speaking.

"I will make no vow!" Dayan replied. "I am the rightful khan. You have no right to my allegiance."

Dayan! But she said nothing, and watched the khan. If she looked at her son, she would lose her self-control. Ketai, she saw, was displeased that Dayan was forcing his hand.

She halted a precise distance from the dais as the khan spoke.

"Unless I have surety that you will never rebel again I cannot let you live, Dayan Fire-born."

"Never? I cannot promise that. Who knows what changes the winds of Heaven may bring?"

Ketai frowned as a murmur of approbation rolled through the crowd of onlookers.

He could have more easily forgiven you if you had childishly ranted about your destiny, Chrysogon thought. This was the wrong time to show a glimmer of the man you could become.

"Then I have no choice—" Ketai began.

"Great Khan!" Chrysogon stepped forward, and Ketai turned. Then, awkward in the unaccustomed movement, she knelt. Daughter of an emperor, sister to an emperor, she was bound to kneel only before him who graced the Pearl Throne itself and then only on great occasions of state, but now her knees touched the earth before the barbarian khan of the Sueve.

"Great Khan, I beg you, for my sake, for the sake of my father, for the sake of my brother—spare my son's life." Had her voice trembled? She wasn't sure. Ketai had seen her start to kneel and chosen to look away. He knew what this must cost her.

Her women murmured in dismay. Tita Maimai tugged at her arm, trying to make her rise, but she shrugged the woman off.

She saw the white flutter of a handkerchief from where the Barajians sat. Did Wiraz use his to keep the stench of her humiliation from his haughty nose? She could hear footsteps behind her. Was Wiraz leaving?

"Kaiyun," Ketai said, still unable to meet her eyes. "For your father, your brother, and you, I would give you your son. But for the Mahar I dare not spare him, unless I can be sure he will not betray us again."

She could see Dayan from the corner of her eye. He stared at her, his mouth ajar, his eyes wide. Was he astonished or ashamed that she begged for him?

"What guarantee can I offer you, Great Khan?" she said. "My blood? My life for his good behavior?"

"Neither blood nor death has ever yet deterred Dayan Fire-born."

What could she say? What more had she to bargain with? Someone crouched beside her.

"Your Highness," the low voice spoke Tarsean. The "clerk"—maybe—who had called himself Enandor Thomas. "May I help?"

"If you can," she whispered.

"Will you translate?"

She nodded mutely.

"Ask the khan this . . . ," and he proposed a plan that made her heart leap in unexpected hope, immediately followed by terror that this plan, the only feasible one, still might not save Dayan.

"The Enandor Thomas has proposed that my s—Prince Dayan—return with me to Barajia, his life to be forfeited should he return from this exile without your express permission."

The khan warily fixed his gaze on Kaiyun Chrysogon again. Dayan looked dismayed and too dumbfounded to protest.

"Would your brother the emperor agree to keep him by force, if necessary?"

"For love of me, he will do what he must."

The khan glanced at Dayan, who was silent. Had he realized that whatever his destiny, it could not be realized if he were dead? *Let him understand!*

"An armed escort must accompany you to Istlakan to

guarantee that your son arrives there as promised."

"Yes. Anything."

"I accept this plan. Please rise, Kaiyun. It is not fitting for you to kneel."

She started to obey, but her legs would not hold her. Enandor Thomas saw this, as did Tita Maimai, and together they helped her to stand.

She turned briefly to the Tarsean. "He has agreed," she said, "though there will have to be an armed escort that the khan can trust to assure that Dayan gets to Barajia. Thank you."

"I am glad I was able to pay our debt to you before we depart," he said, and with a brief bow left her and rejoined his companions.

She looked after him, wishing that this was not to be their last encounter.

Thomas sat through Walter's polite audience with the khan, too distracted to try to guess at what was being said. Kaiyun Chrysogon had been waved to sit at one side of the dais; Thomas watched her instead.

Her actions had cost her. She rubbed her hands as she had when preoccupied at the tuan, and paid attention to the conversation only when she was directly addressed.

The Barajian Royal House held itself very high indeed, descended from the Gods. How many generations of divinities had she just disgraced to save her son? She was a rare woman, to love such an unlovable child.

Walter had to nudge him twice to rise and depart. As they left the palace tent, Thomas shook his head to bring himself back to the Hunt's problems.

"What was that all about?" he asked.

"The khan has asked that *we* escort the kaiyun as far as Istlakan."

Thomas grinned, realized what he was doing, and tried to look solemn. "That was my fault." Walter looked at him shrewdly. *Damn the man. I can't deceive him.* "I apologize for presenting a plan which causes additional complications."

"No need. Ketai's plan all along was for Dayan to accompany his mother."

"What?"

"But the suggestion had to come from the Barajians," Walter explained. "It puts the responsibility of keeping the bargain on them."

Thomas felt much less clever. "Did you agree?"

"Yes."

"Why?"

"Short of telling him we have a time constraint I couldn't refuse. Besides it gives us good cover."

"I understand the roads through the mountains are infested with bandits."

"True, though I doubt we'd have problems alone."

"Yes, but—" He'd give away too much if he said that he was glad that the kaiyun would have their protection.

Time constraint, indeed. He glanced up at the endless sky, Eternal Heaven, moonless last night. Fourteen days. Not nearly long enough.

The first time the cell door opened Payne had been wary, prepared for whatever his captors might do. His fortitude had been wasted on a guard who merely put a wooden cup and bowl near the door and then shut it again. Payne had examined the food, sat on his cot, eaten some of the thin gruel and sipped the beer.

When the keys jangled in the lock again, he expected only the guard come for the dishes. Instead there were a group of russet-clad guards with an officer who gestured for him to come with them. Payne put the bowl on the cot and rose.

He recognized the first part of the way, but this time they took him past—not through—the bronze doors, then down a long corridor with doors along one side and latticed windows on the other. At the end of the corridor two men in blue, not russet, guarded a door. They saluted the officer and opened the door at his order.

The room beyond was an anteroom where four more blue-clad men guarded elaborately carved wooden doors on the far wall. The guards took him through another corridor that turned at right angles, to another guarded door at its far end. There they knocked and were bidden to enter.

The officer and two of the guards led him in. The shawl-

draped woman of the night before was the only other occupant. While she talked to the officer, Payne looked
around. He could see no other exit. The narrow windows
on two walls of the hexagonal room were filled with intri-
cately patterned stone lattices. The walls were covered as
high as the window tops with panels of wood and gilded
leather picked out in red. Payne remembered the spiral
staircase hidden behind a panel in another room of the palace and wondered if this room also had a secret entrance.

The officer bowed perfunctorily and left, taking the
guards with him. The woman crossed to a table where some
papers lay that looked like the notes from the interrogation,
not mystic diagrams. Payne was surprised that she could
read. In contrast to the gaudy decor, the papers lay on a
table of utilitarian plain wood. The room held little more
furniture: a bench, a stool, and an earthenware lamp hanging from a bracket.

"You told the guards you were sold as a debt-slave in
Rayln?"

Payne had not expected her nearly accentless Tarsean.
"Yes."

"Were you a merchant there?"

"A very unsuccessful one, I fear."

"What did you trade?"

"Hides, for luxuries imported from the south."

"Sit down." She waved at the bench. "You were a fac-
tor?"

Payne sat and answered her questions as best as he could.
He wished he had thought up a better cover. She was far
more knowledgeable than he about the mechanics of trade.

She paced the room as she listened and questioned. Finally she turned. "You're lying," she said and dropped her
shawls to her shoulders.

She was Eskedi, as he had guessed, with black curly hair
like Hamon's and swarthy skin, but her eyes were not
brown but intensely turquoise, and she was beautiful. Payne
told himself not to be mesmerized by those eyes; this might
be an interrogator's trick, as usual as the accusation of lying.

"I'm a poor merchant, as my cousins warned me I would
be, but I assure you I'm not lying."

"I don't believe you."

He decided to take the offensive. "Why?"

She refused the bait. "You are no merchant."

"What am I then?"

"That's . . ." She stopped as someone rapped on the door. Payne recognized the Barajian who entered without waiting to be asked as the man who had supervised the ambush. She pulled her shawl up over her head.

The man spoke sharply. "You are to rise and accompany him," she translated.

Payne rose, but the Barajian didn't leave. He walked around the table and looked at the papers on it, standing close to the woman. She stiffened and held herself as though she did not wish to be contaminated. The two exchanged what sounded like a series of brief questions and answers till the man said something dismissively and gestured for Payne to follow.

Once outside, the guards closed in behind them. The Barajian led Payne back down the corridors, past the stairs he had been brought up the two previous times, and down another right-angle corridor which led to a balcony above the courtyard Reynard had described. The guards stopped, but the Barajian led him down a flight of stairs and shouted for a blue-uniformed man to join them. After a barrage of what sounded like orders, the Barajian left.

The uniformed man eyed Payne then asked something Payne didn't understand. Payne shook his head. The man tried again, then finally tried a language Payne did understand—the language of the southern trade caravans. "Do you speak Adiko?"

"Some."

"Good. Follow me. I'll show you where you'll bunk. Your uniform and your kit are on your cot. Your squad is at weapons practice till the midday meal. You will help in the kitchen till they finish the meal and then join them for the rest of the day. Do as your squad leader tells you. Your squad is number four, it has a quatrefoil on the sleeve. The leader knows some Tarsean. I am the officer in charge of the four senior squads."

"So, I obey you and my squad leader."

"Correct."

"And I address you as?"

"Valaker. I am Valaker Amval."

Amval entered one of the doors off the loggia and pointed at a cot. "That's yours. Shave. Change. I'll show you to the kitchen."

Tiramet paced the room one more time, hugging her shawls around her. *What was this man?* Whatever he was, his power was strong. Even without her jewel she could see the red glow around him now.

Tiramet sank to the bench. If only Niret had not left her the jewel! She had not wanted it, but Niret had insisted that of all her grandchildren, she should have it. If she hadn't had the jewel, would she have gone to the governor with her story of the Child? Probably, since it had been the only way to save Edralen from being executed with their father. But would she have been believed?

It didn't matter now. The governor had believed her.

But what was this stranger? She wouldn't find out if Zakar interrupted every time she questioned him. She shivered. No, Zakar must have no excuse to come. But how could she examine this man without Zakar's knowing?

After some minutes thought, she rose, went to the paneled wall, and unlatched the door the paneling concealed. She climbed the steps to her bedchamber, unlatched another secret door, and hurried along the covered wall-walk to the tower of the governor's apartments. She paused to listen before she unlocked the door and entered but heard nothing. The governor should be at work or reviewing the exercises in the southeast courtyard. She let herself into the chamber and decided not to wait. She wanted to speak to the governor before Zakar did.

She arranged her shawls carefully. The governor was not the only Lakandari who was frightened of her eyes. Then she went down the stairs behind the other hidden door and through the audience chamber below to the balcony above the courtyard parade ground.

The governor was alone, surveying the blue-clad troops. *None of them would be here if it wasn't for me. Two hundred men and boys snatched from their lives. What have I done?* She squared her shoulders. It was beyond her power to fix. She must do what she could.

The wind blowing her draperies must have caught the governor's eye. "Did you learn more?"

She bowed. "Unfortunately, no, Your Excellency. Zakar interrupted and took the man to the barracks."

"You will have to try again."

"I intend to." She took a deep breath. "It seems to me, Excellency, that Zakar interests himself too much."

"What do you mean?"

"He does not want me to succeed."

"He is jealous of your powers."

"It is more than that. He is a Barajian. He does not wish the good of Lakandar as we do."

He swiftly glanced at her, then back at the youths below. "You are Eskedi. Why should you wish the good of Lakandar?"

"I was born here, Excellency. It is my homeland too."

He said nothing.

"I would have many opportunities to question the Tarsean if he were one of the guards assigned to my door."

"He has not been trained."

"Zakar would not know what I learned, only you."

The governor watched the youths march. Finally, he said, "Very well, in a day or two."

"But his information may be urgent."

He held up a hand to stop her protests. "He must have some training."

She bowed her acquiescence.

Reynard eyed his wooden cup. The beer was vile. Now that he was no longer thirsty from the morning's exercises he didn't relish drinking more of it. On the other hand, the thick porridge would probably stick in his throat if he didn't have something to wash it down.

He wondered what the afternoon would bring and hoped it would be less stultifying than the morning.

After the strange examination the evening before with the woman waving the jewel at him, he had been taken through the courtyard he had seen from the cell to an eight-bed dormitory where he had been issued a uniform, a wooden plate, cup, spoon, and a poorly made knife. He had been assigned the cot farthest from the door. Apparently the newest man was given the least chance to run. Then he had been left alone with the dormitory's other occupants.

They were all red-haired youths between twelve and sixteen, he judged, dressed in the same uniform he had been issued. He'd greeted them in Tarsean and been answered with blank stares. Then he had tried Suevarna with little better result. One of the youngest had managed a word of reply. The others had laughed and moved in, forcing him to put on the uniform and making what he judged from their braying laughter had been jokes about his build.

He looked down the table at his chief tormentor, a wide-shouldered boy he judged to be the oldest. The youth's hair was curly and he had brown eyes and olive skin. His hair was dark red. Looking around the dining hall, Reynard judged that the majority of the redheads who dined there were of the same race, whatever that was.

Payne had dark red hair, but it was straight. Reynard had heard that Payne had inherited his hair color from his ancestor Amloth so that shade was not unknown among the Sueve. But he was more familiar with brighter reds like his own or Bertz's golden red. Neither color was too unusual in the north of Tarsia. From Marda's description, her son's hair was fox-colored, like his own, and straight.

He looked around. He could see few who had hair that color, and no one younger than twelve. The tables seemed to be grouped by age. At some sat older men, at others men near twenty, at others youths like the one he was sitting at. They had been grouped that way on the parade ground that morning as well. Now that he looked more closely, he could see that there were also minor differences in the uniforms. Belts were different colors between age groups, and some of the trim was different. He hoped he would soon find someone who could explain it to him.

No one had explained anything that morning. They'd been fed the bad beer and watery gruel, then taken to the parade ground in the courtyard, where they had practiced some sort of drill. He'd tried to copy the others, but all too often he had had his spear at the wrong angle or marched in the wrong direction and been cuffed or cursed for his mistakes. He'd finally got the hang of it by the time the old man who had been at that odd examination last evening had come out on the balcony in a golden breastplate to watch them march, but Reynard hoped the afternoon wouldn't be more of the same. That was, unless it helped him find Robin.

The older men were rising now, leaving their table service at their places and filing into the sun-filled courtyard. Reynard eyed his bowl and cup dubiously; if he left them, how would he recognize them again? They had washed their own dishes that morning. This was something else unexplained.

The younger men followed their elders. An apron-wrapped man emerged from the kitchen at the end of the hall and pointed his ladle at a table of youths. They rose and started gathering the discarded dishes. Reynard watched his tablemates. They rose. He scrambled to his feet and followed as they filed out into the courtyard. One by one they were handed swords. Reynard turned to look back into the dining hall as he waited his turn. Boys were filing in to sit at some of the empty tables. At least two had bright red hair.

Reynard hefted the single-edged sword that was handed him. If he was at the table assigned to clear the tables, he would be able to see if one of those boys was Robin. Maybe he could even talk to him. What did he need to do to be assigned kitchen duty?

"Walter isn't here?" Michel asked Marda, who had just finished packing her few possessions—more now, since the kaiyun had insisted that she take more than a single set of garments.

"No, he's out with Garrett and Ulick, making arrangements with the Sueve and the Barajian guards."

Michel sighed in exasperation at her answer.

"What is it?" she asked.

"The Barajians insist we can't start before noon tomorrow, because of some portent or other, and Thomas wants to be sure Walter's told right away." Thomas was acting as liaison to the kaiyun's party, while Walter and Ulick dealt with the Sueve. Michel had been sent to help. "And

I'm to come straight back without wandering around."
Michel was as sulky as Robin when Marda made him stay
within sight.

"I can tell him, unless he's with the khan."

"If he is, go to the kaiyun's tent and Thomas can deal
with it himself."

She nodded—the kaiyun's tent was the least frightening
place besides this one in the camp, but she wanted free of
confinement and she was tired of being told to go sit in the
corner and be quiet. Outside she got her bearings; Walter
was likely to be at the edge of camp, but where, precisely?
The easiest thing to do was to find her way out and circle
it until she found him.

Many Sueve were packing to depart. Ulick had said that
few had left even this late in the spring, because they were
afraid of the shaman. Now the danger was past and they
were safe from his wolf winds.

Their lives were back to normal—when would hers be?
And Robin, what was happening to him in Barajia? She
didn't know anything about that country, except fireside
tales that couldn't be true—these Barajians certainly had
only one head.

She was on the western edge of the camp now—and she
gazed wistfully over the miles of empty land between her
and home. How would she ever get back? They still had
to travel far to the south—six days, Walter had said—and
find Robin. The moon would be full again in less time than
they'd already spent on this journey.

It didn't matter. If she had Robin she'd find a place
somewhere—she could work hard and surely that would
help her find a way home.

The sound of galloping horses and raised voices broke
into her thoughts. She panicked, wanting to hide, before
she realized the voices were children's.

They were racing back and forth on horseback, boys and
girls both, at breakneck speed. A stick substituted for a goat
carcass as they played at the tuan barkha of the adults. Their
riding was incredibly skillful. Someone had told her once
that the southern Tarseans believed that Sueve were joined
to their horses—a kind of two-headed beast. She could believe it of these children.

One of the small girls—barely older than little Anya had been—took a tumble. Marda checked the urge to pull her to safety as the child rolled skillfully away from the horses' hooves. Dirty and laughing, the little one scrambled onto her mount and hurled herself back into the game.

The riding figures grew blurry; she'd seen Robin do that a hundred times—fall and scramble to his feet so intent on the game he hardly noticed his tumble. She turned blindly to continue her journey, barely heeding the rider coming toward her.

Not until he drew up and called her name did she realize that it was Ulick.

She wiped her eyes and faced him.

"What are you doing out here?" he asked.

She started to tell him about Michel's message, then blurted out, "Watching the children."

He studied her face for a moment then dismounted, and, to her surprise, turned to observe the small band of young riders.

After a moment, he said, "That boy in the red jacket—he's good." He watched a little longer. "He rides almost as well as my son Taryan, when I last saw him."

Days ago Marda would have said she could not read his expression, that Sueve kept their emotions hidden, but days in Ulick's company had taught her better. Pride and sorrow mingled in his eyes.

"Was—was Taryan your oldest?"

"No, he was my second son—he was younger than this boy, seven years old—when I saw him last." A year younger than Robin. "Verik was the eldest; Simos the youngest."

"And you had daughters." Peter had always wanted a daughter.

"Two. The youngest had just taken her first steps. And a child who must have been born soon after—" He broke off, she thought, before his voice betrayed more than he wanted. Marda touched his sleeve and turned his attention back to her. "Come now. I'll take you back to the tent. You shouldn't be out here alone—not that I don't think you're more trustworthy than Michel."

She snorted, then remembered the real reason she was wandering outside. "No, take me to Sir Walter instead. I've a message for him."

18

Seventeenth Day

Reynard pushed his sweat-soaked hair out of his eyes and tried to steal a look through the door of the dining hall, but the head cook saw him and swung his ladle. Not wanting to get hit again, Reynard returned to stirring the steaming cauldron of stew that formed the bulk of the evening meal.

Three meals had passed, and he hadn't had a chance to find out if any of the younger boys was Robin. He had approached one the evening before when the group of youths he was assigned to had joined the other squads their own age and younger in a large room after the evening meal. The two age groups had been seated separately and harangued in what Reynard assumed was Barajian by men in fancy uniforms.

The program had been varied at intervals by periods when the audience parroted back what the speaker said. It had been noisy and boring, and Reynard had whiled away the time by narrowing the possible candidates for Robin.

The boys had filed out first, and as a bright-haired boy who looked about eight had passed, Reynard had dropped a button from his uniform jacket into the aisle. He had lunged into the aisle asking for help in Tarsean. The boy had stared at him, then run off to tattle to an officer.

Reynard had been grabbed by two of the officers and hurried out to the courtyard, where his jacket had been removed and he'd been beaten with one of the thin sticks the officers carried. He didn't know if the punishment was for speaking to someone not in his squad or for speaking Tarsean. Then he had been dumped in a cell overnight and brought to the kitchen before dawn.

The cook had kept him busy with the heaviest tasks the whole day. He had chopped and carried firewood, fetched supplies from underground storerooms, hauled water from the well in the cellar, lugged the heavy iron cauldrons to and from the fire, washed them, stirred them till he thought he would melt into the boiling stew—all under the direction of the head cook, who enforced his orders with his hot iron ladle. Reynard rubbed the burn on his cheek, which the rising steam made sting like new. The day's work would be worth the pain if he could just identify Robin, but he hadn't had a chance even to get a good look into the room beyond.

The cook swung his ladle gesturing for the cauldron Reynard stirred to be brought to the door to be served from. Reynard and one of the three youths, who had come to the kitchen late that afternoon, carried the cauldron to the door to the dining hall. But before he could no more than register that the boys were being seated for their meal one of the youths shoved a bucket of dirty wooden tableware into his arms, and the cook waved him back into the kitchen.

Reynard searched for something he could use as an excuse to go back to the entrance but saw nothing of use. The cook yelled at him, and he carried the bucket down to the scullery where the dirty pots awaited. The greasy stew was going to be harder to clean than the gruel and porridge of the day's earlier meals, and he was probably going to be the only one assigned to the job again.

He set to work with rags and sand to scour the dishes that the other youths brought down from the kitchen above. Most dumped their buckets and left hurriedly, but one stayed after his third trip down the stair, picked up a rag, and started scouring. Reynard judged that the boy was about fourteen. He was tall and thin, and had dark-red curly hair and golden-brown eyes.

They worked in silence. The footsteps above became fewer, then ceased. Then a single set crossed the floor and ended in a loud thump.

"The cook's sat down to drink his dinner," the boy said in Tarsean.

Reynard looked up, surprised at the cynicism as much as by the Tarsean.

The boy caught his eye and smiled. "It should be an hour at least before he thinks to check on us. I thought you could use some help. No one has explained anything to you, have they?"

"No."

"Typically stupid. You've been forcibly enlisted in the governor's private guard. Term of service is life or the governor's pleasure."

"No one gets out?"

"No one ever has."

Reynard shook his head. "But what if I don't want to?"

"Doesn't matter. You have no choice. If you obey and do your best to fit in, you will be well treated. Just don't speak Tarsean in front of anyone who might snitch. We're supposed to forget our pasts and become good Lakandari."

"I thought this was Barajia."

The boy nodded. "It is."

"I don't understand. Why is the governor doing this?"

"Too complicated. You don't need to know."

Reynard piled clean bowls on the table by the door. This boy knew more than he was telling, but he did seem friendly. That could be a trap. He decided to take the risk.

"My name is Reynard. My companions and I came in search of a boy stolen by Sueve raiders, and, we believe, sold to the governor. He's red-haired, eight years old. His name is Robin. Do you know if he's here?"

"Two mistakes. Your name isn't Reynard and his isn't Robin. You'll be beaten again if you don't remember that. What name did they give you?"

"Ardrim."

"I'm Ivreim. There is a new boy in the trefoil squad that could be the boy you seek. He's been here maybe ten days."

"How could I get word to him?"

"You can't and what good would it do? There's no escape."

"Maybe I can find some way to get word to his mother. He's an only child. His father is dead. She's frantic with worry. At least she'd know he's alive and safe."

"I can't promise but I'll see if I can find out if he is the boy. Robin?"

"Yes. Thank you."

"I hear you've been assigned kitchen duty for two more days. I'll see if I can join you again tomorrow."

Reynard lifted one of the larger cauldrons to the table top. "I wouldn't volunteer for this."

Ivreim grinned. "Don't count it a sacrifice. I get sent here a lot. This is about the safest place in barracks to talk or be alone."

To be alone. Reynard looked at his companion who was intent on scouring the greasy pot. "So we're supposed to forget our pasts. Have you?"

"No," Ivreim said, without looking up.

The very shortness of his answer made Reynard want to ask more, but the floorboards creaked above.

"Cook's stirring," Ivreim said. "We'd better finish quickly. Is there anything else I can tell you?"

"Yeah. What's the Barajian phrase for 'I don't understand'?"

Ivreim grinned. *"Vey ic ser.* A very useful phrase, under the circumstances."

They swung the heavy cauldron down from the table, filled it with cleaned bowls, and carried it between them up to the kitchen.

The kaiyun's cart was richly furnished; even the carpet on the floor was a wonder, woven in rich red, gold, and deep blue wool. But though the sides were made of elaborate latticework that let in light and air, Marda felt as if she were shut in a box with the other four women. Their perfumed scent half-choked her, and the constant incomprehensible chatter in Barajian put her nerves on edge.

Only Kaiyun Chrysogon and Marda were silent. Marda stared out the window at the miles of waving grass, but from time to time she watched the kaiyun covertly as Sir Walter had asked. The great lady did not seem as untroubled as Marda had expected now that her son was safe. It was obvious that her attention was not on what her women were saying. She spoke little and her gaze often strayed through the latticework. It was not until well into the day that Marda realized she wasn't watching the scenery—she was watching Prince Dayan who rode alongside them.

What does she have to worry about? Her son was safe and on his way to live in a palace, unlike Robin, who was still missing and could be dead, for all she knew.

No. Not dead . . . surely she'd know that. Surely the Huntsmen would know that they'd failed.

Ulick had said they would find Robin. He, if none of the other Huntsmen, understood her fears, the panic that twisted her bowels when she thought of all the things that might be happening to her son.

Strange she'd think of Ulick, though. Sir Walter had lost a son—everyone knew that song. But Ulick had talked to her about his loss, about his children. Sir Walter never would.

She wondered now if the way he felt, the way he acted, was the way Peter had felt when he knew he was going to die. Or had Peter known it? No one had known how he'd died, just that Peter had been another body on the field after a battle.

She looked out the lattice again. Dayan was not looking at the cart. He was scowling into the distance.

This was the man—no, boy—who had stolen Robin, who had been responsible for so much grief, for more bodies, more deaths. He was sleek, nearly plump, as if he'd fed on his killings. Too soft, she thought, for someone who fancied himself a great leader. He hadn't had to do much, just ride to a village or camp when he wanted something, see that his men took it, and ride away. That and hiding were all he had had to do.

He and Ulick were both Sueve, but so different. Ulick was not soft; whatever he had done with the Hunt, he had worked. The body that had shared her bedroll was hard.

He didn't have an oval face, like the kaiyun's, either, as Dayan did. And Dayan was definitely taller. Ulick, however, had more bone to him—his face was leaner and his eyes were more yellow than brown.

Sueve or not, Dayan was like one or two other spoiled youths she'd known. Ulick had said that Dayan's father had let him do as he'd willed, and his mother's women had petted and coddled him. And look what that had led to!

The prince must have sensed her watching, he seemed to look directly at her. Did he shrug before his gaze returned to the horizon in front of him? Marda's hand clenched the latticework.

She stared at the rich carpet. She wanted to rant and scream, but she couldn't among these women, who all loved or worshiped the boy riding beside them. And who outside the cart would brook such behavior? Sir Walter would soothe or perhaps scold; the others would not even bother to listen.

Ulick would, though. He, of all of them—and she wished he were next to her, instead of these jabbering women.

The thought startled her, and she was still grappling with it when the cart lumbered to a halt for the noon meal.

Bertz paced the storeroom, waiting for Reshalon. He was tired of the dark, tired of the closed-in place, tired of inaction.

Reshalon and Naroc, his friend who knew Tarsean, had confirmed when they visited last night that Hamon was being held in the city prison. They had been appalled that he had still been adamant that he needed to talk to Hamon and had tried to dissuade him. What good would it do for him to be captured as well, they had argued. When he was insistent, Reshalon had paced the room, much as Bertz was doing now, muttering to himself, and firing what sounded like occasional questions at Naroc. Then Reshalon had smiled and stopped pacing. He and Naroc had had a rapid conversation in Eskedi, with Reshalon sounding enthusiastic and Naroc skeptical. Then Reshalon had scrambled up the ladder and left. Bertz had tried to question Naroc, who shook his head and said that the matter was not worth explanation. Wait till the seed sprouted before selling the crop. Then he too had left.

A whole day had passed since then; the sun and moon

had risen and set. Except for the women who brought him his meals, he had seen no one. He might as well be in prison—maybe then he could communicate with Hamon.

Finally he heard footsteps heavier than the women's and children's on the floor above. The trapdoor was opened and Naroc and Reshalon descended, followed by a tall man in a grey hooded robe. Reshalon put the lamp he carried on a shelf and gestured at Bertz as he said something to the hooded man.

The man looked Bertz up and down and said in slow Tarsean, "Reshalon tells me you need to get into the city prison."

"Yes, I need to speak to my friend who is imprisoned there."

"For slave stealing?"

"Yes. We were trying to rescue a boy who was stolen from his mother by Sueve raiders and sold as a slave here. We offered to buy him back, but were refused."

"He has red hair?"

"Yes."

"Unfortunate." The man turned and spoke to Reshalon and Naroc then returned to Bertz. "Reshalon speaks well of you. It may be that I can help you see your friend, if you are willing to make certain sacrifices." He dropped his hood to reveal a completely shaved head.

"Sacrifices?" Bertz asked.

"Your hair. I and the other members of the brotherhood tend to the unfortunate, including those in the city prison. If you are willing to live like one of us for the day, we can take you into and out of the prison when we visit and see that you are the one assigned to tend your friend."

"Why are you helping me?"

"As I said, Reshalon speaks highly of you, and we have reason to be grateful to him. In his days of prosperity, he was generous to us, and even now he gives us what he can. Besides, the governor gives us too much to do—there are too many poor, too many prisoners. Perhaps we can help one child be returned to his mother."

"What do I do?"

"Accompany me tonight, live with us until we visit the prison tomorrow. After that we shall see what is necessary."

"Won't people suspect something?"

"The brothers will not talk, and we often take in unfortunates. You were wounded recently. It would not be unusual if you were brought to our hospital."

"It would not endanger you?"

"That is of no matter. Here. I brought a robe. If you agree, and Reshalon or his household have a razor, we can get started."

"Of course I agree." Bertz took the robe and quickly changed into it, as Reshalon—once the conversation was translated—hurried up the ladder.

After a few minutes Reshalon returned, followed by the woman from the bridge who carried towels, a bowl of water, and a razor. Bertz sat on a stool. The woman said something rapidly, and the men laughed.

"She says it is a shame to spoil such a beautiful man," Naroc translated.

"Vanity," Bertz said. "Besides, you have said that the Governor's guards are arresting all red-haired men. I will be safer without it."

The woman left, and within a few minutes, Bertz and the grey-robed man were ready to leave as well.

"We'll tend your horse," Naroc said at the outer door.

"Thank you. Tell Reshalon I cannot thank him as much as he deserves."

Naroc translated. "He says it is he who owes you. If you need further help, ask."

"I hope that will not be necessary." Bertz turned and followed the grey-robed man into the city.

"Exotic," Thomas said to Walter, "and much more edible than anything we've had since we left Tarsia." Walter scowled at the Barajian food, irritated because Thomas was right.

"Yes, but not worth the time it has cost to halt early just to set up the kitchen for the kaiyun and her pet nobles."

It was Thomas's turn to scowl—he had become sensitive to any criticism of the kaiyun—then he shrugged and took another bite of the meal which had been sent to them. "They'll get tired of traveling and want to pick up the pace soon. The kaiyun's women are anxious to get back to civ-

ilization. Most of them haven't been home since she was
wed to the khan."

"You didn't let on that you understood Barajian, did
you?"

"Of course not. I know how to play my hand better than
that."

Walter put his plate down. "I'm sorry. Of course. I'm
not sure what makes me uneasy."

"Hamon?"

"It's different. The other is—" he groped for words,
"—like a warning bell in the back of my head. This problem is something that I can't put a finger on, something
I've seen or missed seeing. Not something from the Goddesses like the other—it's a feeling that anyone might have
in a situation they're not sure of."

"If it will help, I'll keep an eye out."

"Ride with the kaiyun's party, then. Listen, tell me anything you hear."

"Unlikely. You saw the cart."

The cart which conveyed the kaiyun had been a point of
contention from the beginning. It slowed the party down,
but the Barajians had insisted that the kaiyun's modesty be
preserved. The conveyance had closed latticework sides to
hide the kaiyun from the Sueve, the barbarians, and the
commoners of her own people.

"Then listen to the men who ride with her. They must
talk among themselves."

"I wonder what the others have overheard."

The rest of the Hunt were scattered about the caravan.
Some among the Barajian troops, and Ulick with the Sueve
who would accompany the party as far as the foothills.
Walter gave Ellis a sharp mental summons and almost as
he finished the silver-haired Huntsman arrived.

"I was already on my way," he complained.

"I apologize. Have you established any rapport with the
Barajians?"

"A little. Michel isn't much use, but Justin understands
more of the language than he thought—he's only read it
before. And a couple of Barajians speak Adiko. But they're
uncomfortable around us. I'm not sure if it's because we're
outsiders or because we bested them in the tuan."

"Keep trying. Tell Justin to keep his ears open. Is he drinking?"

"Starting to when I left. But not as much as usual."

Walter dismissed him with a wave and rested his forehead on his knees.

"I wish," he said to Thomas, without looking up, "that we were somewhere that spoke a civilized tongue."

"Barajian is very civilized. It has seventeen cases and over a thousand poetic forms. You can't get much more civilized than that."

"Their murders are very civilized, too. Or so I understand."

"Are you thinking of what Michel overheard?"

"I wish I knew how well he understood the language."

"He's not stupid."

"No. But he's lazy. He hadn't studied the language for years before he was cursed and he hasn't had any reason to practice it since."

"Oh, but it was about a woman and a murder. Surely Michel could be depended on to comprehend that."

"I wish I could be that amused."

"Personally, if I had a preference, I'd murder the one the Princess calls Tita Maimai. She's a harridan."

Walter's interest sharpened, and he sat up straight. "Do you think that's likely?"

"I think it's likely that someone would have said they'd like to murder her. Whether they meant it or not is another question."

"Perhaps it's no more than that. I don't feel very trusting, however."

"That's your job, Walter."

Thomas finished the last few bites of food and stood up, finger combing his hair.

"Where are you going?"

"To fetch Marda." The Tarsean woman was traveling with the kaiyun in the most guarded part of the cortege. "If we're to maintain the fiction that she's married to Ulick, she can't sleep there. And Ulick will be late, since he has to see to the pack animals."

"Of course." But as the Madarian wandered off into the

darkness, Walter did not miss the fact that he paused in the shadows to change his clothing to garments less dusty and travel stained. That was not something he'd do just for Marda.

Eighteenth Day

Bertz followed the two members of the brotherhood down the dark stairs to the lower level of the city prison and waited while Reshalon's friend Olm talked with the turnkey. He kept his head down, so that his hood shadowed his face, but the turnkey barely glanced at the three men as they carried their burdens of food and medicine past him into the room beyond the iron-bound wooden door. The locks ground closed behind them.

The room was dim, lit only by grates set high in the wall on one side. Bertz heard the rattle of chains before his eyes adjusted and he could see movement. Outstretched hands reached for the bread they distributed as they worked down the room.

"Ivm thinks your friend is there." Olm pointed to room's dark far end. "Take the water and bandages. They will give you an excuse for tarrying with him."

No outstretched hands awaited him. He could barely distinguish Hamon covered by a filthy cloak in the darkest corner. Hamon didn't stir but lay stiffly, his gaze fixed on the ceiling vaults as Bertz set the bucket beside him. Bertz knelt on the stone floor beside the fetid straw on which Hamon lay.

"Hamon?" Bertz reached to pull back the cloak.

Hamon fiercely clutched it by one hand and slowly turned his head. His eyes, sunken in his unshaved pallid face, focused on Bertz. He tried to speak and coughed. Bertz leaned nearer.

Hamon tried again. "I'm hallucinating."

Bertz sat back. This was no time to joke. "No, it's me."

Hamon wet his lips. "The others?"

"Taken to the palace."

"You? Captured?"

"No. Friends helped me to see you."

"Why?"

Bertz chose to ignore some of the possible meanings to a question he didn't have answers for and didn't want to think about. "What happened to the coin Walter gave you?"

Hamon's eyes lost focus. "Don't know." He frowned, closed his eyes, then opened them again. "The Barajian took it. The one at the ambush."

"Think. Did he keep it or leave it at the prison?"

Hamon didn't answer. Bertz wanted to shake him. "It's important. Robin is almost assuredly at the palace like Payne and Reynard. If they can't be freed, Marda must be brought here. Walter could follow the token elsewhere."

"He swung it in my face. Then . . ." Footsteps approached. ". . . He tucked it in his robe."

Bertz looked up to see Olm, who knelt and eased the cloak from Hamon's hand. Bertz caught his breath. Hamon was naked under it, save for the rags of his shirt. A red burn crossed his trunk from breastbone to lower hip, and his leg was twisted, broken above the knee. He twitched away from the wet cloth Olm was using to wash the filth away, and Bert could now see his other hand. Two fingers were missing, their stumps blistered.

Hamon submitted to Olm's ministrations, his teeth clenched against the pain, his eyes fixed on the ceiling. Bertz mechanically handed Olm what cloths, medicines, and bandages he asked for. He didn't want to feel the compassion that welled up inside him. Everything he'd heard of Hamon of Saroth, the stories of his murders, his incest—

everything he'd seen of his mockery and irreverence told him that this huntsman deserved his cursing, told him that his sympathy was undeserved. But the stark endurance with which Hamon met his injuries stirred his unwilling admiration.

Olm raised Hamon's head to help him to drink, then eased him back down and moved on to the next prisoner. Hamon reached awkwardly for the cloak. Bertz helped Hamon to cover himself, careful of his wounds.

"They were inventive." Hamon's teeth flashed in a grimace. "But I could have taught them a thing or two."

Bertz was silent, not knowing how to respond.

"Why were Payne and Reynard taken to the palace, instead of being brought here with me?"

"From what I've been told, the governor is recruiting red-haired men and boys for a special guard."

"Ludicrous."

"It seems some soothsayer has told him that the 'Child of Fire' will lead his troops to victory."

Hamon gasped, his chest shaking. It took a moment for Bertz to realize that the spasms were laughter and not from pain.

"The Child of Fire shall lead the chosen from the darkness into the land of light."

"What?"

"It's a prophecy of Madromac. Didn't expect to run into it here." Hamon paused for breath. "But why not? Everybody else has used it."

"Used it?"

"For every rebellion, palace coup, and assassination in the last millennium. Everybody sees himself as 'chosen.' "

Bertz was vaguely scandalized. "Isn't it blasphemous to use a prophecy falsely?"

"They exist to be used. Madromac was a court poet. He called himself a mage and a prophet. After Derbran fell, he drifted from court to court with his poems and his prophecies. He even worked for my grandfather at Saroth at one time. Get him drunk enough and he'd spew vague prophecies of anyone's future greatness."

"He was of your people?"

"Eskedi. Fled with the nobles when the capital fell to the Obriki."

"But you're of Saroth."

"My great-grandfather's great-grandfather founded Saroth. He quarreled with his brother, the King of Ascovia, and fled abroad with his followers to found a separate realm—not just a trading port like all the 'lins.' "

"Lin'Merith?"

"One of them. Some Eskedi settled in Barajia and Lakandar as well. Seem to have spread their damned prophecies."

"You don't believe them?"

"Wishful thinking on the loser's part. Some day the Gods will right our wrongs with no work on our part. Willful self-deception."

"But the 'Child of Fire' will be a red-haired man?"

Hamon laughed mirthlessly. "That's one of a hundred interpretations. In Eskedi every word of that prophecy has a number of meanings. That's what makes it so useful. *Bis*, the word 'child,' itself is neuter."

"It could be a woman?"

"Or an it."

"But the governor thinks it's a man or boy. That should keep Robin healthy till we can save him."

"You and the others."

"No."

"Look. Don't waste time on me. I'd be a liability. Rescue the boy. I'll survive only if the task is accomplished. What happens till then doesn't matter. Go. The Barajian had the coin, the last I saw it."

Olm had returned. He put his hand on Bertz's shoulder. "He's right. We'll do what we can for him."

Bertz rose reluctantly and followed Olm from the room.

"Think you know *baed* from *eret* now?" Valaker Amval asked in Adiko.

Payne stopped and saluted the valaker, who was seated with a few other officers on benches under the east loggia, just as they had on the previous evenings. "Yes, sir."

Amval gestured for Payne to sit on the empty bench

across from him. "I'd guess you've seen previous service. Arinese?"

"Yesacroth, sir."

"Infantry?"

"Cavalry."

"Thought so. Cavalry myself, before the governor made me a schoolmaster. See much action?"

"Some." Payne patched together an account of his service from his life before and after his cursing, which apparently satisfied the valaker's curiosity without arousing his suspicion. Soon they were joined by two other officers in an argument about cavalry tactics in an odd mix of Adiko, Tarsean, and Barajian.

"Have some beer," the valaker offered, handing Payne a cup. One of the squad leaders rose to pour from a jug from under the bench, but it proved empty, as did its two fellows on the table inside.

The squad leader swore and yelled at a trooper who stumped across the courtyard to the kitchen. Soon Reynard appeared in the kitchen doorway with a small keg on one shoulder and a full jug in his other hand.

Payne hadn't seen Reynard, except across the courtyard that first day he had been assigned to the barracks, and had been worried about him. Reynard's stringy hair and stained uniform showed that he had been working in the kitchen, which meant that he had probably had no chance to search for Robin. Payne frowned. He had had little chance himself. The younger boys were kept well apart from the men. He would have to think of some way to solve the problem.

"Bring the good beer, boy?" one of the squad leaders asked in Tarsean.

Reynard set the jug on the bench. "Yes, sir." He twisted to swing the keg down from his shoulder. "From the cook's own cellar." He was facing only Payne, and he winked. "I'd guess from the cook's expression that it's as good as that at the Bird in Mayflowers, and that was the best inn in Rayln."

Payne wondered what that was about. But he had no chance to ask as the valaker waved Reynard back to the kitchen. The squad leader filled the cups and the conversation resumed. Payne puzzled over Reynard's words. He had no doubt that it was a message. He tried to picture the inn sign. A bird? He'd seen eagles, hawks, even owls, but a bird? Any bird? Then he got it. A robin was a bird. Robin in mayflowers. He knew of three different plants called that. What would Reynard mean by it? He noticed the five-lobed insignia on one of the squad leaders' sleeves as he gestured to illustrate some famous combat. Mayflowers all had three petals. Reynard must mean he had located Robin in the trefoil squad of boys. Good. Now that they knew where he was, they could plan how to escape and get the boy to his mother.

"What do you think? I say there's nothing that can stand up to heavy cavalry," one squad leader asked.

Payne wished he had been listening. "On level ground, but the Gods don't always give us that luxury."

"Just my point," the other squad leader cut in. "Look at Basarfal, if Velerim had used conventional tactics there, he would have lost."

"Not so." The first speaker launched into a detailed analysis of the battle, which was disputed by Amval and the other. The argument was finally ended when Amval was called aside by a messenger in russet uniform. He was frowning when he rejoined the group.

"You've got a new assignment," he told Payne. "You're to be one of the guards at the Berim tower."

One of the squad leaders whistled and the other said, "He gets to guard the governor's piece of skirt. Why don't I get those assignments?"

"You're too ugly."

Amval waved them to silence. "You're to move immediately. Get your gear. The messenger is waiting."

When Payne returned, Amval was alone. "It's probably unnecessary now, but I wanted to warn you. Don't speak to the youths or boys in anything but Barajian."

"Yes, sir. But why? The men speak among themselves in their native languages, and the squad leader spoke to the boy who brought the beer in Tarsean."

"He shouldn't have. The boys and youths are supposed to become Lakandari."

"Not the men?"

Amval spat. "The governor doesn't think you can be

molded. Count yourself lucky." He gestured to the russet-uniformed man who awaited then at the gate. "Follow him. He'll show you to your new quarters."

The moon had set before Ulick came back to Walter and the others.

Walter and Thomas conversed in low voices by the dying coals of the fire. They quieted at his approach until they saw who he was. Walter's face was grave.

"What's wrong?" Ulick asked.

"The Barajians are trying to slow us down."

"It's not the kaiyun," Thomas said. "It's the men."

"Can you be sure?" The day's journey had been a short one; they had halted well before sunset.

"Because she wants to get her son to the capital quickly. She's afraid he'll do something stupid. The boy is unhappy about the arrangement."

"The other women, then?"

"No. I can't hear much from the cart except Tita Maimai, who is loud and adamant about her hurry to get back home and supervise the wedding of one of her unfortunate brothers' daughters. We'd have stopped even earlier if she hadn't scolded Wiraz into continuing."

"If you can't hear the women in the cart, how do you know that the kaiyun is in such a hurry?" Walter demanded.

"I spoke to her last night. And this afternoon when we stopped to eat." Thomas seemed defensive.

"I see." Ulick tried to stay still and unnoticed. He'd never felt this kind of tension between Walter and Thomas before.

"She wants to practice her Tarsean. She doesn't have much chance, you see."

"You don't have to make excuses to me. I just wanted to make sure your source was legitimate."

Thomas shrugged. "The Barajian men don't like my conversing with her; neither do her women."

"They don't like foreigners," Ulick said.

"What do you hear from this Wiraz and the others?" Thomas relaxed when Walter changed the subject.

"It seemed clear that they were the ones who insisted on stopping."

"Why?" Ulick said. "It doesn't make sense."

"We need to find out. Tomorrow, ride with Eleylin and Garrett and the Barajian cavalrymen. You might be able to worm something out of them."

"I can try. The other Sueve say they look down on us, so I don't know how much they'll tell me."

"Tomorrow I'm going to refuse to stop when the Barajians insist. Maybe I can keep them moving." Walter didn't look at Thomas as he addressed him. "Try to enlist the kaiyun's help. Perhaps if she demands they keep traveling, they will."

"I hope so," Ulick said. "The Sueve say that Silasar Pass hasn't been well patrolled the last two seasons."

"And the other—the Agandar Pass?"

"They didn't know. Even the few Sueve who have business in Istlakan don't use that one. It's too dangerous even without bandits."

He could see the mountains to the southeast, a featureless ebony wall blocking the star-spattered blue-black of the sky. He was going again to somewhere strange and unfathomable. Did he want that or not?

Marda willed herself to sleep but could not help straining to hear the Huntsmen's conversation. The crunch of footsteps coming toward her told her that Ulick had come to pretend to sleep, too.

"Is what they're saying true? That we're going too slow?" she asked as he sat to take off his boots.

"It seems so, but it's not a problem yet. Don't worry. We'll—"

"Find Robin. I know." She rolled over to face Ulick. "But what's happening to him now?"

She saw the wariness in his eyes. He knew something of what she had learned and hadn't told her. But why should he? He was only bound to bring Robin to her, not to warn her of what might have been done to him in the meantime.

"You'll find that out when you see him, won't you?" Ulick said, and bent to turn back the blankets, hiding his face. He was being cagy; she didn't like that.

"The other women having been speaking of things that— that happen to boy slaves in Lakandar."

"How do you know? Only the kaiyun speaks Tarsean."

"I can tell from their giggles and sometimes their gestures. Besides—we knew some men who'd hired out to the caravans. They brought back stories."

Ulick was studying her face; had he learned to read her as she had him?

"Some of the stories are true. But most likely he'll have been sold as a household slave to do menial work. The other is not something even the Barajians think well of."

"But people *do* do things other people don't think well of." She hugged herself against the cold thought, and hardly noticed the comforting hand Ulick put on her shoulder except as welcome warmth.

"You'll soon have him back safe. Then you'll know, and what you know you can face."

"And take him to what?" she said, the question that she had tried to elude facing her again. "Everything's gone."

"You'll have your son, and the rest will work itself out. Now rest. Walter will make sure we travel longer tomorrow."

He drew her down and pulled the blankets up. But though he put his arm over his eyes as if to signal that the time for talking was done, Marda realized that her head was resting on his shoulder. He'd done that deliberately, she realized, and accepted the comfort it offered.

20

Nineteenth Day

It rained in the early morning shortly after the entourage set off. Walter pulled the hood of his riding cloak up and kept away from the Barajians to avoid giving them the chance to find the weather another excuse to dally. The kaiyun had been adamant about traveling as far as possible today—that should curtail attempts to stop before dark this evening.

A Sueve rider drew abreast of him—Dayan Fire-born. Walter had all but forgotten the boy was with them, even though he had been a sullen witness to the attempts to get the Barajians under way each morning and to keep them moving as the day progressed.

Now the boy said nothing, but rode in silence, as if waiting to catch Walter's eye.

Finally, without looking at the Huntsman, he said, "I think my mother has convinced the yellow robes to ignore the rain and continue."

"Excellent."

"They are soft. A few hours on horseback and they complain that their bottoms hurt!"

"They seldom have reason to travel so long and hard."

"I know they prefer to remain rootbound."

187

The boy sounded less contemptuous than apprehensive.

"A fixed dwelling place has its advantages."

"*You* don't stay in one place."

"I don't travel because I have a choice."

"They tell me Ulick chose to move to a village."

"Yes."

"Why?"

"You'd have to ask him."

Silence.

"Ulick Assaga Nu won't speak to me," Dayan finally admitted.

"I see."

"He has something of mine." Walter waited. "I want it back."

"Your medallion? It is his decision to keep it or not."

"My father gave it to me! How can I live in a strange place without one single thing that was his?"

"From what I understand, you abandoned all the property your father left you when you ran off with Aslut."

"I kept the amulet and his sword. Now my mother won't let me carry a weapon."

"Ulick has the medallion. I can't give it to you."

"You can tell him to!"

"What makes you think that I can tell Ulick what to do?"

"I've seen." The boy's face was alight with indignation. "He tries to act as if he's the leader, but he listens to you before he acts." Walter would have to tell Ulick to be more circumspect. "Command him to give it me."

"I can't. He took it from you; it is his decision when or whether to give it back."

Dayan urged his horse forward to block Walter's path and snatched at the Huntsman's reins.

"I will have the amulet! It is mine—my birthright!"

Walter caught his arm and held it in a grip that made the young Sueve grunt in surprised pain. "You forfeited it when you chose to disgrace your father's people."

"Tell him I must have it!" He shook free of Walter. "I'll tell the governor of Istlakan, and he'll make Ulick return it!"

"You've a long ride before then. And I won't suggest it

if you continue to disgrace your parents and both their peoples this way." Dayan started to speak again. "No more. He'll return it when you are worthy of it. Not before."

Dayan started to ride away, but before he did, he loosed one parting shot over his shoulder. "And keep that puling clerk of yours away from my mother! He presumes too much!"

Walter watched him ride away. So Thomas's affinity for the kaiyun had penetrated even the boy's self-obsession.

Walter had recognized the signs himself: Thomas took every opportunity to speak to her, defended her when she didn't need defending, and had seen to her interests even when it wasn't necessary to fulfill the terms of the Hunt's summoning. Women had never been one of Thomas's obsessions, either as individuals or as recreation—not that he had anything against them, he judged them with the same lively intellect with which he judged everyone.

Thomas had been married, Walter knew, and had had a long-term affair with a married woman. Neither relationship seemed to have marked him deeply. He lacked the bitterness of most of the Huntsmen.

What had this woman touched in Thomas? She was beautiful certainly. Walter had no doubt that she possessed intelligence and charm. He could not imagine Thomas loving a woman without both those qualities.

Thomas could be freed; he deserved to be. The Barajians appreciated scholars; he could find a place in Barajia.

Does this woman have the determination to hold him, though? She had certainly been determined when she had pleaded for her son's life. Thomas had explained how demeaning it was for the daughter of an Emperor to kneel before a Sueve.

Would she have the will to free Thomas? That was the difficult part. The best way to encourage that was to make sure they were together often.

As he spurred his horse forward, catching up with his place in the cortege, Walter mulled plans to assure that Thomas spent the maximum amount of time with the kaiyun.

He was some time and a number of miles along the road

when he found himself trying to imagine an existence without the Madarian.

This was the most boring day of his life, Payne thought, as he shifted his weight unobtrusively. He had stood for eight hours guarding a door at the end of a corridor which no one had used since he and his companion had come on duty. Every two hours when the bell sounded, they had changed places from left to right, right to left. Either the woman in the room beyond was very unpopular or there was, as he had suspected, another entrance to her room. Or maybe the governor had other things to do in the daytime.

"The governor's piece of skirt," the squad leader had called her. She was beautiful enough to be an important man's mistress, but neither her bearing on the night of the examination nor the governor's actions had any suggestion of sexuality. What did she do for the governor, then? She had asked Payne shrewder questions than the officers had. Could she be some sort of advisor? Payne discarded that theory. Not in Lakandar; they kept their women locked up. He'd probably never know. *It would be more useful to plan some way to communicate with Reynard and Robin, so think about that, not the woman behind the door.*

Finally their relief marched up the corridor with an officer. Payne and his companion went through the ceremony of exchanging places and fell in behind the officer. Just as they started down the corridor, the door opened and the woman said something to the officer. He barked something at Payne in Barajian.

"You're to stay with me," she translated, and motioned him inside the room.

Payne entered, torn between curiosity and an empty belly.

She walked around him as he stood still. "We had established that you were not a merchant, as you claimed."

"Had we?"

"It remains to ascertain what you are."

"*What*, not *who*? I'm crushed. I thought the interest was personal."

"You're in no position to joke. Both you and your fellow debt-slave made my jewel glow. So, what are you?"

"Debt-slaves from Tarsia."

"Someone's a lucky buyer, then. Or a knowledgeable one, for you are more. Your master," she crossed the room to look through the papers on the table and read from them, "Hamon sar Vedrac, got quite—" She stopped abruptly, frowning, and stared at him.

He wondered what she saw.

She sank to the bench still staring. Her hands shook.

Payne watched worried.

"Why are you here?" she said finally.

"I told you."

"A pack of lies." She pushed her veils back. "You are one of the Wild Hunt. For what were you summoned?"

He considered lying again and wondered how she had guessed. "To return safe to his mother a boy who was stolen."

"No more than that?"

"No more."

She made a noise between laughter and tears. "If only all things were so simple. You think he is here?"

"Reynard, my companion, located him in the barracks, in the trefoil squad."

"My fault." She shook her head.

"How? You didn't cause the Sueve raids or the slave traders' dirty business."

"I told the governor of the Child of Fire."

"What?"

"It's an old prophecy. 'The Child of Fire shall lead the chosen to the land of light.' "

"Why?"

"To save my brother's life. He has red hair as the Child will have." She laughed shakily. "I was so afraid when I saw how my jewel blazed in your presence that you were the Child and that I had put all that power into the governor's hands."

"So you don't serve the governor?"

"I do because I must, or my brother will die."

"Tell me."

"Our father was appointed Treasurer of the Province—the Barajians aren't as prejudiced against we Eskedi as the Lakandari are. He discovered that part of the taxes were disappearing before they got to the capital. Someone was diverting funds from the imperial fisc. Before he could inform the emperor, one of his clerks betrayed him and the thefts were blamed on him. Records were falsified and he was condemned for treason."

"Your brother?"

"Was nine, but all the males were to die under Barajian law."

"Barbaric."

She smiled wanly. "So I went to the governor and told him that my brother might be the fabled Child of Fire."

"He believed you?"

"I made up a good story, did some tricks my grandmother taught me. It worked, even if it had unintended consequences."

"It was a risk."

"I couldn't let my brother die. Besides, the governor is gullible. Zakar has led him by the nose for longer than I have with his omens." She wrinkled her nose. "He reads entrails."

"Zakar? That's the Barajian who was here before?"

"Yes. He has contacts of some sort in the capital who use him to control the governor."

"For what?"

"I've only heard snatches. They're worried about the young emperor, who's not as easily led as his father was."

"Are these the same men who destroyed your father?"

She looked down. When she looked up again her eyes were blazing. "Yes, I think so."

"And the governor?"

"He uses them as much as they use him. He's Lakandari, not Barajian. The appointment was made to soothe the people."

"He listens to you?"

"Because I tell him what he wants to hear—that he is the 'chosen,' that Lakandar will be the 'land of light.' "

"And you are safe?"

"My brother is alive as long as the Governor believes me and not Zakar."

"Why the other redheads?"

"I told the governor that the Child's talents would not be

full-formed until his twenty-fifth year. I thought that I could find a way for my brother to escape in that time. Zakar said that it was too convenient that my brother should be the Child, and the governor has collected the others to be tested. He is afraid to let any go in case I am mistaken, even those past twenty-five. Thus the guard." She looked at her hands. "I never meant to disrupt so many lives, or cause so much heartache."

Payne looked down on her bowed head. She had explained much that had baffled him, but could she help? "The moon is already waxing, and we have an innocent child to free. Do you know a way?"

"I will see what I can do, but it will be difficult. Zakar . . ."

"Distrusts you."

"More. I have little freedom. But I will do what I can to free you and this child."

"Robin. He's eight years old."

She flinched. "My brother is barely fourteen. I will not risk his life and have all this be for nothing."

There was nothing else he could plead. Payne turned the subject. "You guessed who we were. How?"

"I spent the night thinking of who or what might make my jewel glow. Reviewing every spirit and being, every prophecy I knew, without finding an answer. But when I saw that name, I knew. Every Eskedi knows the tale of Hamon of Saroth. What other answer could there be?"

"Does Zakar suspect?"

"He noticed nothing when my jewel blazed. He is as great a fraud," she grimaced, "as I thought I was. As I wish I were. Go now. They will be suspicious if we talk longer. I must think up some false information to say that I discovered from you to placate the governor with."

Payne left but paused in the doorway to look back at Tiramet, huddled disconsolately on the bench.

Garrett was in high form that evening, and Walter couldn't blame him. The cortege had made good time, not halting until it was indisputably too dark to continue.

"We'd have gone even farther if Justin hadn't kept stopping to pick flowers!"

"Not flowers," the apothecary protested indignantly, *"herbs!* I think I've identified a dozen I've only read about."

"Most of 'em stank so bad I'd get well not to have to be around 'em anymore!"

"Some of them are very powerful remedies for—"

"Never mind, Justin," Walter said. "We'll take your word for it. How did the rest of you fare? Have you learned anything from the cavalrymen?"

The Huntsmen who had been riding with the Barajian soldiers fell silent and shifted uncomfortably.

"We've found out why they weren't bothered by the slow pace," Ulick said. "When they reach Istlakan, Lord Wiraz is going to have one chosen by lot and beheaded."

"Just for losing?"

"That's what they have been told."

"He's right." Thomas put down his plate. "I remember I overheard one of the Barajians saying that during the tuan."

"If that's so, it means that the Barajians are much more worried about Michel telling us what he overheard than I thought. It puts much more credence in the threat to a woman than we had previously believed."

"But we might know what woman they were talking about," Ulick continued.

"Who?"

"The troops from Istlakan have mentioned the one they call 'the governor's witch' several times. I gather the Barajians hate her."

"So the governor has fallen prey to a soothsayer?"

"It would seem so."

He turned to Thomas, "Have you overheard anything which confirms that?"

Thomas shook his head. "The kaiyun hasn't been in Barajia since she was fourteen, and what news she has heard has been of the capital, not of Lakandar."

"And from the men?"

"Wiraz and Dovir mostly complain about the pace—as if they wanted us to go slowly."

"I suppose it's possible they want this soothsayer dead— it's not healthy to have too much influence over an Imperial governor, I imagine. In that case it's not our problem."

"They still might mean Tita Maimai, though," Thomas said. "She was quite smug about the distance we traveled today."

"Keep your ears open. If we're lucky, we might be able to make up our lost time tomorrow."

Tiramet walked down the enclosed wall-walk so engrossed in mentally rehearsing the story she planned to tell the governor that she didn't pay attention to the conversation that filtered through the lattice near the door until Zakar said, "Seven more men to kill. Plus the woman."

She stopped her hand frozen on the latch wondering if she had made any noise to betray her presence.

"So," the governor said, "Captain Ferahim will have to have more men at the ambush if the accident doesn't work. I don't see the problem."

"More witnesses, more men who could talk, more risk of failure."

"We'll just execute them later as renegades. That should present us as loyal subjects of the Emperor."

"These newcomers aren't Sueve. They might be spies."

"Zakar, you see problems where none exist."

"Someone might ask questions."

"Who? With the emperor dead and his son in your friends' hands, who will ask questions about the death of the emperor's sister or her escort? The heir is barely two. If your friends are as clever as you say, they will have him believing that they did him a favor long before he comes of age. Don't you trust them?"

Zakar must be pacing, she thought, his voice came from the end of the room. "The kaiyun must die. She could act as Regent."

"Yes, yes. And she will die, and the blame will fall on the Sueve."

"Why did these men appear? Why were they added to the escort?"

"Wiraz writes that they say they are searching for a stolen child."

Tiramet's heart jumped. Could these be more Huntsmen? She almost did not hear Zakar's reply. "I don't believe that.

They bested trained cavalrymen. They are not what they say they are."

"So we add more men at the ambush. I don't see the problem."

Zakar didn't reply. Tiramet could hear his shoes flap on the pavement as he paced. Metal chimed on metal. The governor must be pouring wine.

"What have you learned in the interrogation?" the governor asked. "What was the meaning of the Nolsic coin?"

"The slave-stealer still insists it has no meaning."

"But he tried to steal the Child. Do you think the Nolsic sent him?"

"I doubt it." Zakar sounded like he was trying to cajole an impatient child.

"What if they want him too? What if they know?"

"What?"

"That now is the time. About our plans."

"They couldn't." Zakar sounded impatient now. "Oh, very well. I'll send the coin to our friends; they can make inquiries. Does that satisfy you?"

The governor must have nodded. Zakar continued, "Now, what are you going to say to the council tomorrow? We must seem to agree with the emperor's new edict even while we are delaying implementing it."

Tiramet crept away from the door and back down the wall-walk to her chamber with her mind a muddle of questions. Who were these men who had been added to the escort? Who was the woman who would be killed?

21

Twentieth Day

Bertz sat on the bench in Olm's quarters and let the argument rage around him. Olm and Naroc tried to keep the conversation comprehensible, but Reshalon's voluble protests overwhelmed their abilities to translate quickly.

"Tell him it will work," Bertz said. "The simplest way is usually the best. I need to get into the palace, since you say the Barajian lodges there; so, you will turn me in."

Reshalon sputtered when this was translated to him. "He asks how you will get out again," Naroc translated.

"It's more important that I get in. Both the token and the boy have to be there. I must see that they stay together. Besides, my companions are there."

Reshalon did not seem mollified.

"Let's get our stories straight," Olm said. "One of our rural brothers found you wandering on the far side of the river, dazed from a head wound, and took you in. After a few days when you did not recover your wits, he brought you to our central quarters, hoping that you would be identified, but you were not."

"So you took me in, but now you are suspicious that I might be the man the governor still

197

seeks, so you are doing your duty and taking me to the palace," Bertz finished.

"Why not the prison? Reshalon says they will ask," Naroc interjected.

Olm pursed his mouth in thought.

"Because now that my hair is growing back, you see that I have red hair," Bertz answered.

"That answer could work. The brother could have shaved it to tend your wound. It hasn't healed completely, even now. He would have returned to the country, so he can't be questioned." Naroc paused as Reshalon tugged his sleeve. After a quick exchange of words he went on. "What if someone recognizes you from the prison?"

Olm and Bertz looked at each other, frowning. Then Olm said, "We took him along because he is strong. We needed someone to carry the heavy chest." He grinned and added, "He may be witless, but he is biddable."

"Should we say that I understand orders in Tarsean?" Bertz asked.

"That's probably safe under the circumstances. You look northern, so they would suspect it anyway. But you're slow to respond."

"Like I'm hearing in a fog? Is that how I should act?"

"That's not a bad description. Like the world were at a distance and you were detached from it."

"I think I can do that."

"You are sure you want to go through with this?" Olm asked.

"I must."

"The Gods help you, then."

"When is the best time?"

"This afternoon. Everything slows down; the officials will be less harried and more inclined to listen, I believe."

"Soon, that's good. Too much time has passed already. The boy must be alone and frightened; it's time he was on his way home."

Naroc stopped his murmured translation to Reshalon. "Reshalon says that he will have the passes you will need to escape from Lakandar forged and hopes that you will survive to use them."

"So do we all," said Olm, as he bowed the two Eskedi out of the room.

Walter caught up with Thomas as he rode in the Barajians' train. It was only early afternoon and already, by a mixture of coaxing and bullying, Walter had prodded the cortege into making more progress than they had either of the first two days. The river ahead was a landmark showing that the foothills were only days away.

"What are the Barajians saying?" Walter asked.

"They're very quiet," Thomas answered. "I think you're wearing them out."

"I wish I knew why they are determined to slow us down."

"Perhaps they just like to sightsee."

"They had the entire journey to the Khan's camp to do that."

"Some people are very avid tourists. Perhaps they came via the other pass."

"I can't see these men using the Agandar Pass that even the Sueve regard as too dangerous."

"The Sueve don't like heights."

"You're being facetious."

Thomas sighed. "I know. I'm just tired of trying to determine the motivations of men I don't know and don't understand."

Walter silently surveyed the Barajians riding in a formation that kept the nobles nearest the kaiyun's cart. He could understand Thomas's perplexity. How, for instance, could the Kaiyun bear to ride in the cramped, enclosed cart that jolted so badly it threatened to overturn in every rut in the mud near the riverbank, merely to preserve a modesty that she hadn't displayed in the Sueve encampment?

"What don't you understand about the Barajians?" he asked. Were Thomas's questions about them his own?

"Everything. The way they assume everything in their culture is so automatically *correct* that they couldn't possibly learn anything from anyone else. The way they treat inferiors—I thought the Tarsean nobility were high-handed, but I can't imagine even the worst of them executing a man for losing a game. And the way the Barajians treat women as if they were all fools."

"I could cite you examples of all those faults in every place I've been."

"Yes, but—I suppose it's because they're so infernally complaisant about it."

"Like the Duke of Yesacroth?"

"That wasn't complaisance. He couldn't admit that he might be wrong about his favorite; it would have been too big a blow to his pride."

"Just think of the Barajians as a nation of men modeled on the Duke of Yesacroth."

"What a terrifying thought. I—"

One sharp crack sounded, then another, followed by a loud thud, shrieking, and the sound of wood shattering. Both men whirled and saw the Kaiyun's cart tumble on its side, dragged toward the bank of the river by the frightened horses.

Thomas spurred his horse toward the wagon, and Walter followed. The Barajian nobles were either trying to control their own mounts, startled by the sound and tumult, or staring with haughty surprise at the disaster unfolding.

Luckily, the burden of the cart kept the panicked horses from going far or fast. Walter and Thomas reached the cart at the edge of the rushing water. Walter caught the head of first one beast, then the other as Thomas cut the traces.

The silence from the cart was ominous. Thomas clambered over the wheels onto the side on top and began ripping out broken latticework. Marda was in that broken vehicle.

Walter could see one of the cart's wheels lying some distance back. It had apparently broken off in the ruts and the other had given way when the cart rocked sideways.

No time to worry about why now, though. When he climbed on top of the wreckage, all he could see in the cart was a jumble of bodies and objects. One of the ladies-in-waiting was on top, and just beginning to move; they pulled her out. She was only bruised and stunned. The second had a broken arm, but she seemed more frightened by the strange men who rescued her than by her injury.

Wiraz and Dovir were no help; they sat on their horses

and watched as if it were a faintly revolting show, but not really their business. Walter gave a mental summons to the rest of his Huntsmen, then called to the Sueve guards so he and Thomas could hand the injured women down to them.

A shrill scolding voice emerged from the cart, and the head of Tita Maimai popped through the broken side. A gush of incomprehensible words poured from her.

Thomas hauled her out under her arms and Walter took her legs to lower her into the arms of the waiting guards. She continued to scold without losing a beat and tried to climb back onto the cart, struggling against restraining hands.

"Marda?" Walter called.

"Sir Walter?" came the reply, to his relief. "I think Kai-yun Chrysogon is trapped."

Thomas lowered himself gingerly into the body of the cart. Walter could see now that the kaiyun was pinned under the benches which had stood against the sides of the cart. She had sat on the side that was now on the bottom and almost everything in it had landed on her.

Marda must have been close to her—she was not much easier to reach.

They had to throw a number of objects out before they could lift Marda to freedom. The kaiyun was still pinned by the benches and only her head emerged from a shroud of heavy cloth.

"Highness," Walter heard Thomas say, "Are you hurt?"

"The carpet seems to have protected me." She sneezed. "However, I could wish it gone now."

Walter and Thomas had to hand out some of the furniture for fear of starting an avalanche which might bury her further. She was patiently amused throughout the ordeal.

They turned back the exquisite carpet which had covered the cart's floor. The kaiyun's skirts were soaked with something red. She brushed at the substance and smiled at Thomas, who was very pale.

"Wine," she said, then reached under her side. "From this, I think," and drew out a battered silver pitcher which she hurled away. Then she sat up. "That has tormented me ever since we came to rest. Lift me out now, please."

Prince Dayan had joined the guards and Tita Maimai standing outside the wagon. Ulick was keeping them away from the cart and translating what Marda told him.

At the sight of the kaiyun being handed down to the ground, the Tarsean woman crowed, "I *told* them she wasn't dead, but they wouldn't listen."

"Yes, I am alive and quite well," Kaiyun Chrysogon said. "Where is Nilkana?"

Marda took the kaiyun to where the maid-servant with the broken arm was weeping. Only now did the Barajian noblemen dismount and approach her. She ignored them and talked soothingly to the injured woman.

A loud argument in familiar voices caught Walter's attention. Eleylin and Garrett were quarreling with a Barajian officer. The officer was wresting the wheel which had broken off the cart away from them, and as Walter approached, he rolled it off toward the rest of the wreckage.

"What was that all about?"

"I wanted to show you the wheel," Eleylin said. "But one of the Barajian 'yellow robes' saw us and told the man to take it."

"What did you want me to see?"

"Part of the axle was attached to it. It was broken, but it broke because it had been sawn partway through and the rest must have shattered when it hit a deep enough rut. I wonder if the other is the same way." He started toward the cart, but Walter put out a hand to stop him.

"No, we don't want to make it too obvious that you know what happened. I believe you. They must be desperate to slow us down to risk the kaiyun's safety."

He turned to stare at the wreckage of the cart. Someone could easily have been killed—Tita Maimai, or Marda, or the kaiyun herself.

He cursed himself for a fool. The wrong women! They'd thought of everyone but the kaiyun. She was the most likely target—and it was vitally important she be kept alive.

Traveling further that day was impossible between setting the maid's broken arm and soothing the rest of her escort. Shortly before twilight a Barajian servant arrived in the

Hunt's encampment, inviting Walter and Thomas to dine with her formally that evening.

Thomas found the scene when they arrived irresistibly quaint. The Barajians had set up the center of their camping area to resemble one of their banquet halls—or as much as they could manage in the wilderness. Behind the head table the kaiyun's servants had managed to hang a length of cloth of gold from the conveniently placed riverside trees. Thomas estimated that the cost of the cloth would feed a small Tarsean village for a year. Low tables were set in a square. There were cushions for the guests to sit on—some of which Thomas recognized as salvaged from the wagon a few hours ago.

Lanterns were hung in the surrounding trees to keep back the gloom.

Altogether it made an elegant show—perfectly finished by the kaiyun Chrysogon gracing the head table. She wore a wide, stiff coat of cloth of gold—a textile worn only by the emperor's close kin on pain of a rather hideous death. The princess must meet every standard of Barajian elegance—symmetry being a primary tenet of that quality. She sat with her hands perfectly folded holding a fan delicately carved from scented wood and her robe precisely spread about her. Her face was serene and welcoming, as if she hadn't come near to death that day and had her dignity battered at the very least.

But she was too human to quite bring off the show. Her smile was genuinely warm, not politely supercilious, as Thomas remembered the figures in the few Barajian books that had come his way.

Her servants ushered Thomas and Walter to the head table, where they joined her and Dayan, who looked disgruntled and uncomfortable in Barajian dress.

"I must apologize," the kaiyun said, "the fare for this evening's meal is poorer than I would wish for such an occasion, but it cannot be helped. When we reach Istlakan, I shall have the governor throw a proper banquet."

"Your Highness must be looking forward to returning home," Walter said politely.

"It has been nearly twenty years since I left," she answered. "It is strange being homesick for a place one no longer knows. Where is your home?"

"The southern part of Tarsia, Highness. A place of hills and forests."

"Ah, you must miss it very much."

"I too have been away from home for many years."

"And you, Enandor Thomas, are you homesick?"

Her dark eyes were too observant. Did they notice the hesitation before he answered?

"Sometimes, but I think if I went back to Madaria I would miss the variety of my travels. Sometimes home is a place best left to memory."

"Then you have traveled for some time with Sir Walter?" Where had she gotten that title for him? Marda, of course. Someone was going to have to warn the Tarsean woman to be more discreet.

"A year or two. It seems like more."

"In the military?"

"No."

"But I was told that you had fought with the Ortasjian Ulick recently."

Blast. That was the story Marda had been told to tell.

"Oh, that. I was in the wrong place at the wrong time when the late Grand Duke had anyone handy conscripted. I managed to make myself useful as a secretary to one of his generals and avoided any actual fighting."

"You held a spear well enough a few days ago," Prince Dayan said as he gulped a mouthful of food.

I should have let them kill the bloody young nuisance.

"I was compelled to learn a little before I discovered that the general could barely sign his own name."

"Why would he need someone to write?" the boy asked.

"To tell the Grand Duke that he'd been delayed or defeated and why it wasn't his fault, mostly."

"Didn't the Duke fight?"

"When it made a good show for the troops," Walter said, then diverted the boy's attention by explaining the art of the siege. Thomas blessed him and turned back to the kaiyun.

"What did you do before you were in the military?"

"Advised people on the law."

"I had heard that you allow scholars of the law to speak in courts. In Barajia that is not permissible."

"There are many at home who would wish the same. Usually shortly after they have had a decision made against them." She began to question him on the workings of the Tarsean and Madarian legal systems.

He had not realized how engrossed he had been in the conversation until one of the Barajian nobles left his table and knelt before the kaiyun.

"What is it, Lord Wiraz?"

"Kaiyun, it falls to me to ask if we might be excused. If we are to be able to fetch another conveyance for you quickly, I must write to the governor and have him send one. The sooner I do that, the sooner we should be on the road. If they move very swiftly, we should be delayed only another five or six days."

He had spoken in Barajian, so Thomas tried to look bewildered. But his mind was reeling—five or six days before they could even get under way. This was disastrous.

"That is ludicrous, Wiraz. First of all, if there is one thing I have learned living among the Sueve besides patience, it is to ride a horse. Second, I have no desire to ever ride in one of those wheeled coffins again as long as I live."

"But Your Highness—your brother would not wish you to be put on display for these barbarians. They might—"

"Which barbarians do you mean? The ones I have lived with for nearly twenty years, or the ones who saved my life today?"

"I might remind Your Resplendent Highness that one of the latter was found in your tent with a weapon drawn."

"He was lost in a strange camp—that was proven to my satisfaction. I fear you harbor a resentment because he was so skillful with his knife." She gestured with her fan in the direction of his seat. "You may leave and write the governor to tell him that his carriage maker was ill-chosen, or you may stay and enjoy the meal, Lord Wiraz. I leave the decision to you."

The noble knocked his head against the ground, and Thomas couldn't help thinking that it was as much to hide his face as to admit acquiescence.

The kaiyun smiled at Walter, who must have caught the

tenor of the conversation, if not the meaning.

"Lord Wiraz was merely concerned over the arrangements for our journey tomorrow. He will see that I have a proper mount. We should be home much sooner without the cart." Then, with immense courtesy and good humor, she began to question Walter on how a Tarsean knight happened to be helping a Sueve mercenary find his lost foster son.

With mingled regret and amusement Thomas sat back to watch him try and wriggle out of that one.

It was quite late when the banquet was finished. As he and Walter stumbled toward their hard beds, he wondered if the Barajian wine had been stronger than he had thought at first. He felt a little light-headed. The whole evening had a hazy pleasant glow to it.

"I think we should be careful of the kaiyun," Walter said. "If I didn't need you to keep an eye on the Barajian nobles, I'd keep you away from her."

"Why?"

"She asked all the right questions. I'm not sure she believed anything we told her."

Damn. He was right. The glow faded rapidly.

"Well, the Barajians rarely speak among themselves. Their habit of mistrust is too ingrained. The most significant thing they've talked about so far is the weather and if it will slow our progress. I could be spared from that, I suppose."

To Thomas's relief, Walter shook his head. "It's vitally important that you stay with the kaiyun."

"Why?"

"I think she's the woman they want to kill."

"Why? Why her?"

"Why the soothsayer or the waiting woman? And you heard her tonight. She's too intelligent for her own good. Something is happening in Istlakan—I think Hamon has been tortured."

"Gods of my homeland. You feel it, and you can still talk?"

"I can wall it off—keep it out of my mind most of the time. But if Hamon has stumbled on something bigger than just the sale of the boy—it could explain why these Barajians are not in a hurry to get her back to Lakandar. If at all."

"What could it be?"

"Maybe the governor's smuggling salt, or wearing the wrong badge on his nightcap. I don't know. We'll find out soon enough. But if we're not to burn we've got to keep the kaiyun alive."

"But it's Marda we've got to hand Robin to."

"I'm doing your job for you, Thomas. You're usually the one who points out the verbal quibbles. What did Marda say when she summoned us?"

"Put her son back in her arms again."

"*Safely* back. By the time we get her to Istlakan—even if we get her her son alive and well—there won't be time to get them back to Tarsia before the next full moon. She'll be stranded alone in a country she knows nothing about. That's hardly safety."

"And you think the kaiyun will take them in?"

"I'm sure of it—especially if we all mysteriously disappear."

Thomas nodded. He should have seen all this before. The kaiyun must be preserved.

But I'd save her myself even if it wasn't necessary to Walter, he thought. *Even if I had to do it behind his back.* Then, surprised at his own thoughts, he hurried after the leader of the Hunt.

22

Twenty-first Day

Payne and his fellow guard had already gone through the ritual of exchanging places once when the door to Tiramet's chamber opened and she emerged. She spoke first in what Payne assumed was Barajian, then translated for him. "You both are to accompany me to the gardens and stand guard there."

Payne and the other guard saluted.

"*Baraki!*" That meant "forward!" The other guard preceded her down the corridor and Payne fell in behind. After several doors and corridors, she stopped at a heavy door and ordered the other guard to stay. Payne followed her into the walled garden beyond. It was some twenty paces square, with a multi-level fountain on one wall and geometric beds between stone paths. On the opposite side behind a row of stone benches was a heavy gate.

Tiramet walked to a bench near the fountain and sat. "Guard the far entrance. You may wish to speak with the gardener. He was brought to me for examination last night."

Puzzled, Payne stared at her, but her face was unreadable. He turned and walked to the gate. He had barely noticed that there was anyone else in the garden, but when he turned he could see a kneeling hooded figure grubbing weeds from a bed of herbs. It wasn't until the man turned to drop the refuse in a basket that he recognized him.

"Bertz."

Bertz hastily motioned him to silence, gesturing at the woman on the bench.

"She can be trusted," Payne said. "She brought me to you."

"How can you be sure?" Bertz whispered.

"She knows who and what I am and you as well, yet she didn't tell the governor."

"Maybe she wants to catch bigger fish."

Payne looked at Tiramet who sat watching the water splash from basin to basin. "No, I don't think so. She has her own reasons to help us." He repeated the story Tiramet had told him.

Bertz only nodded when Payne had finished.

"So," Payne asked, "what happened to you after the ambush?"

Bertz kept working as he narrated in a low voice his escape, rescue, and visit to Hamon in prison. "It seemed the best course of action was to join you in the palace, and—" He broke off as Tiramet approached.

"Look like you're standing guard," she warned Payne. "They can see us from the towers on the outer wall."

"I think you should join us," Payne said, as he straightened in his place by the gate. "Bertz, tell Tiramet what you told me."

Bertz's eyes narrowed and he said nothing.

"Tell her."

"No. Her own people curse her."

Payne's eyebrows rose.

"That does not surprise me," she said. "They have good reason. I shall withdraw."

"Stay." Payne turned to Bertz. "Don't be a fool. She's our only friend in the palace. We need her help."

Bertz grunted, jerked up a plant, and threw it in the basket. "And what have you accomplished so far?"

"Reynard has located Robin. He's one of the trefoil squad of boys in the governor's guard."

"Then what? Have you a plan to get him to his mother?"

"Not yet," Payne grudgingly admitted. "Walter should be on his way here with her. He must have found out, long before now, that the Sueve don't have Robin. He knows where we are. I'd rather wait till we have more men before I risk the boy's life."

Tiramet sank to the nearest bench.

Bertz glanced up at Payne. "Can you be sure Walter will come? He should follow the token and Hamon says the Barajian took that. It could be anywhere."

"What token?" Tiramet asked sharply.

"A gold coin pierced to hang on a cord or chain, like a necklace," Payne said.

"Nolsic?"

Both men frowned. "Hamon said it was from some island off the Barajian coast," Payne answered.

"Nolsic," Tiramet sighed. "Zakar—the Barajian you mentioned—has the coin, but he plans to send it to his fellow conspirators in Valadiza, the capital."

"How do you know?" Bertz glanced up from the herb bed.

"I overheard them."

"Do they know you did?" Payne asked. "You could be in danger."

"I don't think so. There is a secret passage between my chambers and the Governor's apartments. I could hear them talking before I opened the door."

"Yes, but could they hear you?"

"The passage was built so that King Ilkirim's mistress could come to him without his jealous wife knowing. I think it was constructed so that the mistress could hear if anyone was with the King before she entered. But that doesn't matter. What about the coin?"

"Walter could follow it," Payne acknowledged, scowling.

"How many men does he have?" she asked.

"Seven men and Robin's mother, Marda."

"I heard more, and it's mostly bad." Tiramet summarized the conversation between the governor and Zakar.

"So the rest of the Hunt is on the way, but there is an ambush planned," Payne said.

"Which could kill Marda. If she dies, we fail." Bertz sat back on his heels.

"Not to mention that time is short," Payne said.

"We've got to warn Walter and make sure he comes here."

"And free the boy as soon as possible." Payne turned to Tiramet. "Can you help?"

She hesitated. "I could get him released." She nodded at Bertz.

"Then I could ride north and warn Walter. You say the Kaiyun Chrysogon's party is to come here?"

"Yes, so that she can go by barge on the rest of the journey to the capital. It is more comfortable and more seemly than the overland journey," Tiramet answered.

"So I should intercept them on the road."

"You will need papers."

"Reshalon promised them."

She smiled wryly at the name.

"You know him?"

"He is married to my great-aunt. He warned my father not to take a government position. He was right."

"About freeing Robin?" Payne cut in.

"I could show you the passageways I know of, perhaps even steal the token from Zakar."

Bertz looked her straight in the eye. "You keep saying 'could'—does that mean you haven't made up your mind, or is there a price?"

"There is a price. Free my brother and take us with you when you escape."

"It will make the whole job more difficult," Bertz grumbled.

"But less difficult than if we had no help. I say it's a bargain," Payne said.

"First I must get him released." Tiramet nodded at Bertz. "He must warn your leader and the princess that they plan to kill her and the Emperor, her brother, too, very soon. Perhaps she will be grateful enough to aid you and to protect those who have aided you as well. The Eskedi and the poor people of this province need someone to speak for them."

"No, the coin is more important," Bertz objected.

"I have no control of when I see Zakar, but I can choose when I speak to the Governor. I will find the coin. Besides, you will warn your leader not to follow it." She frowned. "Is the coin . . ." she searched for a word, "encharmed?"

Payne nodded.

"That should make it easier to find." She arranged her shawls and rose. "It is time we returned." She turned to Bertz. "I will tell the governor that Payne recognized you but that you remained unresponsive, and that since you cannot possibly be the Child of Fire, it would be a charity to return you to the brotherhood. He should release you in no more than two days. Most likely tomorrow."

"I shall tell my friends of your help."

She nodded.

"We may need their help as well," Payne said as they left.

Payne had been off-duty long enough to eat when an officer came and led him back to Tiramet's door. She opened it to the officer's rap. She waved Payne inside and dismissed the officer. She closed the door and turned to Payne. "I talked to the governor. He will release your friend tomorrow."

"Good."

"Don't speak too soon. The governor thinks you are insufficiently trained. He wanted you transferred back to the barracks, but I persuaded him to change your hours of duty instead. Now you will train during the day and stand guard at night. I convinced the governor that there was more I could learn from you."

"That should make it easier to contact Reynard and Robin."

"And my brother. But it would be impossible to coordinate our plans. They will watch you closely and the governor may still change his mind. I thought that I should show you the passageways now in case he does. Wait a moment."

She opened a panel in the wall and disappeared. When she returned, she had changed from the elaborate Eskedi dress she usually wore into a long simple short-sleeved tunic and had bound up her hair in a scarf. She crossed the room and opened another panel. "Come. We must do this before the light fails."

Payne followed her down a narrow spiral stair.

"It is safe to talk in this section," she said, as they reached the bottom. "This was the way the mistress visited her family in the city. Unfortunately, part of the passage has caved in and the door at the far end is heavy and locked, but it is possible to get from here to some of the other passages."

"How many?"

"A number. Apparently the Kings of Lakandar were as suspicious as King Ilkirim's wife. Many of the rooms have spy-holes or entrances, but some of the passageways are dead spaces left when sections of the palace were rebuilt."

"You know them all?"

"I have had little else to do but examine the redheads the governor acquires. But no, I don't know them all." She motioned him to silence and led him down a dark corridor lit only by openings high in the wall. The corridor branched. She pointed to chalk marks on the wall. "That leads to the locked door. This, I think, goes to the barracks. Boost me up."

He helped her to a ledge four feet above the floor then scrambled up beside her.

"Don't talk," she whispered. "We're next to the audience chamber. They might hear."

This passage was too low for him to stand without stooping and lit only by light from the far end, which proved to be a narrow gap between walls left when a courtyard had been built over.

"Down here." Tiramet jumped down and dropped through a low window to the cellar below. Payne followed. His knees buckled and his feet stung as he landed on the stone floor below. Tiramet opened a door into a short corridor and led him up a narrow stair. At the top she opened the door cautiously and peered out, then gestured for him to follow her across a lavishly decorated room to a wooden carved niche in the side wall. She swung a panel open to reveal a passage no wider than his shoulders. "I think this runs along the barracks."

"You don't know?"

"I've never been in the barracks. I wouldn't recognize the rooms. The bottom of the passage is even with grates high on the walls of the rooms. I've measured; they ought to be rooms in the barracks, but I'm not sure." She led him into the passageway, warning, "Don't talk. I know that anyone in the rooms below can hear. At least, I could hear them. Mostly men's voices, usually only in the evening."

The passage was dark but level. They walked for what Payne judged some ninety feet before it jogged right then left. The floor was dimly illuminated at intervals by light seeping through the latticed grates Tiramet had described.

Payne knelt eagerly to peer through the first grate they came to and discovered that he had to lie on the floor to see anything. What he did see was disappointingly just a small room maybe seven feet square with a closed door and a small shuttered window on the far wall. It could be a room in the barracks—there were rooms on the north side of its courtyard with similar doors and windows—or it could be some minor official's quarters off one of the other myriad courtyards that formed the palace.

He crawled to the next grate. This room was much the same, except that he could see the end of a cot covered with a cheap blanket and the shutters were open a crack and let in a rosy bar of late afternoon sunlight. The next five rooms were equally anonymous. They had cots and some had a stool or a small chest, but none had anything that identified its owner or verified that it lay in the barracks.

One grate remained at the end of the passage where Tiramet stood against the wall, out of his way. He stood to let her pass and take her place. They were face to face, their bodies forced to touch. His hand brushed her hip, and she looked up. Her breath warmed his neck. He bent impulsively to kiss her, letting himself acknowledge that he had wanted to do that almost from the day he first saw her. At the last moment, she turned her head. Her whispered "No" was more a warm breath than a word. Then she was past him and the moment was gone.

Payne knelt, then lay on the floor. This room was much like the others. It had the door and window, a stool, a cot, but on the cot lay a blue garment. He twisted to see if it had the embroidered decoration on its sleeve that would prove it was a uniform jacket. He pressed his head against the corner of the grate and looked down. Yes, there were the bands and the diamond that held the squads' insignia. He strained to see through the small space. The grate moved under the pressure and he grabbed it and pulled it back into place. He held his breath, but no one came to investigate the scraping noise.

Elated, he rose to his feet; he had identified the insignia of the squad leader of the quatrefoil squad. That officer, he remembered, had one of the rooms on the north side of the barracks courtyard. The grate was loose but too small for him to get through. Reynard, though, with his training in breaking and entering, could get through the opening, as could an eight-year-old boy. Tiramet had said that her brother was fourteen. If he was built as slightly as she, he could probably squeeze through as well.

Tiramet led him silently back along the passageway and stopped abruptly to push aside a spy-hole in the door at its end. Peering over her shoulder, he could see two white-robed, brocade-sashed elderly men cross the room beyond.

She waited long moments before opening the door after they were gone. Payne was acutely aware of her body inches from his in the darkness and gratified when they could move again. When they reached the cellar and he swung her up to the passage above his hands seemed to burn when he touched her, but she said nothing.

Finally they were back in her chamber. He pushed his hair back out of his face and realized that his hands were filthy.

"You're covered with dust," she said. She had dust on her skirts as well. He took his jacket off and shook it till the dirt wasn't obvious then slipped it back on. He hoped that the evening light would let him get back to his quarters without drawing anyone's inspection.

"You have cobwebs in your hair." She reached up to brush them away but he caught her wrist and pulled her close and kissed her. But after a moment she pulled back. "No." She broke away and put the table between them. "You don't understand." Her hands trembled on the table's edge. "In my position, if I say 'yes' to you then I can't say 'no' to any other man."

He stared down into her magnificent jewel-like eyes. "In my position." Then he understood. Alone, disgraced among her own people, forced into a profession despised by reputable people, her virginity was her only defense.

He turned away to study the leather wall panels. "I'm sorry."

"Just a moment."

He heard a door open behind him, but when he turned she was gone. When she returned, she carried a tray with a basin of water, a comb, and some towels. She had wrapped herself in her gray shawl.

"Here, clean yourself." She set the tray down and retreated to a stool on the opposite side of the room.

Payne dunked a towel in the basin and washed his face. "The passage is above the barracks. Above the officers' rooms, in fact. The grate is so loose that I'm sure the boys could get through it if they knew."

"Then we should hope that you can pass word to them when you go back to the barracks."

"Yes." Did she sound relieved that he would be gone?

She said nothing more.

"I'll need to get word to your brother. What is his name?"

"Edralen. But the Lakandari have renamed him Ivreim. That's one of the few things I've been able to find out, other than that he's alive."

Five years without knowing was a long time. In five years a boy could change. "Is there anything we could say to him that would prove that we spoke for you? Prove that he can trust us."

"Wait." She left by the paneled door. When she came back, she put a small piece of carved jade on the table. Payne picked it up and turned it over. There was a design incised on its bottom.

"It is our father's seal. Edralen knows that father gave it to me to keep safe for him."

"Which you have surely done."

She shrugged. "We will only be safe when we are out of Lakandar."

"Soon. I promise you."

"Promises are cheap."

*　　*　　*

Walter was tired, but triumphant. They had covered more ground that day than he had hoped, and the kaiyun's delight in being that much closer to home made it clear she would brook no more delays. He was still acutely anxious to learn what was happening to Hamon and the others, but the party would reach Istlakan in three more days, with luck, and he'd be able do something about the crisis.

It was nearly full dark; even the fainter stars were beginning to come out; and the Huntsmen gathered waiting for the Barajians to bring the evening meal as they had every evening. Michel and Garrett were arguing over something to do with horses; Justin was studying the leaves on yet another plant he'd found by the side of the road, and explaining it to an obviously bored Eleylin. Marda sat cross-legged next to Walter, conversing softly with Ulick. She seemed to have lost much of her fear of the Sueve, but then she'd been forced to sleep next to him since they had arrived at the great khan's camp ten days ago. Walter supposed that she had had to adapt.

The rattle of pots and cranky orders barked in Barajian signaled the arrival of the evening meal. The smell from the steaming kettles was exotic, but then all the meals had been since they had started to Lakandar. A highly seasoned mix of meat and vegetables was dipped into bowls and passed to the men.

The head servant bowed to Walter and proffered two wineskins.

"Her Highness sends her compliments and this wine from the Emperor's own vineyards."

The kaiyun's gratitude was becoming embarrassing. She hadn't been hurt, after all. Walter conveyed his thanks and put the skin aside. He would ration it to his men later; he didn't want to encourage Justin and Michel to excess.

They ate, discussed the coming day's route, and hardly noticed when the kaiyun's servants gathered up the plates and the pots and departed.

"You're hoarding the wine, Walter," Michel complained. "I'm tired of Sueve horse piss."

Walter hefted a skin in his hands and passed it to Ulick, who sniffed the stopper and grimaced. Then Walter picked up the other, pulled out the stopper, and turned to hand it to Thomas. A few drops spilled on Walter's hand, and without thinking, he started to lick them off. He stopped before his tongue quite touched the liquid. Then he whirled; Ulick had given the skin to Marda, who was already raising it to her lips.

Walter threw himself at her and knocked the skin out of the peasant woman's hands. It fell on the ground, red liquid pouring into the ashes and dirt by the fire.

"Walter?" Thomas was holding the other skin at arm's length as if it might bite.

"Poison," he said and watched as all the Huntsmen stared from Walter to Marda. A moment more and they'd have failed, whether they ever found Robin or not.

"I don't think the kaiyun is responsible for this," Thomas said. Walter took the other wineskin and emptied its contents on the ground.

"Does it matter?" Eleylin asked. "Somebody wants us dead."

"It matters a great deal," Walter replied, and threw the skin away from him.

Marda had realized what had almost happened; she was staring at the skin she had almost drunk from; Ulick had put a hand on her arm as if to keep her from fleeing. Or was that the reason?

The waxing moon would be in its first quarter tomorrow. Seven more days and it would be full again. And Hamon— Hamon was gravely hurt. Bertz as well, though not, he thought, as much so. What was happening in Istlakan?

"We can't continue as we have," he said finally.

"But Walter," Thomas began, "Last night you said—"

"We won't abandon the kaiyun's party," Walter cut him off and noticed that Thomas looked relieved. "*But*, we must make sure someone gets to Istlakan as soon as possible." He scanned the worried faces of the men before him. Eleylin, Justin, Michel, Garrett, Thomas, and Ulick. And Marda, of course.

"Ulick, take Marda ahead. Travel to the city as quickly as you can. Try to find Hamon and the others."

"Just the two of us?"

If he paused for too long, he could feel Hamon's pain beating against the edges of consciousness.

"No. Take Justin with you. I have reason to believe he will be needed."

"When should we leave?"

"At once. Go as far as you can in the dark."

"How shall we find Hamon?"

"A Sartherian and three Tarseans should not be difficult to trace."

Ulick rose, drawing a stunned Marda after him. The apothecary carefully packed his leaves into his pouch as he followed. Walter caught Ulick and pulled him aside.

"Whatever happens," he said to the Sueve, "I will try to make sure that the kaiyun is delivered safely to Istlakan. At the full moon, make sure that Marda and Robin are left in the kaiyun's care. Understand?"

He saw comprehension light Ulick's eyes and hurried the man on his way.

Walter watched the three disappear into the darkness. Sending them ahead was the best thing to do, but he was not easy about it. If Hamon suffered so greatly, the situation must be grave indeed. Was he merely sending Marda and Ulick into more danger? He had no way of knowing, but what else could he do? At least they were safe for now; he would deal with the rest when he arrived in Istlakan.

23

Twenty-second Day—
First Quarter

Marda's horses had carried her all day and were
spent, but Ulick had wanted to get as far as he
could before stopping, so he had taken her up
before him on his mount which would not tire
and led Marda's. She was shivering; he wondered
if it were from fear of him, or if she were chilled
through.

"Do you need your cloak?" he asked. "We can
get it from your pack."

"It doesn't matter."

"I think it does. It will only get colder as we
go into the mountains."

He felt her shrug and drew up.

"Are we stopping for the night?" Justin asked.

"No, I want to go an hour or so more."

"It'll be nearly dawn then."

"Yes, but at this rate we'll be well into the
mountains by sundown tomorrow. That way we
can slip through the Silasar Pass after dark."

"Why?"

"Fewer questions to answer."

He swung Marda down and saw her knees buc-
kle. She had steadied herself by the time he was
beside her, but her hand was over her mouth and
he realized she was retching.

"What's wrong?"

She swallowed and took a deep breath.

"I'm sorry—it's just when I think about the wine, and what might have happened."

It hadn't been cold that made her shiver, but shock. She had come within a swallow of dying a few hours before. He found her cloak and wrapped it around her.

"Don't worry. We wouldn't have let you die."

"What would happen to Robin if I'd died?" She searched his face. "And to the rest of you? I—I know something bad happens if you fail, but no one who told me the stories about you knew what."

"Don't think about it. You didn't drink the wine, and we will find Robin, and he will be safe."

"How? A city is so big—how can we ever find him?"

She was pale with cold and dread. Without thinking, he put his hands on either side of her face to warm it. Then he stepped back, realizing that his next impulse was to kiss her.

"Can you ride any farther?"

"If I need to. I don't know if I could sleep, anyway." He started to help her mount when Justin spoke.

"Someone's coming."

A rider. Ulick pushed Marda behind him and pulled his sword. Justin uncertainly drew his knife as well.

A Sueve rider on a Sueve horse, leading a second mount. The rider drew up, a silhouette against the sky.

"I could hear you half a mile away," Dayan Fire-born said.

Ulick scowled. "Dismount."

"I only—"

"Get down!"

Dayan reluctantly threw himself off his horse and stood with his arms out. Ulick checked; the boy was unarmed—whatever his reasons for running after them, he hadn't bothered to steal a weapon.

"How did you know we were gone?" And if he knew who else might be following?

"I've kept an eye on you."

"Why did you follow us?"

"You have my medallion."

Ulick fought the urge to strike the boy.

"You broke your parole—your word to your own mother for that?"

"If I didn't, I'd be breaking my word to my father. Besides, if you give it to me, I'll go straight back."

"Why should I trust you?"

"I give you my word."

"Which is worth nothing. You've already broken it." Ulick tossed him his reins. "You'll have to travel with us. I'll turn you over to your mother when they get to Istlakan. If you stay out of trouble until then I'll consider giving it back."

"Why did you leave the caravan?" Dayan asked as Ulick mounted.

"We were traveling too slowly; my son could have been sold anywhere and it could take weeks more to track him down at this rate. I told Walter we'd meet him in Istlakan."

Dayan nodded. "The Barajians travel like old women. I'll be glad not to have to listen to them—bad enough when I'm surrounded by their jabbering and nonsense at my uncle's court." He swung up on his horse. "How much farther do you want to go tonight?"

Walter had just finished breaking his fast with the rest of the Hunt when one of the kaiyun's maid-servants rushed into the camp. She looked wildly around and ran to Thomas, who was the only Huntsman she was likely to recognize.

"Come, please! The kaiyun!" she babbled in barely comprehensible Tarsean. Thomas was off like a shot arrow, and Walter a few steps behind.

It wasn't far to the tent the Sueve had furnished for the kaiyun, but it was time for too many possibilities to race through Walter's mind. The worst, and the most likely, was that the attempt to murder the Hunt last night had been part of a larger plan. He cursed himself for not thinking of it before.

Outside the tent, groups of Barajians seemed to be arguing—recriminations and exonerations, Walter suspected. He'd have to ask Thomas later, if the man had actually heard any of it. The only Barajians who seemed calm were Wiraz and his dogsbody, who stood superciliously observing the show, until Walter and Thomas passed them. Wiraz's eyes widened, then he wiped all expression off his face and strolled with studied indifference away from the tent.

You didn't expect us to be alive and hale, did you?

Walter had no time to notice more as he followed Thomas into the gloom of the tent.

The kaiyun was still in her bed, surrounded by her women, and at first Walter decided she must be ill by the way they were fussing over her. But she looked strong enough as she pushed the maidservants aside and reached to catch Thomas's hands in a white-knuckled grasp.

"Your Highness, what . . . ?" Thomas began.

"My son! He's gone! Ketai will surely kill him now!"

"When did he leave?"

"Last night."

"When was he last seen?"

"He said he was going to check his horses and then go to bed."

"Before or after he had eaten?" Was Thomas thinking that the boy might have been poisoned and his body hidden? Not likely; why kill the boy and not his mother?

"After." She shook her head. "He promised he would not go back to Suevia. He's always kept his word before."

Tita Maimai had been clucking in the background, now she draped a brocade robe over the Kaiyun's nightdress. Thomas pulled it up over her shoulders.

"Perhaps he hasn't gone back. Ulick and Marda left last night to ride ahead to Istlakan."

"But why would he follow them?"

Walter thought he knew the answer. "Ulick took a medallion from your son when he was captured."

"Set with a blue stone, surrounded by a fire glyph?" she asked. Walter nodded. "His father put that around his neck when he gave him his first horse. Dayan has always worn it." She nodded. "Yes, he'd follow Ulick for that."

"And Ulick, likely, won't let him return on his own." Thomas assured her. "So he'll be waiting for us in Istlakan when we arrive." But she did not let go of Thomas's hands until Thomas seemed to realize that the nervous fluttering of her maids was aimed at his too intimate proximity. He pulled away, stood, and bowed very formally.

"Is there anything more we can do, Your Highness? Do you want us to send someone to look for your son?"

She folded her hands carefully in her lap.

"I don't think that will be necessary. I—I must trust that Dayan has kept his word not to return to Suevia."

As they left the tent, Thomas was fuming. "That boy should be beaten for the good of his relations."

Walter tried not to smile. He had guessed long ago that Thomas's interest in the kaiyun was something more than a means to an end. What he hadn't realized was that the kaiyun's interest was more than a distant fascination with a different culture.

"The best we can do for Her Highness now," Walter said, "is get her to Istlakan quickly."

Tiramet closed the door gently behind her. She had known that Zakar was lodged in one of the apartments usually reserved for visiting dignitaries, but she had not expected the size and splendor of this room. It was an audience chamber worthy of a prince. But, she reminded herself, an audience chamber was a semi-public room. Zakar would not leave the Nolsic coin here.

He had not had it with him earlier when he and the governor had planned their strategy for dealing with the representatives of the rural tax districts at their meeting that afternoon. She had detected no sign even with her jewel that Zakar wore the coin or any other charmed object. The coin should be here. She had at best two hours to find it before Zakar returned from the meeting.

She crossed the room and opened the door on the far wall. The room beyond was Zakar's chamber, with silk draped bed and dining table. She checked this room's other doors. One led to a dressing room with a servant's room and privy beyond. The servant's room was luckily empty and had a narrow stair behind it that went down. The other door led into an elaborately decorated room empty of furniture.

Tiramet returned to the chamber. Where would Zakar put the coin in this welter of shelves and chests? She half-closed her eyes to block out the mundane properties of the things that surrounded her and tried to see a glow such as surrounded the three Huntsmen she had examined. Nothing. She would have to use her jewel. She pulled it from her sash and slowly pivoted watching its sparks.

The door opened behind her. She stuffed her jewel back into its hiding place as Zakar purred, "An unexpected pleasure."

She turned to face him, smiled, and glanced around the room. "Reading entrails pays well. These rooms are ten times as splendid as mine."

"As I have told you before." He closed the door and walked across the room to stand in front of her.

"Seeing is believing." She wanted to retreat but instead let her veils slip back and looked him in the eye. He must not guess why she was here. He would send the coin to the capital immediately if he guessed.

His hand rose to touch her chin. She tilted her head back and forced herself to smile.

"If I whispered a word in the governor's ear, you could be housed just as well."

"You have said that before."

"And you have refused. Why are you here?"

She swung away from him and sat on the chest at the foot of the bed. "I've changed my mind. I'm tired of the bickering, tired of my cramped quarters, tired of working at cross purposes, tired of Lakandar. You once promised me that if I backed your prophecies with the governor you would take me to Valadiza and introduce me to great people. You promised me that I should be powerful and rich, that you would teach me all you knew."

"You refused that, too. You sneered that there were lores too dark for you to learn."

"I was a fool."

He smiled. "And are no longer? Or are you simply aware your scheme cannot go on much longer?"

"I was younger then."

"But no more beautiful. There was a price."

"I am willing to pay it now."

"Are you?" He held out his hand.

She took it and he pulled her to her feet and kissed her hungrily. His hands circled her waist and pulled her close against him. She forced herself not to stiffen or pull away, not to close her mouth as his tongue invaded it. His hands slid up from her waist and the pressure of his ardor made her back arch. She was forced to step back toward the bed.

Suddenly he stepped away. She wanted to cry from relief but forced herself to step forward and put a hand on his brocade sleeve. "You do not want me?"

He laughed. "In time. It will be worth the wait. But I must attend the governor now. He is the one who provides the room." He crossed the room and took some papers from a table. "Convenient in its way that I forgot these—I would not have met you here today—"

"If not today, tomorrow." She smiled as softly as she knew how. "I would have taken any opportunity until I found you alone."

"But inconvenient that I must go before we have finished our business. We shall do that soon. I will send a guard for you when it is convenient. Come." He held out his hand peremptorily. "I will find you a guard to escort you to your chambers. You should not be wandering the palace alone. You are too valuable."

She smiled as though she took that as a compliment and allowed him to lead her from his rooms.

The corridor swirled with shadows as the torches over-powered the fading daylight that fell through the latticed windows. Soon it would be fully dark. Payne wondered what the night would be like in these already deserted corridors. At least he didn't need to sleep. Keeping watch eight hours after the day's training might lead a normal man to doze at his post. A Huntsman had no need to worry about that.

Instead he worried about escape and the woman behind the door. He had news, but she had shown no eagerness to learn it. The door had not opened.

It was full dark when it finally did, and she beckoned him into the room, the space beyond which was lit by the swinging oil lamp. She dropped to the bench by the table and barely glanced up as he told her of his time in the barracks and his stolen minutes with Reynard. "So, we will manage to get kitchen duty at the same time and there we should be able to plan. Unfortunately, it means I may not be released in time for guard duty, at least not that night."

She looked up at that but her gaze quickly dropped to her clasped hands.

"But," he continued, "Reynard says it is safe. I think he knows your brother." That should have roused her, but it didn't. "Did you get the token?"

"No." She pushed herself to her feet. "It is in Zakar's chamber. My jewel had begun to glow—the purest light I have ever seen from it—but I had no time to find the coin's hiding place. Zakar returned, he found me there."

Payne's muscles tightened. She was here, her room was the same, the guard the same at the door, he reassured himself. "Did he suspect?"

She shuddered. "I don't think so. He does not know that I know of the token, nor does he know of any reason that I should want it, but my very presence was suspicious."

"What did you do?"

"I lied. He has many times offered me bribes to tell the governor the same lies as he does. I told him I had come to accept. I was tired of the struggle."

"Bribes? Your brother's freedom?"

"He never offered that. For that I would pay his price."

"His price?"

"That I would be his mistress in return for wealth and freedom. He has powerful friends who he thinks would be taken in by prophecies he would have me tell."

She looked up and her face was set like stone, rejecting his dawning pity. "It is for the best. It will give me more freedom and access to his rooms so that I can steal the token."

"You could . . ."

"Refuse? No, he would retaliate. This has gone too far this time. I must go to him when he sends for me."

Payne was shocked at the relief he felt. "When?" Perhaps there would be time to escape.

"Soon. That could mean tonight, tomorrow, days hence." She rose. "We have little time and there is something I want from you." She swallowed. "Take my virginity."

Payne's emotions veered from elation to shock as he realized her meaning. "Why?" She wasn't asking as a lover.

"There are stories that a man takes on a woman's powers when he takes her virginity. I do not believe them, but if by any small chance they should be true, I will not yield what powers I may control to Zakar."

She held out her hand and he took it, though part of him wanted to refuse. She led him up the spiral stair to her bedchamber above. It was lit by a single lantern, and the furniture was little better than in the room below: a table, a chair, a carved chest, and a narrow bed.

"Quickly, we have little time." She dropped his hand and started to undress. His hands paused on the buttons of his uniform jacket as she dropped her shawls and unwrapped the sash that fitted her full skirt to her hips. She dropped it on the floor, then unfastened her short jacket and dropped it as well. Her skirt and thin chemise quickly joined them. She reached up to unpin her hair.

He threw his jacket on the floor as her hair spilled down, ebony against her skin. His hand touched her narrow waist and she flinched, then stopped herself.

The bed was behind them. He eased her down, glad that the shadows lay across her face, and tried to be as gentle as he had ever been, to give what pleasure he could from necessity. When he was done, she said, "Go now; if you linger, they will suspect." She sounded composed, but when he rose, the light struck her face and he could see that her eyes glittered with tears.

Ashamed of his own pleasure and expediency, he grabbed his clothes and retreated down the stairs.

Dusk made the shadows of the mountains ahead long and purple and the ravine they rode through dark. Where before there had been trackless grassland, here the foothills had funneled generations of travelers onto well-worn paths. Ulick turned in the saddle to look back at the straggling procession of riders and spare horses he led and worried about how he would explain them if the pass above was patrolled so well he could not slip by the fortress.

Marda looked up from guiding her mare over the gravel of the streambed with an expression between a question and a frown, and he smiled at her with what he hoped was reassurance, then turned back to the track ahead.

The ravine twisted, and the track rose to the hillside above. The summit was bathed in the rose light of the setting sun. Light reflected off the breastplates of the horsemen who were drawn up across the road.

Ulick signaled for his party to halt. These men were uniformed and armed like the Barajian cavalrymen of the kaiyun's escort. It might still be possible to bluff his way by them. He rode forward to be met by two of the cavalrymen.

"State your name and your reason for being on Barajian territory," ordered the fancier-uniformed horseman.

"I am Ulick Assaga Nu, and I am traveling with my wife and kinsmen. We are going to Istlakan in search of my stepson."

"Kinsmen? They're an odd lot."

Ulick shrugged. "My wife's brother, an apothecary, and my nephew."

"Any trade goods that owe duty?"

"No, nothing but necessary food and clothing."

The officer signaled to his remaining men, who rode forward and were soon searching the pack animals. There was nothing to find. Perhaps this would soon be over, and the way would be clear into Barajia.

Marda was repacking the spilled packs. Ulick could tell from her stiff bearing that she was furious with the carelessness of the soldiers. He smiled to himself; she was probably furious with the carelessness of men in general, not just soldiers. Justin looked relieved to be at rest, not riding. Beyond him Dayan was silent, glowering at the cavalrymen.

The soldiers returned to report to their officer then reformed behind him. The officer had a few more questions to ask about whether they had passed other travelers on their journey and about their proposed route.

Ulick answered patiently. The officer didn't seem suspicious. He heard a horse come up behind him and turned to see Dayan.

"We're almost finished. Go back to the others," he ordered.

Dayan didn't move. "Why are we delayed?"

"Border guards just doing their jobs. Go back to the others."

"I can hurry them."

"Go back to the others." Ulick turned to the officer who was watching slit-eyed. Dayan had spoken Suevarna not Barajian, but, if the officer had been long at his post, he undoubtedly knew the language. "Is there anything else?"

The officer frowned and didn't immediately reply.

Dayan glared at him and Ulick wanted to throttle the young idiot.

The officer ran his finger under the chin strap of his helmet. "I—"

"Hurry up and let us pass if you value you career," Dayan ordered. "I'm the emperor's nephew, and he shall hear of your actions."

Ulick swung around in the saddle and slapped Dayan hard in the mouth. "Silence."

Dayan shocked, obeyed.

Ulick turned to the officer. "My nephew is not right in the head. That is why I could not leave him behind. He needs constant watching. He is occasionally delusional, but not dangerous."

The officer eyed Dayan, then signaled his men. "This is too important a decision for me to make. You will have to accompany us to the Silasar fort. Let the captain decide if you should enter Barajia."

24

Twenty-third Day

Head down, hood shadowing his face, Bertz followed Olm through the streets of Istlakan. Olm and his brethren must be a familiar sight; no one seemed to pay attention to their passage, and the watch on the northern gate waved them through after only a few words with Olm.

Supposedly, Olm was taking him to the countryside where he had been found to help the brother who dwelt there. Actually, the Eskedi would be waiting beyond sight of the walls with his horse, supplies, and the forged papers that would let him pass the military posts that guarded the border. Bertz's head came up as they escaped the oppressive shadow of the city walls, and his stride lengthened. How far north would he have to ride to intercept Walter?

The road turned, turned again, and crossed what seemed to be a natural river in this land of canals. On the far bank stood a rare grove of trees. A horse, his horse, whinnied, echoed by others. When they reached the grove, Naroc stood in the shadows and beyond him were two young men who held not just his horse, but five others. Two were laden pack horses; the other three were saddled riding horses, small, beautiful, and restive.

Bertz could hardly contain himself while Naroc and Olm exchanged greetings. "Who are these men? Why are they here?"

Naroc grinned. "These are my nephews, Alsen and Dirac." The young men nodded their greetings. "We will be riding north with you."

Bertz protested.

"Think," Naroc said. "You need someone to translate, especially at the fortress. My brothers and I trade with the Sueve. It's not unusual for my nephews to ride into the Sueve lands, though I haven't made the journey for many years. We'll be much less conspicuous than a Tarsean riding alone."

Naroc was probably right, but Bertz suspected from the gleam in his eye that he relished the chance for an adventure. *God protect them all.* Bertz looked from eager face to eager face; this could too easily prove worse than an adventure.

"I have other news," Naroc said. "Reshalon has located your comrades' horses and brought them to safe pasture. He has arranged for a fishing boat to stay in sight of the palace landing until the signal is given. The boat will take everyone across the river where the horses and supplies wait. He will have the proper passes forged. The boy will soon be on his way to his mother."

Bertz turned to thank Olm for his help. All of these people had given him more help than he would have given to someone not Stros. Saddles creaked as men mounted behind him. More grateful than he had words for, Bertz turned and mounted, then followed Naroc and his nephews to the road to the north.

Silasar Fortress perched high above the pass like a dyspeptic vulture. Inside its towers and walls it was a maze of corridors and small rooms, not a dwelling place, but a watchtower for the pass and a prison.

Time was when even entering its gates would have made Ulick feel that the grey stone all around would collapse on him at any moment. He'd been in too many such since he had been cursed to be unnerved now, but he tried his best to look impressed—as if he had never seen a stone dwelling before.

The captain was a short, florid man who looked more irritated at each word his subordinate said and gulped something from a goblet before he spoke.

"You are Mahar?" His voice was hoarse and unnaturally deep.

"No, Ortasjian."

"What brings you to Barajia?"

"A band of renegades stole my son and sold him to Barajian slave traders. I'm searching for him."

"And this boy?" He pointed to Dayan.

"I am Dayan Fire-born! The emperor's nephew! You will let us go on our way."

Ulick mustered a sigh of pure annoyance.

"I'm sorry. The boy is, as you can see, quite mad. That's why my wife's brother is traveling with us."

"He's a physician?"

"An apothecary," Justin corrected him, apparently proud he knew the Barajian term for his profession. "And the boy is past due for his medicine." He glowered at Dayan. "I can quiet him very efficiently."

Dayan glared back, then turned to the captain. "They are lying."

"He seems rational," the captain said dubiously.

"Last time he thought he was the Great Khan of the Mahar," Ulick assured him. "Before that he was a Tarsean khan he'd heard about."

"Don't forget the nightmares," Justin threw in.

"Besides, why would *we* be traveling with the emperor's nephew?"

"Good question—" the Captain began, then paused to cough.

"*I* am traveling with them," Dayan protested. "He's lying to you out of spite, because I was the one who stole his son."

"Be quiet!" Ulick ordered. "Do you want to disgrace us all?"

Dayan snorted. "I can prove who I am. He has my amulet."

"Amulet?" The Captain asked.

"Ulick took it from me. He's carrying it. A medallion with a blue stone and fire signs around it."

"Geran, search him and see if there is such an item."

Before the officer could lay hands on him, Ulick reached into his caftan and pulled the medallion out. Dayan looked triumphant.

"Here it is. I inherited it from my grandfather," Ulick said. "He's insisted it was his ever since."

"Liar!" Dayan's voice rose. "I am who I say I am!"

Ulick handed the amulet to the Captain. "Keep it away from him. He goes mad at the sight of it."

Dayan snatched at the medallion, and the captain yanked it out of his reach.

"Give it to me! It is mine! My father, Tekar Khan gave it me! I am Dayan—the Fire-born. The Child of Fire!"

The Captain's eyes opened wide, then before he could speak, his entire body was wracked with coughing. He sat heavily in the chair behind his desk, until the spasm stopped.

Then, tears in his eyes and his face redder than ever, he said, "Geran, take them to the quarters for visitors of the third rank. Keep them under guard until I've had a chance to investigate this."

Foothills at last, and country that wasn't a bleak, land-markless expanse. Thomas welcomed the change as he sat silently by the fire staring at the sky. The just-past quarter moon was halfway to the horizon. Six more days and it would be full again.

Too many nights sleepless, too long on the road. The Huntsmen were silent. Were the others toting up the days as he was? Walter was certainly surveying the moon with the intensity of an astrologer. As Thomas watched he shook his head and stood up.

"I'm going to make a circuit of the camp."

Thomas scrambled to his feet. "Do you want company?"

"If you want."

They walked in companionable silence. The camp was quiet; they'd traveled hard that day, and those who could sleep did so. They passed where the horses were picketed; a few of the Hunt's mounts whickered recognition. Thomas was constantly amazed at how horselike the creatures seemed. But he had seen one kept from its rider on the final full moon once. The equine veneer had been very thin then, and he'd wondered ever since what they really were.

"Now what?" Thomas asked, as Walter paused to idly stroke the neck of his mount.

"I don't know."

"What's wrong?"

Walter shook his head.

"Nameless apprehension, as usual?"

Walter smiled slightly. "One of the Goddesses' more dubious gifts. Or is it? I've never been sure if I really sense something is wrong or something in me simply assumes that there's always something wrong and I only remember the feeling when it's right."

"Why don't we check the kaiyun's tent and then go back to the others? I'm considering having Michel teach me some of his gaming tricks. I think it'd be useful. Would you suspect *me* of cheating at dice?"

He'd drawn a chuckle from the other Huntsman.

"I overheard the Barajians today," Thomas said, as they resumed their round of the camp.

"And?"

"They sent someone to see what happened to the wine. They've decided we're mad. Sane men wouldn't pour perfectly good wine on the ground."

"It wasn't perfectly good."

"But they have no way of knowing we knew it wasn't."

They were coming up behind the kaiyun's tent, concealed from the guards by the shadows cast by the watchfire. Walter started to say something more, then put a hand on Thomas's shoulder, halting him.

"Her guard's been cut. There should be twice as many."

"Perhaps some are inside?"

"I don't think so. Where does Wiraz sleep?"

"Halfway across the camp. The servants and the guard are between him and the kaiyun."

"That far? Always?"

"Whenever I've noticed."

"I don't like this."

"Let's—" A whirring sound followed by a solid "thunk"

cut him off. A guard fell to his knees gurgling horribly, an arrow protruding from his throat. The first arrows were followed by a full flight of lethal shafts. Several of the guards went down; the rest dove for the scant cover.

The second hail of arrows found few targets, and Thomas found his wits. An ambush—Wiraz's doing? It would explain much. Well, it wouldn't succeed, if he had anything to say about it.

Walter caught his arm before he could run to the entrance of the tent.

"Wait. I've called the others. They'll have to invade the camp to get to their quarry. They can't shoot into the tent."

He was right; Thomas could hear running footsteps even now.

"Go ahead," Walter told him, and he sprinted around the tent.

Thomas needed a weapon, something more than just his belt knife. He snatched a short sword from the body of a fallen guard and took a position in front of the entrance while Walter waited in the shadows to make an ambush of his own. The guards who had not been killed outright were regrouping, but they needed reinforcements.

The attackers wore Sueve armor, he noticed, as they swarmed around the fire. He kept his place, knowing that he was more useful stopping an assault on the tent than in the press of men. Still, he wished the kaiyun had a more skillful defender.

It was messy, close fighting, too chaotic for strategy. He caught glimpses of Garrett and Ellis as they entered the fray. Where was Michel?

A man got free of the press of fighting and rushed toward the tent. Thomas stepped forward and lashed out. The Sueve—if he was a Sueve; Thomas had his doubts—dodged and struck a blow of his own.

For a while they feinted and parried, then his opponent pushed forward in earnest, but missed his footing. Thomas, almost without thinking, kicked out and hurled him backward into the Barajian guards' fire. Thomas's last sight of him was running away screaming, trying to beat out the flames in his shirt and hair.

Then someone else replaced him, someone warier of

Thomas, having seen him in action. As Thomas focused on this new foe, he was vaguely aware that more people had poured into the area around the tent. Whether friends or enemies, he had no time to learn.

This man was tall—too tall for a Sueve—and had the reach on him. Thomas sidestepped a vicious swing, and half stumbled on the body of a fallen Barajian. The Sueve took the opportunity to charge him, but found himself suddenly up against Garrett as well. Garrett chuckled and caught him a solid hit across the neck.

Thomas caught his balance just in time to see that the entrance to the tent was undefended and several Sueve were converging on it. He called to Garrett and ran forward. The first man fell easily—he simply hadn't noticed Thomas's approach in his excitement at getting close to his objective. Garrett occupied two more, and a clot of Barajians kept anyone from getting nearer.

But only one Sueve had to get through, and one had. Thomas rushed after him. Inside the tent it was pitch dark— who'd the sense *not* to light the lamp? There should have been a brazier of hot coals burning, too. Had it been covered?

It hadn't. With ruthless efficiency, someone was hurling its contents at the first man to enter the tent. The man shrieked, his hands to his seared face, as Thomas unhesitatingly drove his sword into the man's gut.

Then he whirled to find that no one was behind him. He peered cautiously out—if not precisely quiet, the battle had certainly died down, and almost everyone Thomas saw was Barajian or a Huntsman.

"Smother the coals before they start a fire," he said over his shoulder, as he slipped out of the tent.

Walter, breathing hard, but looking grimly satisfied, nodded at Thomas.

"I had Michel raise the rest of the guard."

"It was still too damn close."

"I know."

"Why would Sueve attack the kaiyun?"

"They're not Sueve. I got a good look at a couple of them. They're Barajian."

"Do you think the delays were caused to set this up?"

"Yes."

"Wiraz is to blame, then. No doubt."

"None at all." Walter looked around and summoned Ellis to his side. "Are any of the cavalrymen from the tuan here and alive?"

"A few."

"Bring them here."

Four were easily found.

Walter had Ellis translate, "I understand that Lord Wiraz has ordered that one of you will be chosen by lot and executed for losing the tuan." The Barajian who appeared to be the highest in rank shrugged his acknowledgment. "I have reason to believe that Lord Wiraz has something to do with this ambush. Would you go to where he is camped, and make sure he knows what has happened here, and that he doesn't attempt to leave? Under the circumstances, I'm sure the kaiyun will see that Lord Wiraz's orders will not be carried out."

The cavalrymen seemed quite eager to follow Walter's orders. Thomas took a deep breath and relaxed. He noticed for the first time that he was smeared with blood. There was no help for it, though, so he turned back to the tent.

Inside, it was dark and silent.

"It's over, Your Highness. You're safe," he said to the black interior, which smelled of singed wool, and heard a rustle as someone near him stepped back. A lamp was uncovered, illuminating the tent.

Standing next to him was Tita Maimai, wielding a vicious-looking bench.

"Did she throw the coals?" he asked Kaiyun Chrysogon.

"Yes."

"*Amedu*," he said to her. "Thank you."

25

Twenty-fourth Day

She couldn't hide here forever, Tiramet chided herself. The dark close space of the wall-walk might be a burrow to lick her wounds after her night with Zakar, but it was dangerous to linger. Neither the governor nor Zakar seemed to guess how much she could overhear. If Zakar or some messenger they sent followed her into the passage they would discover her secret, and her last remaining source of power would be gone.

She told herself that she should go back to her chambers, but the sight of them stirred too many memories, made her want to vomit. She huddled on the floor clutching her knees to her chest. Words seeped through the lattice above her head.

"It will be the night of the Full Moon Rite as the emperor returns through the gardens. Our friends," that was Zakar's voice, "have suborned the Captain of the Guard. He will ignore the assassins' presence until it is too late and then make himself a hero by capturing some of our enemies 'red-handed.' A satisfactory conclusion for him and us."

"I wish we had word from Lord Wiraz that the kaiyun and her mongrel pup were safely dead," the governor fretted. His voice was loud. He

239

must be standing in the doorway to the balcony. "I don't like loose ends."

"Even by post it is two days' journey. You must be patient."

"I have been patient for years of your promises, Zakar. It is time they become reality."

"They will be real before the new moon. Our friends will rule for the child emperor and you, for your help, will rule Lakandar."

"Tell me again how this assassination is to be accomplished."

In the dark passageway Tiramet raised her head, alert.

"Every full moon, as you know, the emperor performs the rites of the moon goddess Bakshamai in her temple by the river about a mile from the palace. Since Bakshamai is the goddess of mercy, it has been the custom of the emperor and his father before him to return through the lower palace gardens which are open on that night to respectably dressed members of the public. Anyone who wishes may present a petition to the emperor, so his progress is usually quite slow and the gardens full of strangers. The emperor is heavily guarded but we have taken care of that difficulty as I told you. The emperor will stop to accept a petition and the petitioners—assassins in our pay—will kill him. Simple and neat. The assassins will escape in the darkness. Our friends will make sure that our enemies are implicated in the murder. When the dust clears we will control the government until the heir comes of age."

"Unless the kaiyun survives."

"She won't."

"I wish we had word."

Tiramet eased herself to her feet as Zakar reassured the governor in the room beyond the passage. She retreated down the dark wall-walk feeling that no place was safe from death and its shadows. She could tell the Huntsman what she had heard, but what good would that do? Where could she take her brother that was safe when they escaped? Was escape even possible?

Chrysogon sat with her women, knowing her composure was a comfort to them—they were still frightened from last night's attack. So was she, though she had no one to tell. For once Maimai was silent, though the medicine Chrysogon had insisted she take to lessen the pain of her burned hands was probably responsible for that.

Someone had tried to kill them. At first she'd thought the attackers were Sueve; perhaps a rival tribe trying to take her hostage—they had timed it for the night after the Sueve escort had departed. But once the helmets and armor had been removed, it had been obvious, even to the most prejudiced of her women, that the attackers were Barajian.

Suspicion had immediately fallen on Lord Wiraz, the more so when guards sent to apprise him of events discovered him trying to flee.

They were questioning Wiraz and Dovir now; Chrysogon was glad she was not present. Not just because the screams from the other end of the encampment made her stomach churn, but because Enandor Thomas was there and she didn't want to know his part.

When had he become important? He was intelligent, and thoughtful, rare enough qualities, but beyond that he seemed to value her intelligence, which was almost unheard of.

He had made this difficult journey tolerable, pleasant on occasion. And he had saved her life twice, at least once at risk of his own.

She suppressed a smile her maids would not understand. He had been so urbane when he entered her tent last night to tell her she was safe—urbane, and covered in blood.

But who or what is he? Enandor was a title from Amaroc, not Tarsia, and more important, one which had not been used for centuries. It was a title from Amaroc's period of rule by popular acclaim—she had read of it in her books on the West when she was studying Tarsean.

And Thomas spoke Barajian. She suspected it when he had supervised the arrangements for her departure, and last night when he had thanked Maimai so formally his accent had been excellent. How well did he speak her tongue? What had he learned listening to Wiraz and Dovir? Was that why the attack had been foiled?

One of her maids let out a small cry of alarm and scuttled into the tent. Thomas and Sir Walter were approaching;

Chrysogon could almost read their message in their grim expressions.

"Wiraz has confessed?" she asked.

Sir Walter nodded. "It's more serious than we thought."

"Tell me."

"Lord Wiraz and others—the only one he would name was the Governor of Lakandar—are part of a plot to kill the emperor. Apparently, they felt you were a threat to their plans to rule through his heir."

Kill her brother? The world seemed to spin with the shock of the idea. Emperors had been murdered before, but emperors dead long before her birth and the emperor who had been her childhood companion were two entirely different things. She understood too well now why she had been a target. And Dayan, what would happen to him without her or his uncle?

"It has happened that the paternal grandmother, sister, or aunt of a minor heir has acted as regent. Since my brother has no other kin to take that office, it would fall to me. Sir Walter, how do they plan to kill my brother?"

"Wiraz didn't know. Only that it was to happen before you reach the capital."

"We must hurry." She started to rise, trying to put her mind on expediting their departure. She could leave some servants to pack and be on the road in minutes. But Sir Walter was shaking his head to stop her.

"Your Highness, we can't take the Silasar Pass. The men who attacked you last night were sent by the captain of the fortress."

"Has this conspiracy spread so far?" She looked at Thomas, who nodded as if he hated confirming the news. "What shall we do?"

"There is the other route—the Agandar Pass," Walter said.

"Only goatherds use that. It is treacherous."

"Not so treacherous as the Silasar Pass, with the fortress against us."

She remembered Silasar Fortress. When she had stopped there for one night on her way to her new husband, it had been menacing. Its evil reputation as a prison had contaminated even the quarters intended for the emperor's kin.

She repressed a shudder. "You are right, of course."

"It will mean leaving behind most of your train."

She waved her hands. "That is no matter. Speed is what is important. My brother must be saved."

"Then pack only what is absolutely necessary. Bring one servant and we will be on the road in an hour."

She looked at the brown-haired Madarian next to Sir Walter and decided in the midst of this crisis that she could spare a measure of gratification for herself.

"If Enandor Thomas could help, it would expedite matters greatly."

"Certainly, Your Highness," Sir Walter replied. Had she detected a note of satisfaction in his voice? Why?

She must keep her wits about her. Though she sensed no threat in these men, she wondered again how much more to them there was than showed on the surface.

Justin wanted a drink, but there was nothing new in that. Captain Ferahim wanted to find out whether Dayan was truly mad or Ulick was lying, and there was nothing surprising in that either.

"How long has he had these delusions?" the captain asked for the fourth or fifth time. His voice rasped like a file on metal from coughing and catarrh.

"As long as I've known him."

"How long has that been?"

"Since I went to visit my sister last fall. I found the boy and a dozen other Sueve squatting on her farm."

"If she had all these Sueve with her why was her son carried off?"

"How should I know? They're not one of my interests."

"Why did you come with them?"

"Because they needed someone to dose the boy, and because I've never been to Barajia and thought I'd see what I could learn about Barajian medicine." That should satisfy him, but the captain scowled and looked over his notes again. As he did, a coughing fit wracked his body, and he gulped hastily from a goblet.

"How long have you been coughing like that?" Justin asked.

"All winter. I took a chill at the first snow and it hasn't gone away."

"With all the musk root around, I'm surprised you haven't taken advantage of it."

"Musk root? I've been dosed with everything from honey and vinegar to goose gizzards in broth. I've never heard of that."

"It's a sovereign remedy for lung spasms."

"And it grows nearby?"

"I've seen it growing not half a mile away. I've even some in my pack, I could make a posset in wine, if your men would give it back to me."

Captain Ferahim was overcome with coughing and that seemed to make up his mind. He beckoned to one of the guards and between spasms instructed his man to bring Justin his pack.

The captain sniffed the half-dried root and wrinkled his nose. "It stinks."

"That's why it's called musk root."

"You're sure it's not poisonous?"

"I'll drink the posset if you want me to."

The captain nodded, and had a mortar and pestle fetched from the kitchen, and a pipkin to heat the wine and ground root over a brazier where Captain Ferahim could see him.

It took some time, and while Justin ground the root, the captain wrote at his desk. After he finished, he rose and went into the outer room.

The instant he was gone Justin leaned over the desk and glanced at the papers. The characters were slightly different from those he was familiar with—but he caught the gist of the document. Ferahim was sending Dayan's medallion to the governor to see if anyone could confirm that the emperor's nephew owned such an object.

Shit.

When the captain returned, Justin was stirring the wine and root mixture, placidly staring out the window that overlooked Silasar Pass.

The captain looked at the mess of leaves and stems Justin had stripped from the root.

"Only the root—not the rest?"

"No. That has other uses. I'll save them for emergencies.

I think this is ready." He took a deep draught of the medicine. It tasted as bad as it smelled.

Then, while the captain drank his bitter medicine, Justin carefully gathered the remainder of the musk root plant and scooped it into his pouch. Musk root leaves indeed had uses, and if anyone recognized the medallion he might need them.

Reynard dumped the dirty bowls on the scullery table and stooped to pick up one that he had dropped. He tossed it down with the others. *The only thing I've learned this summoning is which offenses will get me kitchen duty in this godforsaken country and which will get me a beating* and *kitchen duty. Totally useless information. Goddesses, never send us to Barajia again!*

A youth dumped another bucket of dirty bowls on the table. Reynard looked up. It was not Ivreim; he'd have more time to plan what he would say to him. Reynard thought over what Payne had told him while they were locked in the kitchen storeroom last night. Having your father condemned to death, being condemned yourself—at nine years old!—explained something of the youth's silences, of his cool kindness. Ivreim had visited him only once in the scullery, after he had confirmed that Robin was a member of the trefoil squad. He had said he would come if Reynard needed him, had given Reynard a signal to flash. Reynard had used it on the parade ground that morning. Perhaps Ivreim had not seen it.

Another youth dumped a load of bowls carelessly on the table, setting off a cascade of bowls to the floor. Reynard sighed and knelt to gather them.

"You signaled?" Ivreim slid his burden of kitchen tools and bowls onto the table so as not to disturb the rest. "What did you need?"

Reynard scrambled to his feet searching for words. This wasn't going to be easy. If their positions were reversed, he would be skeptical of what he had to say. "I needed to talk to you."

"So," Ivreim stooped to swing the greasy stew cauldron to the table, "talk."

"I have something of yours." Reynard held out the carved jade seal.

Ivreim froze, his gaze locked on the seal. "Why do you think that's mine?"

"Your sister kept it for you. She sends it to prove that you should listen to what I say."

"Sends? How?" Ivreim had still not touched the seal.

"Payne, my companion, is one of her guards. She gave it to him to give you through me."

Ivreim flicked the seal over in Reynard's palm. "So, after all this time, what does Tiramet want?"

"She wants you to know that you can trust us. We have a plan to escape from Istlakan."

Ivreim raised an eyebrow.

"There is a loose grate in the room of the leader of the trefoil squad. Behind it is a passageway through which we can get to the river and steal a boat. Once across the river we have horses ready to flee the province."

"When?"

"When Payne gives me the signal. That will be when Tiramet and he think it is safest. We need to be ready to snatch Robin and go. But it will be soon."

"And if I don't choose to take the risk?"

"You want to stay?"

Ivreim said nothing.

"Then I'll have to take the boy. You will help me with that, won't you?"

"Would he be better off with you?"

"We take him to his mother."

"He speaks of her often," Ivreim said. "I have been tutoring him in Barajian."

"Then you can tell him what I told you. His mother wants him, waits for him."

"Just because I know what it is to be young and alone and have shown Robin some kindness doesn't mean I am going to go along with this scheme. We may be safer here."

"Unless the governor changes his whim."

"True. But he hasn't."

"He could. Your sister has been trying to find a way for you to escape for years. We provide one. We have help available outside the walls of the palace. We may be your only chance. Will you take it? Will you help us?"

Ivreim flicked the seal over to its upper side then picked it out of Reynard's hand. "What is the plan?"

"Payne will give the signal during the afternoon drill before he goes back to be your sister's night guard. He will overpower his fellow guard and he and she will wait for us in the passageway. Meanwhile, in the evening when all the officers are drinking in the east loggia, we will take Robin and go to the trefoil squad leader's room. We'll bar the door and shutters and take out the grate to get into the passages. Then we rendezvous with the others, take a boat, and cross the river to the horses and freedom."

"Sounds simple." Ivreim tossed the seal in his hand before tucking it in his jacket.

"It is simple. Are you in?"

"Yes. What signal will your companion give?" Ivreim asked, as he stooped to get the scouring rags from their bucket under the table.

26

Twenty-fifth Day

Zakar pushed Tiramet into his soft bed until she thought she would smother in the pillows or choke on her hair. Resistance would only prolong the agony; experience had taught her that. She tried to think of something other than his weight on her back, his hands in her hair. *In days it will be over*, she reassured herself. *Endure it till then.*

Zakar's weight shifted. "Come in."

His servant was at the bedside. "The governor sends for you, Master."

Zakar swore, but he got up. "Did he say why?" he asked, as he crossed to the dressing room.

Tiramet rolled over, wrapping herself in the coverlet. With both men in the other room, perhaps she could locate the Hunt's token. She squinted her eyes trying to see with the inner eye her grandmother had told her of, the pure light her jewel had glowed with the first day. Methodically she faced each wall and corner of the room in turn. There was nothing at the bed-head or the chest beside it, nothing near the dining table or its two chairs, nothing near the hangings of the door.

Water splashed in the dressing room; she must hurry. No light glowed from the chest at the foot of the bed or the chest on the far wall. That left only the unfurnished room—surely Zakar would not put the token there—the dressing room with its clothespresses, and the curious tall chest on a table by the door to the balcony. The open door streamed with distracting sunlight. She closed her eyes; the sunlight was red through her lids. *Concentrate*.

The red faded slowly to pulsing white. She opened her eyes to face the chest. Somewhere in its left side was the token.

She had time to do no more than rise to her feet before Zakar strode into the room, followed by his servant.

"I must go," Zakar said. "Minvar will see you to your chambers." Then he was gone, leaving the smirking servant to loiter.

She sat on the bed and reached for her scattered clothes. The servant showed no sign of leaving.

"I wish to wash. Bring me water."

The servant sketched a bow and left for the dressing room. She had time only to put on her slippers before he had returned with a basin and towel.

She looked at the dull water. Zakar had used this. "I want fresh water. Shall I tell Zakar what a poor servant you are? He would not be pleased. I want hot water. Get it."

The servant made a more respectful bow and left. Soon she could hear his feet on the stairs to the lower floor.

She hurried across the room to the chest and tried the iron clasp. She sighed with relief; it wasn't locked; it turned under her hand and the front panel swung down to form a level shelf and reveal a front of small drawers. She opened one and found an inkwell and an assortment of reed pens. She had not expected Zakar to own a writing desk; he might be more clever than she had given him credit for. Where was the coin? She closed her eyes and centered her inner gaze on the light. She opened the drawer that she faced when she opened her eyes. Inside the small drawer were a cylinder seal, a flat shield of carved gold which was a Barajian rank badge, and a thin gold chain. She pulled out the chain and its pendant. The Nolsic coin was cool in her hand. Somehow she had expected it to be hot. She closed the chest quickly.

The servant would return soon. She hurried to the bed

and donned her chemise and skirt. She was winding her
sash around her hips, the coin safe in its folds, when
Zakar's servant returned with a basin of steaming water.

"Thank you." She fastened her jacket.

The servant didn't leave again as she washed her face
and hands and bound up her hair but made a show of making the bed while he watched her. He smirked as if he knew
every distasteful thing that occurred there. Tiramet shivered. He probably did know; his room had only a curtain
as a door. She swung her shawls around her as though they
would hide her shame. Did all the servants know? She
wished that tonight were the night they would escape. Then
she could take Edralen and flee to somewhere safe, somewhere no one would know them.

The quarters for visitors of the third rank were small, and
smelled of moldy neglect. Six beds were crammed into a
room which would have been barely comfortable for four—
the only concession to privacy was a curtain hung between
two of the beds and the rest, presumably for the modesty
of female lodgers.

Ulick's hatred of stone buildings provided a discordant
background to concerns far less trivial. He felt like a man
embattled, and all the battles were within himself.

He had failed Walter, and probably doomed the Hunt.
He should have sent or taken Dayan back the night the boy
had run away. If he hadn't brought him along, they would
not be imprisoned here now.

Dayan sprawled on his bunk scowling, undoubtedly plotting to have the three who had tried to keep his identity
secret imprisoned, when word came that his amulet was
recognized. Then how would they get Marda to her son, or
her son to Marda?

Marda sat on her bed beyond the half-open curtain, silent, angry, despairing, as she had been since their enforced
stay here had begun. She was too wise not to understand,
too angry to believe any words of comfort Ulick might have
had the temerity to offer.

That gnawed at him worst of all.

When had her fears become his? When the Hunt was
summoned his only concern had been that they not fail.

Now he regretted that he could not solve her problem, that in five days she would be abandoned in an alien land, her son lost to her. Not because the Hunt might fail, but because he would fail her.

He'd always found the Tarsean obsession with a single woman to the exclusion of all others a quaint and foolish idea. He wondered now that he hadn't understood before. It was kin to a blood tie, a clan tie. An obligation beyond personal need. When had it grown inside him? What had fostered it?

Marda's knuckles were white as she clutched the bed frame. Her head was down, but he doubted that she was weeping. She was, he thought, beyond that. He rolled to his feet and sat beside her.

She stiffened. "You're going to try to tell me again that we'll find Robin." Her voice was flat.

"I can't promise you now."

He'd surprised her. She met his gaze with a shocked glance so full of hurt he wanted to hold her.

"But Walter is with the kaiyun," he continued. "They have to come this way; the other is too dangerous. She can free us, even if Dayan's amulet is recognized."

"There is so little time."

"The others may have Robin waiting for you even now. I won't try to tell you that success is certain, but it is not out of reach."

She nodded, not as if she were convinced.

"This shouldn't have happened," she said. "None of it. We only tried to live our lives, Peter, Robin and I. And now Peter is dead, because the Duke was an arrogant fool, and—and—" Something in her snapped. She gestured to Dayan, "And because this conceited whelp thought he was above everyone, my son is lost."

Dayan glowered; his Tarsean was good enough to understand what Marda had said. "Keep your woman quiet, Ortasjian," he snarled in Suevarna.

"She speaks the truth; she has cause to feel as she does."

Dayan snorted and said in heavily accented Tarsean, "I only follow the destiny the gods laid out for me."

"Then your gods are vicious fools to let a willful child lead them!" Marda exploded.

Dayan was on his feet.

"Shut up!"

"I will not! What else can you do to me? You've stolen my son and other innocent children. You killed people who never did you any harm and never would. A great leader is supposed to help his people. All I can see is that you've hurt everyone you've ever touched!"

"I was born to lead the Mahar!"

"Then you'll destroy them! You've never a thought to anything or anyone but yourself!"

"I am—"

"I don't care what you are. You will only become great by standing on the backs of the people you've killed. What you are is a murderer and a thief!"

Dayan's arm flew back to hit her, but Ulick caught him. The boy had let himself get soft during his months of raiding, and he was no match for the Huntsman.

"Are you going to add striking a woman to your list of cowardly acts?"

"This one needs striking." Dayan shrugged elaborately and unconvincingly and strode out of the room, doubtless to complain to the captain.

Marda was shaking; Ulick tried to think of something to say. But words would not serve, and he did not dare do any of the things he wanted.

She recovered herself. "I shouldn't have said that—he'll be more vindictive than ever."

"I don't see how," Ulick answered. She smiled faintly in return. "Besides, you didn't say anything that shouldn't have been said long ago."

"He won't believe it." She sat heavily on the bed. "I want my son. I feel so alone."

"You're not." He sat beside her, and finally, unable to leave her uncomforted, put his arm around her shoulders.

She was going to be alone, though, in five days.

27

Twenty-sixth Day

The bell that summoned her to the governor's apartments was jangling insistently as Minvar escorted her into her chamber. Tiramet wondered how long it had been ringing and hurried Minvar back into the corridor. She straightened her clothes, wishing she had time to change into garments unsullied by Zakar's touch.

The bell vibrated on its cord. She had no time. She opened the panel in her upper chamber and tried to compose her mind as she hurried down the passageway. It was barely dawn. How long, she worried, had the governor been summoning her, and what had happened that he summoned her at this strange hour? Her imagination supplied only disasters, and she prayed for her brother's life.

She heard nothing through the lattice at the passage end and tentatively opened the door to the governor's chamber. He was alone, pacing from chair to window, papers clutched in his hand. She quickly crossed the room to kneel at his feet. "I crave a thousand pardons for my tardiness, Excellency."

"You may need that and many more." He walked past her and sank into a chair. He looked over the papers he held. "What do you know of the kaiyun's son?"

"Nothing, Excellency." She did not rise from her crouch. "Is there something about him I should know?"

"I don't believe you."

She shook her head. "What should I know?"

"He calls himself the Child of Fire," he spat at her. "You have deceived me."

Her mind raced. She had not heard this claim before, had barely been aware the kaiyun had a son. For a cold moment her stomach knotted. *What if it is true?* Then reason overcame her fear. This claim was no more likely than the ones she had fabricated. She wondered why the governor was concerned about the prince. He had called the boy a mongrel just days ago and had fretted that he had not been killed. What had changed the governor's mind?

"Excellency, why should I know of claims made by a barbarian Sueve? I do not know why he should think himself the Child of Fire. That is a prophecy of my people which I have shared with you."

"Deceived me with!"

"No!" She crawled nearer his chair. "I shared what I knew. The wise ones of the Eskedi know the time is near. The Child has been born."

The governor looked down at the papers now dropped in his lap and took a medallion from among them. "Fireborn, this prince was fire-born, when the comet blazed across the sky."

She sat back on her heels and said slowly, as though considering the matter, "That *was* one of the portents. . . ."

"Then *he* is the Child."

"Many boys were born in the comet-year, and that was only one of the portents which stretched over many years. There needs to be further proof."

The governor's eyes were hollow with despair. "The heavens blaze with portents only for princes. He is the Child and I have been a fool. You have made me a fool."

"Excellency, were there not three suns in the sky when you won the battle at Egril? You are as a prince, better than a prince, for you alone are the 'chosen.'"

His head came up a little at her words, so she continued.

"That is why I shared the prophecy with you. The Child of Fire is only a tool for the 'chosen' to use to gain his goal and you are the chosen. You must find your tool. I had always assumed, because my people assumed it, that the Child would be one of us. Zakar has already pointed out that I may be wrong about that. You must find a way to test this prince as you have tested the others."

"He is a prince; how can he be my tool?"

She scrambled to think of an answer. The boy was not dead; the governor spoke of him in the present tense. She did not want the prince dead, but neither did she want the governor so convinced that he was the Child that he would discard the others. He might execute her brother before they could escape. "Perhaps gratitude would bind him to you."

"Gratitude! Why should he be grateful? I—" The governor stopped, his eyes narrowed, and in a few moments he began to stroke his beard—his usual gesture when lost in thought. Finally he said, "Yes, with some manipulation he could be made to feel a useful gratitude." Ofarim smiled slowly. "Zaker shall bear the blame and I shall appear his saviour."

"If he *is* the Child. But what if he is not? He must be tested."

The governor smiled. "Oh, he will be tested, never fear. Be ready to do that soon. Not immediately, not till I know more of other matters."

His words promised her more time, but she was afraid to trust them. She prostrated herself again but there was a rap on the door before she could ask to return to her rooms. Zakar entered at the governor's command and walked across the room to bow shortly to the governor, ignoring her presence. He said eagerly as the governor waved his dismissal of her, "Excellency, there is news?"

The governor folded the papers quickly and stuffed them and the medallion into his sash. "Not that which you await. This is minor, unofficial."

Tiramet closed the passage door behind her. Through the lattice she could hear the governor say, "I need you to write a letter to your friend Captain Ferahim, send it immediately by post. This is what you should say." His words faded behind her as she fled down the corridor and opened the door to her chamber.

She dropped her shawls and splashed water into the basin, grateful finally to be able to wash Zakar's touch from her body. She wished she could cleanse it from her soul as well. She pulled the pins from her hair, then froze. Her comb was not where she had left it, and now that she looked closely, other things had been moved as well. Who had been here while she was gone? She twisted up her hair and thrust the pins back in, grabbed her shawls, and was halfway down the stairs to ask the guards before she thought better of it. She was a prisoner here; would they tell her? Minvar had escorted her from Zakar's rooms that morning. It would have been easy enough for him to make an excuse to reenter. He would have known from the jangling bell that she must go to the governor.

She shivered with revulsion. It was bad enough living with the way he looked at her as though he expected her to be passed along to him, another servant's perquisite like his master's old clothes or the candle ends, without the thought of the man touching her things. She slowly climbed the spiral stair to her bedchamber. Worse, what if Minvar didn't act on his own but on Zakar's orders? The walls seemed to close in.

The door to the guest chamber opened. Though the thin privacy curtain was closed, Marda recognized the brisk step as Ulick's. He and Dayan had gone in search of breakfast, or rather, Ulick had gone and taken Dayan with him, so she wouldn't be left alone with the prince.

The search must have been successful; Ulick carried a bowl of a porridge which, if experience was any guide, would be highly seasoned.

She took it and listlessly stirred the mess as she sat crosslegged on the bed. "Talk to me."

"About what?" She could see he was surprised at the request.

"Anything. Tell me a story. I think I will go mad just sitting here."

He sat on the narrow bed they shared and leaned his shoulders against the wall. "What kind of story?"

She peered around the curtain.

"Where is Dayan?

"Trying to get an audience with the captain. I think the captain's tired of listening to him, too."

"He only says one thing—how great he is."

"All he's been taught."

"Tell me how you made the new king."

"That wasn't what we did."

"Then what did you do?"

"A Tarsean noblewoman summoned us to kill off the old king and his family. At the end of the moon she kept Alesander from returning to Walter. He was of the Tarsean Royal line, so I suppose she managed to put him on the throne somehow."

"Why did she want the old king dead?"

"Revenge for her brother who'd been killed by the old king's son Leot."

Marda nodded; she'd heard garbled bits and pieces of the story. She took a bite of the porridge; it was worse than usual. She made a face and put the bowl down, but Ulick put it back in her hands.

"You need to be strong. Walter should be here soon."

"If you say so." She was beginning not to believe him, but she didn't want Ulick to know how defeated she felt. "What did you do to kill the old king?"

"Stood watch while Leot did it."

"So the son killed his father?"

"Yes."

"If he truly killed the lady's brother, I'm glad they're both dead."

"Why would it matter to you?"

Why would it?

"I guess because she couldn't get anyone to help her, either."

"She had us kill too many." Ulick's wooden spoon scraped the bottom of the wooden bowl. "The king, his sons, his wife. She would have had us kill his daughter if Brian hadn't rescued her. She had the right and reason to kill Leot, but the rest?"

"And what would the ones left behind have done to her?"

"If they'd known—probably killed her."

"What was she to do? Sit in a corner and wait after her brother was murdered? She didn't have anything to lose, did she?" She turned to dangle her legs over the edge of the bed.

"I know why so many of you are cursed by women." Ulick sat silent; had he guessed that somewhere along the way? "Women don't get weapons. We're expected to sit quiet and let the men act. Cursing must have been the only weapon left; just like summoning you was for me."

"A poor weapon. Most of the women who cursed were dead before the full moon."

"Yes, but they *knew* they'd done something that would last." What was she thinking? It had been a woman who'd cursed Ulick. She put out a hand, quickly apologetic. "I'm sorry. I forgot."

Ulick shrugged. "Perhaps I deserved it. I could have stopped some of the killing, I suppose. She had reason. I think my wife would have done the same."

"But you're not—you're—" What did she want to say? "You're different."

He was amused by that. "I'm Sueve."

"No." She wanted to tell him he was more real than the others. "You talk to me—not at me."

"That's only so you won't hate the nasty Sueve any more."

"You're making fun of me."

He shook his head. "I'm just the only one nearby you can trust, that's all." Was that true? He wasn't laughing.

"I'm sorry I was so stupid at first."

"You had reason."

Marda scowled down at the porridge bowl. "Do you have to be so broad-minded all the time?"

He laughed. "First I'm too barbaric. Now I'm too tolerant. What do you want?" He brushed a stray wisp of hair from her face.

"I—" But she didn't finish. It was if something was hanging in the air between them, something that had been there which they hadn't seen until now. Ulick leaned a little forward, and Marda closed her eyes waiting for what he'd do next.

Dayan did not raise his credit in her eyes one bit by stomping into the room at that moment. But she was not sure whether it was a fortuitous interruption or not.

*   *   *

The trail was narrow and steep and worsened with each mile they traveled, so Walter knew that the rider foolhardy enough to ride at breakneck speed was Garrett. He'd been left with the decoy cortege with orders to report if, as expected, it was attacked.

"When?" was all Walter asked when Garrett caught up with him.

"Yesterday near twilight, just before we were to stop for the night." He grinned. "Wiraz went down first."

Thomas's plan had worked. They'd dressed Wiraz in the kaiyun's traveling clothes, surrounded by the cavalrymen from the tuan. Dovir had been dressed as Tita Maimai.

The kaiyun listened intently. "My maids?"

"I saw the cavalrymen hot-footing it out of there with your ladies, as planned, Your highness." They were to flee to the fortress, pretending they thought they'd been attacked by Sueve.

"How much time do we have?" Walter asked Garrett.

"Depends on how long it took them to guess where you went. If we're lucky, half a day."

Walter surveyed his little party. Besides the four Huntsmen there were the Barajian cavalryman who was their guide, the kaiyun, and Tita Maimai.

He'd have to push them faster. He didn't like the road, and from their guide's description it would only get worse. More important, there was no place to camp until they'd crossed the pass unless they stopped soon.

He looked up at the mountains, black and jagged against the grey sky. It was impossible to turn back now.

Bertz and Dirac watered the horses at the caravansary below the fortress while Naroc and his other nephew dealt with the officials inside. This caravansary was much the same as the one he had been at with Hamon, Payne, and Reynard, but three weeks had changed the countryside. Even high in the mountains there was no hint of snow now. Bertz's eyes swept the sunlit valley; the grass below was fresh gold-green and pink flowers nodded in the crevices of the rock. Would they be plowing at home? Would the trees be budding?

Dirac prodded his arm. "Might as well sit down," he said in Suevarna. "They'll be a while."

"Could you take the horses? I want to stretch my legs."

Dirac nodded. "I don't like closed places either."

Bertz walked out the gate. The fortress on its cliff loomed above the caravansary buildings; the road it guarded clung to the mountainside weaving between meadow and steep hillside. He gazed north through the gap in the mountain wall, wondering how far away Walter, Marda, and the other Huntsmen were. Only four days remained to reunite Robin with his mother.

Bertz looked for a path to the stream below. Down by the free-running water he could feel alone, ignore the buildings and their occupants above. Sunlight reflected off metal. No, he wouldn't be alone. A spearman stood below watching another man who stood on the hillside, gathering plants. Bertz walked down the road to stand above him. That grey tunic looked familiar.

Justin didn't look up when Bertz stopped five feet above him. Bertz spoke softly so the spearman wouldn't hear. "What are you doing here?"

Justin jumped, almost losing his balance. Shackles linked his ankles.

"Not so loud," Justin whispered. "He might hear."

"Are the others here? The woman?"

"Marda is in the fortress with Ulick and that damn Prince Dayan. The rest are back on the plain. They're escorting the Emperor of Barajia's sister home. Walter thinks her protection will ensure that Marda will be 'safe,' since we can't get her home to Tarsia. He sent us ahead to find you and the boy. We would have been well on the road to Istlakan if the Prince hadn't opened his mouth. Now we're stuck till the governor decides what to do with us."

"And you?"

"Gathering herbs to treat the captain of the fortress's lung spasms. Proves I'm an apothecary and earns his gratitude. At least in theory."

"Not entirely." Bertz indicated the shackles.

Justin grimaced. "Wave your arms as though you were asking directions. The guard is watching."

Bertz did as told.

"Why are you here?" Justin asked. "Did you locate the boy?"

"Yes, he's in Istlakan, imprisoned in the palace with Payne and Reynard. We'd hoped to have the help of rest of the Hunt to free them. I was riding north to find Walter but we won't have time." Bertz sat on his heels. "You say Marda is here?"

"Yes."

Bertz studied the fortress, the road, and the guard. "Could she gather whatever it is you're gathering in your place?"

Justin jerked up a plant while he thought about his answer. "Yes, but I don't know if the captain would allow it."

"Couldn't you say that you needed time to prepare your concoction? It took all kinds of complicated steps when I helped you in Tarsit."

"This isn't a poison."

"But it could take preparation only you could do. To save time, the woman could gather the herbs for you."

"I could say that these need different preparation because they are fresh. Yes, it might work."

"And I could snatch Marda and ride with her to Istlakan. Payne has a plan to escape with Robin. All we would have to do is make sure mother and child are together and safe for the summoning to be fulfilled."

"It could work. I'll try to convince the captain to send Marda out tomorrow."

"The guard's coming. I'll be waiting." Bertz waved to the approaching guard and made a half salute to Justin. He returned to the caravansary to tell the Eskedi of the change in plans, and convince them to ride into Suevia out of reach of arrest when he snatched Marda.

"No one told me Barajian goats had wings," Ellis said from the rear.

The sun was nearly down, the path narrow and steep. Thomas could sympathize with his fellow Huntsman. Even goats would be hard-pressed to follow this trail. And goats were not usually chased by a band of bloody-minded Barajians still smarting from being humiliated.

The Hunt could see their pursuers when the path twisted in the right direction. The Barajians must be using their energy to catch up before full dark—they couldn't be eager to traverse this at night either.

The kaiyun rode immediately behind Thomas; he didn't dare turn to see her face, shadowed though it must be. She was afraid and Thomas didn't want to see it.

Far back in the line of riders he heard a grunt and the clatter of stones rolling down the steep slope. Someone had stumbled—Ellis or Garrett, he wasn't sure.

"Walter?" he said.

"The sky may clear, then the moon will light us."

"*If* the sky clears."

Walter didn't answer. For a long while everyone was silent, as if listening to each step of the Barajian leading them. The sky did not clear, and the last daylight faded to nothing.

Thomas wished the path were wider, then he could have ridden outside of the kaiyun. But the path was too narrow to ride two abreast, almost too narrow for one. Ellis was right—even goats would have to fly to take this path safely. He wished that wings were something the Goddesses granted their Huntsmen.

But they hadn't given them *that* power.

Walter was only a black shape in front of Thomas, but the taut set to his shoulders was as readable as words on a page. How stubborn would Walter be? Success depended on getting the kaiyun through this pass, as Walter had understood the words Marda had spoken.

He wanted to tell Walter he must yield, must use the one power that would give them a fighting chance of crossing safely, but there were boundaries to their friendship Thomas knew better than to test. He'd learned that last summons, when he'd not been able to raise Walter from his sickbed.

But now Walter endangered more lives than his own and his Huntsmen's. Tita Maimai was praying, her voice too low to understand; her intonation was unmistakable in the silence. She wouldn't be praying for herself, either. Thomas wanted to join her, but he'd been the tool of three deities for too long to depend on their mercy.

The Barajian guide swore as his mount stumbled. There was the scrabble of falling stone, heavy at first, then slowing as the horse started to regain its footing.

Thomas was too far back to see what happened next. The guide cried out, rock shattered and fell heavily, and the guide's horse trumpeted terror. Something heavy fell with the rocks, hurtling down the steep slope.

The darkness was a blessing now; they couldn't see horse and rider plummet. Frozen, unable to do anything to help, Thomas heard the Barajian's scream fade, then cease.

Stunned silence followed as the party froze. It was, Thomas only realized later, the wisest thing they could have done. They had no way of knowing how much damage had been done to the crumbling path.

"Walter . . ." Thomas said, after an eternity of silence.

"I know." The answer was curt, angry. Or was it the realization of how close he had brought all of them to their deaths that colored Walter's voice?

He could see Walter massage his hands as if he'd been clenching them too long. Then he cupped them in front of him—where had Thomas seen that gesture before? It took him a moment to remember that it was the way the Goddess Elun held hers in her statue at Reasalyn.

The glow of light was dim at first, growing brighter slowly. Of course, anything else and they'd be as blind from the sudden light as from the darkness. Whatever else Thomas thought of them, the Ladies were no fools.

The light was round, a small silver moon, and illuminated the path directly ahead.

Behind him the kaiyun showed her surprise only by one slow intake of breath. Tita Maimai prayed more quickly.

The path ahead was not as bad as Thomas had feared. The guide must have strayed too near the edge where water had eroded the rock. The way was narrow, but passable if they hugged the wall.

"Be extremely careful," Walter called. "The trail is still treacherous."

The riders slowly began to pick their way uphill again, each wondering how much further until they could rest.

28

Twenty-seventh Day

Chrysogon tucked her hands into her sleeves against the morning chill. Lakandar was spread below her, the fields a delicate green. It looked so serene—she found it difficult to believe that corruption was rife among the beauty. Had it always been so? Her memories of home were so distant, filtered through time, forgetfulness, and childish impressions.

Tita Maimai was still asleep, exhausted after the long treacherous journey and two sleepless nights. Chrysogon had slept fitfully, her dreams and waking moments alike filled with worry and unanswerable questions.

"Kaiyun?" Thomas's voice. At first it filled her with warmth as it had for days, only to be replaced with all the consternation that last night's events had engendered. "Walter needs to know how we should proceed. It wouldn't be advisable to just go to the governor's palace."

He looked so ordinary this morning, except for the smile in his eyes when he looked at her. The smile she wanted to answer with her own.

"Who are you?" she asked, unable to think of words less blunt. Before he could make fools of them both by pretending he did not understand, she continued. "You have introduced yourself with a title which has been unused seven centuries, and Sir Walter"—she emphasized the title—"can use the moon for his personal lantern. Who are you? *What* are you?"

He frowned fleetingly. "It is hard to explain. We are tools of the Rensel Goddesses. Called up to perform tasks in their names."

All the pieces fell into place. "There is a name for you. The Hunt—the Wild Hunt." She smiled at his surprise. "Poetry is one of my studies. Need I explain that much Tarsean poetry has been written about you?"

"No. It has caused difficulties before."

"You are summoned, as you say and as I have read, for a task. What is it?"

"Marda summoned us to rescue her son."

"And the rest is all coincidence?"

His smile was ruefully crooked. "Not the first time we've become enmeshed in matters unrelated to our task."

She was relieved, almost giddy for a moment. They were no danger to her brother, then. She pulled poetic scraps from her mind. *Moon to moon.* Full moons—the stretch of one to another. How much longer did they have to succeed? What if they failed?

The moon was nearly full.

"You have little time," she said.

"Three days. And there are more difficulties ahead. Four of our party were sent to Lakandar to trace Robin when we found evidence that he might have been sold to a Barajian caravan." They were approaching the other Huntsmen sitting at the fire finishing a meager breakfast. "They may have stumbled onto something, perhaps more of the plot. Walter has reason to believe that harm has come to them in Lakandar."

Sir Walter heard the words and frowned. Thomas turned to him. "She's not a fool, Walter. Or blind."

Walter was not pleased, but he seemed to understand what was beyond his fixing.

"And the waiting woman?"

"Tita Maimai was raised in the same court as I. She knows when to ignore what doesn't concern her."

He nodded briefly, reluctantly. "Where should we take

you, your highness? I would suggest that the palace is unsafe."

"Dayan may be there." And if he were, what was happening to him?

"What good would your falling into a trap do him?"

"None. But what should I do? We could never get to the capital unnoticed."

After a pause for thought, Thomas said, "Walter, couldn't we send someone ahead to warn the emperor? One of us could make the ride in time."

"And who would believe a Tarsean riding out of nowhere?"

"A letter from the kaiyun?"

"Written on what?" Walter answered.

"Is there anyone you can trust in Istlakan?"

She considered. "The old governor's brothers. They tried to warn my father that Governor Ofarim was not trustworthy despite his military successes—Ofarim's appointment was so resented by the Barajians that the news spread even to Suevia. They would know who else we can trust."

"We could leave you with the old governor's family."

"Then what? If they kill my brother, the governor will merely take me into 'protective' custody."

"Perhaps you could be smuggled home," Walter said.

"But my brother will be dead."

"He may already be dead, your highness."

"I must try to save him until I know it is futile. No, the governor must be shown for what he is!"

Walter was scowling now. "Your highness, my priority is to find Marda's son."

"And to assure that both of them are safe," Thomas said. "You said that yourself, remember."

"Your highness," Walter said, "if we help you save your brother, will you promise to take Marda Trefsdottir into your care?"

Beside her she felt Thomas bristle for her sake. "It was not necessary to ask," she replied. "I would have in any case. I take it the Ortasjian is *not* her husband and is bound to leave when your task is done?"

"Yes, at the full moon, whether we succeed or no."

"I will ensure her safety and her son's."

"Then we will help you." Walter rubbed his face, a tired frustrated gesture. "Thomas, what should we do? You understand this kind of politics. I'm only an old soldier."

"Barajian imperial politics is not exactly my area of expertise, but I should say that with a sufficient backing, her highness could confront the governor with her accusations."

"With sufficient backing."

"Barajia has held Lakandar for many centuries. Most of its nobility will lose greatly if this governor breaks from Barajia. How many of them do you think she could rally at a moment's notice?"

Chrysogon stayed silent, answering only such questions as they sent her way. Thomas and Walter's conversation flowed as if with each succeeding idea the other's mind took flight and raced ahead. An old soldier Sir Walter might call himself, but he understood Thomas's meaning immediately and refined on it.

How long had these two men worked together? Long enough to almost read each other's minds. Long enough to enjoy each other's thoughts. They were too different to appear as halves of one man, but they had learned to use their differences to complement each other.

They spoke so quickly, stepping on each other's words, that she lost all but the basic shape of the discussion. Details were blurred. At length the two men nodded, like artisans who have finished a work to their satisfaction.

"Explain, please," she said. "You were going too fast."

Thomas leaned forward and told her what they had devised.

"Tell me again what Bertz said," Marda asked eagerly. "Robin is in good health in Istlakan and he will take me to him?"

Justin repeated yet again the story he had told when he'd returned from treating Captain Ferahim late the night before. Ulick wished he could make her smile like that, that he could at least have been the messenger if he could not be her rescuer, as Bertz would be.

"Tell me before the soldiers come. What am I to do?"

"You are to dig roots for me. These." Justin pulled a leaf

from his pouch. "Bertz will wait until the guard has relaxed his watch and snatch you before he can intervene. Then he will take you to Istlakan."

"Aren't the guards late?"

"They have other duties," Ulick said, "but. . . ." He was beginning to worry about that himself, just as he was worried about Dayan, who still sprawled on his bed across the room. They had kept their voices low and spoken Tarsean, but he could have overheard the eager tone of Marda's voice.

"We're a low priority. They'll come," Justin assured Marda. "Don't seem too eager."

"I'll see if I can find some food," Ulick said in a normal tone of voice as he stood. "The Barajians are poor hosts, but they must provide something for their guests to eat."

Dayan rolled over. "Get some for me too. I'm hungry." Ulick cursed the ambition that had led the brat to learn the languages of his enemies.

"Get it yourself. You have two legs."

Dayan glared at him, then stood. "Why not? It's less boring than staying here." He started for the door with Ulick right behind him worrying what he would say and to whom if he left him alone with the Barajians.

Dayan stopped short at the door. Captain Ferahim stood outside with a letter in his hand and a dozen men behind him. "Good," Dayan said, "You have word confirming my identity. I want—"

Ferahim cut him short. "Come with us." His gesture included all the room's occupants.

Ulick helped Marda to her feet. They followed Dayan and Justin from the room. Dayan was talking to the captain who did not seem to be paying him much heed. They were speaking Barajian. The captain escorted them to the main tower of the fortress where his quarters were, but once inside he led them down a spiral stair that seemed to worm itself into the rock. What had Dayan said about them? He seemed unconcerned. Ulick slowed, looking for some escape, and was shoved by the soldier behind him.

The stair ended at a heavy wooden door that stood ajar. The room beyond seemed cut from the mountain itself. Its floor was rough stone, save for some planks in the center;

the same stone formed all but one section of the walls. There the dressed stone had high narrow windows which let in feeble light. Ulick knew this was a prison from the smell even before his eyes adjusted and he saw the chains. Marda knew too; he could feel her shoulders tremble.

Dayan was arguing with the captain. Ulick heard Marda's name.

One of the guards put a torch in a bracket on the wall. Two of the guards shoved Ulick to where a mass of chains hung down in the center of the room. A stooped old man emerged from the shadows with a hammer and anvil. The captain pointed at Ulick and the guards jerked his leg into place as the old man pulled an iron pin from his leather apron and riveted the shackle on.

In the only jail Ulick had been in before the prisoners had been chained to the wall, but Ulick had guessed the reason for the strange arrangement even before the Captain explained it to Dayan in Suevarna.

"Some prisoners we want to keep, some we want to rid ourselves of quickly." The captain kicked the planks aside revealing a gaping hole in the center of the floor. Ulick stared down into blackness; no bottom was visible and a smell worse than a cesspit rose from the depths. "The chains ensure the prisoners stay," the captain continued, watching Dayan's face, "but if we release the weight above, it plummets and pulls anyone chained to it into the pit. They're gone beyond sight, let alone rescue, long before the fortress can fall to ruse or siege. For the price of a little ironwork," he pointed at the weighty ring that hung from the ceiling, "anyone the emperor desires can be disposed of."

"Clever," Dayan said tightly, "but these prisoners are not so important; a cell—"

The captain signaled to the guards. "But you may be, and they are witnesses."

Dayan went white as the guards pushed him to the chains. "You have the proof of my identity! You would not dare to treat a prince this way."

"You would not be the first prince, if prince you are—I have no confirmation—who has taken that drop. Higher blood than yours has spilled there."

"But the emperor, my uncle—" Dayan fought the guards who held him as he was shackled.

"Would be better off without mongrel kin."

"He will break you for this."

The captain glanced down at the letter he held. "I think not. I have my orders. The woman next."

"My wife—"

"She has done nothing!" Ulick and Dayan spoke together. "This is not necessary."

"But it is," said the captain, as Marda was pulled from Justin's protective arms and shackled. "The floor slopes. We would not want anyone to fall into the pit prematurely, as she might if unchained. Besides, two can pull another out where one would not be strong enough." The captain walked close to the pit and coughed from the fumes that rose from it. "I still have need of his remedies."

"And I need her to gather the herbs," Justin managed to sound angry rather than frightened. "I don't care what you do with either damned Sueve, but I can't both gather the herbs and brew your damn possets."

"Teach one of my men what to gather. You can bring them their food to assure yourself she's safe." The captain took one last look and shepherded Justin from the room.

The rest of his men followed, taking the torch. In the dim light Ulick sat against the wall and pulled Marda down beside him. She huddled into his shoulder, crying quietly. On the far side of the pit Dayan sank slowly to the floor staring up at the window slits.

Sunlight still glowed on the mountain tops, but the valley was dissolving into shadows as Bertz paced yet again between the stables and the caravansary gate. The gates would be closed for the night soon and it was increasingly unlikely that anyone would come out to gather herbs in the fading twilight.

Bertz considered his choices. He could wait another day to see if Marda emerged from the fortress to gather Justin's herbs. There could be a good explanation for a day's delay. Perhaps the captain's health was better. But then there would be no need for herbs and another day's wait would also be in vain. The officials would grow suspicious, especially if Bertz kept his horse saddled, supposedly impatient to be on with the journey to Tarsia. No, he would have to go. The problem was deciding which road to take. He could go north to try to intercept Walter as he had originally planned. He discarded that idea. The time was too short.

He knew where Marda was and he knew where Robin was. He couldn't bring Marda to her son; he would have to bring the boy to her and in some way ensure their safety. Perhaps it was a mercy of God that Naroc had refused to go when Bertz had urged him. Naroc traded in the Sueve lands; perhaps he or his fellow Eskedi could devise a way to get her safely back to Tarsia. Bertz must ride back to Istlakan and fetch the boy.

Naroc and his nephews were full of protests when he explained his plan to ride back alone, but subsided when he proved adamant in his refusal to involve them further in his scheme to free the boy. Naroc sank back on his pretended sickbed with a groan that caused the other travelers at the caravansary to look up from their evening meal. Alsen rushed to arrange the pillows under his uncle's head, while Dirac poured liquid from a bottle into a cup and helped Naroc to drink. Naroc grimaced as though the good wine was foul medicine and let Dirac ease him back on the bed. The other travelers' attention returned to their meals.

Naroc winked at Bertz. "You underestimate us."

Bertz persisted. "It would look too suspicious if I didn't go somewhere after leaving my horse saddled all day. Besides, if that post-rider who rode in this morning brought orders concerning the woman or my comrades, I could wait here days to no purpose." Days he didn't have to waste; he'd seen the rising gibbous moon from the gate, but he didn't tell the Eskedi that.

"Then let me ride with you," Dirac pleaded.

"No." Bertz intended to use his horse's uncanny powers to ride through the night. Dirac's mount could not keep pace. "I need someone to keep watch here."

"I can do that," Alsen cut in.

"Yes, but if anything happens and you need to send word, who then would carry it? It would look too suspicious if Naroc rose from his sickbed and galloped off. It would be suspicious, too, if you both abandoned him. The most useful thing you can do is remain here and find out what has happened to Marda, the boy's mother. But don't endanger yourselves. If the officials become suspicious of your tarrying, do what you told them you intended to do, ride on into the Sueve lands as if to trade. You might be able to tell my other comrades of the woman's and the boy's whereabouts and our plans."

"We will stay here," Naroc said firmly.

"Don't be foolhardy."

"Oh, I'm not." Naroc wriggled his toes under his blanket. "Has anyone suspected so far that I am faking being ill?"

Bertz admitted that no one apparently had.

Naroc grinned covertly. "You see?" His nephews traded glances and sat on the bench by his bed. Bertz suspected they'd heard this story many a time. "I studied under a master." Naroc continued. "My great-uncle Mashalec controlled the family for decades with his strategic illnesses. He was the richest trader in Istlakan. All the relatives wished to be his heir, and he knew it, had them all dancing to the tune he whistled. If they tired, he'd conveniently become ill. They'd all come running to his sickbed and he'd change his will to reward the most obedient. Our mother had my brother and me apprenticed to him in hopes that one of us would be the fortunate heir. We served him for fourteen years."

Naroc paused for effect and Bertz fed him the question he obviously expected. "Did it work? Were you the heir?"

"Of course not. He married a young wife three months before he died." Naroc grinned. "Left everything to her."

Bertz couldn't imagine such folly as leaving wealth to a woman. It wouldn't occur among the Stros. "Weren't you angry?"

"At first. But he'd taught me my trade very well. I made my own fortune."

"And your brother? Was he also so content?"

Naroc's nephews grinned at each other even before Naroc spoke. "He married the widow. Kept the money in the family."

Bertz could only shake his head.

Naroc clutched his belly as though in pain, and Alsen

rose to lean over him. After a few whispered words, Alsen sat on the edge of the bed and rummaged a set of tablets and a stylus from his pack on the floor, then wrote at Naroc's dictation. When he was finished writing and the tablets were properly tied and sealed, Naroc took it and handed it to Bertz.

"Here's your excuse to return to Istlakan. May the Gods ride with you and prosper your cause."

More false gods! Will good wishes in their names help or hinder me? I am already bound to demons. Bertz reassured himself that their intentions were good and God himself knew that the cause was pure. The boy must be saved. Even demons' help could be used in such a cause. He thanked Naroc and went out to mount his waiting horse and ride under the caravansary gate onto a road illuminated by the waxing moon.

Payne stood guard outside Tiramet's empty rooms and tried not to think of where she was and why. He felt as useless as a statue frozen in place. Tiramet had been escorted past him hours ago in the early evening shadows by Zakar's smug servant. Her shoulders had been slumped under her shawl and her jaw set as she had passed him.

Unwilled pictures formed in his mind of Zakar's hands on her body, Zakar's smile. His hands tightened on his spear. He had had a mad impulse as the servant had shoved her along the passage to put that spear through his gut. That would wipe the smirk off the oily little man's face.

It wouldn't help Tiramet, though. Nor would it relieve his own guilt. She was in Zakar's power because she had helped him. Every degradation she endured—Payne tried not to picture how Zakar might be using her—was his fault.

He could no longer bear the guilt, the unwanted images his conscience presented. Or, he asked himself, his jealousy? It had to end. Tomorrow he would give the signal to Reynard, tomorrow night they would escape. Walter could find them as easily on the road as in the palace. And she would be free.

If only she would return so he could tell her his decision. Less than an hour remained. Last night she had not returned during his watch and he had spent the day with worry about her ever-present in his mind.

The door at the end of the corridor opened. Payne fought to remain impassive as Tiramet walked swiftly down the passage with Minvar scurrying a pace behind. Zakar's servant opened the door to Tiramet's chamber and would have accompanied her inside, but she dismissed him with a few short words and closed the door. Minvar left, but paused midway down the corridor to look back at the closed door and its guards, then shuffled to the far door. Its latch clicked after him.

In the lengthening silence, Payne strained to hear sound beyond Tiramet's door. She had carried herself so tensely when she passed that he searched for any excuse to open the door he guarded. He had found none when a crash, followed by another, echoed beyond the door.

The other guard beat him to the latch and threw the door open. Payne gaped over his shoulder. The room beyond was lit only by moonlight through the lattices, and as his eyes adjusted, Payne could see Tiramet standing alone by the table. She answered the other guard's questions sharply, pointing to the oil lamp that lay spilled on the floor and the overturned stool under the lamp bracket. She picked up the broken lamp and shoved the pieces into the other guard's hands. He ducked a bow and left.

She hadn't moved as if she were injured, Payne reassured himself, and there had been two crashes, not one, as there would have been if she had fallen while adjusting the wick. She must have thrown the lamp and kicked the stool over. It was a good ruse to send the other guard away so they could speak. A good way to relieve her anger and frustration as well.

"Clean it up." She shoved a towel from the table into his hands. "He'll be back. We haven't time to waste. Is there news?"

Payne knelt to mop up the spilled oil. "I'll give the signal tomorrow."

Her eyes widened with hope. Even in the moonlight he could tell they were blue. Then she frowned. "Is that wise? Are all the arrangements made?"

"There is no time to wait. The moon waxes with every night that passes."

"But your leader, has he come? How—?" She broke off as the other guard returned, carrying a lamp more ornate than the one she had given him. The man had stolen one from an empty chamber rather than fetching one from storage. Payne cursed his ingenuity.

At her order, the other guard hung it from the bracket and lit it. He hovered, waiting, as Payne finished cleaning the floor. They bowed and returned to their posts. Payne watched the moonlight pattern the corridor as it fell through the lattices. For a moment she had almost smiled.

29

Twenty-eighth Day

Bird songs heralded the first dim light of morning. Ulick shifted carefully, trying not to wake Marda, who slept with her head on his shoulder. He turned his head. Dayan still sat on the other side of the room, his hands between his raised knees, staring up at the windows. Ulick wondered if he had moved at all since the guards had left. His bowl of stew sat untouched where Justin had left it the afternoon before.

Marda shifted and the chain bound to her ankle rattled.

Dayan turned his head and met Ulick's eyes. "Could we jump the man who comes to release the weight?"

"No."

"Why not? I would help."

"It doesn't release from here. Look up. There is a flange that goes through a slit in the ceiling. Whatever holds it must be in the room above. There was no other door on the stair that led here. Who knows where the access to that room is? We will not even have the warning of feet on the stairs—our fates are at the whim of Heaven."

Dayan studied the ironwork. "Or the captain. I'm sorry. I tried to convince him, ask her brother what I said."

276

Ulick just looked at him.

"I know, too little, too late. I should have kept my mouth shut with the patrol."

"Yes."

"I didn't know they would take it that way. I thought it would hurry them."

"It didn't."

Dayan said nothing and looked back at the windows. The sky was blue through the slits. Dayan said finally, "I know nothing."

Ulick let that piece of adolescent self-abnegation pass without comment.

Dayan swallowed. "I'm sorry. You and your wife are paying the price for my folly."

"Her son as well."

"I know. I can't fix it. Tell me what I can do. I will do as you ask. You are wise in the way of the outlanders. Tell me what I should do."

"Why should I help you?"

Dayan started to speak, then stopped himself. "No reason at all, I don't deserve it."

"Everything you say is *I*."

Ulick looked down at Marda in the lengthening silence and pulled her cloak up where it had slipped from her shoulder. She murmured something in her sleep. *Let her sleep and not wake to this reality.*

On the far side of the room Dayan spoke again. "They will use me against my mother. Even if we escape this, everything I do, every misstep I make, will be held against her. My ignorance will be a whip to beat her. She has helped you; for her sake, will you help me, Ulick Assaga Nu?"

He wouldn't be here to help; he would burn. Ulick said nothing.

The remnants of the kaiyun's cortege arrived at the gates of a Barajian country villa. If the directions the people in the village had given were correct, this was the home of Rakir, brother of the previous governor of Lakandar.

A porter emerged to greet them, looking askance at the

bedraggled group. Thomas, bristling at the contempt in the man's eyes, leaned down to address him.

"Tell Lord Rakir that the kaiyun Chrysogon is in need of aid and shelter." Since they had crossed into Lakandar the kaiyun, as a noble Barajian woman, had had to fall into habits she'd long neglected. One was not speaking to men below a certain rank.

The porter turned to stare at the kaiyun, who gave him a look of frosty hauteur. The man jerked a bow and backed through the gate.

Within minutes a small army of people, led by a man hastily pulling on a deep-blue silk robe replete with insignia, spilled through the gate. In this costly garment he fell to his knees in the dust and knocked his forehead on the ground, as did the servitors who followed him.

A very noble Barajian woman.

"Please, Lord Rakir," the kaiyun said, "there is no time for formality. My life and my brother's are in danger."

The Barajian noble scrambled to his feet. He was a portly man in his mid fifties. He gave swift orders and the ragtag group was escorted into a room that overlooked sumptuous gardens whose fountains sang in the early morning sun. They were an outrageous luxury in a land so devoid of water that canals were necessary to irrigate the crops. The room itself was a medley of brightly colored tiles, scant furnishings, and brocade hangings that partially hid the whitewashed walls.

Lord Rakir bowed again. "You honor my house." He escorted the kaiyun to the seat of honor on the dais. "Food is being brought. Your escort will be attended to immediately." He didn't add "elsewhere," but that was implicit in his gestures and his unwillingness to ask the obvious questions in their presence.

"These men were appointed by Ketai Khan," the kaiyun said firmly. "They saved my life."

Rakir looked at the five Huntsmen with more respect.

"They are the ones who discovered the governor's conspiracy. Enandor Thomas speaks excellent Barajian. He can tell you what they know."

Rakir's eyes had flickered at the mention of the governor. Now he reluctantly made seats for the Huntsmen on the floor before the dais, before seating himself there nearest the kaiyun.

No one said anything as the servants brought low tables and trays of food and wine. When they had gone, Rakir asked, "Resplendent highness, will you tell me of this conspiracy?"

The kaiyun and Thomas told him what they knew.

"You came by the Agandar Pass? The governor doesn't know you are in Lakandar?" She nodded. "It may be safest if you stay hidden until the emperor has been warned."

"No! I cannot hide and do nothing."

"Her highness had thought to confront the governor, remove him, but she needs backers. People willing to show whose side they're on."

Rakir smiled as he sipped his wine. "Ofarim has made enemies. He saves the best appointments for Lakandari like this Ferahim who has proved a traitor. I can think of fifty nobles who would enjoy witnessing his fall."

"But can they be summoned quickly?" Thomas asked.

"Not all immediately. But I can think of ten nobles who could raise their men to add to the kaiyun's entourage between here and the city and at least twenty who dwell in Istlakan."

"Time is important. We must catch the governor off guard and send immediately to warn my brother."

"I will send messengers immediately, but it is more than a two-day ride to Valadiza. Wait while I talk to my secretary." Rakir pushed himself to his feet and left.

Thomas translated the conversation for the other Huntsmen. He had barely finished when Rakir reappeared.

"My men will be ready within the hour," Rakir said, as he bowed and took his seat. "The messengers are being sent. We should reach Istlakan before midnight. I will confer with nobles in the city and all should be ready to confront Ofarim tomorrow."

"Is that safe?" Thomas asked.

"He does not expect her highness. He will have nothing planned. If she does not seem to suspect him, he will be off guard. Besides, it will give me time to rally support."

"So, I should go to the palace as though I suspected nothing."

"It will get our men within the gates in case Ofarim tries to resist." A movement in the doorway caught Rakir's eye. "Ah, highness, here is my wife. Perhaps when you have eaten, you will wish a bath and clean clothes."

The bell had rung, the shuffle of feet outside the door had signaled the new guards coming on watch. She had only to wait for the sun to fade. Tiramet tightened the cord on the small bundle of belongings she had finished packing when she returned from Zakar's chamber. He had insisted on coaching her upon what she was to say to the governor and had questioned her at length about what she knew about the governor's message from the north. She had managed to evade his questions. Soon it would be over, and she would be on her way to freedom. Soon she would see Edralen. She wondered what he would be like. Would he understand what she had done and why? It didn't matter what he thought of her. They would be free. Still, she was afraid to hope; too much could go wrong.

The last pink sunlight glittered on the gilded panels by the east windows when she heard the scuffle outside her door. She ran to open it. Payne dragged his unconscious fellow guard inside. She handed him the cord she had prepared and knelt to tie the guard's feet as Payne gagged him and bound his hands. Payne dragged him into the shadows behind the door as she opened the panel that led to the lower passage.

"Quick!" She grabbed her belongings.

"And I thought the door to your bedchamber was on the other side of the alcove. Do you prefer to do it in the dark?" Zakar had eased open the outer door. Behind him stood russet-clad guards.

She said nothing as Zakar entered and made a show of peering down the spiral stair. "Or were you leaving us?" Two of the guards had seized Payne and hauled him to his feet. Another two untied the unconscious guard and carried him out. The others remained outside the small room in the corridor. Zakar circled her. "I'm not sure I approve of your traveling clothes." He ran his hand from her breast to her hip. "Your others are much more exotic."

Payne stirred between his guards and Zakar looked him

up and down. "You really have bad taste, my dear, to let this barbarian seduce you into helping him. I thought you had more care for your brother than that."

"Why do you think I was helping *him*? I was trying to escape *you*."

"Think of a better story for the governor when he comes. I'm not so easily fooled. I wondered why you so suddenly changed your mind, why you were in my rooms. And soon enough, something was missing. Would I find the Nolsic coin on him if I had him searched?" Zakar waited for an answer, watching her expression. Unsatisfied with her silence, he goaded, "Or does his fellow slave have it? Or your brother? They're so chummy."

Her fists clenched at her sides.

Zakar smiled. "You'd be surprised how much you can learn when you have enough gold to offer. The guards talk." He took a step closer. "They know who goes in and out your door."

"I questioned him for the governor."

"But did you tell the governor all your activities? I'm sure he will be dismayed at their extent."

The door at the end of the corridor opened and more russet-clad guardsmen emerged. Zakar put his hand on her arm. "There he is now. Shall we tell him how you have betrayed him?"

There were only the two guards who held Payne within the room and they had been avidly following the conversation. Tiramet turned toward Zakar as if she would plead with him. Instead she swung her hand to slap him in the face. He easily deflected her blow as the guards stepped forward. She pulled Zakar's ornamental dagger from his sash and stepped back, breaking his grip on her arm. Payne took advantage of the guards' inattention to bash one guard's head against the wall, then slam the door and lock it. The other guard jumped him and they wrestled on the floor, their bodies barring the door.

"Saving yourself from a fate worse than death?" Zakar sneered coming at her. "It's a little late for that."

She kicked the stool and he stumbled over it, falling to his knees. She stepped behind him, grabbed him by the hair, and slowly and lovingly slit his throat. She loosened her grip, and let the body fall.

Payne had finished the other guard and was pushing the table against the door. It sounded as though the guards outside had improvised a battering ram. She picked up her bundle and turned to run for the passage door, then froze. The door that led to her bedchamber was open and guardsmen were spilling out. Resistance would be useless against these numbers. Payne surrendered his weapons and Tiramet dropped Zakar's dagger in the blood beside his crumpled body.

The officer in charge called up the spiral stair and the governor emerged. He surveyed the room as the lamp was lit. He paused beside Zakar's body. "He told me not to trust you." He kicked the body onto its back. "I should have listened."

Tiramet saw one hope. She flung herself on her knees before him. "No, he was the one you could not trust."

The governor turned from pondering Zakar's body and sat on the bench. "You killed him and tried to escape, and yet he is the one I should not trust? Incredible."

"I was escaping from him, not you!"

"Why? He was my servant."

"He didn't think so. To him you were a tool to be used." The governor frowned. Tiramet took heart. "He wanted me to aid him in deceiving you, but I refused. I could not betray you so I tried to run."

"And him?" the governor jerked his head toward Payne. "I am told he is your lover. That does not fit with your supposed loyalty to me."

Tiramet bowed her head as if in shame. "I am a woman and weak. He is handsome, and as I discovered when I questioned him for you, kind. I admit he is my lover. I have been five years alone." If the governor had not been afraid of her strange eyes she would have raised them tear-filled and pleading; instead, she let her voice tremble. "Zakar found out. He said he would have him killed if I did not do everything he wanted. I would not lie to you. We had no alternative but escape."

"So you care about this man?" She nodded. "More than your brother?"

That was the weak point of her story; she had hoped he would not see it. "I trusted your justice, Excellency. That you would not punish the innocent before I could find a way to inform you of Zakar's treachery."

The governor tugged at his beard as he looked from her to Payne. "Take him to a cell while I decide what to do with him." The guards hustled Payne from the room and shut the door on the group in the corridor. "Now tell me of Zakar's treachery."

"He insisted that I tell you things that were not true." Feet shuffled behind her as the guards ascended the stair. "He would have me feed you lies."

"She's lying now," Minvar said behind her.

She turned. Minvar knelt beside his master's body. His eyes blazed with hatred. "Ask her why she offered herself to him. Ask her how she eluded her guards to get to his chamber to thieve."

"Eluded her guards? I did not know of that." The Governor leaned forward.

"There's a lot you don't know," Minvar sneered. "You should lurk in these passageways as I have these last few days when she was absent. You would be surprised at what you can hear, at where you can go."

"Hear?" The governor rose from the bench as though stung. He gestured to the officer of the waiting guard. "You, take as many men as you need and search these passages. See where they go and what you find in them."

Tiramet tried to hide her fear. The boys must already be in the passage. The governor turned back to her. "As for you, I still need you to test the kaiyun's son. I don't think you will mislead me, now that I have two hostages for your good behavior. I can kill your lover before your eyes and still have a threat to hold over you." He signaled to the remaining guards. "Take her to the room prepared for her."

Reynard waited outside the dining hall door for Ivreim to join him with Robin. The officers and some of the older men sat in the shadows of the western loggia enjoying their beer, and some of the youths were practicing with their weapons in the courtyard while there was still light. Enough people were moving about that the three of them could cross to the north loggia without being conspicuous. Everything was perfect for their move, but Ivreim was late.

Someone yelped in the courtyard, and Reynard turned to see one of the youths who shared his dormitory down on the ground, while his former opponent picked his sword from the ground some feet away.

"Serves him right. He always thinks he's better than anyone else."

The words echoed his own thoughts. Reynard turned to smile at Ivreim. His smile froze. "Where's Robin?"

"I changed my mind. Take this." Ivreim caught his hand and pressed something into it. Reynard looked down and saw the Nolsic coin.

"But you said—"

"Don't you sense they're watching us? I've known since afternoon."

"You're imagining things. Get the boy."

"I've lived with this for five years. I know when something's off."

"You won't even try?"

"No."

"At least bring the boy."

"I won't let you endanger him. I tell you, wait for another day. It's better to stay alive."

"Coward!" Maybe that would provoke him to action.

Ivreim stared at him coldly. "Perhaps, but I've lived under sentence of death for five years. I count my life precious. If you persist in this folly, at least don't implicate me or the boy. Give me enough time that I don't seem your accomplice." He turned and walked toward the dormitories.

Reynard eyed the waxing moon, pale in the darkening sky. Sentence of death? He'd lived with one longer than Ivreim had. In two nights it would be executed. He had to act; he couldn't wait passively.

He could think of no excuse to fetch Robin, no way to quickly convince the boy to trust him. He would have to escape with Payne, then find Walter. Walter would think of some way to bring mother and child together.

The shadows were deepening. Reynard pushed himself away from the wall and sauntered across the courtyard. No one seemed to pay heed. He reached the north loggia and opened the squad leader's door. Still, no one seemed to notice anything amiss. Reynard shut the door and barred it and the shutters. Ivreim was a slave to his fears. Reynard put the table under the grate and stood on it to tug loose the grate. He judged the small opening; he'd wriggled through worse.

He thought he heard footsteps outside and pulled himself up to the opening. His shoulders were through and his feet sought purchase on the wall beneath when someone rattled the door. The sound encouraged his efforts. Soon he was lying on the floor of the passage. He listened, but heard no further sounds of anyone trying to enter. He rose to his feet. The passage ahead was dark, with only dim patches of light to mark the other grates. Payne said it was level and straight. Reynard stepped out quickly, balancing himself with his hands against the walls.

Darkness closed in when he passed the last grate. He slowed automatically and cursed his instincts. *Don't slow down when you can still touch wall.* He sped up—then one hand and the other felt no wall. Payne had said turn right. His hands found the wall again and he edged forward. The next turn was to the left.

The passage seemed to go on for eternity although only minutes had passed. When one hand found emptiness, it was the right, not the left. He turned and felt the walls ahead and to the left. He must have missed the turn. He heard voices and froze, then realized they were from a grate in the passage ahead, not from the passage behind him. He took a long breath to still his nerves and turned back the way he'd come. His hand scraped a short metal stake driven into the wall. He licked the blood away as he inched back down the passage feeling for the turn he'd missed. Shouldn't Payne and the woman who was to guide them be here already?

He found the turn and hurried along that passage. He heard nothing through the small lattice near the door at its end and eased the door open. No one was in the room beyond. His eye appraised the hangings and the furnishings as he crossed it. Plenty of fine pickings here. This was definitely not the servants' quarters.

Where was Payne? He'd said he'd meet him where the

passage ended, that they'd come from another passage. Reynard stuck his head out the door. There was no one in sight, so he started down the corridor. He was trying a likely door when someone shouted and he could hear running feet. He ran back to the room he had come from and into the passage. He listened at the lattice. Someone was shouting orders and he could hear the shuffle of feet. He was wondering if he could wait them out and worrying about Payne when a thump under the lattice made up his mind for him. If they were searching for hidden passages, he dared not stay. He hurried up the passage. Damn! He could hear scraping noises to the right from the barracks and see the flicker of torchlight on the far wall. He turned left, almost running. He hoped there would be a loose grate along that passage. What if there wasn't? He'd be trapped. Beaten. Maybe worse.

He remembered the spike almost too late. He sidestepped and scraped his temple on another, higher one that was inches from his eye. Why two? To climb? He reached up. There was another higher. Would the men chasing him think to look up or blindly follow the other passage? To follow the other passage was more likely. The spikes were short, inconspicuous, but they must lead somewhere. The crash of splintering wood from the side passage prodded Reynard. He began to climb.

30

Twenty-ninth Day

Even after battling the governor's objections about the protocol of honoring the Hunt by lodging them in the apartments adjoining the kaiyun's own, settling five men in a suite of rooms meant for one man and his servants was a noisy undertaking. One that made it hard to think. Walter left Thomas and Veran, the young official the kaiyun had assigned to aid the Hunt, to direct the servants and escaped onto the balcony.

The palace gardens lay below him, colorless in the moonlight, with the river beyond. The river lay to the east of the city. That gave him his bearings. Walter faced north. He must locate his other men. He flinched away from contacting Hamon. Hamon could do nothing, he rationalized, then he acknowledged his cowardice. He did not want to touch that pain.

He sent his thoughts to Justin. He was somewhere northeast. Ulick and he must be together, for Walter sensed him in the same direction. Were they still on the road from the Silasar Pass? Walter wished he could judge distance as well as direction.

Bertz? Bertz was east. *Why?* Walter thought, looking at the fields beyond the river. At least he no longer felt pain from Bertz; his injuries must have healed.

Payne was northwest, possibly in the city, if not the palace itself. Reynard? Reynard was southeast and up, as was the coin he had sent to mark Robin. Walter looked up at the flat roofs of the palace. He was on the top story. How could Reynard be above? He gave a summoning call and waited.

Soon he heard scrambling noises overhead and Reynard hung by his hands from the roof. Walter helped him swing himself onto the balcony. The boy was wearing a blue version of the uniform worn by the palace guard and was covered with dirt.

Reynard pushed his hair out of his face. "Thank the Gods you're here."

"Have you found Robin?"

"Yes. He's in the barracks, in the trefoil squad of boys."

"The barracks? A boy of eight?"

"Yeah." Reynard explained what he knew of the governor's corps of red-haired males. "The governor bought him from the slave-dealer who brought him from the Sueve lands. Kept us as well after the ambush."

"Us?"

"Me and Payne. Bertz got away, though he's been in contact with Payne."

"Ambush? Tell me."

Reynard told about Hamon's negotiations and how he had been set up. "So they took Hamon to prison for slave-stealing and brought us here. Payne knows more. We were supposed to escape tonight to go and find you, but Payne never showed."

Walter had sensed no physical pain when he had mentally touched Payne earlier. Whatever had delayed Payne must not be urgent. His priority was Robin. He reentered the main room of the suite to talk to Thomas and Veran and soon the three were following Reynard's directions to the barracks.

"It seems a lot longer in the passageways," Reynard said, as Veran high-handedly commanded the blue-clad officers.

"Passages?"

Reynard described his journey. "And Payne says there's even more."

One of the blue-clad officers returned, leading an obviously sleepy redheaded boy.

Walter knelt to his eye level. "Are you Robin Peterson?"

The boy nodded, wide-eyed and apprehensive.

"Your mother sent us to find you."

"Is she here?" His face brightened.

"Not yet. We'll take you to her."

The boy peppered them with questions as they returned to the suite and got him settled for the night.

Now he must locate Payne. Walter summoned Thomas and Veran. He had a better idea of Payne's location from the changes he had sensed in his direction as they had walked to the barracks. Soon they were outside a row of cells and Veran was arguing with the turnkey. Veran prevailed.

Payne jumped up as they entered. "Are Robin and Reynard all right? They could be—"

"They're fine. The boy's probably asleep by now, upstairs, in the rooms provided us."

"You can't trust the governor."

"We don't. But why do you say so?"

Payne ignored the question. "You've got to find Tiramet."

"Who?" Payne started to push past him. Walter stopped him. "Sit and explain. What do you know about the governor?"

Payne subsided onto the cot. "Bertz was to ride north and warn you. Didn't he find you? The governor is part of a plot to murder the emperor."

"We know that."

"At the full moon tomorrow night."

"How do you know?"

"Tiramet overheard them—the governor and Zakar—discussing the details. She could tell you, but I don't know what the governor did with her."

"Why?"

"Zakar caught us trying to escape. She killed him, but the governor came with more guards. When the guards brought me here, she was trying to convince the governor that we were merely lovers trying to escape from Zakar. But I don't know if he believed her."

Walter picked the essential point out of this welter of surprising information. "She knows the details of the plot to kill the emperor?"

"Yes."

"Then we must find her." Walter turned to Veran, whose face showed that his Tarsean was good enough to have followed the conversation. "You know the palace. Find this woman."

Payne gave a quick description and Veran left with Thomas. Walter turned to Payne. "Now, tell me from the beginning everything that has happened to you—who is Tiramet, and what was Bertz's part in this?"

Walter had sorted out the answers to his questions from Payne's complicated narrative when Thomas and Veran returned to report that Tiramet was not to be found.

"Someone must know something." Walter rose and signaled Payne to follow. "Let's see if the kaiyun can offer any help. She needs to hear what Payne has told us."

Chrysogon could see Robin's mother in him, in his grey eyes and in the way he held himself with staunch pride. Just now he sucked nervously on his lower lip, but he took in everything about her chamber in furtive, swift glances that always returned to her face.

"Are you hungry?" she asked in Tarsean.

His eyes widened and he started to speak, stopped himself, then, hunching his shoulders, answered quickly in Barajian, "*Vey ic ser*"—"I don't understand."

Somewhere he had learned to be frightened. She repeated the question in Barajian, and he answered carefully in that tongue. He had grasped the language quickly, as children did.

She offered a tray of candied fruit—an unfamiliar delicacy. He hesitated, studied the selection, chose one, and nibbled at it tentatively.

"You've traveled a long way," she said. "I know you must miss your mother. We will get you to her as soon as we can." Even as she made the promise, she wondered if she lied. Sir Walter said that the men he had sent with

Marda had not contacted him, but seemed to be northeast, still on the road. Was Dayan with them? Was he safe? What if he had gone back? Would Ketai kill him?

Robin was looking at her strangely. Did her fear show on her face? She asked in Tarsean. "Do you like it here?"

He shrugged and answered in that tongue, "Mostly. Sometimes the other boys—" He broke off and put his hands over his mouth.

"It's all right, Robin. Has someone told you not to speak Tarsean?"

He nodded slowly.

"We get punished," he whispered in Barajian.

Had they set traps for him? His reaction indicated it. She entered another item in the list of the governor's crimes.

"You won't have to go back."

"Am I going home?" he asked.

"Perhaps. If you and your mother wish to. Perhaps you will stay here with me."

"The houses are strange here."

"Are they?"

She allowed him to ramble. He was an intelligent boy; he had noticed a great deal and had apparently reasoned out what he saw.

Tita Maimai swept into the room, eyed Robin, and said, "Tertiiar Veran and those Tarseans want to see you."

Sir Walter's glance rested briefly on Robin, then slid away. Was there bad news about Marda, or was that due to some older hurt? She had one of the maids return the boy to Sir Walter's chambers.

"What has happened?" she asked.

"I've talked to another of my men," Walter said. "Payne has been in the palace and has learned a great deal of the plot, but not all."

"Tell me."

"The assassination is to be tomorrow night."

Her heart caught. Was there time to warn her brother? "How?"

"We don't know. Payne knew a little, but not enough." Walter summarized what Payne had told him.

"How does he know?"

"He had suborned the governor's fortune teller—an Es-

kedi woman. She learned the details and they had planned
to escape with Robin last night and ride to warn us."

"We must talk to this Eskedi woman—if she is alive."

"She must be. There was no reason to keep Payne alive
if she's dead."

"Then where is she?"

"We don't know. Veran found her old rooms, but she
was not there. She is not in a cell or anywhere else Veran
thought of."

"A woman fortune teller?" She turned to Veran. "No one
knew her whereabouts in the women's quarters?"

Veran looked shocked. "I would not have presumed—
the governor's wife would never answer my questions
about such private matters. And why would he send a prisoner there?"

To keep anyone from finding her.

"Tita Maimai." Chrysogon switched to Barajian. "Go to
the women's quarters. Find out where the governor keeps
his Eskedi fortune teller. Tell them you've heard she's very
good and that you want your niece's fortune told."

"An Eskedi, tell my niece's fortune?"

"She's been telling the governor's. I'm sure she's excellent. Go quickly." She turned to Walter. "Tell me what you
know of this woman."

"Payne seems fairly besotted," Walter was finishing,
when Tita Maimai escorted the woman into the room. The
fortune teller looked from person to person as she walked
forward, then stopped abruptly, her gaze locked on Walter.
Tita Maimai pushed her and the woman crossed the room
to kneel before Chrysogon's chair.

"You wished a fortune told?" she asked, and looked up.

"Besotted" ought to have warned her that the woman was
beautiful, but Chrysogon still was surprised by the woman's
looks and bearing. Those eyes would lead many a man
astray.

"We have been told you know the details of a plot to
assassinate the emperor, my brother. Is that true?"

The woman gave a slight nod as though a suspicion had
been confirmed. "Who told you, Highness?"

"Payne is not here, but he is safe, Tiramet. Tell us what

you know. He said you overheard the governor and another plotting."

"Zakar. Yes, I heard them. They said the assassination was to be in the Imperial Garden as the emperor returns from the Full Moon ceremony. The captain of the guard had been suborned."

"The captain of the guard? The officer in charge for that night, or the officer of the whole guard?"

"Captain of the guard was all they said."

"Did they mention any names?"

"No. Zakar said, as he usually did, 'Our friends.' "

"So you know nothing more?" Walter asked.

"I might, but I want two things in return."

"I have already sent to the barracks to free your brother," Chrysogon said. "What else do you want? Your fortune returned?"

"That would only be just, since my father was innocent; but no, I ask for justice for the Eskedi. They have aided your men." She looked at Walter, then back to Chrysogon. "And been more loyal to the Empire than the Lakandari and many Barajians. Yet they are treated like dirt."

"As far as it lies in my power, I will see that they are treated justly."

Tiramet weighed the promise, then said, "That is as much as you could honestly say. Zakar mentioned no names when he spoke of the assassination, but he mentioned names before." She listed those she had heard, giving as much context as she remembered, then said, "He corresponded with these 'friends' as well, so you may be able to confirm names from that. I doubt the governor had time to destroy Zakar's papers."

"Which would be where?" Thomas asked. A short conversation elicited the location of Zakar's rooms and which of the kaiyun's supporters had been lodged there. Veran was sent to make sure the papers were safe and taken to his uncle Rakir.

"We will need your testimony as well when these men are tried in Valadiza," Chrysogon said.

"No."

"Don't you want them punished?"

"All I want is to take my brother and go where no one has ever heard of Lakandar or Barajia!"

"Does your brother feel the same?"

Tiramet was silent.

"In Valadiza the case against your father could be reopened, the men who falsely accused him punished. Don't you want that?"

"He would be no less dead."

A shrill male voice in the next room made Tiramet jump to her feet. "Highness, I—"

"Take her to the other room, Maimai. Quickly."

Chrysogon settled into the great high-backed chair and composed herself. Sir Walter and Thomas moved to flank her chair.

The governor's color was high as he performed the necessary obeisances. Chrysogon wondered if he had looked this impassioned before his military victories. "Your excellency? To what do I owe the pleasure?" she asked.

He had swallowed considerable bile, she noticed, as he knelt before her. She did not permit him to stand.

"Your highness, why have you seen fit to countermand my orders?"

"Which orders?"

"You have freed a prisoner who has acted against the state, and have commandeered two members of my personal guard."

Ah, he didn't yet know she had Tiramet.

"Your personal guard includes an eight-year-old boy?"

"Soldiers are more loyal if they are raised to serve."

Aslut used to tell Dayan that.

"I promised to return this one to his mother."

"If you insist, kaiyun, but the other boy—"

"Is no longer your concern either."

The governor did not like that; he struggled with the urge to protest.

"A great deal will cease to concern you in the near future, excellency," she said.

"I don't understand, Your Highness."

"My train was attacked on the way here, and my carriage sabotaged on another occasion."

The governor scowled. "I shall root out the perpetrators at once, Your Highness."

"There is no need. We are perfectly well aware who is to blame. You see Lord Wiraz was too quick to try to run away. That is not an opportunity he will have again, excellency. Before his untimely demise the bodyguard Ketai Khan so kindly sent with me questioned him." She gestured to the Tarseans on either side of her.

"He told us," Thomas said in Barajian, "that he had been sent to supervise the attempts to kill the kaiyun and he named the person who had given him his orders, excellency."

The governor's face was stony.

"I can guess why you wished me dead, Ofarim. You wanted to be sure that I could not act as guardian to His Resplendent Majesty's son after you and your friends have my brother murdered."

"Your brother? That was not my doing. Zakar gave the orders! I told Ferahim to protect your party at the fortress."

"Ofarim! Not all the attackers died immediately; we know that they were sent *from* the fortress."

"Zakar told me nothing of a plot against His Majesty! He said that an unsuccessful attack on you would force the Emperor to start a campaign against the Sueve! That was all I was told. You know I have been a loyal soldier. I owe all I am to the Resplendent One."

"Nicely spoken. I would be very touched if I did not have a witness who says otherwise." Chrysogon clapped her hands. "Tita Maimai, please bring our guest to see the governor."

Tiramet stood like a stone in the doorway, staring at the governor.

"You see, governor, she has told us all she has heard. A messenger will be dispatched at once and should foil your murderous plot. You will be beheaded as befits a traitor!"

The governor stared at Tiramet, then he turned back to the kaiyun.

"I doubt that, your highness."

"We have her brother and her lover safe."

"Do you?" He should have been defeated, but he looked

as if he held victory in his palm. What was wrong? "No matter." He rose to his feet. Sir Walter, and Thomas bristled, ready to protect her. He thrust his hand into his sash and drew something distressingly familiar from it.

He held it before her eyes and swung it a little.

Dayan's medallion.

"I don't think you wish to act except as I tell you, your highness."

"Where did you get that?"

The governor dropped the amulet into her lap.

"You will wish to keep it. If you don't follow my orders precisely, it will be a remembrance of the departed." He smiled. "We shall have a great deal to discuss following the welcoming banquet. I will return in an hour to escort you."

As the door closed behind him, Thomas caught her shoulders as she sank back in her chair.

Walter caught Veran's eye and nodded at the door. The young official spoke to the man next to him at the banquet table, then rose and left the hall. Walter waited a few minutes before joining him and calling Michel to follow.

The governor found them small fish, now that he had the kaiyun to do his bidding. He seemed eager to send them on their way with Robin. Walter judged it wise not to call attention to his comings and goings; he waited till the next course was served and the entertainers claimed the diners' attention.

"You could have waited till I finished the *covas*," Michel grumbled, when he joined them in the corridor.

Walter ignored him and told Veran what he wished to do. Veran seemed to have lost his capacity to be surprised. He made the necessary arrangements and they were soon outside the palace on their way to the prison.

Payne pushed himself away from the wall he had been lounging against and crossed the street to meet them. "There's been no suspicious activity. No obvious messengers or any officials."

"Good. Stay out here." Walter nodded at Veran to precede him inside. After a short argument with the warden they were escorted to the lower floor. As the door swung open Walter braced himself for what he would find.

"The warden says your man is over there." Veran pointed to the far corner of the room.

Hamon didn't stir as Walter stopped beside him. From the pain he had sensed, Walter judged that even momentary unconsciousness must be a blessing.

"It took you long enough to get here." Hamon half-opened his eyes.

"I'm sorry." Walter knew the words were inadequate.

"Are you?"

Trust Hamon to be offensive in such straits. "You'll be cared for now. We've a doctor waiting—"

"How do you know I need one?"

Walter said nothing.

Hamon made a sound that might be a laugh. "Oh, so you feel my pain. That accounts for your unaccustomed solicitude."

Walter turned to Veran to discuss arrangements and the official left to carry them out. Walter found Hamon staring at him when he turned back.

"You've a long face for someone who has brought mother and child together. Haven't you found the boy?"

"He's at the palace in Eleylin's care."

"And the woman, where is she?"

"I don't know," Walter finally said.

"You've lost her."

Walter said nothing.

"So you're giving me a night and day of tender care before we all burn."

"I sent her ahead with Justin and Ulick, but they aren't here yet."

"Is that all?"

"They may have been joined by Prince Dayan and we know he is a prisoner of the governor. We don't know where. Bertz may know more when I find him."

After a moment Hamon said, "You think you've failed. That you won't find her."

Walter nodded curtly.

Hamon stared at the ceiling. "That last day at Onsalm, Amloth told me he knew that he had failed—that the boy was dead, the task could not be fulfilled—and his heart was like an iron weight in his chest. Do you feel that?"

"No."

"Then the woman is still alive. You have only to find her."

"In time."

Whatever else they might have said was cut off as Veran returned with a litter and attendants. Walter waited till the painful transfer was over and the litter was on its way to the palace with Veran in charge before he started to rejoin Payne and Michel in the street outside.

A grey-robed man stopped him near the door to the prison chamber. In halting Tarsean he said, "Your man?" He pointed after the litter that carried Hamon.

Walter nodded.

"Perhaps, you speak to Olm. He tell more."

"Olm?"

"Olm. House of Pity. Know more."

Walter wondered if this were a waste of time, but he told Payne and Michel, and Michel soon discovered the location of the House of Pity. It seemed to lie in the same direction he sensed Bertz.

Michel inquired for Olm at the door and they were ushered inside. After only a few moments another grey-robed man emerged from the back of the building. He looked at the three men and slowly smiled.

"Would you be looking for a man named Bertz?"

"Yes. Can you send us to him?"

"I can take you to him. He is here. I have had a hard time keeping him from doing something foolish since he returned." He motioned for them to follow and led them to a small room off an inner courtyard.

Bertz rose as they entered. "Do you have the boy?"

"Yes."

Bertz sighed. "His mother is in Silasar Fortress."

Walter sat, weak with relief. "How do you know?"

"I talked with Justin. He was gathering herbs to treat the fortress commander's illness. They were taken into custody because some prince they were traveling with irritated the patrol."

"Prince Dayan?"

"That sounds like the name."

"Is he there too?"

"Justin said they had sent to the governor to decide what to do."

Walter nodded. That explained how the governor had the medallion. Had Dayan boasted about being the Child of Fire? If he had, it explained a lot. It also meant they might solve the kaiyun's problems as well as their own. "Are they still at Silasar?"

"I left men there who were to send word of any change. I have heard nothing."

Bertz had apparently been busy; he seemed to have a network of people helping him. Walter postponed his questions to ask a more vital one. "Where are the other horses?"

"The Eskedi are tending them in a pasture east of the river."

"Take us to them. Payne and Michel have a ride to start."

Bertz had answered some of Walter's questions by the time they arrived at the pasture. The four horses trotted to the fence. "Michel," Walter ordered, "take Hamon's horse. We won't waste time going back to the palace." While Bertz helped the Eskedi who had watched the horses to saddle Hamon's and Payne's horses, Walter took the kaiyun's letter from his robe and handed it to Payne. "See that this gets to the emperor. If he dies we will burn. Do whatever is necessary." Payne took the letter and stuck it in his jacket.

Bertz brought the horses and soon he and Walter watched the two men disappear on the road east.

"I want you to meet the rest of us at nightfall on the road to the Silasar Pass," Walter said. "Bring Reynard's horse. We have a hard ride of our own to make and I have arrangements that must be made first."

31

Thirtieth Day—Full Moon

"You don't understand the Barajians," Michel complained, as they stood across the square from the entrance to the Imperial Gardens. People were beginning to mill about in the darkening twilight, waiting for the gates to open. "You don't just charge in waving a letter. Everything has to have a pretty speech attached. You can't make one, so give me the letter."

"We should have taken it to the palace," Payne said, handing it to Michel.

"We don't know who we can trust. Now, change your clothes to be like mine. Different colors, of course. They'll get us into the gardens."

Payne changed his clothes to a robe and a hat like Michel wore. "I still say my uniform will lend more credence to the message."

"Change back once we're inside."

"Are you sure you know where to go?"

"My tutor was sickeningly nostalgic about his hometown. I heard his description a hundred times. The Moon Altar wouldn't have been moved, and the palace is in the same place it's always been. The emperor has made the same journey every month for a thousand years. The only difference is that now he takes petitions. We need to get into the gardens. Keep your mouth shut and follow me."

Once they were inside, Michel led them down a paved path to the east. "Stroll. Don't look so furtive."

"We're wasting time."

"No, we're going to the Moon Altar without drawing the wrong attention. See where the lanterns form a solid row ahead? That's the wall of the terrace where the altar stands. We won't be allowed up the steps but we can position ourselves where we can be the first to speak to the Emperor when he descends."

"What if they assassinate him on the terrace? We shouldn't wait."

"Too much light. I'd wait till he was in the gardens and there were more people around and a better chance to get away."

"And how many assassinations have you planned?" They stood in the shadows near the foot of the steps. Payne said, "I have no wish to burn," changed his clothes into the uniform of the Lakandar guard, and started up the stair. "Follow me and translate."

Michel hesitated, then did the same. They were challenged at the top of the steps. "We bear word for the emperor from his sister the kaiyun Chrysogon," Michel announced.

The guards looked dubious and sent one of their number for their officer. From the gilded decoration of his parade armor, the officer who came must be the captain of the guard himself, Michel judged. The officer looked them over, then waved them onto the terrace. "This way," he said, and led them to a group of guardsmen. The altar was in the other direction. "You bear a message from the kaiyun to her brother. Give it to me, I will deliver it."

"It is for his hands alone."

"He is absorbed in the ritual. Only those of highest rank may approach him."

"Honored one, our orders are to deliver it to him and him alone."

"In the circumstances, you should defer to one of higher rank."

"We follow the kaiyun's orders. Her rank is second only to the emperor's."

Beside him Payne had grown increasingly impatient with the incomprehensible talk. Now he interrupted in Tarsean. "Tell him the Emperor will be killed."

By the small flicker of his eyebrow Michel inferred that the captain had understood Payne's words, but he made no move to hurry. That confirmed Michel's suspicions that the captain's stalling was more than an exercise in protocol. Was he part of the plot? How could he extricate them from a false position? "My colleague grows impatient. He has not served long enough in Lakandar to understand polite ways. I apologize for his abruptness." Michel jabbed Payne and pointed to the stairs. "We must obey the kaiyun's orders. We will await the end of the ritual."

"The message," the Captain held out his hand.

"Is for the Emperor alone."

"I insist you give it to me."

"No, that is against our orders." Michel was bowing his way to the stair. Payne was slow to follow. "Move, you idiot, they're part of the plot," Michel muttered in quick Tarsean, as the captain gestured for the guards to surround them. Instead of running, Payne grabbed a sword from one of the guards and tried to cut his way toward the Altar.

Michel didn't stay to watch the inevitable conclusion. The honest idiot had just made his job much harder. He jumped the wall and ran until he found a shadowed arbor. He changed his clothes into Barajian robes and hat, wished he could change his blond hair as well, and blended into the crowd.

Walter had told Thomas to guard the kaiyun and to make sure that Hamon was tended to. They both knew that the kaiyun was safe for now. The governor would not let this most important pawn be injured.

But he hadn't seen her all day until now. She had received formal visits from every person in the city of sufficient rank to claim her attention. But now that the formal tide had ebbed, she was alone, looking weary and frightened in a beautifully decorated chamber. She offered him spiced wine and fruit and bade him sit.

"Will you know if Sir Walter succeeds in getting the boy to Marda?" she asked.

"I will know if he fails."

She studied his face. He thought she could read him as well as Walter did.

"Have you failed before?"

"The Hunt has once. I was not with them, or I would not be here now. The Ladies do not tolerate failure."

"How long have you—" She broke off, at a loss for a word for what he did.

"I was cursed, as you have surmised, nine hundred years ago. But I have only experienced eighteen months of that time. We only come awake when we are summoned."

"How terrible." She frowned. "You must feel so alien each time."

Did she feel alien, here in her homeland after twenty years among the Sueve?

"It is easier to think of myself as an agent of the La-dies—sent on tasks where and when they will. It makes the abrupt changes easier, and," he sipped the warm wine of Barajia, "I have learned to enjoy the variety."

She nodded. "Who is the man Sir Walter had sent from the prison?"

"Hamon. He is from Saroth."

Her eyes widened. Where had she heard of Hamon? From the poetry about the Hunt, or from history of the lands which traded with Barajia? Both, probably. Almost everyone had heard of Hamon.

"My physicians say he is horribly injured. His hands . . ."

"His body will heal, unless we fail."

Did she understand what he had not said, that if they failed what had been done to Hamon would pale beside what would be done?

"But Sir Walter knows Marda is in Silasar Fortress?"
And your son.

"Yes, but we have learned not to assume victory. Too many impediments may arise." He smiled ruefully. "This task, for instance, seemed so easy. We thought all we had to do was find the boy, give him to his mother, and return them home safely."

She drank her wine without speaking, then put the cup down carefully.

"Why are you one of the Wild Hunt?"

"What did I do? That is a long story, and shows me in a very poor light."

"Tell me!" Thomas was surprised at her vehemence.

He swirled his wine in the porcelain cup.

"You have deduced that I was an Enandor—one of the ruling council of Amaroc. In theory, any landed man could be elected, but in practice, most of the Enandrin were from a few families. I was not of that exalted number—my great grandfather had been a dealer in donkeys who had known how to invest the money he made. We had not squatted on our particular plot of land for nearly enough generations.

"I had earned my seat. Worked far harder for it than the men who despised me. I allowed myself to be nettled and I wanted more than anything to be acknowledged as their equal."

Chrysogon listened gravely. He saw no judgment, either good or ill, on her face.

"There was a war. There is always a war when it suits the ends of men in power. At my request, my patron, the man I had served for years, helped me to get appointed to the governorship of one of the frontier outposts. I knew if I governed it well I would win a following."

He made a face, laughing at himself. "It was a relatively quiet post—the military wouldn't allow someone with only a cursory history of service to be appointed to anyplace strategically important. But it was a good first step. The Selinians were the only threat."

"Selinians?"

"The survivors of the old Rensel Empire who live in the mountains north of Madaria. They are an eccentric people. Very insulated. Their land is harsh and they supplemented their larders by raiding.

"The war made them bolder, so my predecessor had negotiated an exchange of hostages. The raiding had slowed, not ended. Our local landholders took matters into their own hands. They conducted a counter raid—one that did more damage to the Selinians than the Selinian raids had done to us. The Selinians retaliated by killing the hostages we had sent them."

The Barajian wine suddenly tasted sour.

"Our landholders were as much to blame as the Selinians, but word reached the capital and there was a great outcry. The Enandrin misinterpreted my dispatches for their own ends and solemnly condemned the Selinians. They demanded I execute the hostages we held.

"I knew that the honest course was to explain that the blame lay as much with our people. But in Amaroc, popular acclaim was the road to power, and I wanted power. I rationalized that I could use that power to good ends. So I had the hostages killed."

"I see." The kaiyun's face was closed. What did she think of him?

"It was swift, and tidy. Amarocean public stranglers were well trained, even in a frontier outpost. I had to be present, to count the bodies. I had the acclaim I desired in my hand."

"And you were cursed?"

"I was sitting in the public forum, hearing petitions and congratulations because the Enandrin had summoned me back to Amaroc. A woman worked her way through the crowd, it wasn't until she was upon me that I realized she was Selinian. She spoke seven words of a curse." He took a deep breath. "I think I know what a man whose heart stops feels like. For an instant everything stopped around me, and my heart gave one great leap and then was cold as a stone for five days until the full moon."

"You feel that you deserved punishment?"

"Yes."

"Why?"

She saw too much. Like Walter. Where was Walter? Had he reached Marda yet?

"A stronger reason than mere ambition made me want to win power. I had been having an affair in Amaroc; we both wanted to divorce and marry."

"And you could not because of your status?"

"Not precisely. Divorce was common. But it would have been unwise. My marriage was a political match. It was Mencia's marriage we had to be careful of." He paused remembering her, thinking of how much of her he could see in the woman before him. "She was my patron's wife. Had he found out he would have broken me, ruined her. The affair was dangerous. Too many people paid the price for it."

But how could he not have loved Mencia? How could he not love Chrysogon? They both had the same clear, shining minds and souls.

Through the window onto a walled garden Thomas could see the moon. In only a few hours Walter would summon him.

"You will leave tonight," Chrysogon said, as if she read his thoughts.

"Yes."

"When?"

"Close to sunrise. Walter will call. I will go. It will take us no time to reach the place we were summoned to be judged for success or failure."

"What if you do not answer Sir Walter's call?"

"I must answer it. My whole will must be bent on reaching Walter."

"And if someone holds you?"

"You have read too many stories, your highness."

"They told me of Amloth. He was held and he escaped."

"Yes. It has happened three—no, four—times." He smiled briefly. "The king of Tarsia was one of us. And the king of Canjitrin."

"Would you mourn if I held you?"

"I—" Would he? He would have something so near to what he had wanted. But Walter—Walter needed him, his counsel, his friendship. Walter had come so close to giving up in Tarsit last moon. Terrifyingly close. To have Walter burn because he had no one to help him—that would be as hard to endure as losing Chrysogon.

"You are torn. Why?"

"Walter—"

"I understand. You are very close."

"Freedom is not something I have wished for. But—"

"You have time to decide. Must you leave the instant he summons you?"

"The pull grows stronger with the growing power of the sun. I can resist it for a time."

"Come to me then. Tell me your answer."

He bowed, took her hand and kissed it very lightly before he left her sitting in that still, perfect chamber.

Riding. Walter had spent too much of his existence riding. Riding to war, riding to find Cassimara, riding to inspect his fields, riding to war again, riding as a prisoner taken to the Duke, riding since that night to places that blurred in his mind for reasons that were all too clear.

Ahead of him was Silasar Fortress. Behind him was Istlakan, and Valadiza, the Barajian capital. Payne and Michel. And Thomas.

Had he been too obvious when he had told Thomas to guard the kaiyun? Thomas knew him too well. He knew Thomas too well. Thomas had been too obviously pretending he agreed with the need.

Would that woman hold him? She was strong—the journey had shown him her character. She knew what they were. Did she know what to do? She must know—did any story of the Wild Hunt omit Amloth's freeing?

Moonlight shone on the grim walls of Silasar Fortress. Think of the task—not of the endless years with no one to confide in. Think of Thomas free, able to turn his mind and heart to more than the endless round of summonings.

The road that wound up the mountain to the fortress was well kept. Generations of Emperors had made sure that the most important defense against the depredations of the Sueve, if nothing else in the hinterlands of Lakandar, was well maintained. The Sueve were not a people to underestimate.

Sueve. He turned his mind to the fortress and sought his men. Yes, Ulick was there. And Justin. And therefore presumably Marda and Dayan.

Robin rode with Reynard. Walter could see the boy tightly gripping Reynard's waist. Had he dozed? Walter doubted it—the boy had been bright-eyed and fascinated since they had told him they took him to his mother. His mind was like a small beacon, bright as his hair.

Walter desperately wanted away from him. He reminded

him of too much he could not spare the time to think of. Made him remember the haunting voices the shaman had summoned.

"This task will cost you something you do not value enough," the shaman had said, and Walter thought of Thomas. He had learned to survive loss; he could again.

The guards at the gate quickly opened them when shown the kaiyun's letter, and the five Huntsmen and Veran rode into the courtyard beyond. It was late, only a few men were still about. One was a cavalryman from the tuan who ran to them.

"The kaiyun's women, are they safe?" Walter asked, as they dismounted.

"Yes. No one suspected our story."

"Good. Where is the captain?"

"At this hour he would be in his quarters, there." The man pointed to the central tower.

"Gather the men who came with you and wait outside his quarters in case we need you."

The man jerked a half salute and left.

Walter looked at Veran; they had so few men. Would the captain be caught sufficiently off guard to obey? "Ready?"

Veran nodded and led the way across the courtyard. The guard on duty at the door called on another to lead them to the captain's office. The captain soon entered, buttoning his jacket. He looked from Veran to Walter, hesitated, then spoke to the guard who had escorted them. The man left. The captain said something smoothly to Veran in Barajian.

"Refreshments are not necessary. This is not a social call, captain," Veran replied in Suevarna. "We bear a letter from the kaiyun which asks for the release of prisoners, her son among them."

The captain took the letter Veran proffered and read it quickly. "The kaiyun is mistaken. I have no such prisoners."

Walter knew that was a lie. "Then we will search. We have good information that they are here. Perhaps the prince did not identify himself."

The captain dropped the letter on the table and began to pace. "You put me in a difficult position, Veran Samesar.

My loyalty is to the imperial family but my orders come from the governor, my commander. I cannot allow you to search a fortress under my command without his orders."

Walter and Veran exchanged glances; they had hoped that the captain would realize that the dice had not fallen his way. Veran reached into his robe for a second letter as Walter opened the door for the cavalrymen and the other Huntsmen.

Reynard held Robin back in the corridor as Veran said, "Captain Ferahim, this letter relieves you of your post and appoints my uncle in your place. I will act as his deputy until his arrival tomorrow. Surrender the keys of the fortress."

Ferahim snatched the letter and retreated under the hanging lamp to read it. He threw it on the table. "It seems I have—" he darted into the adjoining room with Bertz and Garrett on his heels. They caught him but not quickly enough. He tossed the keys that had hung at his belt through the window. "I will never surrender to you, Barajian."

Veran sighed and ordered him placed under guard. "Overdramatic Lakandari. Now we'll probably have to wait till morning to find them."

"We can't wait. We've got to find the prince and my people," Walter said.

"Of course. Do any of you," Veran addressed the waiting soldiers who numbered more than the cavalrymen, "know where prisoners would be kept?" Several men volunteered. "The rest of you, take lanterns and find the keys."

"On the hillside?" one guard ventured.

"Yes, the man who finds them will be well rewarded. Hurry."

The Huntsmen split up to speed the search, each with one of the volunteers. They were soon back to report that they had not found Marda or Dayan in the usual prison or the visitors' quarters, though such people had been lodged there recently.

"Are there other prisons?" Walter asked Veran.

"I've heard rumors."

"Some of these men should know. Impress upon them that it is the emperor's nephew we seek."

Veran gave what seemed to be an emotional speech in Barajian. At the end of it a grizzled veteran stepped forward.

"He says he knows where they might be."

The old soldier led them only a short way from the captain's office to an obscure door that opened on a spiral stair. Walter grabbed a torch and scrambled down to be stopped by a heavy wooden door. Ulick was behind it, he sensed. He saw no way to take the locked door off its hinges and the space was too confined for a battering ram. Even in this enclosed space he could feel the moon descending to the west.

"Veran, hurry the search for the keys. See if there are any that the captain didn't have. Eleylin, find Justin; he is somewhere above this room. He may know more."

Michel watched the throng that waited at the foot of the steps. The moon was at its zenith, the ritual was ending; the Emperor would come soon. He would have a better chance to reach the Emperor farther along in the garden, but so would the assassins, who would likely be first. No, he had to get the kaiyun's letter to the Emperor here and do it without getting a spear in the gut.

It wasn't really his problem; the woman had only asked for her son back and this had nothing to do with that. Michel wanted to fade into the crowd and forget about emperors and assassins, but he remembered that one word, "safe." He could burn if the emperor wasn't warned. He edged along the rear of the jostling crowd looking for an opening. The guards were probably on watch for him.

He collided with a young girl who was shoved back out of the crowd. He started to swear at the inconvenience then focused on the girl. She looked to be about eleven and clutched a folded paper in one hand. She was carefully if shabbily dressed. The press of the crowd had knocked her glass hair ornaments askew and she looked ready to cry as she adjusted them.

He drew her back from the crowd and knelt to her eye-level. "Having trouble delivering your petition? Me too."

She looked at him warily then nodded. "It's about Papa's

pension. It hasn't been paid. Mama sent me. She won't be pleased . . ."

". . . if you don't deliver it. If you will do something for me," Michel drew a gold coin from his purse and held it between his fingers, "I'll make sure you get to the emperor."

"What?" Her eyes were as round as the coin.

"Present this letter to the emperor. Tell him to read it first. Can you do that?"

"Yes, but, my petition?"

"Give that as well. Take this coin now." Michel pressed it into her hand. "There will be more when you succeed. Bargain?"

She nodded.

Michel looked up. Lanterns bobbed on the terrace near the steps. "Take this, face up, and run forward and kneel when I make a way for you." He shepherded the girl to the back of the crowd at the stair foot. There must be twenty guardsmen beside and behind the Emperor as he started to descend. The captain of the guard stood right behind him.

Michel elbowed the man on his left, stepped into the place he vacated, and pulled the girl to stand in front of him. As the crowd started forward, pressing against the guards who lined the path to keep order, Michel jabbed the man in front of him in the back and pushed him when he turned. The man staggered back into the crowd. Michel shoved the girl through the hole he had made. She didn't hesitate and ran forward and knelt just as the emperor reached the bottom step.

She made an affecting picture and the emperor stopped for her. He glanced at the papers she held out, started to hand them to the official behind him, who carried a gilded box, then stopped and opened one and read through it quickly. Michel sighed with relief. The emperor was questioning the girl now. She turned and pointed to where he stood. The emperor waved him forward.

The captain of the guard whispered in the emperor's ear as Michel bowed himself up the path. "You brought this letter?" the emperor asked. "Do you know its contents?"

"Yes, Majesty."

"Do you know where this attempt is to take place?"

"In the garden was all we were able to discover in Lakandar."

The captain whispered more urgently.

"We tried to deliver the honored kaiyun's letter earlier but were prevented by the captain."

"He says you attacked my guards. That you are the assassins."

"Majesty, that is your sister's handwriting. Do you doubt her word? My companion fought when he thought the letter was being taken from us to be destroyed. There was talk of some of your guard being disloyal. Perhaps the captain is one of them."

The emperor thought for a moment. He turned to the man with the box. "Asvar, collect the petitions in my place. Tarach, you came by barge, will you lend it to me? I will return to the palace by a different route. Captain, you will consider yourself relieved of duty until this is inquired into. Cerach, find out what happened when they tried to deliver the letter earlier. You," he waved at Michel, "come with me. I want to know more of this conspiracy and my sister."

Michel was mounting the steps when the girl tugged at his sleeve. Impatiently he pulled his purse from his robe and threw it to her, then hurried after the emperor.

The wine was good in Tarach's barge; that at the palace was better. The emperor gave him reason to keep his throat moist; he asked many questions. "So, you know that governor Ofarim and the captain of Silasar Fortress were part of this plot, but you don't know the names of the conspirators here?" he asked, after hearing Michel's narrative of everything that had happened since his first encounter with Wiraz.

"We know that they corresponded through an omen reader named Zakar."

"He has been questioned?"

"He is dead, but his servant will be questioned and his correspondence is being searched. I told you that the governor holds her son's life over the kaiyun's head. We had to be discreet in our inquiries. Their plan was to rule in your son's minority so they must be powerful men." Michel remembered something. "Oh, they were involved in the accusation of an Eskedi named Andritos some five years ago. Does that help?"

The emperor smiled grimly. "Yes. Yes, it does." He rose and left the room. Michel looked about at the silk hangings, the ebony lattices, and the gilded furniture. There could be great rewards in saving the life of an emperor. Next time he did it he hoped it would be earlier in the moon. He wasn't going to have more than three hours to enjoy this.

The emperor rejoined him. "Cerach says they dumped your companion's body in the river. We will search in the morning."

His horse will find it first, Michel thought, as he settled back to savor the wine and the lush surroundings.

Justin ground the diced root methodically, then dumped the grindings into the pot to steep. He had persuaded his guard that this batch contained tainted roots and must be ground one by one, lest one bad root contaminate the whole. The guard would not lock him up till the medicine was finished, and he had grown so bored that he had drifted off to the kitchen next door to talk to the cook.

The moon was full. The Hunt had not come. He would burn if Marda was not reunited with her son. Burn, cease to exist, never have to remember. He'd wished for this. But when he burned, he wanted some reassurance that Marda could still be safe with her son. It would be some recompense to his wife, his sons. A small atonement.

He glanced at the leaves on the table. If he added them to the medicine, could he convince the captain that he had been poisoned, bluff that he alone knew the antidote and the price was Marda's freedom? Would the captain capitulate before moonset or kill them all?

He heard the commotion in the kitchen still then grow louder and he glanced through the door. A man in a guard's uniform was arguing with the cook—the guard was Geran, the captain's shadow. What was he doing here at this hour?

Geran won the argument, for the cook turned away from supervising the baking of tomorrow's bread, but the guard didn't leave. He told Justin's guard to fetch beer and the two sat talking.

There was something about the man's demeanor that

worried Justin. He seemed impatient, waiting for something. Justin continued dicing, but kept a surreptitious eye on Geran. For a long time nothing happened. Justin chopped, the cook sent food upstairs, and Geran sat drumming his fingers.

The duty gong sounded in the courtyard below. Justin checked the kitchen; Geran had risen, abandoning his second, unfinished beer. He walked across the kitchen and slipped through the door to the storerooms. Justin frowned. Why would a soldier go there? Justin's guard had his back to the door and was drinking and talking to the cook. Justin grabbed the small knife he had used on the roots and followed the soldier. The man was not in sight when Justin closed the door behind himself, so he tried door after identical door. The last one led not to a room full of bags, casks, or jugs, but to a short straight flight of steps. Justin ran up them and opened the door at their head.

He stopped short. Geran was there, his hands on a wheel attached to a gigantic screw. Justin looked at the flange that emerged from a slit in the floor and knew this had to be the release for the dungeon weight. He had only the small knife but the man had not heard the door open. It had been drowned out by the squeal of machinery beginning to turn after disuse.

Justin walked quietly across the floor, wondering where he should strike. He was an apothecary, not a surgeon, and he had never won a fight in his life. He lunged at Geran's back but the man turned, somehow alerted, and the knife only sliced through his jacket sleeve, drawing blood.

He grabbed Justin's knife hand in his other hand. Justin gasped at the painful grip, kicked him, and pulled back. The maneuver knocked the man off balance and both men stumbled into the wall. Justin thought his wrist would break. He kneed the soldier, who staggered back. Justin looked for a better weapon as the man came at him, dagger drawn. Justin grabbed the only shield he could see, the iron pot that held the oil to grease the machinery. Oil spilled down his arm onto the floor as he backed away from the soldier. The dagger clanged on the pot as the man swung. Justin slashed ineffectively with his knife. Geran smiled and closed in. They were circling the mechanism when

Geran slipped on the spilled oil. Justin pushed, the man's head made a satisfying *thunk* as it struck one of the iron uprights, and he sank to the floor.

Justin dropped the pot. Geran was unconscious, not dead, and was muttering already. Justin took him by the legs, dragged him from the room, and pushed him down the steps. If he put him in the storeroom corridor, someone might find him. Justin hurried back to the room that held the mechanism and found that its door didn't lock from the inside.

Maybe there was some way to jam the mechanism. Justin circled it, wiping his oily hands. The flat flange was closely held between two half-round posts. Each had a hole and the three aligned holes had a great metal screw screwed through them. The screw ended in a hand wheel. Unlike the crude ironwork in the dungeon, this was as finely finished machinery as he had ever seen. But why not? This was permanent, the other disposable.

He could see no way to jam the screw or take the wheel off to make it unturnable. The screw protruded equally on both sides of the posts. He could screw it all the way to the wheel. That would at least take more time to take out. He bent his strength to the mechanism. Even oiled it screeched.

Two turns more, he thought, then he sensed movement behind him. He had no time to dodge as Geran brought the iron oil pot down, crushing his head against the wheel.

Walter's summons came later than Thomas had expected and was a relief—his own plans hinged on speaking to the kaiyun before dawn.

Chrysogon was awake, sitting where he had left her. She had changed her robe for a simple one like the ones she had worn while traveling. Otherwise, she might not have moved in all those hours.

He had spent that time making sure that the officials who had rallied to support her were told why she had seemingly changed her mind. When word came tomorrow that Dayan was free, they would be at her side.

She smiled at him, her dark eyes sad and frightened, but she did not speak.

"Your highness."

"Will you stay?"

"No."

He'd hurt her. The change in her was barely perceptible, but it was real.

"You cannot leave Sir Walter."

"That is one reason. But not the only one." He picked up a porcelain cup from the table beside her and fingered it. "Your highness, what will you do once your son is free and your brother's life secure?"

"Return to the capital."

"To the palace."

"Yes."

"And live in the scrutiny of everyone at court, and your brother, and all his enemies." He turned to look at her when she didn't speak. She nodded and he could see she already understood.

"What would they think of you," he continued calmly in spite of Walter's call clamoring in his mind, "if you brought back a foreigner? How soon would your brother seek to keep us apart? How soon would His Resplendent Highness's enemies seek profit from whatever relationship we had?"

"Too soon."

"I risked a woman's happiness because I loved her once before. I should have forgotten her, dealt with the separation for her sake. I do not think I could stand knowing the danger I put you in."

"If I chose to risk that?"

"I do not chose to risk *you*. Put the blame on me. Say, 'Thomas Chadener was a coward. He was afraid that love would wither in the heat of your brother's disapproval.' "

"I cannot do that. But I understand. You are no coward and I will honor your decision."

He turned to her and smiled briefly. Soon, Walter, he told the insistent summons. Was he going to the flames and then oblivion? No matter, that would not change his decision—it was her fate that decided him.

"It is time I go, Your Highness."

Chrysogon nodded. He could see her fight not to make

parting more painful than it must be. He knew her too well. He would always know her too well.

There had been nothing between them but the exchange of thoughts. That was, perhaps, more lasting than anything physical. He bowed, kissed her hand as he had before, and left her.

He checked his sash—these Lakandari were clever to turn a decorative object into a giant purse. The item he had prepared earlier was there. *Good.*

Thomas walked through the halls quickly. Walter's call was insistent; Thomas fought to ignore it. He knew where the governor's chambers were. Two red-haired guards stood up straight and tried to pretend they had always been at attention. They eyed the foreigner suspiciously.

"I bear an urgent message."

"Can't it wait until morning?"

"Would I be here now if it could?"

One of them shrugged, went inside, knocked on the door, and gained a peevish, sleepy reply.

The guard opened the door.

"Deliver your message, then."

The governor's servant took him to a side chamber, then lit a lamp on a table next to the governor's bed. Thomas scowled and said, "The message is private."

The governor eyed Thomas for a moment, took in his obviously unimpressive stature, must have remembered that he had been introduced as a secretary, and shrugged in annoyance.

"All right, then." He waved the servant out. Thomas closed the door, and tossed a letter he had confiscated from Zakar's collection earlier onto the table by the lamp.

The governor's eyesight must be failing. Thomas smiled as Ofarim bent to hold the letter to the light. *Perfect.* He reached into his sash and pulled out a scarf with Barajian viels tied into the corners.

He had overseen all those executions in the frontier outpost of Amaroc and distracted himself by taking careful note of the public strangler's technique. It was not a difficult art. Later he had learned other ways to achieve the same end with a tool more easily found than the strong cords used in his homeland.

The governor flinched as he felt the scarf fly round his throat, but he was sluggish with sleep, and not anticipating the attack, so Thomas was able to jerk the ends tight before Ofarim could grab it.

The governor clawed at the scarf and made a soft unpleasant noise. His neck was thick—a typical soldier—so it took more force than Thomas had anticipated.

But it was quick and neat. Thomas broke the fall of the governor's body, and lowered it silently onto the floor. He checked for a pulse—there was none. He blew out the lamp.

Putting a look of discreet annoyance on his face, Thomas left the room shaking his head as he softly closed the door.

"Mark my word," he said to the guard who led him out. "He will regret having ignored that warning and gone back to bed."

Chrysogon was safe, whatever happened to him. He ran through the passages to where his impatient steed waited.

Marda woke and felt Ulick restless beside her. As she lay curled against him, she reckoned the days. If she was right, the full moon rode high in the sky and the Hunt's time was up. What would happen? Would Ulick just die?

He was still a warm, falsely reassuring presence next to her, and she wished she could see him in the unnatural blackness of the dungeon. Was there a hint of daylight in the window slits? She started to ask if Ulick saw it too when a shrieking metallic sound from above made her heart freeze. It continued ominously.

"I said we wouldn't hear footsteps," Ulick said. "That is our warning." Marda clutched him and his arm tightened around her. But the noise stopped and didn't resume.

"The captain is playing with us." Dayan sounded tired.

"I'm not sure, but—" Ulick began.

With a more familiar jangle and creak, the door to the cell opened. Lamplight blinded her at first, then she heard a familiar voice.

"Get the smith," Sir Walter ordered.

"Robin?"

"My mother?" Dayan demanded.

"Both safe. Robin is waiting above." Marda sobbed and

buried her face in Ulick's shoulder. "The kaiyun is in Ist-lakan."

"The governor . . ." Dayan began.

"We know what he's done. He will be arrested when you are free."

Lantern raised, Sir Walter inspected the chains to the great iron ring and the yawning pit below. He turned to a man in Barajian robes.

"Veran, have the guards put those planks over the pit." The Barajian nodded. Guards soon had the boards over the hole.

"They won't stop the weight if it falls. Hurry, her first," Sir Walter ordered the stooped old smith who bent to re-move Marda's shackle. She had to strain to hear the con-versation over the noise the blacksmith made. "What happened?"

"We—" Ulick began, but Dayan overrode him.

"It was my fault. I told the border guards who I was and they hauled us here. They'd have been in no danger if I hadn't opened my mouth."

Walter surveyed him impassively. "We guessed as much. The governor tried to control your mother with threats to you."

Dayan flinched and did not speak.

"Dayan tried to keep Ulick and me from being brought here, but the captain didn't want witnesses," Marda said. Her leg was free. "Robin?"

"Eleylin, take her to her son." The fair-haired Huntsman helped her hobble up the stairs. Robin was in the room where they had first been interviewed. He sat behind the desk, sharing a plate of food with Reynard. The red-haired Huntsman nudged the boy, who looked up and ran to her.

She was holding him too tightly, he was squirming—or was he just embarrassed at getting so much attention from his mother in front of all these men?

"Are you all right?" she asked. "What happened?"

"I lived in a palace. They made me a soldier. Do I have to be a soldier? It was dull. I like the food, most of it. I—"

Reynard interrupted. "He's well, Marda. He's been in the governor's palace with all the other red-haired boys in Lak-andar." He nodded reassuringly, as if he understood what she feared. "Nothing really bad happened to him."

She let her breath out and hugged Robin again. Then she heard the sound again—the shriek of metal scraping against metal.

"Keep him safe." She pushed her son back to Reynard and ran to the dungeon. But everything was as she had left it. The iron ring hadn't hurled down and Ulick and Dayan waited patiently as the smith finished cutting the shackle off Dayan.

"Didn't you hear that noise?" she asked.

"No," Walter answered. "We can hardly hear each other over the smith."

"Someone is releasing the mechanism."

"Veran, have someone find out where." Sir Walter turned to the window. The sky was deep blue. "I must leave." His grey eyes met hers briefly and he nodded, a benediction in its way, then turned to Ulick, who stood as the smith bent to his shackle. "Follow when you can."

Ulick nodded. The Huntsmen who had crowded the chamber followed in Walter's wake. They must depart now. Ulick would leave when he was free. Abruptly she felt as bereft as she had when Peter left, when Robin was taken.

Before the smith could put chisel to metal, the horrible noise from above began, and this time it did not stop.

"They're releasing the weight!" Marda and Dayan grabbed for Ulick, but the great iron ring dropped with terrifying speed and plunged downward. For a bare instant she thought the planks would stop it, but it smashed through as if they were kindling.

Ulick was yanked from their grasp, knocked off his feet, and plunged into blackness. Marda screamed and stared in numb horror at the gaping hole. Dayan knelt at the edge and peered down. "He's still alive!" the Prince shouted. "The loose chains have snagged on the remaining planks."

It was true, but she could hear the boards splintering "Haul him up!" she said. "Grab his ankles."

"No. If the weight goes, he will be ripped in half. We execute enemies that way—with horses."

"Then what can we do?"

"We'll have to haul the weight up by the chains." He turned to issue orders in Barajian. Veran and the guards reluctantly moved to the pit. They disentangled the chains snagged on the splintered planks and pulled against the weight.

The shock when he reached the end of the chain sent Ulick into momentary unconsciousness. When he came to, the pain shooting through the leg by which his body was suspended overpowered even Walter's summons.

But then the fetid blackness pulled at him. Anchytel's darkness would softly swallow him and set him on his horse at the summoning place; he had only to fall into it. Like a fish on a hook he squirmed, trying to free his ankle from the shackle or his foot from the boot. But it held him fast.

Above he heard Marda's shout. "Don't move. The planks will break if you struggle."

That was how to free himself. Ignoring the searing pain in his leg—that would end soon enough—he swayed, his body swinging like a huge pendulum. The sound of splintering wood and cries of distress from above rewarded him.

But not for long; he was rising, dragged away from the welcoming darkness. He was furious till he remembered that the smith was there. The smith would break the damnable shackle that kept him from falling to the Goddess who pulled him so seductively.

Marda stared into the pit, hating it as fiercely as she would a living creature. She was scarcely aware of the guard gripping her ankles to keep her from sliding into the pit, or of the flesh the chain ripped from her palms as they hauled Ulick up. When he came in sight, she breathed a sigh of relief. She had had the unreasonable fear that he somehow wouldn't be there. She shouted at Veran to grab the chain as she helped haul Ulick over the edge.

Her touch stirred him to look at her and her gaze held his fiercely. His face was impassive and she wondered if he had forgotten who she was. "Ulick?" she said. He didn't answer, his eyes were on the pit.

It pulled him, she knew suddenly. *It* wanted him. She clutched his arm. It couldn't have him. She would keep him as she hadn't been able to keep Peter, as she hadn't been able to keep Robin. This one she would hold until he had to stay.

Her mind raced. What had the stories about the King said? That the King had been a pillar of fire the Queen had had to embrace all night.

Then she'd do the same. The sky outside the window was rose. It must be nearly day. It was the moon that had summoned him—would the sun keep him? She was afraid to pray that it would, for what god would answer?

Dayan stood speaking to Veran, and the guards were inspecting the chains and the iron ring gingerly. Didn't they understand what was going to happen?

"Ulick?" He turned with that same blank gaze. "Stay with me." He shook his head almost imperceptibly.

The shackle came free and Ulick launched himself toward the abyss. But Marda blocked him, held him. They slid together to the pit.

At that instant Ulick seemed to notice her—to truly see her. He scrabbled his feet to check their fall and tried to push her off him and away from the hole. For an eternity she thought they must fall, then Dayan grabbed Ulick's ankles and dragged him back. Ulick squirmed, trying to escape, and Marda threw her weight on the Huntsman's chest.

"He has to go to Sir Walter. Help me hold him!" she cried, and though he obviously did not understand why, the Prince didn't let go in spite of Ulick's furious kicking.

Sunlight struck the top of the window slit, and Ulick abruptly went limp under her hands. His chest rose and fell; she knew he was alive. Then his eyes opened and, bright as a lynx's, focused on her as they had not earlier.

"Did I do it right?" she asked. "Can you stay?"

A smile tugged at the corner of his mouth, and he touched her face and hair as if making sure she was real. "You did it right." He winced and twisted to scowl at Dayan. "I think my leg's half-ripped off. Let go of it."

Dayan did and asked suspiciously, "What was that about?"

"Later," Ulick answered, as Marda helped him sit up.

Dayan waited until she had finished. "What will you do now, Ulick Assaga Nu?"

Ulick stared at him. "I don't know."

"Will you go back to your turned dirt in the West?"

"You left precious little to return to."

Dayan looked at the floor. "Will you stay and teach me not to be a fool?"

Ulick snorted. "That's a life's work."

"I'll see you're well rewarded."

"Indeed you will." Ulick put an arm around Marda's shoulders and hugged her against him. "Start by helping me stand. I want to meet my son."

AVON EOS PRESENTS
MASTERS OF FANTASY AND ADVENTURE